INTO DEATH'S ARMS

THE WILD FENS MURDER MYSTERIES

JACK CARTWRIGHT

ALSO BY JACK CARTWRIGHT

The DCI Cook Murder Mysteries

A Winter of Blood

A Secret to Die For

The Wild Fens Murder Mysteries

Secrets In Blood

One For Sorrow

In Cold Blood

Suffer In Silence

Dying To Tell

Never To Return

Lie Beside Me

Dance With Death

In Dead Water

One Deadly Night

Her Dying Mind

Into Death's Arms

No More Blood

INTO DEATH'S ARMS

JACK CARTWRIGHT

Had Kyle Butters been in the Dales or the Peaks, the spectacular view before him would have been one of a thousand. But he wasn't in either of those places. In the mostly flat and sprawling Lincolnshire fens, the view from Viking Way was unique, spectacular, and one to behold.

Despite the wondrous view, the early morning walk was the bane of Kyle's existence. It wasn't even his dog he had to walk, yet whether by Faye's skilled manipulation or his desire to avoid an argument, he'd agreed to go with her, trudging through the village and the paddock into trees, down the hill, and then along a little way so that when they climbed the hill they emerged on the far side of the village, having completed a full, yet pointless, circle.

It was a fruitless exercise made even more laborious by having to go down the hill only to climb it fifteen minutes later, and to top it off, the dog didn't care if they went near the hill. He had usually done his business within five minutes of being outside, which Kyle then had to carry in a warm, little bag for the remainder of the walk.

"You're quiet," Faye said, as they passed the last of the houses in the village and entered the woods that lined what the locals referred to as the Lincoln Edge – a steep escarpment that runs south from Scunthorpe through Boothby Graffoe like a scar on the otherwise flat and fertile farmland.

"Am I?" he replied, making little effort to sound enthused.

"Have I upset you?"

"I've been awake for ten minutes," he replied. "I haven't had a coffee, I haven't cleaned my teeth, and in fact, I think these are the first words to leave my mouth today, other than, 'Yes, dear,' so how on earth could you have upset me?"

"I don't know," she said. "You just seem quiet."

"Should I sing?" he said. "And if so, what would you have me sing?"

She smiled weakly at his rhetoric, her eyes tracking Bramble, the overweight and undertrained labrador, as he burst from the bushes and into the trees as if he'd never been there before. Surely the poor sod shared Kyle's sentiment and was bored of the same old walk every morning.

The evening walks, which Kyle was happier to do, were a little better for two reasons. The first reason was that Faye was rarely back from work in time to join them, so he could avoid the ridiculous hill, walking a slightly longer but flatter route that happened to take them past the second reason – The Tempest Arms. It was, of course, rude not to pop in and support the local businesses, which was all the excuse Kyle needed.

"Beyond the Sea," she replied. "I always used to enjoy it when you sang that one. You do a good Bobby Darin."

"Well, I might need a coffee before I attempt that," he grumbled, then found her watching Bramble again and saw the reason he came on the bloody walks – the love and kindness in her eyes as she watched Bramble barking at a squirrel in a tree.

Regardless of how much he loathed the morning walks, she adored them. It was their time together, she had told him on numerous occasions. Time for them to discuss things, if his mood allowed, or to just be out together if, like today, it should not.

"I've been thinking about this cost of living crisis," she started, which he recognised as both a tease into a conversation he didn't want to have and the premise of one of her ideas.

It was, in his own words, a marital trap. Should he ignore her, she would only fall into a long silence, finding some other means with which to ruin his empty day. Should he enter into the conversation and agree to go ahead with whatever deranged plan she had constructed, then he would likely be setting himself up for either endless phone calls and correspondence to facilitate her plan, or endless phone calls and correspondence to reverse the failed idea. Or both. But should he enter into the conversation yet decide to oppose the idea, he would risk being ignored and berated for an indefinite period of time.

"Ah, I wouldn't pay too much attention to all that," he said. "We've plenty to live off."

"It's all over the news, Kyle. I don't think we can just ignore it."

"Listen, love, there may be a cost of living crisis for the youngsters who are struggling to get by, but we've had our day. The house is paid for, my pension is enough for both of us, and we still have your little job at the library for anything extra. Although, I don't think I need to remind you of my feelings about that."

"I know but I was thinking–"

"We're okay, Faye," he told her. "Blimey, if I thought we were in trouble, I'd have said something, wouldn't I?"

"Well yes, but–"

"And I wouldn't have let you book that bloody cruise either, would I?"

"I suppose," she said, a little deflated.

"Well then, let it go," he said. "Leave the worrying to the youngsters. God knows we've had our fair share."

"I just thought that we could shop around for our electricity and internet. You know, shave a few pounds off here and there. Geoff does it and he managed to bring their monthly bills down by fifty pounds."

"Darling, after what happened last night, I think Geoff has other things on his mind, right now, don't you? Besides, you spend fifty pounds on having your hair done every month, plus whatever it is you pay for your nails. If you want to save a few quid, why don't you start shopping around for a new hairdresser?"

"That's not fair," she said, apparently taking the comment to heart far more than Kyle had intended. "I've been using Janice for years. I can't change now. What if she found out?"

"Well, we've been with our electricity company for years," he replied, as he stepped over a fallen branch and began his descent a few yards behind her. "I dread to think what they would say if we told them we were going elsewhere."

"It's not the same and you know it," she said. "Janice has two kids to feed, not to mention a husband who..."

She stopped mid-sentence, which Kyle took as a sign she was about to say more about Janice's husband Steve than she had intended.

It took a few seconds for Kyle to catch her up, and he came to stand beside her as she peered out into the trees.

"Go on?" he said. "What about Steve? What's he done now?"

But before she could answer, she pulled her phone from her coat pocket and answered it.

"Is everything okay?" she asked, without even greeting the caller. Her eyes widened as if she had seen something in the trees, but Kyle could see nothing of interest amongst the copse, and by the time he looked her way, trying to gauge the mood of the conversation, she had ended the call.

"Faye?" he said. "Everything okay?"

"Listen, Kyle," she said, slowly turning to face him. "There's something we need to talk about."

"That sounds rather serious," he mused, and he watched as Bramble caught sight of a squirrel and chased it into the thicket.

"It is," she told him, the tone of her voice far graver than it had been. "It's something

I've been meaning to tell you for a while now."

The call had made her jittery, nervous somehow, and she glanced up at the top of the Lincoln Edge as if she expected somebody to be there.

"What is it?" he said, feeling a sudden rise in his heart's tempo. "Why haven't you said anything before?"

He reached for her arm, but she shook it off and then averted her eyes.

"I couldn't bring myself to do it," she replied softly, and she squeezed her eyes closed, forcing a rogue tear from where it had perched to begin its journey south. "I know you're going to hate me, Kyle."

CHAPTER ONE

The curtains had been opened and the morning was fine and bright with the type of sky that fools a woman into leaving the house ill-prepared for the waiting chill. From the warmth of her bed, Freya pulled herself up to a seated position, the view through the window as new as the ruffled sheets on the other side of the bed. The village church dominated the view, with the beck running from left to right and the old, red phone box that some kind soul had converted into a book exchange. Before all of that was a small village green with a bench which, even in the short time she had owned the house, Freya had noted was the meeting spot for two lovers, who sat closer than two friends might, but refrained from any obvious public displays of affection.

As if on cue, the landing floorboard creaked and with a bare, outstretched foot, he toed the door open enough to edge through with a tray, which he laid down beside her.

"You might have dressed," she told him, as he strutted around to his side of the bed in nothing but his briefs. "What if a neighbour sees you?"

"So what if they do?" he replied, carefully lying down beside her with the tray between them. "Or are you afraid that I'll be tempted by a better offer?"

"A better offer? Do you mean from the lady with the two spaniels?"

"What lady?" he asked, and made a comical show of scampering over to lean on the window ledge to peer down at the road. "What time does she come past?"

Freya chose not to pursue the conversation. Instead, she took a moment to savour the new addition to her view and then poured a coffee from the cafetière when he had sloped back to bed.

There were two cups, but she only poured one, much to his obvious amusement. While he poured his own coffee, adding in a lump of demerara sugar and a splash of milk, she took a slice of toast from the rack.

"Aren't you going to butter it?" he asked, to which she shook her head.

"No."

"Dry toast?"

"Yep," she said, taking a second polite bite.

"That's just wrong," he said and began buttering himself a triangle of toast of his own. He watched as she took the final bite, and then wiped her hand on one of the little napkins he had added to the tray. "Blimey. You worked up an appetite."

"Don't be so vulgar, Ben," she told him. "Besides, we're not eating lunch until twelve-thirty. I need something to keep me going."

"Yep, you'll need all the energy you can get."

"Ben," she snapped, and he laughed to himself.

"What are you cooking anyway?" he asked. "What culinary delights have you in store for me? Something French, I suppose?"

"What makes you think I'm going to cook you dinner?"

"Because you always cook dinner, Freya," he told her. "Because for some reason, you think that beans on toast cannot be classed as a nutritious meal."

"It can't."

"Hence, if we are to eat, then I can only premise that it will be you who does the cooking."

"What if I told you that I don't feel like cooking today?"

"Then I'd tell you to prepare yourself for the best beans on toast you have ever had," he said proudly. "Honestly, by the time I'm finished with you, all those fancy cookbooks of yours will be in the bin and you'll be bulk-buying baked beans."

"That's not going to happen," she told him. "I was thinking of letting you buy me lunch at the pub."

"What pub?"

"The Red Lion in the village," she said. "They do a mean carvery, so I'm told."

"By who?"

"The woman with the two spaniels," she said, as she rose from the bed and moved the tray onto the floor beside the bed, leaving him holding a half-eaten piece of toast and a coffee with nowhere to put them down. "Well, her husband told me, anyway."

"I haven't finished," he said, but she ignored him and checked the mirror on the wall.

"Besides, if we go to the pub for lunch," she continued, "I won't have to spend all morning in the kitchen and you won't have to spend all afternoon washing the dishes."

"Right," he said, stuffing the rest of his toast into his mouth and then speaking with his mouth full. "And what are we supposed to do in the meantime? I'm no good at crosswords, you know that, don't you?"

She shook her head in dismay, and then in one smooth motion she let her robe slip from her shoulders, catching hold of the satin belt and gripping it with both hands, which soon put a stop to his complaints.

"Well, first of all, I'm going to teach you some manners," she said, as she knelt on the end of the bed.

He swallowed his toast hard and set his coffee down on the bedside table beside him.

"And how do you plan on doing that?" he

asked, as she slowly began working her way up his legs, catlike in her movements.

"There's only one way to teach good etiquette, Mr Savage," she said, as she breezed over his midriff, letting her hair tease his skin so that tiny pimples formed in its wake.

"Go on," he said, his voice a combination of delight and trepidation.

"Repetition," she told him. "I'm going to teach you again and again."

Only when her hair grazed over his chest, did she reach up until her lips were just inches from his.

"I'm a slow learner," he replied, the glint in his eye belying his schoolboy grin.

"Well, then I shall have to be patient," she said. "Because if you are to be with me, then you must demonstrate good manners."

That alluring grin of his faded a little, taking with it a healthy portion of the heat that had developed.

"What is it?" she asked.

"Nothing," he said.

She studied him for a moment.

"Ben, do you know how many times I have sat in an interview room opposite a liar?"

"I'm not lying," he said. "Nothing's wrong."

But she didn't move. The trick to exposing guilt was not to press. Rather, she would let the truth find its own way out.

"It's just..." he began, seeming to fumble for words. "You talk about us being together."

"I see," she said, and whatever remained of that heat was doused.

"I just think we should tell the others, that's all."

"We've been through this, Ben," she said.

"I know, but it doesn't feel right. It feels like we're betraying them, that's all."

"My love life is no concern of Gillespie or Cruz, or any of the others. And as for it being a betrayal, why?"

"Well, they're good mates, aren't they?"

"No, they are members of my team. A team which I lead, and can only do so effectively if my love life is not the topic of conversation," she said. "Can you imagine the lewd and vulgar comments Gillespie would make?"

"I suppose we should be grateful that Standing isn't around anymore."

"Do you know what? I'd give anything for Chief Inspector Standing to find out about us. He only caused me trouble because I wouldn't give him what he wanted."

"Which was?"

"Use your imagination, Ben," she told him.

"Well, thank God he's in prison, then," Ben said. "I'm not sure I could cope with you and deal with competition."

"There is no competition," she told him. "There never has been. He was a liar, a cheat, and he was corrupt, and he's in prison for all of those things. By the time he's out, he won't even be capable of walking without aids, let alone–"

"Okay, okay. Thanks for that," Ben said, cringing at the image of their old boss she conjured.

"Not to mention what Granger would say if he found out about us. We'd be split up. One of us would be sent to another station to work with another team and let me tell you something, that person wouldn't be me."

"So I'll go," he said. "I don't mind. I can work elsewhere."

"That's just it," she said. "I don't want you

to go and work somewhere else. You're the bloody reason I'm here in the first place."

"How do make that out? You came up here because you split up with your husband."

"And I would have gone right back to him if it hadn't been for you."

The comment silenced him for a moment.

"I don't get it," he said.

"You really don't know a thing about women, do you?"

"Not a thing," he admitted.

"Well, then," she said, resuming her position over him. "It looks like I have my work cut out, doesn't it?"

She reached up to plant a kiss on those big, thick lips of his, and then sat back, straddling him as she reached for the hem of her nightie and swiftly slipped it over her head.

"I told you I'm a slow learner, didn't I?" he said, admiring the view, and she was just about to reply when a familiar buzzing noise stopped them both.

They exchanged glances, both of them asking the same unspoken question, and neither one of them replying. Ben answered the call with obvious trepidation.

"Ben Savage," he said. She listened hard trying to place the tinny voice on the other end of the line. "Oh, you're kidding me," Ben said. "It's Sunday bloody morning." Freya stayed where she was but pulled her nightie back on and Ben gave an audible sigh of defeat. "Okay. Thirty-minutes. We'll be there."

That was when the voice on the other end of the line became clear. It was gruff with a heavy Scottish accent that, even though just one syllable, was as clear as the horror on Ben's face when he realised what he'd said.

"We?" Gillespie said.

"We? I mean, I," Ben said. "I'll give Freya a call now. I'm sure she'll be up and about. You know her."

"Aye," Gillespie said. "But not quite as well as you do, eh?"

CHAPTER TWO

"Just take a seat over there, Mr Mason," Gillespie said to the man, who was clearly in some distress. "I'll see about getting you a wee coffee, eh?"

The elderly man followed Gillespie's invitation and sat down on the rear bumper of one of the police Astras, and then stared down at the ground in silence.

"Excuse me," Gillespie called out to a nearby female officer wearing a fluorescent yellow police jacket. He clicked his fingers a few times, until she turned towards him, her face like thunder. "I don't suppose you could take care of Mr Mason here, could you?"

She stared at Gillespie in disbelief, and then at Mason, and she relented.

"Do you find that snapping your fingers often gains you friends?" she mumbled under her breath as she pushed past him.

"Now you come to mention it," he replied, smiling to himself, as she pulled a blanket from the kit in the car boot and wrapped it around the old man's shoulders. "You might want to see about getting him some coffee. The poor fella's had quite the shock."

"Not quite the shock that you'll have when you're called into your superior's office tomorrow morning," she replied, tugging the blanket tightly. "Facing a complaint."

"Aye, well," Gillespie replied. "Maybe I can get the coffees."

"That would be a help," she said, turning her attention to the old man. "Now then, Mr Mason. Are you warm enough? Perhaps you'd like to sit inside the car?"

"Sorry, love?" he said, cocking his head to one side and holding a hand up to his ear. "You'll have to speak up."

"I asked if you're quite warm enough.

Would you like to sit inside the car while we wait for the SIO?"

"Sit in the car? With you?"

"No, I just meant–"

"Absolutely no problem at all," Gillespie muttered loud enough for her to hear. "In fact, it's my pleasure."

He strolled back to the little paddock that led down to the footpath which ran along the cliff top. The cliff wasn't much of a cliff. It was more of an escarpment, but throughout the area, it was widely referred to as the cliff or the Lincoln Edge. Turning left onto the footpath led into a small copse of trees where the CSI team were busy examining the area. Turning right, however, would lead a walker along Viking Way to Coleby, where Gillespie knew of an extremely nice pub with a beer garden that exploited the wonderful view. On any other Sunday, that might have been an option. But the sight of a lone figure trudging through the field from the footpath below reminded him that the chance was an unlikely one.

"Bloody hell," Cruz said when he was within earshot of Gillespie. "I'm bloody

knackered. I thought Lincolnshire was supposed to be flat."

He came to stop and immediately
grabbed hold of Gillespie's arm while he used
one boot to scrape the mud off the other, and
then reversed the process to clean the other
boot.

"Get off, will you?" Gillespie said when
Cruz was done. "What do you think I am? A
bloody leaning post?"

"Look at the state of me," Cruz said.
Standing straight, the little chap barely
reached Gillespie's shoulders, even with his
messy, dark hair that seemed to point in all
directions. "You haven't even been down
there."

Gillespie reached into his pocket and
pulled out his wallet from which he handed
Cruz a crisp ten-pound note.

"Coffees," he said.

"Eh?"

"Coffees," Gillespie told him. "One for
me and one for Mr Mason. Poor old bloke
has been out here for hours. He must be
freezing."

"I'm filthy," Cruz said, to which Gillespie said nothing and instead snatched the

ten-pound note back and retrieved a twenty.

"Better get one for Ben and the boss, too. They'll be here soon," he said. "What's the news from down there?"

"The news?"

"Aye, the news. Have they found anything?"

"I don't know," Cruz said, as he trudged off towards the cars. "Maybe you should go down and have a look for yourself?"

"Aye, well, there's no need for that," Gillespie replied, calling after him. But any thoughts of retaliation faded when he saw a blue Ford Focus pull into one of the few free spaces on the dead-end lane named Far End.

A familiar figure climbed out, pulled on a thick jacket as he greeted Cruz, and then approached Gillespie.

"Ben," Gillespie said. "How's it going?"

"Maybe I should be asking you the same?" he replied.

"Well, I won't be attending the sermon today," Gillespie replied, as he noted a familiar black Range Rover pull into the space that Cruz's little hatchback had just vacated. "Look lively. Here she comes."

"Here who comes?" Ben asked, and he turned to see what Gillespie was talking about. "Ah, it's Freya. She made good time."

"Arriving moments after you," Gillespie said.

"She must have left as soon as I called her," Ben replied.

"Aye," Gillespie replied. "Must have been dressed and ready, just waiting for the call."

Ben turned to stare at him quizzically.

"What's that supposed to mean?"

"Oh, nothing, Ben. Nothing at all," Gillespie said and he put his hand up to wave at the boss. "Over here."

She pushed the button on her key fob and the Range Rover's lights flashed once as it locked. But instead of approaching them, she walked in the opposite direction.

"Where's she off to?" Gillespie muttered.

She walked to the end of the road, where she stopped with her hands in her pockets, and seemed to study the houses. The village was affluent, and the houses were mostly detached and well-kept. Being off the main road from Sleaford to Lincoln, the village offered very little cause for through traffic, which on a Sunday morning, gave the place a sleepy feel.

"I suppose she's getting a feel for the place," Ben replied. "She's a Londoner, remember? She's probably wondering where all the people are."

———

"Good morning," she said to them, after a good ten minutes of studying the local houses. She flicked her hair from her collar, worked the zip up to her chest, and came to stand beside them. "Gillespie, what do we have?"

She brought with her a fragrance that seemed to hang in the cold air as if the flowers had bloomed early, despite the only things growing in early winter being grass and weeds.

"Female," Gillespie began. "Early sixties. Looks like a head wound. Blunt force trauma. We're still waiting for the FME to give us confirmation."

"ID?"

"Nothing," he replied.

"Photos?"

"They're coming. It's a wee bit muddy down there, so I prioritised scene preservation until CSI have done their thing."

"And where is the CSI team now?" she said. "I saw their vans parked down the road."

"They're down there already," Gillespie replied, pointing down to the bottom of the paddock.

"Doing what, exactly?"

"They're doing what they always do, boss," he said. "I did ask the lass in charge for some kind of update, but due to the conditions, I think she had other things on her mind. Namely, not falling over. Besides, they're not exactly talkative, as you know. I asked them to keep us informed, but you know what they're like."

"Right," she said. "And where is Cruz going? Didn't I just see him leave?"

"Coffees, boss," Gillespie replied, nodding at the old man sitting on the back of the Astra. "That's Mr Mason. He's the man who discovered the body. I sent Cruz down to get him something warm to drink. Poor bloke has been out here two hours already."

She peered down to the end of the field

and at the vista beyond, before tracing the muddy path through the middle of the grass and then finally rested on Gillespie's feet.

"What colour is the victim's hair?" she asked.

"Her what?"

"Her hair, Gillespie. What colour is it?"

"Her hair? Oh aye. Um, grey, I think."

"Grey?"

"Aye, grey."

"Shall I tell you what I think, DS Gillespie?" she said.

"Aye," he replied.

"I think you haven't even been down there," she began. "I think you sent Cruz down there to talk to CSI, they saw him and fobbed him off with some rubbish about being busy and preserving the crime scene, and then instead of conducting an interview with Mr Mason, you chose to send Cruz off to get some coffees, in the hope that I might be fooled into thinking you had the crime scene under control." He stared at her, unable to hide the wonder in his eyes. "Let me guess. You also asked him to get yourself a coffee, plus one each for Ben and I?"

"Aye, well–"

"So perhaps we should wait for DC Cruz to return? Perhaps he might be able to shed some light on the situation."

"Well, I wouldn't go that far–"

"Is Mr Mason our only witness?" she asked.

"So far," he said.

"Have we asked anybody to go door to door?"

"Well, not yet, no–"

"Get to it," she said. "It's a small street, you can handle it alone."

"Eh?"

"Unless, of course, you have something even more pressing you need to attend to, Sergeant Gillespie?"

"No," he said, as Cruz's car emerged at the end of the road and slipped into the spot behind the boss's car.

"Good. Start with this house here, work your way along one side, and then back along the others. What is that? Twenty properties? You should be done in an hour."

"No problem, boss," he replied, and he watched as Cruz ambled up the street carrying a cardboard tray of coffees and sporting a beaming smile.

"Alright, boss?" he said, genuinely pleased to see them, despite the occasion. "I got you a coffee."

"You got it, did you? It was your idea?"

Famously ill-equipped to deceive, even a child, Cruz flustered and broke.

"No, it was him," he said, holding out the tray for her and Ben to take their drinks, which they did and then turned to watch Gillespie bask in the only moment of glory he was likely to have that day.

"Well, there's something," Freya said. "Is that one for Mr Mason?"

"It is, boss, yeah," he replied.

"Good. Well, you can take it to him, and then conduct an interview. Find out if he recognised the victim, what he was doing out here, and if he saw anybody else in the area."

"Me? Conduct the interview?"

"That's right. DS Gillespie has been tasked with managing the door-to-door effort, while DI Savage and I go down and see what all the fuss is about."

"Right," Cruz said, and he looked up at Gillespie, clearly fearful the whole affair was going to backfire on him. "Okay, I can do that. Thanks, boss."

"You don't need to thank me, Cruz. Thank Sergeant Gillespie," she called over her shoulder as she and Ben made their way through the mud. But before she had taken a dozen steps she stopped and looked back at them, catching Gillespie giving Cruz a filthy look. "Oh, and Cruz?"

"Boss?" he said, his little voice nearly lost to the wind.

"What colour is the victim's hair?"

"Her what?"

"Her hair, Cruz. What colour is it?"

He shrugged.

"Brown, I think," he said thoughtfully. "Yeah, brown."

"Thank you, Cruz," she replied and eyed Gillespie with obvious disdain. "Thank you very much."

CHAPTER THREE

"I'll be right with you," one of the white-suited individuals called out from where she and her colleague were crouched in the trees. She made a show of finishing what she was doing and then traversed the line of stainless steel platforms they had put down to preserve any footprints in the mud, snapping off her glove as she walked. Finally, as she approached them and stepped onto drier land, she pulled her mask down and her goggles up to reveal bright blue eyes, and then finally offered a slender hand for each of them to shake.

"It's Katy, isn't it?" Ben asked, and he

watched Freya as she scanned the scene before them. "Katy Southwell?"

"You have a good memory," she replied, and then pointed at them both in turn, shooting from the hip. "Bill Savage and Freya Bloom."

Her build was that of a long-distance runner. Even with her disposable, white suit on, her lean frame was evident. Standing at around five foot six, the average height for a woman in her mid-thirties, she relied on her confidence for presence. And she seemed to have that by the bucket load.

"Close enough," Freya said. "What do we have?"

"Female, late fifties or early sixties. She has a severe wound to her head, no identification, and no real identifying marks that I can see. Of course, we'll know more when the medical examiner has a look at her."

"Have we heard anything from him?" Ben asked.

"He called a while ago. He's a few minutes away," Katy said. "But as you can see from the site, we need to limit the footfall. We'll give him room to get in and do what he needs to do, but I'd appreciate it if you would hold off a detailed search of the area until we're done. Last night's rain was particularly heavy."

"Fair enough," Freya said. "Do we have a timeline or a sequence of events?"

Southwell turned to gesture at her colleague.

"Pat's just finishing up with the footprints. It's a bit of a mess with all the mud, but we think we can identify at least six individuals. We've eliminated the paramedics already, as they were first on site and confirmed the victim's death. Of those six, two are definite males and one is female. The other three are unknown due to their size. Could be a man with small feet or a woman with large feet. We won't know until we can match the prints to a particular shoe."

"Presumably the female is the victim?" Ben said.

"Correct," she replied. "And of course, one of the males is the man who found her."

"Mr Mason?" Ben said, to which she nodded.

"We've taken images of his boots. One of the challenges we're facing is the site being a public footpath."

"What about a dog?" Freya asked. "Presumably, she was walking a dog if she was out here this early."

"There are dog prints further down in the trees," Katy replied. "But again, there are numerous, and even some of those could belong to a fox."

"Well, it didn't start raining until late last night, and it had stopped by six o'clock this morning," Ben said. "So that gives us at least a six-hour window."

"Correct again," Katy said, seeming impressed. "Thankfully, we've had a dry spell, so I think it's safe to presume that any fresh prints we found were made sometime between last night and the early hours of this morning."

"Okay, so we have one definite male to find, plus three more individuals. But we can't know if our victim was out walking her dog or if she was here for some other reason. That's a good start," Freya said. "Anything else? Possible murder weapon?"

"That's hard to say at the moment. There is some debris around the wound, tree bark to be precise, which might indicate that she was hit with a fallen branch or a log or something. But until the pathologist gets hold of her, we really won't know. And of course, we won't know if the blow to the head was what killed her. All the signs suggest so, but I'm hesitant to commit, as I'm sure you can appreciate."

"Fair enough," Freya said. "Well, at least we have something to go on."

"Sorry, I'm late," a voice said from behind them, and they each turned to find Doctor Saint picking a dry path along the precarious track. He wore a light waterproof jacket, perhaps one size too small for his lean and lengthy frame. So much so that the cuffs stopped before his wristwatch, and then pulled up to his forearm as he extended a hand for Ben to shake. "How are you, Ben? Congratulations on your appointment to Detective Inspector."

"Thanks, Peter," he replied, unable to not beam up at the giant of a man who, in all the time Ben had known him, had never said an unkind word – a real testament to his character given the man's occupation. "We're doing okay, thanks. I trust you're keeping busy?"

"Busy enough," Saint replied. "I seem to

be covering a larger area every morning. I spend more time on the road than doing my job, which if I'm honest, isn't necessarily a bad thing."

"Good morning, Doctor Saint," Freya said, and she greeted him with all the charm of a gentrified peer. "It's a pleasure to see you again. Or should I say that I'm grateful that it's you who came to our aid?"

"My pleasure," he replied and he glanced up at Katy, who had begun the rather laborious process of pulling on a fresh set of latex gloves, a task she might carry out a dozen times whilst working the scene due to the various interruptions. "Well, shall we get to it, Katy?"

"You're already acquainted?" Ben asked.

"Doctor Saint and I met a month or so ago," she explained, and she smiled up at the Doctor. "Perhaps one day we'll meet in an environment more conducive to a conversation that doesn't involve death, bodily fluids, and grisly wounds."

"I hope so," he said, his aged voice cracking. "But I doubt it. I tend to attract the more morbid anecdotes wherever I go."

"Just as those intent on a discussion on

bodily fluids tend to gravitate to me," Katy said.

"Well, that's certainly a change from the liars, vagabonds, and thieves we deal with," Freya said. "On that note. We'll wait for you here before we take a look. We don't want to crowd you."

"Thank you," he replied, and with a sweeping invitation, Katy let him lead the way onto the platforms.

"It's amazing, isn't it?" Ben remarked. "There's a man who's seen more corpses than any man I know, more acts of savage brutality, yet he doesn't seem to have a bitter bone in his body. You'd think he'd be a grouchy old so-and-so, wouldn't you?"

"Where does this path lead?" Freya said, ignoring his comment and pointing north along the top of the rise.

"Well, the path is Viking Way and it'll take you to Coleby," Ben replied. "It's a ten-minute walk. Popular with dog walkers and joggers, that sort of thing. Aside from going up to the main road, this is the only real way to get there from Boothby Graffoe."

"And the other way?" she said, pointing

south along the path, past the crime scene and through the trees.

"Castle Lane, I suppose," he said. "It leads down to–"

"A castle?" she said, and he grinned.

"What's left of it, yes. Somerton Castle. It's a way off though."

"But our culprit could have left the scene that way and headed back into Boothby Graffoe, or they could have taken the path to Coleby to make their escape?"

"Or they could have simply walked back through the paddock into the village," Ben said.

"So, three possible means of escape," she mused aloud. "No ID on the body, no murder weapon, and multiple sets of footprints."

"And no Sunday dinner," Ben said. "Let's hope Katy finds some bodily fluids. Failing that, Gillespie might stumble on a doorbell camera."

"Have some uniformed officers search the footpath all the way up to Coleby," she said. "If our killer went that way, they might have tossed the weapon away. When they're done, have them search in the other direction down to Castle Lane."

"Will do," he said. "It might be worth having somebody go door to door in Coleby, too."

"Quite right. Send Gillespie when he's finished. That should keep him occupied for the day," she said.

"And Cruz?"

"Yes, I suppose so. We need somebody with their head screwed on to make sure Gillespie doesn't cut corners."

Ben smiled his acknowledgement.

"What about the others? Do we need to spoil their weekend?"

"Let's see what happens," she replied. "The first thing we need to do is find out who the bloody hell our victim is."

CHAPTER FOUR

"Hello, Mr Mason," Cruz said as he approached the man who had given up sitting on the rear bumper of the Astra and now paced up and down to keep warm. Cruz held out the tray containing the remaining coffee. "Thought you might like a warm drink."

"Who are you, then, the apprentice?" the old man said but still collected the drink from the tray. Cruz tossed the empty container into the back of the car and cleared his throat.

"No, I'm not an apprentice. I'm Detective Constable Cruz, Mr Mason," he replied as politely as he could. "I've come to take your statement."

"My statement?"

"I'd like to know exactly what happened. You know? What you were doing out here, when you came across the...that is, when you made the discovery. Perhaps you saw somebody on your travels? It doesn't matter who it is. We need to know so we can speak to them."

"I see," he replied, taking a sip of the coffee and pulling a disgusted face. He looked for somewhere to put it down but found nowhere suitable. "Thank you, but I'm more of a tea drinker."

"I'll take it," Cruz said, reaching to take the cup from him. He tipped the drink onto the verge, then tossed the empty continuer into the back of the car beside the tray. He retrieved his notepad from his pocket and clicked open his pen. "Now, where were we?"

"I was just out for my constitutional," Mason said.

"A walk?"

"Aye. Same time every morning," he said, his accent offering more than a hint of Yorkshire. I walk up from the village, through the paddock, and then down to the fields. There's a track that runs down there at the edge of the field. Leads up to Coleby, it does. All the way from Castle Lane."

"That's a nice walk," Cruz said. "What is that, a mile?"

"Two, more like," Mason replied proudly. "I come back along Viking Way just to change things up, you know?"

"But you do the same walk every day?"

"I do. You have to keep moving at my age, you know?"

"I wish I had the time," Cruz said. "What time did you set out this morning? It must have been early."

"Oh, six-fifteen-ish. Give or take, anyway. All depends on when it gets light. No good walking out here in the dark. Not at my age. I like the hour before sunrise. Light enough to see but still peaceful and dark. If I'm lucky, I get to see a deer or two in the fields," he said, and he eyed Cruz knowingly. "I know what you're wondering, you know?"

"Oh?"

"You're wondering how I found her if my

route takes me around the trees and not through them."

"Well, it had crossed my mind."

"Aye, well. I can show you if you like?"

"I think it's best if we stay out of the way," Cruz replied, keen to stay out of everybody else's way.

Mason seemed to study Cruz, unnerving him a little. It was as if he was sizing Cruz up, determining how what he had to say would be received.

"Next time you get a chance, you follow the path down the hill and around the trees, young man," he said. "As if you're heading to the track at the bottom of the field."

"Okay..." Cruz said, slightly unsure of where the man was taking the conversation.

"You'll find a spot there, sheltered from the noise of the wind. It's like a little pocket of peace."

"Is that where you saw her?" Cruz asked, to which the old man shook his head. "Through the trees, I mean."

"I didn't see a thing. Not at first anyway," he replied shaking his head soberly. "But I heard it."

"Heard what?" Cruz said, watching as the

man's face paled and his eyes were lost to a memory. "What did you hear, Mr Mason?"

"Something I'll never forget. Until the day I die," he replied and he stared down the paddock at the vista beyond. "I heard death."

CHAPTER FIVE

"Well," Saint said, just as he stepped off the line of platforms snapping his gloves off as he walked. "That's one of the trickier crime scenes I've had to deal with. I feel like I've just been to one of my wife's yoga classes."

Freya watched as he meticulously folded the used gloves and put them in the opposite pocket from which he had retrieved them. She mused he was a man of systems and procedure, of routine and habit, a perfect set of traits for a man in his occupation, but rather lacking in spontaneity for her liking. In contrast, Ben tapped his jacket pockets and then reached into his inside pocket to retrieve an old, gnarled Biro and his notepad.

"Death was almost certainly caused by asphyxiation," he continued. "Severe cyanosis, petechial haemorrhages in the skin, in addition to some slight conjunctival haemorrhage, probably caused by the increased blood pressure at the time of the attack."

"So, she was conscious when this happened?" Freya said, to which the doctor nodded.

"I also found some bruising on her shoulders which could only have occurred antemortem."

"Before she died?" Ben said, for clarification, and again the giant of a man nodded gravely.

"Can I give you my appraisal of the series of events, for what it's worth?"

"Of course," Freya said.

"She was hit on the back of the head. Hard enough to knock her to the ground, but not hard enough to render her unconscious. It's a miracle really. Her skull has been fractured and suffered heavy blood loss, but she knew what was happening. Most of us would have succumbed to that severity of injury," he said, and he took a deep breath. "But she didn't.

She lay on her back staring up at her attacker, who then knelt on her shoulders, straddling her and proceeding with the asphyxiation."

"The scene supports that theory," Southwell said, as she joined them, pulling off her mask and goggles. "There are scrapes in the mud by her feet indicating that she struggled or tried to get away somehow, but was held down. There's also a build-up of mud on her boot heels, as opposed to the consistent spread of mud I'd expect to find had she been on her feet."

"What did they hit her with?" Freya asked, tentatively. Rarely did the question ever result in an affirmative response, but it was always worth asking.

"Something heavy," Saint said. "Heavy and broad."

"A log?"

"Maybe, but I don't think so," he said. "The wound isn't consistent with the rough edges a blow from a log might produce. Of course, there is a fair amount of debris, so the pathologist might say something different when she's cleaned up."

"What about the prints?" Ben said. "If

somebody straddled her, wouldn't there be prints on either side of her?"

"There are," Southwell said. "Sadly, they look like they belong to a generic Wellington boot."

"But the size. Surely we can see how big the boots were?"

"Sadly not," she replied, and she dropped gracefully to her knees, and then pointed to the angle of her feet. "The boot heel doesn't touch the mud. We have a very skewed print of the toe end of the boot, but no heel. Even if I could determine a size, any barrister worth paying would argue the evidence unsafe."

"So whoever did this was wearing Wellington boots? That should narrow it down," Freya said.

"I'm sorry I can't be more specific," Southwell replied. "We may find some traces of DNA. If there was a struggle, then a fingernail scrape could produce re-sults. Plus we might find traces of saliva on her face or in her hair. Despite what the movies might depict, murdering somebody by asphyxiation can take up to a minute or more. She would have been fighting for her life. The struggle would have been real."

On that sombre note, the four of them each imagined the scene.

"Do you want to see?" Southwell asked. "We're nearly finished."

"No. No, you finish what you're doing. We'll come back before the body is removed," Freya said. "I think we're going to be relying heavily on DNA evidence with this one, so I don't want to create delays."

"Ten minutes isn't going to make much difference," Southwell countered.

"I'm sorry, Katy, I don't think I made myself very clear," Freya replied. "I'm going to need that report, or at least the bones of it, this side of the six o'clock news."

"I see," Southwell replied.

"We can't even begin to question suspects until we have a positive ID. What I'd really like is some lines of inquiry ready to pursue if and when her identity is known."

"Understood," Southwell said, and she bowed her head respectfully, before making her retreat back along the platforms, leaving just the doctor to answer the remainder of Freya's questions.

"What time frame are we talking about here?" she asked, which was a slight variation of the standard time of death question but equated to the same thing.

"Hours," he said, checking his watch. "It's ten past nine now. My gut tells me she died three hours ago. However, determining the time of death is not an exact science. Not yet, anyway. But that doesn't help you, does it?"

"It certainly doesn't," she said.

"Between five a.m. and seven a.m.," Saint said. "Again, the pathologist may be able to narrow that down."

"Well, Mr Mason found her at six-thirty," Ben said.

"There you go, then," Saint said. "It's narrowed down already."

"Okay, thank you, Doctor. I understand you can't commit to a time," Freya said and then looked across at Ben. "That's enough for us to work with right now. Shall we get on?"

"You're the boss," he replied and then shook Saint's hand.

"Thanks, Peter. Have a safe drive back, yeah."

"Take care, Ben," he replied. "And once more, well done. You deserve it."

Ben smiled a thanks and then turned to head back to the cars with Freya. The route took them through the paddock, where years of footfall had carved an informal footpath from the end of the dead-end road down to Viking Way.

"Somebody hit her, then panicked," he said.

"What are you getting at?"

"I'm saying that it wasn't premeditated. It was spontaneous. It was emotional," he said, as he leapt across a muddy patch to walk on the much drier grass Freya had found.

"Okay," she replied, liking the direction he was probing. "So maybe she argued with somebody."

"At six-thirty in the morning?" he replied. "We don't all share your enthusiasm for early morning heated debates, Freya."

"What if she was walking her dog and it bit another dog or a person? You hear about that sort of thing all the time, don't you? People become very attached to their dogs."

"I suppose it's a possibility. But there's no guarantee she even had a dog," he replied.

"And it does feel like a stab in the dark. What we really need is a positive ID."

"Alright, boss," Cruz called out as they reached the top of the paddock. He was beaming but trying hard to appear professional. He tapped his notepad in his breast pocket. "I've spoken to Mr Mason. I'll write his statement up as soon as I'm in the office."

"And?" Freya said, walking past him, and forcing him to catch up with them both.

"Six-thirty, boss," he said, taking large steps to keep up with them. "That's when he found her."

"We know that already," she said, stopping at her car to remove her jacket, which she tossed inside. "We need leads, Cruz. Did he see anybody?"

"No."

"Great," she said. "Really helpful."

"But he did hear somebody."

Freya stopped and then stared at the young DC who, despite certain weaknesses had the potential to become a good officer, an observation she reserved for when Gillespie had driven his morale down into the mud.

"Hear somebody?"

"Well, something really," Cruz said. "I'm not sure what you'd call it."

"You're not explaining yourself, Cruz," Freya said.

"Death, boss," he replied. "He said he heard death."

"Death?" Ben said.

"Like a..." he began, then checked to make sure they weren't being overheard. "You know?"

"No, Cruz. I do not know," Freya said, and he shuffled his feet.

"Like an orgasm," he said, reddening at the mention of the word.

"A what?"

"Well, like that, but not quite," Cruz explained in his own round-the-houses way. "He said it was like a release. An exhale. Long though."

"Jesus," Ben said, clearly disgusted at whatever images his imagination had conjured.

"He heard the killer?" Freya said, to which Cruz nodded.

"He said he went back up into the trees when he heard it. But nobody was there. I mean, it was six-thirty. It would have to still be a bit dark, and if I'm honest, it would have taken him a few minutes to get up there. He's not exactly Usain Bolt, is he?"

"He heard death?" Freya said. "Is that what he said? Death as in the process, or death as in..." She could hardly bring herself to speak to the words, but said it with reluctance. "Or death as in the being?"

"I didn't ask that," Cruz said, looking alarmed. "He's being taken home now. Should I go and ask him?"

Before Freya could respond, a commotion halfway up the short street caught her attention.

"What the bloody hell is going on?"

Gillespie was walking backwards along Far End, his arms outstretched to make himself as wide as possible, while half a dozen locals let their curiosity get the better of them. The group consisted of mostly middle-aged individuals with a couple of pensioners behind them.

"Come on now. There's nothing to see," Gillespie called out, but every time he stepped in front of one small group, another moved forward, each of them peering into the paddock to see what was going on. "If you could all just move back so we can do our jobs."

"Gillespie?" Freya called out, her voice loud in the quiet street. He turned and shrugged at her, conveying his helplessness.

"We've got a right to know what's going on," one of the men called out. He was perhaps the youngest of the group, mid to late thirties, wearing a light, olive green raincoat.

"Actually, you don't have any right to information whatsoever," she replied, stepping forward. "And if you take one more step, the only rights that any of you will have will be the right to remain silent and the right to call a solicitor."

The slow-moving group came to a stop, and she pointed at two uniformed officers who were making their way back through the paddock from the crime scene. They looked as if they were about to go on a well-deserved break.

"You and you," she said, and they startled a little. "Get those people out of here, and get the bloody road cordoned off. Nobody in or out unless they can prove they are residents."

"Right away, ma'am," one of them said.

"And Gillespie?" Freya added.

"Aye, boss," he replied, clearly pleased to have the extra support. "Before you go door to door, take all of their names and addresses." A few of the group looked worriedly at each other. "And make sure you don't miss anybody."

The atmosphere that followed what could have been a disaster was soon quenched by the damp air. It was no longer raining, but the moisture seemed to cling to Freya's clothes and hair.

She studied the group of locals, as Gillespie corralled them into a line and began taking their details.

"Well?" Cruz said.

"Well, what?" Ben said, clearly speaking on Freya's behalf and protecting Cruz from her wrath.

"Should I find Mr Mason and ask him about what he heard? You know, the hearing death bit?"

"No, I'm sure we have what we need for now," Ben said, and he tapped Freya's shoulder, then nodded down the road where a man was ambling along the road with a dog, being accompanied by one of the uniformed officers she had asked to cordon the road off.

"Oh, for God's sake, not another one. What is it with these people?" she muttered.

"Chief Inspector Bloom?" the officer called out, and she held her tongue for a moment.

"What is it?"

"This gentleman wants a word with you," he said, presenting the dog owner. "Says his wife hasn't come home from a dog walk."

CHAPTER SIX

He wore walking boots, muddied and well used, and a long jacket, which unlike Doctor Saint's appeared to be a size or two too large for his slight frame. But where the doctor stood tall and proud, fastidious in his posture, the man who approached Ben and Freya seemed to be carrying the weight of the world on his shoulders.

He looked between Ben and Freya as if together they intimidated him.

"This is Mr Butters, guv," the uniformed officer said and then waited for an instruction. "Should I stay or..."

"We'll take it from here, thank you," Freya told him. "I'd appreciate it if you could keep them behind the cordon. The last thing we need right now is all this getting into the papers."

"Very good, guv," he replied, then turned to head off back to where the tape had been drawn off to close the street.

"Mr Butters," Freya said, seeking somewhere more suitable for a discussion, "I'm afraid I can't offer much in the way of a seat."

The comment wasn't meant to be taken literally. Instead, she hoped it would encourage him to begin. Which it didn't. He just stared at them, wide-eyed, a posture that remained even when the patter of light rain became heavier.

"I'm sorry," Freya said, quietly, which took Ben by surprise. It wasn't often she apologised for anything. "You said you're worried about your wife. Is that right?"

He nodded, and Ben took the opportunity to open the tailgate on Freya's car.

"Would you like to sit down?" he asked. "There's no point standing in the rain."

He nodded again and ambled over to the car, his dutiful labrador far more appreciative of the shelter the tailgate offered than he.

"When did you last see her?" Ben asked.

"My wife? This morning," he said. "We took the dog out." He gestured weakly at the dog, then stopped as if realising there was no need. "We split up while we were out. I came home early. I thought she'd probably just gone on a longer walk. She often does that. You know? Takes a different route. Stretches her legs. But she was supposed to be back an hour ago. The library opens at nine. What do I tell them?"

"The library?"

"Sorry," he said. "She works there. Part-time, like. But she never misses it, you know? It's just so unlike her."

Ben caught Freya glancing at him but refused to acknowledge it for fear of disrupting the sobriety of the conversation.

"And the dog?" she said. "You said she went out with the dog."

"That's right. He came back with me."

"You left your wife out here?" Freya repeated.

"Then I saw you lot," Butters said, a little over emphatically. He pointed back in the direction from which he had walked. "We're down at the end of the road, see? I waited for her. Walked to the top of the drive to have a look down the road. That's when I saw that fella in the uniform tape the road off. Well, I thought…" He paused. "Well, I don't know what I thought. All sorts of things. The worst mostly."

"Is there a chance your wife came back and left without you knowing?" Ben asked.

"No," he replied. "We've one of those doorbell cameras. I checked the footage."

"Mr Butters, do you happen to have a photo of your wife?" Freya asked. "If not, perhaps a description?"

He rummaged through his pocket and produced a well-worn wallet, held closed with a browned elastic band that he probably began using when pound notes were in circulation.

"Here," he said, holding out a passport photo. "This is her."

Ben took the image before Freya could get her hands from her pockets, glanced at it, and then handed it to Freya to see if he could see any response in her reaction. But he couldn't. She remained impassive.

"Do you mind if we keep this?" she asked. "Just for the time being."

"Of course," he replied, clearly expecting more. "Is it her, then? Have you found her?"

Even the dog picked up on the alteration in the mood. His head cocked to one side and his ears flattened against his head.

"I know you've found someone or something," he said. "There wouldn't be all this drama if you hadn't."

"You're right, of course," she said. "A woman's body has been found."

"Oh my God."

"But we haven't been able to identify her yet."

"Well, is it her?" he said, holding his hands up to his face. "Oh, Christ. I knew it. I bloody knew it when I saw you all arrive."

"Mr Butters," Freya said, calmly, but assertive enough to cut through his whining. He dropped his hands to his lap and waited, and then accepted the photograph from Freya. "I'm sure your wife will be home soon."

"What do you mean?" he said, a confused and worried look spreading over his face. "What do you mean? It's not her?"

"I'm quite confident that your wife is fine and well somewhere," she told him. "Perhaps you should wait at home for her. You never know, she might be home now wondering where you are."

He reached down and stroked his dog, who welcomed the attention and stood, making it clear he'd had enough of sitting on the cold, wet ground.

"Can I ask you something?" Ben said. "If you don't mind, that is."

"Of course," Butters said.

"Why did you come home alone?" he said.

"Sorry?"

"You said you split up while you were out walking," Ben said. "Why? Why would you leave your wife out here when it was barely light?"

"Oh, you know," Butters replied. "We've been married for forty years. You get to learn when to walk away, don't you?"

"Do you?" Freya said, in that tone that only she could master, which had a way of forcing the recipient onto their back foot.

"All right," Butters said, holding his hand up. He shoved himself off the car and gave his dog a tap to follow him. "You said it isn't her. That's enough for me. I don't need to go into detail about my marriage."

"No, you don't," Freya said, making space for him to leave. "But I wouldn't mind seeing your doorbell footage."

"My what?"

"You said you had a doorbell camera," Freya said. "I wonder if you could let us see the footage. I mean, I'm quite certain that it isn't your wife down there. But she is somebody's wife, daughter, or mother, and I'm sure somebody is out there wondering where she is." She left a pause, long enough to study his reaction. "Just as you were, Mr Butters."

CHAPTER SEVEN

Freya slapped a brand new file onto her desk, then shook her jacket from her shoulders and flung it onto the back of a nearby chair.

"Are we calling them in?" Ben asked, referring to the rest of the team. "Or do you think we can manage with just Gillespie and Cruz until tomorrow?"

"I think we could manage better without Gillespie and Cruz if I'm honest," she said. "But let's not rally the troops just yet. Let's wait until we've at least got a positive ID. If we're going to pay overtime, I want to give them something to do for it."

She stared up at her whiteboard with its clean surface. Three pens had been left in the little tray beneath it, and aside from the name of an old man who claimed to have heard death, and a man who thought his wife was missing, she had nothing to write.

"Gillespie just messaged me," Ben said, obviously sensing her mood. "They've removed the body. It's on its way to the hospital."

"Well, that's something, at least," she replied. "Hopefully we can get in and see her this afternoon. What about the photos from the crime scene? Has he sent those over yet?"

"Check your emails," he replied. "He sent them ten minutes ago."

"And the door to door? Anything to report?"

"Again, he sent an email," Ben replied. "But the short answer is no. I told him to pay a visit to Mr Butters to look at his doorbell footage, so we should hear back soon."

"That's if the big oaf actually gets out of his car," Freya said. "If he's sending emails and catching up on correspondence, then I can imagine him sitting in his car, sending Cruz to do the dirty work."

She opened her emails on her laptop and then double-clicked on the mail from Gillespie containing the photos of the crime scene.

"Do you want to go through these together?" she asked.

"Not the most enticing of offers I've had this morning," he replied. "But go on then. You never know, we might see something we haven't seen before."

He shoved himself out of his chair, grabbed his phone, and then perched on Freya's desk.

The first image was a wide shot of the scene, looking south as the path entered the trees along the top of the rise. Very little detail had been captured in the shot, but then such images were rarely taken to demonstrate creative ability.

"This is a good one," Ben said. "You can see where Mr Mason must have been standing when he heard what he did—"

"Death, you mean?"

"If you believe that, you'll believe anything," Ben said, and then placed one of his fat fingers on the screen. "Look, if he was standing down here when he heard whatever it was, that's a good twenty or thirty metres down the hill from the path that runs along the top. Given how muddy the place was, that must have taken him at least a minute or two. Uphill in the mud?"

"To quote Cruz, he certainly wasn't Usain Bolt."

"Right," Ben said. "But if the killer ran along the path towards Coleby, or if he ran through the paddock back to Boothby Graffoe, it was light enough that Mason would have seen him."

"Which means he must have run south towards Castle Lane," Freya agreed. "There's no other way."

"I think we need to extend our door-to-door effort," Ben said. "Open up a map, will you?"

"I thought I gave the orders?" she said.

"You were happy to take them last night."

"I told you before, Ben. Vulgarity is no substitute for humour," she replied and opened a map as instructed.

He shoved himself off the desk and crouched beside her, while she found Boothby Graffoe on the map.

"Look," he said, pointing at the crime scene. "This is the Lincoln Edge here. This is Viking Way. And these are the trees where the body was discovered. It's wide open. No-body could have got from the crime scene to Coleby without being spotted by somebody standing here where Mr Mason was."

"All right, all right, I agree with all that," she said.

"Okay," he continued, unperturbed. "But if you take the path south through the trees, it brings you out into this little field. If you cut through there, you're onto Castle Lane."

"Where there are no houses, unless, of course, the killer turned left and walked up the hill back into the village that way."

"Or they could have turned right," he said. "Towards the old castle."

"I thought you said that was a long way to walk."

"It is a long way to walk. But it's a few minutes by car," he said and then pointed to a series of metal sheds halfway along the track. "This place here."

"What about it? What is it, a farm?"

"They supply animal feeds. My dad uses them every now and again on the farm."

"Great, we'll send Gillespie down there to get his lunch."

Ben laughed but didn't argue the point.

Instead, he reached over, tapped her hand out of the way so he could control the laptop, and then zoomed in on the industrial premises.

"What do you think that is?" he said, pointing to a black dot at the corner of the plot beside the road.

"Gillespie?" she said, and he laughed again.

"It's a camera," Ben said. "Pointing directly at the gate."

"I had no idea there was a black market for animal feed."

"There isn't," he said. "Not among the farmers around here anyway. But thieves are always looking out for machinery. A forklift or an earth mover for example. Talk to CID. It's one of the biggest crimes in the area. One earthmover is worth ten times what a thief would get for a BMW."

She slapped his hand away, far harder than he had tapped hers, and regained control of the laptop, on which she traced the narrow lane back to the crime scene.

"So if our killer turned right out of the field, heading away from Boothby Graffoe, they must have passed the camera. Get on the phone to Gillespie. Get him down there."

"Hold on, hold on," Ben said, taking back the laptop. He adjusted the map so they could see Boothby Graffoe in its entirety. "If the killer turned right, then the camera at the feed suppliers will have picked them up. But if they turned left and headed back towards Boothby, they could have gone into any one of these houses. Look, there can't be more than fifty or sixty houses in the entire place."

"Are you saying we need to speak to every one of the owners?"

"I'm saying that at six-thirty in the morning in a place like Boothby Graffoe, you'd be hard-pushed not to be noticed. That's prime dog walking time. Trust me, if somebody saw a stranger in the village at that time of the morning, they'd remember. Boothby is one of those places where people tend to look out for each other. It's a close community, and they don't take kindly to newcomers disrupting the status quo. And to be honest, I don't blame them. It's a stunning little village."

"Disruptions such as three police cars, an

ambulance, crime scene investigators and detectives, you mean?"

"It'll certainly ruffle a few feathers," Ben replied. "But then I imagine there will be those keen to help. Eager to let us know if they saw or heard something."

"Good, well that settles it," she said. "Get Gillespie down to the food place, and then he can finish off the day in Boothby. Cruz can come back here and help us."

"You want Gillespie to do all that on his own?" Ben said.

"It's less than sixty houses," she replied. "That's what you said, isn't it?"

"Well, I haven't counted, but—"

"So, he can handle it. The man needs something to get his teeth into."

"I know, but going door to door all day. He'll be unbearable tomorrow, and God forbid he actually finds something of any use. He'll be standing on his desk singing Scotland the Brave."

Containing the laugh proved fruitless, so she let it come and then die naturally before she spoke. "Get him on the phone. We'll deal with his reaction tomorrow."

He resumed his perch on the desk and

routed the call through the phone's loudspeaker while he watched her. But she didn't rise to his stare and thankfully Gillespie answered the call after just a single ring.

"Aye, Ben," he said, and then groaned a little, as one might as they stretched their legs out and leaned back in a comfortable chair. "How's it going?"

"We were wondering how you're getting on over there?" Ben said.

"Oh, you know," he replied. "The body left a while back. CSI has wrapped up. Are we leaving anybody here? You know, to protect the crime scene? No doubt the boss will want to make some poor wee blighter stand out here all night."

"That's right," Freya said. "I do want someone out there. I'll be arranging for a team of uniformed officers to do a detailed search of the immediate area this afternoon. In the meantime, I want the crime scene to remain untouched."

"Well, I could always leave Cruz here," Gillespie suggested.

"No, I actually thought you could do it," Freya replied, and a short silence followed.

"Eh, boss? Me?"

"That's right," she said. "Send Cruz back here. You can wait for the search team and instruct them."

"Right," he said slowly.

"And when you're done with that, we've got a few addresses we want you to look into."

"A few addresses? Suspects, you mean?"

"Until we have a positive ID, Gillespie, we cannot have a suspect," she said. "No, there are a few addresses in the village I want you to look at. Talk to the owners, you know? See if they remember seeing anybody this morning."

"Right," he said, again slowly. "What addresses are those then, boss? I've already knocked on every house on the street."

"The rest of the village," she said, matter of factly.

"The what?"

"The rest of the village. It's less than sixty houses and you've already done ten of them."

"On my own?" he said, clearly forgetting any respect for rank.

"Oh, and before that, I want you to visit the animal feed place halfway down Castle

Lane. They have a camera on the gate. See if you can access the footage."

"What do you think I am, boss? An octopus?"

"The Lord tempers the wind to the shorn lamb, Gillespie. Remember that."

"Eh?"

"Just let me know when you're done," Freya said, smiling up at Ben, satisfied with her efforts.

Gillespie didn't reply, but amidst the silence, the sound of scuffling was clear, as if he was moving about in his seat.

"Jim?" Ben said. "You okay, mate? Can you handle all that?"

"Aye," he replied, a little panicked. "Listen, something's come up."

"What's going on? What are you doing?"

"I'm getting my bloody shoes on," he said. "What do you think I'm doing?"

"Why are your shoes off?"

"Does it matter?" he said. "They were off and now they're on. I've got to go."

"Gillespie, what's going on?" Freya asked, and this time the smile was missing from her glance up at Ben.

"They've got through the barrier, boss,"

he said. "The bloody uniform at the top of the road has let them through. Wait until I get my hands on the useless sod."

"Who? Who have they let through?" she asked, as they heard his car door squeak open and the hiss of wind over the call.

"Who do you think?" he said, breathless with the sudden spurt of action. "The press, boss. The bloody local rag is here."

"Who the bloody hell called them?" she said.

"Well, not me," he replied. "I've got enough on my plate. They're the last people I want to see."

"Well, you'd better get them out of there, Gillespie," she said. "Or they will be the last people you ever bloody well see."

CHAPTER EIGHT

Freya had just pulled onto the new bypass, and Ben had finally figured out how to turn the heated passenger seat off when she called Cruz through the in-car system. He unbuttoned his jacket, wafted some cool air into his shirt as the call connected, and then moments later, Cruz's light and youthful voice came loud and clear over the line.

"Boss," he said. "Sorry, I'm running behind. I was just about to leave when that reporter turned up. I'm on my way, though."

"You've left, have you?" she said.

"I have, boss, yes."

"And does Gillespie have it all under control?"

"I wouldn't say he has anything under control," Cruz replied, which Ben figured was the young DC speaking before his brain had engaged. "He's been sent back behind the cordon. Bloody lucky though, if you ask me. If Gillespie hadn't sent me back down to the crime scene, I wouldn't have seen him. Tomorrow's paper would have been filled with God-knows-what photos."

"I thought Gillespie caught them," Ben said. "That's what it sounded like to us."

"Jim? He was too busy sitting in his car with the engine running. He only came out when he saw me and one of the uniforms escorting them away from the crime scene."

"I see," Freya said. "Well, thank you, Cruz. Did you say you were on your way back to the station?"

"That's right. I'll be there in twenty minutes."

"I thought you'd be keen to get home, seeing as it's a Sunday."

"Not really, boss," he replied. "No real point now Hermione is gone, is there? I'd rather be at work than sit at home on my own."

Ben caught Freya offering him a sideways glance to check his reaction before replying.

"Yes, I heard about the break up. Are you okay?"

"Oh, you know how it is. You just have to keep your mind busy, don't you?"

"You do," she agreed. "You do indeed. Listen, if you want to keep busy, perhaps you could do something for me. It'll save Chapman a job in the morning, and you never know, it might just give us a leg up."

"Of course, boss. Happy to."

"I need somebody to call the local hospitals and medical centres. We're looking for anybody with injuries to their face, scratches and the like. It's a long shot, but you never know. It's one of those tasks that rarely produces results but if we don't tick it off the list we'll be shot later down the line for negligence."

"Okay," he said, sounding enthused. "I can do that. I'll call you when I'm done."

"Call me if you get a hit," Freya said. "Otherwise, just type it up for the file."

"Will do, boss," he said. "Anything else?"

He sounded keen, like a puppy pawing its owner's legs for a walk or to play.

"I think you'll find that will take you a good part of what remains of the day," she said. "Get it done and get home. If I'm right, this is going to be a busy week. You'd better make the most of your evening."

There was a pause, during which Ben imagined the young DC contemplating the empty place on his sofa that Hermione used to occupy.

"Okay, boss. I'll speak to you later then, yeah?" he said.

"Cruz?" Freya replied.

"Boss?"

"Keep your chin up. She clearly doesn't realise what she had," she told him, and then ended the call.

"Wow," Ben said, almost immediately, and made a show of staring at her chest. Then grabbed her wrist to feel for a pulse.

"What on earth?"

"I can feel it," he said. "I can bloody feel a pulse."

"So?" she said, snatching her hand back, and he stared at her wide-eyed, enjoying the bemused expression she wore.

"You have a heart," he said slowly. "I

never knew. I always thought you were dead inside."

"Oh, bugger off," she told him, and he laughed loudly. "The poor boy needed a lift. We all need a lift every now and then, don't we?"

"I suppose," Ben said. "But you can hardly call him a boy. He's nearly thirty."

"He's a fifty-year-old man in a boy's body."

"And I suppose calling around the hospitals is a critical part of the investigation, is it?"

"It's critical to keep his brain occupied," she replied. "Besides, I find Cruz far more likable when he isn't in Gillespie's shadow. I think we should give him a better chance. See how he does on his own for a while."

"You're forgetting something," Ben said. "Cruz keeps us abreast of Gillespie's antics. Without him, we won't have eyes on what I can only describe as our loosest cannon."

"That's why we need to keep him busy," Freya countered as she pulled into a space in the hospital car park. "Without Cruz to lean on, he'll have to pull his weight, won't he? It's sink or swim time for our Celtic friend."

"That's a risky strategy. He's already let the bloody press into the crime scene."

He pushed open the car door, and they spoke over the bonnet, as per the habit that had developed over the past year or so.

"Oh, I don't think Gillespie let them in," she replied, fastening her jacket up to her neck. "He might have been too bloody bone idle to see them coming, but it wasn't him who lifted the tape, was it?"

"What are you saying?"

"I'm saying somebody else lifted the tape," she said. "That's all."

She turned on her heels and started towards the hospital building at a brisk pace, forcing Ben to take a few lengthy steps to catch up.

"So, who did?"

"Somebody else," she said, cutting him off and checking her watch. "Now then, let's get our game plan together. It's one-fifteen now. Our victim has been dead for seven hours, give or take. That's a seven-hour headstart and we haven't even got a bloody ID yet. Before we go home today, I want a name. A name we can research over dinner tonight." She stopped, allowing him to open the door for her, and for him to catch up again once through.

"Tonight?"

"Yes, over dinner," she said. "Just like the old days. Let's face it, what else are we going to talk about? The weather?"

"Tonight's not good for me, Freya," he said. "I've made arrangements."

"You've what?"

"I've made arrangements," he said.

"Well, who with?"

"My dad. I can't get out of it. He wants to go over some farm stuff. He's finally got around to making a will."

"Can't it wait?"

"Freya, it's one night. It's not like I'm going out on the town with my mates. I'm having dinner with my dad."

"You don't have any mates."

"Precisely. Besides, it'll be a day or two before the DNA results come through, and that's even if she's known to the database."

"So, we should just sit and wait, should we?" she replied, her heels clicking on the corridor floor. She stopped again to let him open the door to the mortuary corridor, a long, glass-walled walkway that led to perhaps the most isolated part of the complex. "I see."

"I am an adult," he said. "I can make my own decisions."

"It's fine. I can mull it over on my own," she replied, as he reached up to push the little button to announce their arrival. She checked her watch, then unfastened her jacket and checked her hair in the reflection in one of the windows, eventually turning back to face him. "But it does mean we need to be in and out of here in under an hour."

The lock clicked just as she said those words, and in the time it took Ben to read the expression on the somewhat unpredictable forensic pathologist's face, he knew that being in and out in under an hour was certainly not going to be prescribed.

"I might have known it was you two," Doctor Bell said, her Welsh accent somehow elongating the succinct sentence.

Unusually, she was wearing casual clothes, yet to have donned her smock and mask. Her t-shirt was black and adorned with the graphics of some kind of death metal band in a font that Ben couldn't read. The accompanying image depicted a skeleton riding a

Harley Davidson, smoking something that certainly couldn't be bought over the counter, somehow with tattoos on its bony arm. And on the topic of tattoos, the tail of a great Welsh dragon reached up from her ample cleavage as if it had somehow taken a nose dive into the Grand Canyon.

"See something you like?" she said, and Ben snapped out of his little trance.

"Sorry?"

"How would you like it if I stared at your groin?"

"Oh," he replied. "No, I wasn't–"

"Does he stare at you like that?" she asked Freya, who remained completely un-perplexed and stoic.

"Of course, I don't–" he argued.

"Listen. I may not be a woman of the world, Benjamin Savage, but I don't live under a rock. I know what you men are like. You're all the same, aren't you?"

"Eh? Pip!"

"Don't deny it. Just because I caught you."

"I wasn't–"

"Pippa, I appreciate we've arrived unan-nounced but we really need to progress with the woman found this morning in Boothby Graffoe," Freya said, which under normal circumstances might have cooled the situation. But in light of her mistaking Ben's interest in her tattoo for something very different, she was on the offensive, and it would take something similar to the Versailles peace treaty to calm her down enough to make progress.

"You must be referring to the delivery we took this morning," Pip said.

"I am, yes," Freya replied. "Early sixties. No identification."

"How many deliveries do you think we get?"

"I was just clarifying."

"Well, you can clarify all you like," Pip said. "I haven't even cleaned her up yet, and as you can see, I'm not even dressed." She glanced at Ben. "And don't you run away with your smutty ideas."

"Eh? I didn't–"

"Sorry, Pip," Freya said. "I don't think you understand. We need to do what we can to expedite a name. We need to know who she is so we can begin our investigation. All we have right now is an idea of how and when she died, neither of which has been confirmed. So right now, whoever was responsible for the atrocity lying on your bench is out there, seven hours ahead of us. They could be bloody anywhere, and the sooner we understand who she was, the sooner we can bring that poor lady justice."

It took a lot to silence Pip, but somehow Freya had managed it. She let the echoes of the emphatic rant die off in the far corner of that long corridor, and then cleared her throat.

"You just need an ID, do you?" Pip said. "You do realise it'll take a day or two for the DNA analysis, don't you?"

"We are aware, yes," Freya said. "Which is why it's important that we get the process underway. We'll even take the samples to the lab if it helps."

"I usually like to swab them and clean them before we open them," Pip said. "You know? To give them little dignity."

"I'm not interested in witnessing an autopsy right now," Freya said. "If you need us to be present for that, then we'll return. But right now, it's imperative we understand who she is and how she died. We need facts, Pip. We need your help, and I'm sorry if Ben allowed his schoolboy lust to overcome his professionalism–"

"Eh?" he protested.

"But what I need now is for the three of us to work together," Freya said. "We are, as they say, under the pump."

Again, the speech was emphatic, offering a display of emotion far greater than was usual for Freya. But clearly, she had done it for a purpose, and it seemed to have done the trick.

Slowly, Pip nodded, took a step back, and held the door.

"Ten minutes, all right?" she said, letting the R roll off her tongue like she was gargling a marble. She pointed up at Ben with a tattooed index finger. "And don't you go getting any ideas. I've got my eye on you, Savage."

CHAPTER NINE

"I didn't," Ben said, as soon as Pip had left them alone in the reception, letting the double doors swish closed behind her.

"Anything you say," Freya replied, unable to conceal her amusement. She tied her gown behind her back and then snapped her mask into place. Ben raised his arms, clearly still reeling from the incident and reluctant to admit that, despite his experience, he still struggled with the gown strings. She made her way over to him, snatched the strings tight, and then tied a knot like she was tying a child's shoelaces. "Don't let her get to you."

"Just..." he began with a heavy sigh. "Just leave it."

"Listen, I know you better than anyone," she said. "Or at least, I hope I do."

"You do," he said.

"So, I should know," she replied. "You would never allow yourself to be caught staring at a woman's chest. You have far more decency than that."

"I'm glad you think so," he said, as he opened the heavy double doors. She edged through the doors, pausing briefly to look him in the eye.

"You do look. But you're far too subtle to get caught."

"You what?" he said, as she left him standing there.

The air in the room was as cold as the outside. A row of stainless steel benches, each wiped down and gleaming under the fluorescent lights save for one on which a mound lay beneath a thin blue sheet. Behind the bench and now wearing her white smock, Pip was waiting for them, watching them as they approached, as a schoolmaster might appraise a delinquent duo.

Freya smiled to herself when she saw Pip's eyes tracking Ben's every move. Not because she no longer trusted him, of that Freya was sure. Even Pip couldn't believe that Ben would have done such a thing. But the watchful eye was designed to put him ill at ease. She was toying with him, and he was falling into her trap.

"Now then," Pip then, leaning on the bench as a celebrity chef might before introducing the ingredients. "I haven't had a chance to have a good look at her yet, so you'll have to bear with me."

"Have you read Doctor Saint's analysis?" Freya asked.

"I prefer to draw my own conclusions before being swayed. I'll compare notes before I open her up," she replied, as she drew back the sheet to reveal the woman's face, then laid it gently on her shoulders. With a gloved thumb, she pulled back the lips to examine the teeth, then moved quickly on to open both eyes. "Female. Somewhere between fifty and sixty-five years old. More likely the latter judging by the excessive wear on her molars. Haemorrhaging in the eyes, discolouration of the lips."

"Asphyxiation?" Freya asked.

"Looks to be, but I'll need to open her up, of course," Pip said, without looking up.

She opened the victim's mouth once more, pulling the lower lip down. Then without saying a thing she reached for a stainless steel tray containing various tools, and grabbed a pair of needle-nosed forceps which she then inserted into the mouth, leaning over the body, and blocking Freya's view. Eventually, after a brief exchange of confused glances between Ben and Freya, she retracted the forceps and held them up to the bright light hanging above them.

"What's that?" Ben asked.

"Fibres," Pip said thoughtfully. "I'll need to get it under a microscope, but it looks to be wool of some kind. Dark blue, if I'm not mistaken."

"Wool?"

"It was in her teeth," Pip said, and she looked up at them both. "Not the most nutritious of breakfasts."

Freya considered her conversation with Doctor Saint and Katy Southwell, but said nothing, choosing to wait for Pip's assessment before adding any potential unconscious bias into the mix. Pip placed the fibres into a Petri dish, then laid the forceps down before gently lowering the sheet to the woman's mid-riff. Each shoulder bore a faint mark like the early onset of bruising, which Pip picked up on almost immediately. She moved back up to the head, turning it to examine the wound through a magnifier that hung, like the light, from an arm overhead.

Eventually, and clearly in deep thought, she covered the woman back up and snapped off her gloves.

"The head wound is not the cause of death," Pip said.

"That's what Doctor Saint said," Freya added, to which Pip didn't react in the slightest.

"The weapon was smooth," she said. "You might be surprised to learn that striking a person's head isn't as easy as you might think. Rarely do blows land directly unless the weapon is rough like a log or a piece of wood or something. It's the curvature of the skull, you see? The blow to the head was glancing. It removed more skin than it did bone damage. That's why there was so much blood. But typically a log or a piece of timber would leave fragments behind. There's nothing here but debris from the ground. Found in a forest, was she?"

"Kind of," Freya said. "More of a small copse of trees."

Pip nodded.

"The wound looks worse than it is. Had the killer not acted, she would have had a splitting headache and she would have worn a bandage for a week or so," she said.

"Smooth, like a baseball bat or something?" Ben suggested.

"It's possible," Pip said. "Although, how many people do you know in this country that own baseball bats?"

"True," he said.

"My professional analysis," Pip continued. "And please bear in mind that this may change when I've completed the autopsy, is that the killer struck her from behind, knocking her to the ground but not killing her. He or she then knelt on her shoulders, stuffed her mouth with a scarf or something, and held it there until she stopped struggling."

"Well, Pip," Freya said. "There's no point in reading Doctor Saint's analysis. Of course he wouldn't have been able to examine the wound in the field as you have."

"I'll check for any signs of sexual interference," Pip continued. "And I'll swab her for DNA. The swabs will be at the lab before lunchtime."

"That's great," Freya said. "Thank you."

"Until I've opened her up though, I'm afraid I can't tell you much more."

"Actually, you've been a great help," Freya said. "We at least have a direction to pursue."

"The wool?" Ben said.

"And the weapon," she said. "Let's leave Pip to do what she needs to do and get Gillespie to organise a detailed search of the area. At least now we have an idea of what we're looking for. If the lab receives the swabs by lunchtime, then we might even have a name to work with by the end of the day."

CHAPTER TEN

There had been a time when Freya had first arrived in Lincolnshire that Ben did all of the driving. But since she had purchased her new car, rarely did Ben's old Ford get a look in. It didn't bother him too much. The ride was nicer in her Range Rover, the seats were far more comfortable, and most importantly, the heater warmed them far faster. No less than thirty seconds after she had started the car, warm air was spewing from the vents, and they both savoured the feeling, flexing their fingers and toes before saying a word.

"If she's on the database, then we could have a name by dinner time," Ben said. "Until then, wool and a weapon. Not much to go on."

"Not much, but if you can excuse the pun, it's a thread to pull on," Freya replied. "And the more we pull, the more we'll unravel."

She eased the car out of its spot and then made her way to the hospital exit.

Seizing the moment, Ben called Gillespie, routing the call through the loudspeaker, and setting the phone down on his knee so they could both hear.

"Aye, Ben, the big Scotsman said. "You'll have to be quick, mate. She's got me running ragged."

"By she, I presume you're referring to me, Gillespie," Freya said, which was followed by an awkward silence. "It's okay. I'm pleased to hear that you're earning your keep for a change. What do you have for us? I presume you managed to eject the press successfully?"

"Aye, boss. I did. Had a sharp word with the blighter, too. I tell you, if I hadn't seen them, they'd have been down through the paddock with their cameras and we'd have the top brass all over us slapping us about the head with the front page of tomorrow's paper."

"Oh, so it was you who saw them, was it?" Freya said. "I was under the impression that it was Cruz who managed to stop them."

"Aye, well..."

"While you were warming yourself in your car, catching up on emails."

"Well, I wouldn't say I was–"

"Have you managed to review the footage from Mr Butters' doorbell camera?" she said, leaving him no further room for a tiresome and fictitious explanation.

He paused, and Ben could picture him planning what he'd say to Cruz when he saw him next.

"Aye, boss," he grumbled. "Nothing. They left together in the morning when it was barely even light outside. He returned about thirty minutes later on his own. He didn't say much, but I got the impression they'd had a wee barney."

"A barney?" she said. "Are you trying to tell me they had an argument? And if so, what gave you that impression?"

"Ah, just the way he was," Gillespie replied. "You know? Cagey. Like he didn't want to say too much and the fact that she hadn't come home was irritating him more than anything else."

"Right," Freya said. "So, she still isn't home?"

"Not as far as I know, boss."

"What about the farm, Jim?" Ben said, hoping to diffuse the atmosphere. "Have you popped down to the feed supplier?"

"I did, aye. I'm just on my way back now. They let me take a wee look at what they had. But there's bugger all to see. I mean, it's a single-lane track that leads down the castle and a few other farms, but I didn't even pass a dog walker, let alone another car."

"So, whoever did this didn't go down there?" Freya asked. "Which means they went into or through the village. Is that right?"

"Aye, boss," he said. "If they walked south from the crime scene, they had to have turned left when they hit Castle Lane. There are a few other footpaths they could have taken, such as the old railway line. But if I'm honest, boss. It's a bloody quagmire after all that rain. You'd have to be out of your mind."

"I agree," she said. "This was spontaneous. Whoever did this walked there. So, we can only presume, at this stage anyway, that they walked home afterwards."

"So, I guess you need me to hit the rest of the village, aye?"

"Yes, I do," she said. "But before that, find me the name of the officer who was supposed to be keeping the public and the press out."

"Ah, come on, boss. He didn't mean it. He was just taking a–"

"I don't care what he was doing, Gillespie. I want his name."

"Well, don't tell him I told you," Gillespie said. "He's out of Lincoln HQ. The last thing I need is them lot against me. They have a tendency to stick together."

"The name, Gillespie."

He sighed, and the phone's speaker rattled.

"Godfrey. He's a sergeant. Good bloke, too."

"Thank you," Freya said. "I suggest you get hold of this Sergeant Godfrey and persuade him to provide a few more officers."

"A few more? There's a dozen of them there already."

"Well, if you're going to do a detailed search of the entire area, you'll need a few dozen more."

"A detailed search? Today? I thought you were kidding."

"I want the immediate area searched before the sun goes down at four-thirty. The wider area can be hit tomorrow."

"Ah, come on—"

"I also want the rest of the village hit and any relevant reports sent over to me tonight," Freya said. "We're having a briefing first thing tomorrow, and unless you want another day like today, I suggest you ensure the reports are comprehensive. Impress me, Sergeant Gillespie. Impress me."

"Aye boss," he said heavily. "Just one more thing. What exactly are we looking for?"

"Doctor Bell thinks the weapon was rounded and smooth," Freya said. "My initial thoughts were that a glass bottle could have been used. I think I saw signs that teenagers have been using the trees as a refuge from the weather. Perhaps there's a few discarded bottles."

"Anything else?"

"Yes. A woolly scarf or a hat. Dark blue."

"Right," Gillespie said, sounding unsure.

"It was forced into the victim's mouth to suffocate her," she explained.

"Leave it with me, eh?" he said. "If it's out there, then we'll find it."

"Good. Thank you, Gillespie."

"Just one more thing," he said. "While I've got you on the line."

"Go on?"

"Is Cruz coming back to help at all? He's been gone a wee while now and I could really do with him."

"I'm sure you could," Freya said, beaming at Ben. "It's pleasing to know you think so highly of him. But sadly, I've set him a task that should take him the rest of the day, so you'll have to make do."

"On my own?"

"I'm not sensing dissatisfaction, am I?" she said, to which Gillespie clearly bit down on his lip to refrain from saying what he really thought.

"Leave it with me," he said eventually. "You'll have your reports. It'll take me all night, but you'll have them."

"That-a-boy," she told him and winked at Ben, signalling the call was over.

Ben ended the call and pocketed his phone.

"That went well," he said, purposefully adding a healthy sprinkle of sarcasm to his tone. "You really know how to get the team on your side, don't you?"

"It did go well, as it happens," she said. "Gillespie has the means and motivation to demonstrate his competence. Plus, he's out of our hair for the day. There's a chance the search team might find a potential murder weapon. Cruz will be feeling much better about himself, and tomorrow morning, we'll have enough information to develop some kind of plan. Considering we don't even have a name to work with, I don't think that's too bad."

"Right," Ben said. "So, what do we do in the meantime? Go through the phone book calling every name we see to see if they're missing a family member?"

"Don't be facetious, Ben. It doesn't suit you," Freya replied. "Besides, while we're in town, I thought we could spend the afternoon doing a little light reading."

CHAPTER ELEVEN

Lincoln Library was located in the heart of the city, in the shadow of what was once the tallest building in the world – Lincoln Cathedral.

"Ah," Ben said when he saw the building ahead of them.

"Ah, indeed," she replied. "You got there in the end."

"It's a bit of a long shot, though, isn't it?" he said. "The library, I mean."

"You heard what Gillespie said," she replied. "Mrs Butters still isn't home."

"And Mrs Butters doesn't fit the description. For one thing, she's a redhead and our victim clearly has dyed-brown hair with grey roots."

"Okay," she said, as they approached the door to the library. "Husband and wife take the dog for a walk on a Sunday morning. Husband and wife have an argument. He storms off home and she disappears. Less than half an hour later, Mr Mason hears something in the trees."

"Death," Ben said.

"And then he finds our victim," Freya said, ignoring his rhetoric. "Now, you tell me that Mrs Butters disappearing and our victim being murdered aren't linked, and before you say it, you know how I feel about coincidences."

"Okay, so what are we hoping to find out here?" he asked, as he held the door open for her.

"I'm simply scratching at itch, Ben."

"Scratching an itch?"

"Yes. Something isn't sitting right with me."

"Well, scratching an itch or not, I still think it's a long shot."

"Well, what do you suggest we do, Ben?"

she said, letting his negativity spark her irritation into play. "Eh? Should we go back to the station and just pray that the lab has her DNA on file? Or maybe we should go and watch the search with Gillespie? We could even get down on our hands and knees ourselves."

"All right," he said reluctantly. "All right, you've made your point."

"Good," she replied. "Shall we get out of the rain, then?"

She edged past him into the foyer and waited for him to follow.

"You see, Ben," she continued, "despite what the television might lead us to believe, people very rarely go missing. In fact, people very rarely break their habits. And when a married couple argue, very rarely do they miss work as a result."

"So, if she's at work, then she's in the clear?"

"If she's here, then I'll consider my itch scratched," she replied as she took in the huge room before them, spying a help desk near the centre of the space. Four individuals whom Freya assumed to be students had formed a queue, yet nobody was working behind the desk. The youths silenced when they approached and eyed them curiously.

"Is anybody working?" Ben asked a young man and two girls.

"Denise is in," one of the girls replied. "She's just helping somebody."

"You must be a regular," Freya said, hoping to spark up some kind of conversation. "If you know her name, I mean."

"I'm here a few times a week. The university library gets quite busy," the girl said, with a nervous glance at her friends. "Everyone in the uni must know their names. Everyone who gets their books from here, anyway."

"Oh, so she isn't on her own then?" Freya asked, to which the girl seemed slightly confused. "You said their names. I'm guessing that means there are other members of staff."

The girl, hugging a pile of books to her chest, looked sideways at each of her friends and took a step back.

"I'll, erm, come back later on," she said, before turning her back, and then, before Freya could argue or explain, her two friends both followed her, each glancing over their shoulders as if Freya was some kind of weirdo.

"Have you always had that effect on people?" Ben asked.

"Oh, be quiet."

"Geoff," a voice said, a slightly older man who had been behind the threesome in the queue and who was now positioned at the front. He was a bookish-looking man with narrow shoulders, and somebody who Freya deemed would benefit from a good, sharp razor and a copy of Men's World. "That's the bloke who works here."

"Geoff?" Freya said.

"Sorry, I don't know his last name," the young man explained. "There's Geoff, Faye, and Denise. I think there's a manager but you don't see her often. She usually stays in her office." He looked around the room and then nodded at a middle-aged lady standing near one of the many bookshelves, talking to a man in his mid-twenties. "That's Denise over there."

"You're very knowledgeable," Freya told him. "Are you also from the university? And if so, what are you studying?"

"Art history," he said. "This is my last year."

"Art history. Wow," she replied. "Are you looking to work in–"

"A curator," he said. "Maybe a lecturer if I have to. But the aim is to build a name for myself."

"Right," Freya replied. "So, is Denise on her own today?"

"She is," he said, sounding a little unsure as to why. "They're normally all in on a weekend. It's the busiest time."

"Perhaps they went for lunch?" Ben suggested.

"No. No, I've been here all day," he said and then leaned in closer enough for them to catch the warmth of his coffee breath. "Poor old Denise has been run off her feet. I thought she was going to cry earlier."

"Oh, the poor thing," Freya said, turning to Ben. "Well, perhaps we should come back later. I wouldn't want to add to her burdens. I only wanted to make an enquiry."

"Are you a student here, then? What are you studying?" he asked, which raised a smile on Ben's face, so much so that he had to turn away.

"I'm hoping to learn a few things," she

said. "We're all students, after all. In life, I mean."

He listened to the response and seemed to delight in its cryptic nature.

"You could always try the office," he suggested, and he nodded towards the far end of the room where a single door stood between walls of books. "If it's information that you're looking for."

"Oh," Freya replied, doing her best to sound interested. "Is that where–"

"Shelley," he replied, cutting her off. "The manager. That's where you'll find her."

"But of course, you don't know her last name."

He shook his head apologetically.

"Afraid not."

"Well then," she said, catching Ben's attention with a solid clear of her throat and wide-eyed silent threat. "We'll pay a visit to Shelley. You've been a great help."

"My pleasure," he replied, just as Denise returned to the desk.

"Oh, Graham. Not you again. Honestly?"

"Sorry, Denise, I was hoping you could help me with a few articles I'm looking for."

"Thanks again," Freya said to the young

lad, and she locked eyes with the rather frustrated and exasperated Denise for a moment.

"Who was that?" Freya heard the woman ask when she and Ben were heading towards the manager's office.

"I don't know," he replied. "Maybe she wants to retrain in something? It's never too late, is it? My mum changed her career when she was in her fifties too."

Ben laughed out loud at the comment and then silenced when Freya placed a discreet elbow into his ribs.

"It's never too late, Freya," he said, as he reached up and tapped on the door in question.

The blood pooled into her cheeks bringing with it a burning sensation, and she called upon every ounce of self-control to prevent an outburst to both Ben and the spotty nerd with breath like a baboon's backside.

"Enter," a voice called, shrill and by the sounds of it, educated.

"Leave this to me," Freya said, and she pushed into the room, finding a squat lady with short grey hair in a side-parting, large glasses, no makeup or jewellery, and wearing a man's white shirt. "Shelley?"

"Yes?" the lady said, pulling her glasses off her nose and letting them hang by a plain, black cord that looked more like a shoelace.

Ben closed the door behind them and Freya held up her warrant card.

"Detective Chief Inspector Bloom," she said. "We're with Lincolnshire Police."

"Police? Whatever for?"

"We're looking for a Faye Butters," Freya said. "I understand from her husband that she works here."

"She does," Shelley replied, sitting back in her seat and taking the time to study them both in turn. A wry smile formed on her face as, Freya believed, she understood that Freya outranked Ben. "But for how long, I don't know."

"She didn't come into work this morning?" Freya asked. "Did she call to give a reason?"

Shelley shook her head.

"And has she done this before?"

"I'm sorry, may I ask what all of this is about, please? I suddenly feel like I'm being interrogated."

"You're not being interrogated, Mrs...?"

"James. Shelley James."

"Thank you," Freya said. "Her husband reported her missing this morning."

"This morning? I thought a person had to be missing for twenty-four hours before the police took it seriously?"

"Typically, yes," Freya said. "And that is because most people reported as missing turn up within that time."

"So, what's different here then?" Mrs James asked.

Freya glanced up at Ben, who offered a slight shake of his head as a response to the unspoken question.

"I wonder if you might know where she might be?" Freya said. "It's quite important that we speak to her."

"How should I know?" Mrs James replied. "But if you do find her, tell her not to bother coming in tomorrow. This is the second time in as many weeks the pair of them have done this."

"The pair of them?" Ben said, and the squat lady behind the desk cocked her head as if she was delighting in imparting knowledge.

"Oh yes. I'll be conducting interviews as soon as I possibly can," she replied. "To replace both her and Geoff."

"Geoff?"

Her eyes narrowed, and she smiled wryly, perhaps considering how much information to impart.

"Geoffrey Wilson," she said. "Thick as thieves, they are."

"Do you think they're together somewhere, Mrs James?" Freya said.

"I don't think they are together. I know they are," she replied. "They're worse than the students. They must think I'm daft, you know? Always refilling shelves together, taking coffee breaks together and whatnot. Poor old Denise is run off her feet out there, and as for Linda–"

"Linda?" Freya said.

"His wife," she replied, with an expression of absolute abhorrence.

"I see," Freya replied, then softened her tone. She took a step forward and, without invitation, dropped into one of the two wooden carvers that served as visitor seats. "Mrs James, I wonder if you'd care to help us in our investigation."

CHAPTER TWELVE

The address that Shelley James had provided led Ben and Freya to a detached property in Coleby built, or clad at least, with local stone. The driveway was gravelled and the lawn had been mowed short. In one corner, perhaps the corner with the best light in the summertime, stood a wooden loveseat with an arched trellis reaching above it. The woodwork was exquisite, and once the hydrangeas, which had been planted on either side, had taken to the frame, to sit there on a warm summer's day with a gin and tonic would be a dream.

Ben rang the doorbell and then stepped back to stand beside her and the two waited in silence. That was, at least, until the urge to pry was too overwhelming for Freya to ignore.

"What are you cooking?" she said.

"Sorry?"

"Tonight. What are you cooking your dad for dinner?"

"Oh, I don't know. He's a meat and two veg type of guy," he replied. "I'll pick up some sausages and mash on the way home. I think I've got some frozen peas."

"You can't buy mashed potatoes, Ben," she told him, stepping back to look up at the windows. "You buy potatoes and then you mash them."

"You might buy potatoes and then mash them, Freya," he replied. "I prefer to buy the ready-made stuff. Add a bit of hot water and it's done."

"Savage by name, savage by nature," she muttered, loud enough for him to hear. "I do hope you are, at least, planning on making real gravy. A nice onion gravy would work well."

"Gravy?" he said. "My speciality. Four teaspoons of gravy, one teaspoon of Marmite, and a pint of hot water." He kissed his fingers and gave a 'mwah' imitating a cliché French chef.

"For God's sake," she said. "One day I'll show you how to cook. Maybe that's something we can do together? Something to help us through the long winter nights."

"You can try," he said, as he reached forward to give the doorbell another try, and was shortly after distracted by his phone which began ringing from his pocket.

In Freya's experience, two strangers knocking at a door rarely had to wait long if the occupants were home and a second attempt was often futile. So, while Ben answered the call, she edged into the narrow front yard and shielding the daylight with her hand she peered through the front window.

The living room was high-ceilinged with decorative, moulded coving. The walls had been papered with a light, floral design which wouldn't have looked out of place in nineteen-seventy, and the floor appeared to be the original exposed boards, sanded and finished to provide warmth and texture. The television and lights were off, and there was barely an item out of place, despite the mantle and shelves housing a variety of ornaments and photo frames to the point of appearing cluttered.

But of all the adornments and intricate pieces on display, one photo caught her eye.

"Hang on," Ben said, to the caller, and he tugged on Freya's jacket, gesturing at the phone, which he then set to loudspeaker. "Can you say that again, Katy? I've got DCI Bloom with me."

"We've got a partial match for the victim's DNA," she said.

"Already?" Freya replied. "You can't have had the DNA samples more than two hours."

Shielding the phone from the wind, Ben rolled his eyes at her and shook his head.

"You said you needed a name," Katy replied. "So, I'm giving you one. A Thomas Wilson. Male. Mid-thirties–"

"Thomas Wilson?" Freya said, finding Ben staring into her eyes, trying to read her expression. "Son of Geoffrey?"

"And Linda, yes. How did you know that?" Katy asked.

"Easy," she replied. "I'm looking at a photo of him with his parents right now, and his mother looks strikingly like the lady in the forest."

Ben leaned in beside her and found the photo she was looking at.

"That's her," he said.

"Thank you, Katy. You've been a great help," Freya announced and then gestured for Ben to end the call.

"Thanks, Katy. Let me know when you get anything else, will you?"

"Will do," she replied. And then she offered a friendly, "Good luck."

Ben ended the call and pocketed his phone, then peered through the window alongside Freya.

"We have a name," Freya said. "Do you still want dinner with your dad?"

"I told you," he said. "I can't get out of it."

"Shame," she replied, stepping back to take one last look at the house. "I suppose it's down to me then."

"What is?"

"To make a plan for tomorrow," she said, as she began walking back to her car.

"Can't you just wait until the morning?"

"I could. But we're behind already."

"There's nothing I can do, Freya."

"It's okay," she replied. "You go and make

your dad dinner and talk about farm stuff. I'll put in the requests for access to their financial information and the relevant search warrants."

"Whose financial information?" Ben said. "And what search warrants?"

"Geoffrey Wilson and Faye Butters," she replied. "As you said, we have a name to work with. Now we need to understand why somebody might have wanted Linda Wilson dead."

"We'll need him to identify the body," Ben said, as they climbed into her car. She pulled the door closed and savoured the relative silence of being out of the wind. "If it is Geoffrey's wife, then we can bring him in to make a statement."

"We've got to find him first," Freya said. "And we aren't going to do that sitting down to dinner with your father, are we?"

"Oh, leave off."

"It's okay," she said, clearly amused at how easy it was to flick his switches even after all this time. "I just thank my lucky stars that I'm all alone in this world or we'd never get any work done, would we?"

CHAPTER THIRTEEN

The light was fading outside and the wind was tugging at the tips of distant trees. Ben filled the kettle before leaning on the counter while the water boiled, and Freya's words raced around his dizzied mind like a cyclone.

He'd already laid the table for dinner. It wasn't exactly to Freya's exacting standards, which resembled the diligent touch of the Downton Abbey butler. Instead, Ben's preparation was more akin to a roadside cafe, with a selection of sauces and condiments, and a few knives and forks in a cup.

He checked his watch before opening one of the bottles of beer he'd bought. He didn't need the beer. Not yet, anyway. But he might do in a little while and it proved a worthy distraction.

The kettle boiled and clicked and he stirred it into the pint jug containing the mash. He'd seen Freya cook mash potato, and despite what she thought, of course, he knew how to make real mash. But why bother when it can be made with far less fuss, and far less washing up? He'd seen her press perfectly good Maris Pipers through a sieve, one at a time, adding the butter and milk at the end and somehow ending up with far less mash than the quantity of spuds should have produced.

He stirred with vigour, adding a touch of butter for that creamy taste he enjoyed. He wasn't a complete philistine after all. The microwave, which had been whirring away for the past few minutes, pinged loudly, and he set the mash to one side to remove the mug of frozen garden peas that he'd boiled. Using a teaspoon, he tasted one, deemed it passable, and then drained the water into the sink.

Sizzling away under the grill was his pièce de résistance. Six Lincolnshire sausages, which upon closer inspection appeared to be slightly more cooked than he'd hoped for. One side of them was charred, which didn't matter too much, as he'd simply put them on the plate with the less charred side facing up.

Lastly came the gravy. Four teaspoons of granules into a large mug, topped with water, and then a teaspoon of Marmite for that extra meaty kick. He'd just finished stirring the gravy when the doorbell rang. Again, he checked his watch and wasn't surprised to find his guest a few minutes early.

Wiping his hands on a tea towel, he strode the hallway to the front door and then, recognising the figure through the little frosted window, he pulled the door open.

"I hope you're hungry," he said, stepping to one side. "Come in."

"Ravenous," Anna replied.

Despite the drop in temperature and the rain, she wore the same leather jacket all year round. Her hair was dark and pulled into a ponytail, and her jeans were tight against her slender frame. She was the epitome of a modern woman − tough, no-nonsense, yet vibrant and naturally pretty. Her dark features matched her hair, giving her an almost Latino look, and in case her appearance hadn't delivered the message, the confidence with which she walked was enough to ward off any potential suitor not up to the challenge. She stopped at the intersection of doors as if to ask where she should go, and with a sweep of his arm, Ben led her into the lounge, where his small dining table had been prepared.

"How's it going?" she said. "I heard you got called out."

"Who told you?" he asked.

"Gillespie," she replied, tossing her jacket onto one of his armchairs. She tucked her hands into her jeans pockets. "He called to moan about the boss."

"Ah, you mean he called to moan that we asked him to do some work?"

"Same thing," she said.

"Beer?"

"Love one. What's for dinner?"

It was as if she was purposefully avoiding asking anything further about the reason he was called out. As if she was making a point of keeping this strictly non-shop talk.

"Oh, just sausage and mash. Nothing special," he said, making his way into the kitchen. He pulled the lid off of a bottle, tossed the opener onto the side, and then called out. "Glass?"

"No, thanks," she replied, and he snapped around to find her standing behind him. He passed her the bottle, which she took before inspecting the meal he'd prepared. She pointed to the pint jug. "Mash?"

"Yep," he said. "You okay with peas?"

She said nothing. Instead, she bent to peer under the grill.

"Sausages?"

"Lincolnshire's finest," he replied, to which she appeared less than convinced. She pulled the drawer out from the grill and sucked in a breath. "Well, they used to be Lincolnshire's finest, anyway."

"What are they now?"

He stared down at the now completely charred sausages, then leaned forward to switch the grill off.

"I might have some bacon in the fridge," he told her.

"Do you mind if we skip the meal?" she replied, then gestured at the burned sausages. "I'm actually vegetarian."

"Oh? I didn't know. How long have you been–"

"About forty seconds," she said with a grin.

The defeat was evident. The sausages were far from ruined, but he knew enough about Anna Nillson not to push her into doing something she didn't want to. Instead, he clicked off the grill and then set the remaining jugs and dishes by the sink

"How's the new boyfriend working out?" he asked.

"Well, you'll find out when I mention him," she replied. Although her tone was harsh, her demeanour was far warmer. "I'm not one for discussing my relationships. Not with work colleagues, anyway."

"Probably for the best," he said and drank his way through the awkward silence that followed.

"Shall we go upstairs? I mean, if we're not going to eat, then we might as well, right?"

Disappointed, but keen not to let it show, Ben nodded and pulled his tie off, tossing it onto the kitchen side.

"After you," he said, presenting the doorway with another sweep of his arm.

"Has she been asking questions?" Anna asked. "Does she suspect anything?"

"This is Freya we're talking about," he replied, as they made their way upstairs. "Guilty until proven innocent. I told her I was cooking dinner for my dad so we could discuss his will. I knew she wouldn't be interested in joining us, so we're safe for a while."

Anna laughed a little and stepped to one side, allowing him to unlock the spare bedroom. He shoved open the door and invited her to enter first, then followed and tossed his keys down onto the desk.

"This is cosy," she said. "

"It's safer in here," he told her. "I keep the door locked, so she won't find anything."

"Aren't you the rebel," she said, searching his eyes as if remembering his look of deceit for future reference. She stepped closer to him, and although she was taller than Gold, Chapman, and Anderson, she still had to look up to his six-foot-something height. "Well, you'd better let me see it, then," she whispered.

At this, Ben held his hand out, presenting the desk against the inner wall, above which was a corkboard, and the two of them stared at it for a while.

"Recap?" she said.

Ben mentally prepared himself to go over the facts before pointing up at an old photograph of a man leaning on an expensive-looking walnut desk. He wore a suit of olive-green tweed, a Tattersall shirt, and a red tie. Even if Ben did not know Freya's heritage, the image marked them out as quintessentially of the British upper middle class.

"Archibald Bloom. Fifty-nine years old. Died from trauma caused by several blows to the side of his head. This was back in the eighties. Freya would have been ten or eleven years old at the time."

"And the murder is unsolved still?"

"Yep. Surrey Police have it as an open investigation."

"A cold case? And are they willing to help?" She picked up a file that somebody had given to Ben a few months ago.

"I haven't got that far. I'm cautious that if I reach out, then some busybody might look into me."

"And if they do that, they'll find Freya and put two and two together?" she surmised and gave him a questioning stare to follow.

"I don't want to do this, Anna. I don't want to suspect her. I'm doing this for my own sanity. Because it's my bloody job. Because if I don't and somebody else does, then God knows what could happen. If I know what happened, I can do something about it."

Anna put the file down on the desk and nodded.

"Or you could spend the rest of your life wondering if the woman you love, the woman you spend all day catching killers with, is a killer herself?"

She stared up at him.

"Are you going to help me or not?" he said.

"What do we have on Freya?" she asked.

"Nothing tangible. Not yet anyway. We cornered a suspect a few months ago on that job in Mablethorpe. It was something he said. It was as if he knew what she'd done, somehow."

"A suspect will say anything when he's cornered and looking at twenty years inside, Ben."

"No, it was more than that. It was her reaction."

"You told me all this before, Ben."

"I know, but it was what she did, or what

she didn't do, I should say. His words were like a blow to her. Like her secret was out. I've never seen her react to anything like that."

"Wow. I doubt the jury would even have to leave the courtroom to deliberate on that one, Ben."

"Oh, come on. Don't mock me. This is hard, you know? I don't enjoy doing this. I feel like I'm betraying her."

"Well, at least your morals are intact."

"Don't laugh, Anna. Please. I just need to know if what happened to her uncle had anything to do with her."

"But you spent last night with her. And I'm guessing you've spent other nights with her. Are you acting normally?"

"Well, I thought so," he said. "And how did you know I spent last night with her?"

"Because I'm a detective, Ben," she said. "Your house is tidy. You haven't been here all weekend, which means you must have been in another place."

"Right," he said. "She knows something is wrong. She's intuitive like that. I've just been telling her that nothing is wrong, and I suppose I'll have to keep telling her that nothing is wrong until it either is or it isn't, won't I?"

"I suppose," she said, turning back to the corkboard. "So, we've got the file on Uncle Archie, and we've got the dribbling monologue of a cornered serial killer. What else do we have to go on?"

There was a sincerity in her eyes. A look that only a true friend could offer, in light of the colossal mess Ben was getting into. Only a true friend would give somebody a leg up into a field with a raging bull in it.

"She's had therapy," he said quietly.

"Right? So did I and I never killed anybody. Although, I've often thought about throttling Gillespie."

"When she was a kid," he said, shaking his head to rid the image of Anna with her hands around Gillespie's neck. "She mentioned it once but didn't go into details."

"Right, so she accidentally murdered her uncle and had therapy about it?"

"No, of course not. But he was abusing her."

"According to your theory."

"Can you imagine how something like that could affect a young girl, or anybody come to think of it? It's got to do some damage, hasn't it? I mean, you hear about it all the time. How events in people's past shape them as adults. It's not uncommon for abused kids to steer clear of sexual relationships when they get older, in the same way that it's not uncommon for abused boys to become gay in later life, or for abused girls to become highly sexed. I mean, it's not a blanket statement, but it happens–"

"Ben."

"What?"

"Highly sexed?"

"Look, I don't know why, but it happens more often than you might think. I'm not an expert in the effects of sexual abuse in later life, and if I'm honest, I'd rather not become one."

"Clearly–"

"But I've been in the force for long enough to see fairly indisputable trends," he said, and then let the words permeate.

"And is she?"

"Is she what?" he asked.

"You know? Highly sexed, as you put it."

He sighed and fought the grin that was emerging.

"She is, isn't she?"

"That's not the point. The point is that if she was being abused, Anna, then there's every chance she would have sought some kind of mental help."

"Are we proving that she was abused or proving that she killed her uncle?" Anna asked.

She folded her arms, clearly happy that she had made her point.

"Neither," he said. "We're proving she's innocent. We're hoping that she's innocent. That's all."

She took a few steps forward, closing the gap between them, but keeping her arms folded to maintain a barrier between them.

"Do you want my advice?" she said.

"You're here at my invitation, aren't you?"

"Bin it all," she told him.

"Eh?"

"Bin it all. All of it. You clearly like her. Does it really matter what she did when she was young, especially if she did while in the process of—"

"Okay, I get it," he said, cutting her off.

"Just let it go, Ben. No good can come of this. No good at all."

He closed his eyes. She was right. He knew she was right. Even if Freya had done something terrible as a child, that was no reflection of her personality today.

"You're right," he said. "I know you're right."

"So, you'll stop all of this nonsense?"

He glanced across at the board. It was like the boards they put together in the station at the beginning of an investigation when details were few and far between and theories were developed.

"How about I pause it?" he said. "At least until she says something else about it."

"A cold case, you mean?"

"Something like that," he said, hearing the weakness in his voice.

"I'm happy to help you, Ben. I mean, I'm not sure what we can do. Her medical records will be thirty years old and confidential, so any research would be limited or illegal," she said. "But why not just lock the door, walk away, and bloody well love her for who she is now? Enjoy your time with her. You never know what's around the corner."

He nodded unconvincingly.

"What is it?" she said, studying his eyes

for a clue. "What aren't you telling me?" He said nothing, of course, but failed to hide his deceit. "You've found something, haven't you? Ben, if you're hiding something–"

"Lock the door, you say?" he said, and she obviously saw he wasn't prepared to divulge anything else.

"Lock it and walk away," she replied. "Forget all about Uncle Archie and the vile fantasies of a maniac and walk away, Ben." She stepped closer to him to underline the point she had made. "Bin it all before this gets out of control and you lose everything."

CHAPTER FOURTEEN

In the time it had taken Freya to compose several emails requesting warrants to obtain financial information on Geoffrey Wilson and Faye Butters, plus search warrants for each of their houses based on almost no evidence at all, the night had drawn in. She contemplated giving Ben a call to vent, but thought that time spent with his father would be time he'd appreciate, and after all, who wanted to be the nagging girlfriend checking up on him? Who wanted to be that woman?

She closed her laptop and walked over to the window to close the curtains. A sliver of light still graced the sky, throwing hues of yellows and oranges among the clouds. They were cirrus clouds, she thought, streaks of moisture that allowed the remnants of the sunlight to shine through. Gorgeous. If that was the type of sky she could expect to see more often from her living room, then her choice of house had been a fine one. To top it off, the village church was silhouetted against that watercolour sky and somehow that signified peace. She was by no means religious, but a church was a church. It represented so much more than religion. The most devout of atheists can still enjoy an old church and the imagination they conjure.

Beside the little village green outside her cottage, a pair of headlights shone. Perhaps it was the lovers she'd seen before. Perhaps they had arranged to rendezvous there, before heading off somewhere that offered a little more privacy.

She tugged the curtains closed and then arranged them so they hung neatly. It was something that she knew she did but hated the reasons behind it. It wasn't that she was particularly house proud, although ironically she had been particularly pleased with herself for finding the curtains. It was more to do with chaos. The chaos in her mind, in her life, in everything she did. The files on her desk at work, the mess in the kitchen, the mess in her head. It was the little things in life, small touches of order that showed themselves despite the chaos. Ben was orderly. Perhaps that was why she was so drawn to him. Perhaps deep down she hoped his orderliness, if that was even a word, would rub off on her, or drag her from the melee of information, things, ideas, and passions that was her mind.

Leaving her laptop on the dining table, she grabbed her work bag and ventured upstairs, snatching her wine glass from the table as an afterthought. However orderly she wanted to be, what was the point if there was no wine to enjoy?

Her bedroom was just that, a bedroom. And being the first house she'd owned and lived in alone, she'd made the decision to use the larger of the spare rooms as a dressing room. Her space. Not that anybody else could lay claim to another part of the cottage, but it was her space. Her dressing table, her wardrobe, her clothes, makeup, and her table. It was an old thing that she'd bought from a second-hand place on Lincoln High Street. The owner had been quite charming and had agreed to deliver that and a few other bits and pieces to bridge the gap between buying the house and for the furniture that she'd ordered new to arrive. She'd been tempted to get rid of the table, having very little use for it. But now that it was in her dressing room, she saw a charm in it. A charm that no new thing could ever offer, regardless of cost.

But her attention on that evening was not on the table itself, but the spread of paper on top. In particular, a large A3 sheet on which she had begun to make a list.

The first item was simple. Three words. Road Traffic Accident. From those three words, she'd drawn a line to a name. PCSO Harris.

The second item was even simpler. One word. Complaint. From which she had drawn a line to another name. Sergeant Sanderson.

And now it was time to add a new line. She scribbled on the paper, Press Leak, then drew a line to a new name. Sergeant Godfrey.

Three names. That was enough for her to work with for the time being. Every one of them worked out of Lincoln Police Station, and every one of them had made, or at least tried to make, her life difficult in one way or another.

She picked up her phone, found Ben's number, and hit the call button. The phone rang, and it rang, and then before it could ring any more, she ended it. Nothing was worse than hearing that annoying, stuck-up cow informing her that the person she had called was not available.

She sat there for a moment, eyed the half-empty wine glass, and then padded down the stairs. In a jiffy, she had her shoes on, had dragged her coat onto her shoulders, and snatched her handbag from the dining table. Bugger it, she thought. She didn't mind being that woman. She'd been called far worse in her life.

———

Ben had his hands in piping hot water when he thought he heard something. He switched off the tap and listened, and then heard it again. A gentle knock on his front door. He was barefoot and the shirt he'd been wearing was hanging over the banister. He wiped his hands on the way out through the hallway and peered through the frosted glass.

"Freya?" he said when he saw her on his doorstep. She didn't wait for an invite. Instead, she smiled and breezed past him and went straight into the living room. "Come in, why don't you?"

"I need help," she said when he had closed the door and was leaning against the doorframe, tea towel in hand.

"You finally realised–"

"Somebody is out to get me," she said, and he sighed.

"Nobody is out to get you, Freya."

"First, it was the car thing. Do you remember? The RTA I was supposed to have been involved in."

"I remember, yes."

"Right, that was a PCSO something or other."

"Harris," Ben said, recalling the name with relative ease, mostly because he had felt sorry for the poor bloke, being told to knock on Freya's front door and arrest her for leaving the scene of an accident. "PCSO Harris."

"Then there was the complaint," she said. "Sergeant bloody Sanderson."

"Ah, yes. Well, to be fair, you did belittle him in front of half the East Midlands Police Force."

"So instead of coming to me, he went above my head. The next thing I know I'm being pulled into Granger's office," she said. "And now this press thing. God knows what's going to be in the papers tomorrow. But one thing is for sure, I'll be spending the afternoon in Granger's bloody hot seat again."

"Nothing's going to happen," he said. "The boys managed to stop him."

"Don't you think it's a bit of a coincidence?"

"Not really," he replied. "You have a way of attracting this kind of thing. Trouble seems to find you, doesn't it?"

"I think they're connected," she said. "I think somebody is out to get me. And what do you mean, trouble seems to find me?"

"Well, it does. I don't know how. It just does," he said. "You have a way of..." He faltered, deliberating on the correct word to use.

"A way of what?" she said, her tone sharp and her words succinct. Never a good sign.

"Of rubbing people up the wrong way," he told her, in as nice a tone as he could. "Some people just don't understand you. But I do, and the team does. Who else matters?"

"I rub people up the wrong way, do I?"

"Look Freya, I can't paint it in any prettier a picture. Some people don't like you. Some people don't like me. So what? I don't care."

"Everybody likes you, Ben."

"Doctor Bell doesn't," he countered.

"Doctor Bell loves you," she said. "She just has an odd sense of humour and knows how easy it is to wind you up."

"I was not staring at her..." He faltered again and gestured at Freya's chest.

"Her what?" she said, seeming to enjoy his struggle.

"Her lady parts," he said. "I wasn't. But it's pretty hard not to look when she wears those t-shirts with slogans on, and there's half a Welsh dragon sticking out of her top."

"So, I've upset somebody," Freya moved on. "And it's somebody working out of Lincoln."

"Oh, behave."

"I mean it, Ben. I am not going to let this go. Nobody takes advantage of me and gets away with it. Nobody."

He stared at her, reading far more into that statement than she likely intended.

"And you want me to help you find out who it is that you've upset?"

"I do," she said. "And if you do this, I'll never forget it."

"And if I don't?" he asked rhetorically.

She smiled a smile that conveyed something far from pleasure and stepped towards him.

"Why don't I answer that question with a question of my own?" she said. "Am I staying here tonight or am I going home alone? Big day tomorrow. We're going to need our game faces on."

"Did you request the warrants?" he asked, aware that she was edging closer.

"I did," she said, her voice low and authoritative. "And I must say it was a work of art. Dickens would have been impressed at the rubbish I had to write."

She moved closer still.

"Busy day tomorrow, then," he said.

"Oh, very," she replied, as she took the final step and peered up at him, her eyes seeming to be everywhere at once.

"Nobody is out to get you, Freya," he said, and she stopped, the mood dying in an instant.

"So, you won't help me?" she replied. "You're not going to help me. Is that right?"

"If I thought there was a problem, then I'd help. You know I would, Freya. But I feel like if I help you look into, what, three names?" He shook his head at the very idea of it all. "All I'd be doing is feeding this whole thing. I wouldn't be helping you. It's not the help you need."

She didn't say anything – not at first anyway. She just kind of stared at him quizzically.

"How very disappointing, Ben," she said, softly, and she moved past him to leave, looking back over her shoulder. "Just when I thought you were on my side."

"I am on your side–"

"If you were on my side, then you would support me, Ben," she told him. "I'll see you in the office."

"Freya–"

"Don't push me, Ben," she said. "Perhaps this whole thing has been a mistake after all."

"Don't do this."

"Goodbye, Ben," she said. "At least we didn't go too far. It's not like we were married, is it?"

"No," he replied softly.

"Then, I'd say we got off pretty lightly," she said. "Wouldn't you?"

CHAPTER FIFTEEN

The disappointment lasted throughout the long night. Instead of sleep, Freya found a hundred different things to think about. The names, the mistakes she'd made, her move to Lincolnshire, and even her past, which she had somehow managed to put to one side for the past year or so. She must have nodded off eventually, as she had woken in a daze, groggy, and instantly reminded of her disappointment.

She checked her phone to see if he'd sent any messages, perhaps apologising for his betrayal. But there was none. What the man knew about women she could write on the back of a cigarette packet. Even if he did believe that she was wrong, the decent thing to do would have been to at least go along with it. Support her in her hour of need.

She dropped her phone onto the bedside table and rolled over to stretch. The slice of light that shone between the curtains was weak and heavy raindrops drummed against the window.

All in all, she'd had barely three hours of sleep and the day was already heading south.

She rose, then ran the shower while she chose what to wear, laying out her favourite trouser suit with a white blouse.

The water was hot but did little to rouse her from her mood, and it was thirty minutes later when she was showered, dressed, and made up, that she ventured downstairs into the kitchen and inhaled the aroma of coffee that she felt half human.

With her coffee cup in hand, she strode across the wooden floor and pulled back the curtains one at a time, stopping for a moment to savour the view, remarking on how different it was from the previous night. There was no beautiful wash of oranges and yellows, only shades of grey through a window dotted with raindrops, each one creating its own path downward. Even the church seemed to have shrunk back into the shadows of neighbouring trees.

A man with a dog passed by, slowing to admire her front garden, for which she could take no credit. The little cottage garden was small but the previous owner had done an incredible job of creating something of beauty. Plant names were not Freya's forte, but she did pride herself on style, and whoever selected the plants clearly shared a vision. No sooner had the man stepped out of view than a car passed by, slowing at the end of the road and then speeding off towards the church, to Lincoln beyond.

She stayed there a moment. The bench was empty. Too early and wet even for lovers. An estate car came and went, heading in the opposite direction this time, and much slower. Slow enough for Freya to notice the last three letters of the registration plate: BFG. It was an easy one to notice. An age ago, when she'd had a husband and raised his boy as her own, little Billy had loved Roald Dahl stories. The Big Friendly Giant had been a particular favourite.

She swallowed her coffee and began

packing her bag. Her laptop, files, and pens went into her work bag, while her phone, purse, and keys went into her handbag.

The dark green Barbour jacket she wore rather sullied the look of her smart trouser suit, but it was warm and waterproof. Perhaps her time in Lincolnshire was rubbing off on her after all. A function-over-form approach was seeping in. But she'd spent too many days standing out in a field or on a country lane, freezing to the point of not being able to function to disregard the warmth and practicality of country clothing. That didn't mean that she had to walk around like a vagrant, however. She could still show these country boys a little style.

She locked the house and climbed into her car, prioritising the engine and the heater before doing much else, all the while wondering how the weather had turned from a blistering summer to an arctic winter in the space of a few weeks. The seasons seemed to be shifting. The environmental issues, perhaps, she thought rather guiltily, as her Range Rover's huge engine grumbled away. The moment she felt heat on her feet, she began the process of demisting the windscreen. At least it wasn't icy. Those mornings were yet to come.

The roads were quiet and she made her way through Metheringham at a reasonable pace. Thirty-three miles per hour. Not exactly speeding, but not dawdling either. She wanted to be the first into the office to devise a plan so they could hold a briefing almost immediately. The less amount of time she spent around Ben, the better.

She pictured the scene of the crime, more for a distraction than anything else. Three routes in and three routes out, only one of which was a viable option. According to Gillespie, the killer had moved south from the scene, through the small field and onto Castle Lane. From there, they could only have turned left back into Boothby Graffoe. The question is, what did they do then? Did they have a car parked nearby, or did they live close enough to walk? Were they a regular face? People didn't see regular faces. They didn't notice them the way they might notice a stranger, especially in a small village like Boothby.

She crossed the railway tracks at Metheringham, grateful to have missed the seven-thirty train which could back the traffic up a fair way. She despised being held up by the train. It wouldn't be so bad if it was carrying hundreds of commuters, but the train was only two carriages long. A shuttle that ran from Peterborough to Lincoln. But of course, it was still a train, and the authorities still demanded the barrier to close for what seemed like an eternity before the two carriages rumbled past.

She passed the sign for the national speed limit and put her foot down, peering in her mirror and noticing only two cars behind her. The first was a pickup truck used by thousands of drivers across the county. The car behind it was a newish Volvo. An estate car. She put some distance between her car and the pickup then settled into the short drive.

Linda Wilson's body occupied much of her thoughts. The woman in the photo she had seen through the window was unmistakably her, and she pictured the straight nose and deep-set eyes, but her mind led her to the head wound covered in debris from the forest floor. The smudged and disfigured footprints on either side of her. Her last moments. Having a scarf forced into her mouth and the full weight of her killer pinning her down. She would have kicked. She would have tried to scream.

And of course, there was the sound of death to consider.

The sound Mason had heard. Death. Relief. Relief that it was over? Or satisfaction in the moment?

She turned off the main road as she usually did, pondering her last thought.

Relief that it was over? Satisfaction in the moment. Satisfaction?

She glanced in the mirror again. The estate had taken the same turning as she had and was a hundred metres or so behind.

Fumbling for her phone and keeping one eye on the road, she opened her voice notes app and hit record.

"Relief or satisfaction," she said, by way of introducing the sound clip. "Relief. The killer was relieved. Relieved that she was dead, or relieved that the process of killing her was over? Satisfaction. Orgasm. There was no sign of sexual assault, but did the killer satisfy himself? Did he masturbate?"

She set the phone down in the centre console, aware that she had slowed a little while speaking. The car behind was larger in the mirror now. Still a reasonable distance, but closer. Close enough for her to read the last letters of the number plate, which caught her attention, and instinctively, she braked. The other driver followed suit and hung back.

"Go past," she said, slowing to a stop and pulling onto the verge. "Go past me."

But the driver slowed to a stop in the middle of the lane. She couldn't make out the rest of the registration plate. But she was certain of those last three letters. The headlights were on, as they nearly always were on a Volvo. It was something to do with being a Scandinavian car. Something she had been told once. She indicated and pulled back onto the road slowly, and the Volvo moved with hers.

"You bastard," she whispered to herself, then gunned the engine.

The lane was mostly straight, as they often were in those parts, tracking the edge of a field or a ditch. She took the car to fifty, far too fast for the road, but manageable, and still the car behind maintained its distance.

She took the car up to sixty, monitoring the Volvo as often as she dared, until she rounded a corner and came across an on-coming car. The driver braked hard, sounded his horn, and flashed his lights, and it was all Freya could do to keep her car on the road, using the verge at the last minute, and praying that she didn't roll into the deep dyke that ran alongside it. Once around the corner, she slammed on the brakes, opened the door, and climbed out, ready for the Volvo to follow. She fished her warrant card from her pocket, ready to bring them to a halt.

But nobody came. No car emerged from around the corner. Slowly, she walked back up the lane, hugging her jacket around her and half expecting to find the Volvo coming careering around the bend.

But nothing came. The road was empty. She could see all the way back to the main road in the distance.

Then a car approached in the distance, moving slowly. It was black or dark blue. She couldn't quite tell yet. She tried to make out the shape, but it was difficult to do in the low light. It was only when the car was within a few hundred metres that she saw it wasn't a Volvo.

It was an old Ford Focus, and the driver pulled up beside her, lowering his window as he did.

But he said nothing.

"Did you pass a Volvo?" she said.

"Eh?"

"A Volvo, Ben. Did you just pass one on this road? A dark blue estate. It would have been less than a minute ago."

"I don't know," he replied casually. "I wasn't really paying attention. My wiper blades need changing. Why?"

She stared along the lane back to the main road.

"No reason," she told him, avoiding eye contact. The adrenaline still coursed through her body, and the onset of sweat formed in the small of her back.

"Freya? Are you all right? Listen, if it's about last night–"

"Just leave me alone, Ben," she replied, taking a deep breath and turned on her heels. "Just bloody well leave me alone, will you?"

CHAPTER SIXTEEN

The incident room was rarely a joyous place to be, especially on a Monday morning, and especially when Freya was in a temper. And today was no exception. Ben had parked beside her in the car park and felt her fractious mood the moment she climbed from her car. She had slammed the door and brushed past him without so much as a hi or goodbye, leaving him to follow after her, shaking his head.

Typically, whenever Freya was out of the office, the rest of the team would chat while they worked, and often entered into heavy debates on rudimentary matters; the best chocolate bar was a favourite, or the cold pillow or hot pillow debate. And today was no different, although he never did find out what they had been talking about. All he had heard from the stairwell was the rumble of Gillespie's laughter, a shrill whine from Cruz, and then silence when the incident room doors had slammed closed, denoting Freya's entrance in a flurry of coat tails and dark clouds.

"Listen up," she said, as Ben pushed into the room quietly, nodded a greeting at a wide-eyed Anna Nillson and Jackie Gold, and then slipped into his seat, knowing full well not to speak until spoken to.

Freya dragged the whiteboard closer to where she was perched on the edge of her desk and snatched up a pen, scrawling a name in barely legible writing. In fact, had Ben not already known the name she had written, she could have written I'm a moody cow in Urdu and he'd have been none the wiser.

"Linda Wilson," she said, drawing from it a horizontal line a few inches long, and then adding some more possibly Sanskrit symbols. "Geoff Wilson. The husband. Missing, or at least trying not to be found, along with..."

she said and scrawled yet another name. "Faye Butters, wife of Kyle Butters. Also missing, or at least trying not to be found." She stabbed a full stop, clicked the lid onto the pen, and looked up. "Any questions so far?"

Nobody said a word.

"Good. Linda's body was found in a small copse of trees at the top of what I hear is called the Lincoln Edge, or the Lincoln Cliff. Do we all know it?"

"Aye, boss," Gillespie grumbled, the only one to respond.

"I know that you know it, Sergeant Gillespie. You were there with us yesterday."

"Aye, I know. I was just–"

"Are we all familiar with the geography?" she said, cutting him off.

"Yes, boss," Nillson said, never one to shy away from danger.

Freya waited for more responses and took the smattering of nervous nods as a positive.

"Good. Cruz, print me a map, will you? And while you're at it, you might as well print the photos of the crime scene."

Cruz, the youngest and least experienced of them all, said nothing and opened his laptop. A few tense moments followed, during which time Freya stared at each of the team in turn, except for Ben. That was okay. He could handle a cold shoulder if it meant a warm hand was to follow, which it undoubtedly was. If anything, a period of separation might make the day easier. He might even be assigned somebody else to work with. Moments later, the printer whirred into life, and Freya stood, walked over to the great big, outdated machine, and snatched up the A3 sheet. Silently, she strode over to the large board on the back wall and, using magnets, she fixed it into place.

"Gather round," she said, which was followed by a cacophony of scraping chairs, fluttering notepads, clicking pens, but not a single word was uttered.

She circled the crime scene with a red marker, then drew a line east, through the paddock to where they had parked the cars.

"Entry point one," she said, and then drew a line that tracked Viking Way heading north to Coleby. "Entry point two." Finally, she drew a line south, through the trees, across a field, and out onto Castle Lane. "Entry point three," she said, then struck a heavy pen mark through lines one and two. "Due to heavy rain on Saturday night, the crime scene was a mess. Thick mud. Not good for forensics. Impossible, in fact. But what DI Savage and I deduced from the footprints and our one witness, was that the killer had to have left using the southern path onto Castle Lane."

The printer stopped, then clicked off, and seemed to sigh like an old rhinoceros in the baking sun.

"Boss?" Cruz said, and Freya looked his way, eyebrows raised. He pointed to the printer. "Do you, erm, want me to–"

"Don't wait to be asked, Cruz. Let's see some initiative."

"Right," he said and glanced around as if still unsure if he should get the photos from the printer or not. Ben gave him a discreet nod and he slipped from the huddle and made his way across the room.

"However," Freya said, regaining their attention, "that's not to say the killer approached from this direction." She circled the feed store further along Castle Lane. "We know from CCTV at the gates of this premises that nobody drove or walked along

Castle Lane in either direction during the given time frame. Which means that whoever did this, either had a car parked somewhere in the village of Boothby Graffoe or..."

"Or lives there," Nillson said.

"Exactly," Freya replied, as Cruz returned with a stack of printed photos which he nervously began fixing to the board with magnets. "Sergeant Gillespie has been through the entire village, going door to door. So perhaps he can enlighten us with his findings?"

"My findings?" he said. "I put them in the report."

"Which report?"

"The one I sent you at one o'clock this morning, along with the results of the search, boss."

"Okay, so let's assume I haven't managed to read them yet."

"Right," he said, doing his best to hide his irritation. "The short answer?"

"It would be my preference, Gillespie," she said.

"Nobody saw a damn thing. Nada. No dog walkers. No cars. Nothing."

"Cameras?"

"Oh, plenty of cameras, boss. Plenty of

money in Boothby, I can tell you. But with big expensive houses come big expensive driveways, tall gates, and concealed entrances."

"So, nothing that faces the road? Nothing we can use?"

He shook his head.

"Afraid not, boss."

"And the search?" she said. "I presume you did get the resources you needed to finish?"

"We searched every inch of the space between the crime scene and Castle Lane. There's a list of the finds in the report."

"Again, let's assume I haven't had a chance to read the report yet."

"I was up all night doing those."

"No, you weren't," she told him. "You just said that you sent them at one o'clock this morning. That's hardly what I would call an all-nighter, so if you're going to log the overtime, I'd be mindful of that if I were you."

"Jesus," he muttered to himself, but loud for all to hear. Then he made a show of trying to remember what was on the list, running his hand through his thick, long hair and closing his eyes. "Plenty of rocks, a traffic cone, a few old beer cans so faded you can't even read what beer it used to hold, broken bottles–"

"What bottles?"

"Wine," he said, with a shrug, and for the first time, Freya looked at Ben.

"Where are they now?"

"Evidence locker, boss," Gillespie said.

"Right, first job for you. Get them to the lab."

The task seemed to please him. Going to the lab for a man like Gillespie was an invitation to procrastinate, have a little chat with the techies, and maybe stop for a coffee on the way back to the station. "You can do that before you head back to the crime scene."

"Eh?"

"I want the rest of the area searched. North along Viking Way all the way up to Coleby, and east across the paddock."

His expression said everything he was thinking.

"And no stopping for a little chat or a coffee on the way."

"Do I get Cruz this time?" he asked. "It's a big area."

"No. Contact Lincoln again. Tell them we

need the resources. Any issues, tell whoever it is to contact Ben."

The mention of his name came as a surprise, and Ben looked up from his notes but chose to stay silent and nod his agreement. That was enough.

Cruz, who had spent far too long fixing the images to the board, finally stepped back to admire his work, only for Freya to step in front of him and immediately start to reorganise them, collating the images of the victim and the close-ups of her injuries separately to those of the wider crime scene. Cruz appeared deflated, but if anyone was used to being overruled in all aspects of his life, it was him.

"Kyle Butters, husband of the missing Faye Butters, stated that he and his wife went for their normal dog walk around five-thirty to six o'clock. They had an argument or a disagreement, and he walked away. She hasn't been seen since."

"So, she could be lying out there as well?" Nillson said.

"She could be," Freya replied. "Or she could be hiding somewhere. Hiding somewhere with this man. Geoff Wilson. Husband of the victim. They both work at Lincoln Library and according to their boss, they have recently been thick as thieves."

"Oh, not another affair," Cruz said, then reddened. "Sorry, boss."

"No apology needed."

"It's just that nearly every time we investigate a murder, whether it's got anything to do with the murder or not, somebody is having an affair. I mean, why do people even bother with relationships?"

"Why indeed, Cruz?" she replied. "Why indeed? Perhaps it's a sign of the way society is heading. Perhaps we aren't meant to be in relationships, after all. Perhaps we're meant to be non-monogamous."

Cruz said nothing, clearly not knowing the meaning of the word, leaving Freya to continue.

"As you can see by the wound to her head, Linda Wilson was hit with something hard. But what you can't see, because of all the debris that is stuck to the blood, is that the wound was inflicted by something round and hard. Something round enough that it glanced off her head."

"You mean, it didn't kill her?" Nillson asked.

"No. The killer had to get a little more hands-on than perhaps he or she was hoping to," Freya replied. "CSI found footprints from a pair of Wellington boots on either side of her midriff. Sadly, there were no discernible prints."

"They sat on her and throttled her?" Nillson said.

"Close. Suffocated. Pippa Bell discovered a thread of blue wool in the victim's teeth. So, we're assuming it was a scarf or a hat, or even a pair of woolly gloves."

"It's not cold enough for gloves, surely?" Gillespie said. "A hat, maybe. A scarf? Doubtful. Gloves? Definitely not."

"Blue wool," Freya repeated. "That's what we've got." She looked across to Ben. "Am I missing anything?"

He studied the images and his notes then closed his notebook.

"She was found by a Mr Mason," he said to the team. "Elderly chap—"

"Don't tell me, he was out walking his dog," Cruz said.

"He was indeed."

"For God's sake," he replied. "Affairs and dog walkers. There should be a law against them both, then we'd see a drop in murders. You watch."

"You can't ban dog walking, you idiot," Gillespie said.

"And if they banned affairs, then Gillespie would have to find a real girlfriend instead of borrowing other peoples'," Gold chimed in, her soft Edinburgh accent somehow adding to the humour.

"It wasn't what Mr Mason was doing that was odd," Ben added. "It was what he heard."

"What he heard?" Gold said.

"Death," Ben replied.

"What?"

"Death," Freya said. "The sigh of relief. Like an orgasm. And those were his words, not mine."

"Oh, for God's sake, you're not saying–"

"There's no evidence of sexual assault from what we understand. But that's not to say that he didn't pleasure himself. It's not uncommon for offenders to do such a thing."

"What a sicko," Chapman said, the first words she'd said so far. She was a polite young lady who was far older than her years, and who rarely ventured out of the office.

"There's nothing to suggest that it was a he or a she, and there's nothing really to go on at all, except the musings of an old man." She pointed to a spot on the map. "He said he was walking around here when he heard the noise, and then walked back up here to the break in the trees, which is when he found the body in a little circle of stones." She tapped the photo of the rocks that had clearly fallen from a nearby wall and had been placed to form a large bonfire. "Which supports our theory that the killer exited south to Castle Lane. Mr Mason is an older gentleman. It would have taken him a minute or so to climb back up the hill, meaning that if somebody had walked either north or east, he would have seen them."

"Makes sense," Nillson said. "Gillespie, did you make a note of the names of the people you spoke to?"

"Of course I did," he said. "It's in the report."

"Maybe we can cross-check the list with the database to see if anyone has previous?"

"Good call," Freya said. "But before we

get carried away and make a plan, I want you to think about this." She took a few steps away from them and then turned. "Mr Mason said he heard a sound like an orgasm. I'm sure we all know what that sounds like—"

"I don't suppose you could just be a wee bit clearer on that, boss, could you?" Gillespie said. "You know? Give us an example?"

She ignored him and regained control of the room, snuffing out any laughter.

"In my mind, the sound of an orgasm signifies one of two things," she said. "Relief or satisfaction."

"Relief?" Anderson said, who had been quiet up until now. "As in relief that he or she had killed her? That it was over?"

"Perhaps," Freya said.

"Satisfaction would be creepy though," Cruz said. "I mean, that would mean that they enjoyed it, wouldn't it?"

"Precisely my point," Freya said, nodding emphatically at him and then pausing to look them all in the eye. All except Ben, that is. "We'd just better pray it was the sound of relief that Mr Mason heard. Because if whoever did this enjoyed the sensation of snuffing out Linda Wilson's life, then we're not dealing with an act of desperation here. Her death won't be the result of an emotional reaction. It will be something far worse, and our jobs are going to get much harder."

<hr>

CHAPTER SEVENTEEN

<hr>

"Right then," Freya said, as she stepped through the huddle and back to her desk, where she perched once more. The rest of the team ambled back to their desks, all apart from Cruz who remained there, staring at the images and the map. "Cruz, come on," she said. "Lots to do."

"Sorry, boss," he replied. "It's just..." He stopped as if he daren't voice what he was thinking for fear of being ridiculed.

"It's just what?"

"Well, did Linda Wilson live in Boothby Graffoe?"

"No, she and her husband have a house in the next village. Why?"

"Well, what was she doing there, then?" he said. "You told us that…" He paused to check his notes. "Kyle Butters and his wife Faye went out to walk the dog at around five-thirty. Mr Mason went out at six a.m. and discovered the body."

"Right," Freya said, seeing where he was going, and for once was pleased it was he who had posed the question.

"So, what the hell was she doing out there so early in the morning? Does she have a dog?"

"Maybe she was waiting for Faye Butters?" Nillson said. "Maybe she had learned of the affair and was waiting to give her what for? Maybe Faye Butters saw her and maybe Faye Butters hit her?"

"With a bottle?" Cruz said. "Is there any sign of a fight, other than the head injury?"

"No," Ben said, but Freya refused to look his way. "We saw the body. Her hands were fine. You'd expect somebody who had been fighting to have scratches, swollen knuckles, or even a broken fingernail. There was none of that. In fact, both the FME and Pip suggested she was hit from behind."

"Okay," Cruz said, as he stepped away

from the board. It was odd to see him ask so many questions. He walked as if he was leading the investigation and was prompting his team to generate ideas. "So, if it was Faye Butters, then she must have found the bottle on the ground, crept up on her, and whacked her? But why?"

"Maybe they were talking and Linda turned her back?" Nillson said.

"Even so, Faye would have had to pick up a bottle and clobber her with it," he said. "I mean, if Faye Butters was the victim, then yeah, sure. I'd get it. Linda might have whacked Faye for seeing her husband behind her back. But Faye was the one in the wrong. It was Faye who was, according to our theory at least, sleeping with Linda's husband."

"That hasn't been confirmed," Freya said. "But I understand the point that you're trying to make. Faye Butters is missing and is linked through her potential relationship with Linda's husband. But what's the motive?"

"Right," he said.

"Well, perhaps we can bear that in mind," she told him and the rest of the team. "First things first, we need a formal identification.

For that, we'll need to find her husband, Geoffrey Wilson. Failing that, Katy Southwell, the new CSI lead, matched the DNA to a son, Thomas Wilson. Chapman, can I task you with finding him?"

"No problem," Chapman replied, making a neat note on her notepad.

"Also for you, Chapman," Freya said, pointing her pen in Chapman's direction. "I want Geoffrey Wilson and Faye Butters' financial information. Credit cards, bank statements, the usual. I've requested warrants, so just keep an eye out for them to come in, will you?"

Chapman added the note but said nothing leaving Freya to keep the momentum going.

"Gold, until we've got something more for you, can you get in touch with the phone providers? I want to know who Geoffrey Wilson and Faye Butters spoke to or messaged in the past few days, and if they're active on social media, let's see it, please."

"Yes, boss," Gold said. "What about when we find the husband?"

"If we find the husband, then you'll be assigned as Family Liaison Officer in the first instance, so make notes in case you have to hand over. In fact, Cruz, help her, will you? I need attention to detail on this."

"Sure," he said, very obviously pleased with the task.

"What about us, boss?" Nillson asked, referring to her and Jenny Anderson, a London-born detective whom Freya had first encountered during a prolonged spell out of a South London station.

"The list of names that Gillespie created during his door-to-door exercise," she said. "I'd like to add your idea of cross-checking them against the database. Run the names past Chapman and Gold. I know I haven't lived in a little village for long, but I do know that small villages develop communities. People talk. People share things, they socialise. Find out if Faye Butters or either of the Wilsons spoke to anyone in the village."

She tapped the whiteboard on which she had scrawled a few names, which on a second glance she realised was barely legible, due to the mood she had been in less than an hour ago.

"These people all have friends and family.

I want to see this network expanded. I want to see if there's a common denominator."

"Sounds good, boss," Nillson replied, which left only one duo yet to be assigned a task.

But Ben said nothing. He waited patiently for Freya to speak.

"In the meantime, DI Savage, I'd like you to revisit Pippa Bell. Let's see what she found out yesterday. When you're done there, I want you at the lab. Stick a firework up their backsides and let's have some answers."

"Right," he said.

"And when you're done there, I'd like you to join DS Gillespie on the search," she said, daring him to argue. But he didn't. He simply shrugged.

"Okay."

She had expected him to raise some kind of argument, or even suggest an alternative angle. But he didn't. He seemed content to follow her instructions.

"Well," she said, "that's that then. Let's debrief this afternoon and make a plan for tomorrow. I want a name on that board with an MMO and a plan to bring them in. Understood?"

"Aye, boss," Gillespie said, almost habitually.

But Ben stayed quiet. He simply stared up at her, just as the others did.

"Right then," she said, feeling a pang of resentment at his indifference to not spending the day with her. "I'll see you all at two p.m."

"Ma'am?" Chapman said. "Sorry, before we all split up. I've got something."

"Go on," Freya said.

Chapman turned her laptop so the rest of the team could see.

"Thomas Wilson," she said. "He's currently one year into a three-year sentence at HMP Lincoln."

"He's in prison?"

"Looks like it. Pleaded guilty to several charges of tax evasion and fraud."

"Well, there goes our positive ID," Gillespie said. "Looks like we're going to have to find the husband and his secret lover."

"What's the matter, Gillespie?" Nillson said. "Scared she's going to recognise you as one of her previous conquests?"

"Funny," he replied. "Have you thought of a career in comedy? You wouldn't have to say much. You could just stand on the stage and people would laugh at your face."

Nillson rolled her eyes.

"You know what they say about unmarried middle-aged men, don't you?" she replied, waggling her pinkie finger at him.

"Any details?" Freya said to Chapman, raising her voice in the hope of cutting the vulgar and offensive tangent off because it gathered momentum.

"I can dig them out," she replied. "I'll have them ready for this afternoon."

"Good," Freya said, nodding her approval. "Good, thanks, Chapman. That's something to work with."

"There's something else," Chapman said. "I've just received access to Geoffrey Wilson's credit card statement."

"I'm tempted to ask if you've even been listening to me for the past half an hour," Freya replied with a smile.

"Sorry, ma'am," she said. "I saw it come through and couldn't help myself."

"Multitasking eh?" Nillson said. "The last time Gillespie multitasked, he was turning the pages of a magazine with one hand and–"

"Okay, okay," Freya said. "I think we all

have an idea of how Gillespie spends his free time."

"Steady on," he said, clearly hurt.

"Go on, Chapman," Freya said. "Geoffrey Wilson's statement?"

"Oh right. Well, it all looks normal. He pays the credit card balance in full every month. There are a few subscriptions. Gardening magazines, woodturning, and model trains—"

"Ah, Christ," Gillespie said. "He sounds interesting. How the hell does a man like that not only have a wife and a son, but a lover as well? I'll bet his bloody sock drawer is even organised by colour."

"My sock drawer is organised," Cruz said. "What's wrong with that? I've always wanted a model train set too. Never had one, but I've always liked the idea."

Gillespie flung his arms into the air and let them drop onto his lap.

"I rest my case," he said. "So says God's gift to singledom. The man who had, quite possibly, the best-looking female in the station – no offence, girls – as his girlfriend and managed to mess it up."

"That's enough," Freya said, and she

glanced across at Cruz, who despite his efforts, had clearly taken the words to heart. "I don't mind a little banter but that's too far, Sergeant Gillespie. You should know better."

"Aye sorry, boss," he grumbled.

"It's not me you need to apologise to," she replied, then turned back to Chapman. "Anything else?"

Chapman grinned.

"Will an Airbnb do?" she said.

Freya stared at the timid young woman, who in the past year had proven to be a better researcher than any she had worked with in the Met.

"Do you have an address?"

Chapman hit a button on her keyboard and the printer whirred into life again.

"Looks like a converted farm out near Ashby de la Launde," Chapman said, standing to make her way over to the printer. She snatched up the piece of paper, checked it, and then handed it to Freya. "The owner's details are on there, too. Do you want me to call them in advance?"

"No," Freya said. "No, thank you, Chapman." She glanced down at the piece of paper, and then folded it in half, before waving it in the air in front of Gillespie. "That's police work."

"No argument from me, boss," he said.

She stared at them all in turn, even Ben this time. She'd tried so hard not to be the bitch she knew she was. To be a good boss, a fair boss. Not like all the chauvinists she'd had to deal with in London. She wanted to be someone her team would look up to, but every time they behaved as they did, she felt that little grip of what she wanted to be slip away.

"Two o'clock," she said quietly. "Let's get to it."

CHAPTER EIGHTEEN

It was as if each of them had been counting the seconds from the moment the incident room doors had closed behind Freya. Like they were all imagining her journey down the fire escape stairs, then out to her car, and out of their hair.

Nillson savoured the temporary peace.

"Jesus bloody Christ," Gillespie said, always the first to voice his thoughts. "What the bloody hell was all that about?"

"I have no idea," Gold said. "But thank God for you, that's all I can say."

"Thank God for me? Why?"

"Because if you weren't here opening your

big mouth, then one of us would have got it in the neck. You're like our hero, Jim."

"Bloody hero. I feel like a bloody whipping boy."

"Same thing," Nillson said.

"I don't know what you're talking about," he said. "You were the instigator. It's your fault she went off on one."

"My fault? You were the one who started spouting your mouth off."

"Oh right. Was it me who brought up the whole 'Gillespie the unmarried middle-aged man' malarkey? No, it was you. Was it me who said about the whole multitasking thing?"

Nillson laughed.

"No, that was me. Pretty good, eh?"

"She said she doesn't mind a bit of banter, but every time I get involved, I end up getting it in the neck."

"You were a bit harsh on Cruz," Gold added.

"Yeah, I'd have to agree," Anderson said.

"Oh, come on," he said, waving his hand as if presenting Cruz for the first time. "He organises his sock drawer. You heard him. He wants a bloody model train set."

"There's nothing wrong with that, Jim," Chapman said, usually one to keep out of the banter and arguments but clearly brave enough to stand up for Cruz. "I think it's a good hobby. I think we need hobbies, considering what we have to deal with in here every day."

"What's your hobby, Jim?" Anderson asked.

"My what? My hobby?" he said, growing more infuriated. "I don't have one and if I did, it certainly wouldn't be playing with toy trains, that's for sure."

"And why not? What's wrong with model trains?" Nillson said. "We spend our lives going from one investigation to another. Somebody finds a body and we get called. We research, we question, we go door to door–"

"Correction, it's usually me and Gabby who go door to door."

"We go door to door," Nillson reiterated. "We gather information until we have enough to make an arrest. Then we build a case for CPS. We remand them, hand them over, and then we're done. Occasionally we have to attend a trial, but more often than not that's it. That's the extent of our involvement. We're onto the next investigation. We don't see any of them to the end, Jim, not really. So, if Gabby wants to build a model railway, then let him. At least he'll get to enjoy the end result. And if he wants to organise his bloody sock drawer, then who the bloody hell are you to pass judgement? I'll bet you could eat your dinner off his floor. While I'll wager that your place stinks of takeaway and empty beer cans. I'll bet that your sock drawer hasn't been closed for at least a month. I bet there are so many mismatched socks and God knows what sticking out of it that it won't close. You know you should really sort it out but you're not organised enough. You don't allocate the time to doing the important things because you're unhappy with who you are. So don't insult poor old Gabby just because he is organised. Just because he wants to go places. The last thing he wants to do is end up being a sad, old man who finishes work and has to go the pub to talk to the other sad, old men just to have some conversation."

She finished and found herself slightly breathless. Then she realised that she'd actually entered into the realms of a rant and that all eyes in the room were both wide and staring at her.

"I like to knit," Chapman said as if it was a meeting of Alcoholics Anonymous and she was making a confession. "Most people my age would think that's quite sad. I don't really care."

Nillson nodded at her.

"I do puzzles," Gold said. "Jigsaws. I do them when Charlie is in bed. It takes my mind off work."

"Good for you," Nillson said. "Anybody else?"

Anderson raised her hand with a smile.

"Old films," she said.

"Like what?"

"Anything. Richard Burton, Oliver Reed, Rex Harrison. I don't mind as long as it's old."

"Jesus, I'm working with a bunch of psychos," Gillespie said.

"No, Jim. No," Nillson replied. "You see, we're ordinary people. When we leave here, we're just ordinary people doing what ordinary people all over the world do."

"I suppose there's no point asking what you do, is there?" he said, turning to Cruz. "I doubt you'd have time to play with a toy train even if you had one. You'd be too busy organising your socks. No wait, you've done that."

"It won't work, Jim," Nillson said. "You're not going to embarrass him. If anything, you're the one who should be embarrassed. You're the one with nothing to live for. You come in here every day and you make fun of him. But do you know what? I know your secret."

"Oh yeah?" he said. "Is that right?" He settled back into his chair, making a poor show of not being bothered by what she had to say, but she could see it in his eyes.

"He's the best friend you've got."

He laughed out loud, and then let it fade when he replied nobody else was amused.

"What?"

"Gabby is the best friend you've got. He's the only one who stands up for you, he's the only one who says nothing when the boss is grilling you both, even though he knows, and we all know, that the reason she's mad is very likely all because of you."

From the corner of her eye, she saw Ben stand. He'd been silent throughout the heated debate, despite him being able to pull rank and tell them all to shut up and get on with their jobs. He edged between the desks and took the spot Freya had vacated, perched on the edge of her desk, where he folded his arms and watched.

Gillespie clearly wanted to say something to Nillson, but Ben's movements had intrigued him, just as they had caught the attention of the rest of the team.

"It's none of your fault," Ben said. He spoke quietly and calmly. A contrast to Nillson's rants and Gillespie's wild jabbering. "Freya being mad, upset, pissed, whatever you want to call it, it's nobody's fault but mine. I'm the reason she's upset. I'm the reason she's bad-tempered. Today, at least," he said and gave a little laugh. "It's time I was honest with you all. It's time you all knew what's been going on."

"Ben, you don't have to–" Nillson said.

"I can't knit," he said, cutting her off. "I'm crap at jigsaws. And I don't have a TV. And as for train sets, sorry, Gabby. You're on your own on that one."

"What are you saying, Ben?" Gillespie said, matching the sombre tone of Ben's voice.

"I'm her hobby. I'm Freya's hobby. The boss's bit on the side," he said. "Or at least, until last night I was. And she was mine. My hobby. And last night, I tore up the jumper I'd been knitting. I threw my jigsaw in the bin. And I kicked a big hole in the front of my TV. So instead of blaming each other for pissing her off, just stop. Blame me. I should have been more honest in the first place."

"Ah, Ben," Gold said, but he held up his hand to stop her.

It was probably the largest display of emotion Nillson had seen from him. She glanced across at Gold, who had always maintained a soft spot for Ben, though she never had the courage to admit it. She was biting down on her lower lip, wearing the type of expression a child might when their parents sat them down to tell them that the pet dog had gone to heaven, that it was living a better life and no longer suffering.

"Freya," he said, then stopped himself. "DCI Bloom is going through some stuff right now. Some personal things. So, let's just do what we're paid to do. Let's try not to upset her anymore."

He took a breath and held it before releasing it slowly through his nostrils.

"And seeing as it was me who broke the telly, I'll do what I can to fix it. I just wanted to be honest with you all. You're all my mates. Every one of you. And for what it's worth, she thinks the bloody world of all of you. Even you, Jim."

CHAPTER NINETEEN

Pippa Bell made a show of leaning through the door into the hospital corridor, peering all around. She held the door open with one of her Crocs, and then physically shifted Ben aside to look behind him.

"Where is she?" she asked, her Welsh accent slowing the question and even adding a Y into the sentence somewhere.

"I'm on my own, Pip," he said, maintaining eye contact so he couldn't be falsely accused of anything.

"Allowed out on your own, are you? You surprise me."

"We were expecting a report," he said. "I was wondering if you'd managed–"

"You're giving the hurry up, are you?" she said. "I suppose Freya sent you down here, did she? To hurry me along, or how do you lot call it? Lean on me? Is that it?"

"We're struggling," he said.

"You're always struggling. I can't remember the last time you lot came in here and told me to take my time. You're all the same, aren't you?"

"Busy, you mean?"

"Had another one of you lot in here last month, I did. Said the same to him. DCI Cook, his name is. Works out of Lincoln ."

Ben shrugged, growing tired of the back and forth already.

"And what did he do to offend you?"

"It's like you all want the answers right there and then. The body's still warm half the time. You breathe down my neck, demanding me to make all these, let's face it, stabs in the dark, and when it's not the answer you're looking for, or if – God forbid – I need to take some time, you get all hot and bothered."

"Is it a full moon?" he asked.

"What?"

"A full moon?" he said and stepped over

to the glazed wall to peer up at the sky, then stared back at her. "Has everyone gone mad today, or what?"

She pulled a face to suggest what he had said was absurd.

"I'm always mad," she said, then nodded sideways, gesturing for him to follow. "Want to see her?"

"Do I need to?"

Her head bobbed from side to side for a moment, like a metronome.

"I think you should."

She stepped inside, letting the door close behind her, giving him a few seconds to make the decision. Go in and enter into yet another hostile environment or leave and just tell Freya that Pip would send a report?

The door banged against his shoe just in time and he pushed it open to find the little reception area empty and the heavy doors into the morgue just swishing closed.

It took a few minutes for him to kit himself out with the appropriate PPE – latex gloves, a face mask, and a gown, which in the absence of Freya to help him, he tied blindly in a knot behind his back, knowing full well that he'd need to ask the Welsh dragon to help him out of it.

A rush of cold air hit him as he pushed through the doors and he was immediately aware of Freya's absence. He felt like he was walking into the line of fire alone with no one to cover him.

Pip knew he'd come, of course. She knew he wouldn't walk away. She didn't even look up from her work to see him. Instead, she just prodded away at the mound beneath the thin, blue sheet. It was only when Ben drew closer that he got a good look at what she was doing.

The debris in her wound had been washed clean, as had her face and neck, across which a heavy trickle of blood had run after her attack. The sheet had been pulled down to the woman's naval, protecting most of her modesty, but not all. Naked, she looked just as Ben would have imagined a woman of her age to look. In her day, she would have been trim, but with age and that beautiful gift that women have that men do not came scars. Not just physical imperfections of the skin in the form of stretch marks, but a looseness in her form. She wasn't overweight by any means, but fair play to her, she'd probably enjoyed a little indulgence, just as anybody reaching retirement age should.

"They look different cleaned up, don't they?" Pip said. He had expected some sort of comment about his appraisal of the victim's body, but even to her that would have been vulgar. "For what it's worth, you never really get used to it."

"Now you're the one surprising me," he replied, but she just shook her head sadly.

"I talk to them, you know."

"I think you're genuinely mad enough, Pip," he said. "No offence."

"Somebody's mother. Somebody's sister," she said, then laid her forceps down on the wheeled tray beside her. "That's what I always think. Not the young ones. It's obvious. But when they're this age. When they've lived a life. I like to remember them. Strange, isn't it?"

"No," he said.

"It's not strange that I like to remember them even though I never knew them?"

"No," he said, after a pause. "No, I think you've earned that."

"She was young once. A child. People tend to forget that when they're this age. People tend to forget that somebody nurtured that child so well that she reached adulthood. She got married. She lived a life. God knows what she did in her time, but do you know what? I'll bet she had some stories to tell. Stories that nobody will ever hear again."

"You okay, Pip?" he said, and she nodded.

"My theory still stands," she said. "I've been over her twice."

"Hit on the head and then asphyxiated?"

"I'd bet my lunch on it," she replied. "And in case you're not aware, I'm not pleasant when I skip meals."

"Noted," Ben replied. "What's for lunch?"

"Pot Noodle," she replied. She said it as if she'd just listed an item from the lunch menu at Fortnum and Mason. "Beef and Tomato."

"Wow."

"Toxicology came back," she continued. "As did the fingernail scrape."

"I'm guessing she wasn't out of her head on meth?"

"No, but she liked a drink. Gin. Most likely from the previous night, but her liver suggests long-term use. Do you want to see it?"

"I'll take your word for it," he replied. "Nails?"

"No sign of a fight. No sign of a struggle. No skin or blood."

"But?" he said. "I'm sensing a but coming."

"I've asked the lab to examine the debris I removed from her head wound," Pip said, stalling. "And the debris I found in her clothes when I cut them off."

"Pip, look, I'm sorry, but it's been a pretty crappy morning—"

"They're different," she said, then let him digest that snippet of information.

"Different how?" he said. "Different as in smaller bits of crap? Or different as in—"

"Different different," she said. "As in, the trees that the bits of bark came from are different. As in the soil is different. As in—"

"Okay, okay," he said, closing his eyes to deal with the conundrum in his head before he provoked her temper. He opened them after a moment, and she made a show of waiting impatiently. "What does that mean to you?"

"No," she replied. "What does it mean to you?"

"The dirt in her clothes was different to the dirt where her body was found? It tells me she liked gardening. Her husband likes model railways. Maybe she did the garden while he was in his garage playing choo-choo?"

"Look at her, Ben. Does she look like the kind of woman who would do her garden in the evening, in the rain I might add, and then put the same clothes on the next day? Unless, of course, she did a spot of gardening before she travelled from, where was it?" She checked the topmost sheet of paper on her little clipboard. "Oh yeah, Coleby, at five in the morning, Ben?"

"You've made your point," he told her, nodding appreciatively.

She snapped off her gloves and walked over to her bench where she dumped them in a medical bin with a large pedal that lifted a heavy steel lid.

"That woman, whether by choice or not, rolled around in dirt and leaves and all kinds of crap, somewhere other than that little spot beneath the trees at the top of the cliff in Boothby Graffoe, Ben. The debris I found on her head stuck to the wet blood and tissue," she said. "That doesn't mean she died there."

"Anything else?" he asked.

"Yes, as a matter of fact," she replied. "No sexual activity, so any ideas you might have had about her rolling around on the ground–"

"Let's keep it decent, Pip, eh?"

The bench from where she was talking to him was a good ten to twelve yards away, but even from that distance, he could see the look in her eye. It was soft. Understanding. Not like Pip at all.

"Are we done?" she asked. "I'll send the report through after lunch."

"A bit early for lunch, isn't it?" he said, checking his watch. "It's only ten-thirty."

"It's a Pot Noodle, Ben," she replied. "You can eat them at any time. Don't you know anything? Christ, no wonder Freya gave you the elbow."

"What? How on earth do you know–"

"Look in the mirror, Ben," she said, as she made her way over to the office door. "You look like a little puppy who had his favourite toy taken away for peeing on the carpet."

CHAPTER TWENTY

Wyatt's Farm was as neat as a pin. Even in the incessant drizzle, when the rest of the county was bathed in mud, the place appeared to have been wiped down and polished.

The block-paved courtyard at the top of the drive offered at least half a dozen parking spots, three of them with little signs bearing building names in white letters: The Barn, The Stables, and the Toolshed, which Freya presumed were the two arms of the courtyard, with the main house in the centre. Two dormers protruded from the roof of the largest building, one on either side and atop the double-door entrance. An array of solar panels sprawled across the roof and between the dormers, stretching even to the lower and shallower roofs of the courtyard's arms, the stables, barn, and toolshed, as depicted by matching signs to those on the ground in the designated parking.

The place had been finished with an eye for detail. If it had been converted from an old working farm, then it had been done with great vision and at great expense. The windows and doors were all new UPVC and the roof tiles had either been cleaned or were also new.

None of the parking spaces with signs were filled. The only car was a Volkswagen SUV parked closest to the main house in one of the three spots likely reserved for the owner's friends and family. The car was connected to an EV charging point on the side of the building by a thick black cable that snaked across the paving.

Freya parked beside it, and no sooner had she switched off the engine when her phone began to ring.

Ben's name flashed up on the screen, and for a moment she considered ignoring it before her thumb hit the green button. She activated the loudspeaker and took a breath to prepare herself.

"Ben," she said, neither a greeting nor an invitation for him to speak. It was just a confirmation that she knew who was on the other end of the line and that he had her attention, however briefly.

"I'm on my way to the lab," he said, which meant that if he had followed her instructions he would have been to the morgue already.

"What did Pip have to say?" she asked.

There was a short pause before he spoke, and she imagined his expression. She could picture him hoping to get things back to normal. Perhaps hoping that she would apologise for her behaviour and that she would agree that she had overreacted.

"She found some dirt and debris in Linda Wilson's clothing, down her back and in her underwear. It's the closest thing we've got to any sign of a struggle."

"Okay," she said, keeping her tone nondescript.

"But the debris in her clothing doesn't match the debris that was in the wound."

"What do you mean it doesn't match?"

"It's different. The tree bark is different, the soil is different."

"Has it been analysed?"

"She raised it with the lab."

"Right," Freya said. "So, nothing really to report, then?"

"Well, no. I just figured you'd like to know," he said. "It means she wasn't killed where she was found."

"No, it means that after she was hit, she subsequently rolled around on the ground in one place, for one reason or other, and was found in another."

"She was found at six-thirty in the morning, Freya. She either went to bed wearing the clothes she'd been rolling around in, or she rolled around in one place and was killed and then moved, or she rolled around in one place, moved, and was then killed."

"My point exactly," she replied. "Nothing conclusive to report. Why don't you give me a call when you've got something to tell me? Or did you just want the opportunity to speak to me? Were you perhaps going to transition onto the topic of us?"

"What? No. Freya, for God's sake, this isn't about us."

"No, it's not, Ben," she said. "The debrief is at two p.m. If you've something to share, I suggest you do so then."

"You're being a child, Freya."

"Excuse me?"

He paused again and then spoke with disappointment in his tone.

"I'll see you in the office," he said and ended the call.

She held the phone in her hand, staring at it like it was a gateway to him or into his mind. Like she could somehow get inside that head of his, but only as an observer. It offered her no control.

She let her head fall back onto the headrest and then opened her eyes once more, only to find a face staring through the window at her. She started and then composed herself, shoving open the door to force the stranger to step back, allowing Freya to slip out of the car with dignity.

"Now then," the woman said.

She was pretty with a motherly, hourglass figure whom Freya presumed was in her late forties. She had all the curves in all the right places and was dressed in slim-fit jeans, expensive trainers, a knitted sweater, and a check shirt open at the front. Her hair was a dark blonde, which she wore up in a playful top knot. Freya presented her warrant card.

"DCI Bloom," she said. "I'm looking for Harriet Gray."

"That's me," the woman replied, slightly suspicious, but not in the least bit worried.

"I was hoping to talk to you about one of your guests," Freya said. "I understand you run an Airbnb. Is that right?" She pointed to the two arms of the structure. "Are these the guest houses?"

The woman nodded.

"The barn, the toolshed, and the stables," she replied. "Plus, we've got some shepherd's huts at the bottom of the field, if that's your thing."

"And Geoffrey Wilson?" Freya asked. "Which of those did he stay in?"

"The barn," she replied. "Sorry, is he in some kind of trouble? I don't really feel comfortable talking about him when he's not here."

"He's not in any trouble, Miss Gray."

"Mrs," she corrected her. "It's Mrs Gray. My husband died."

Freya took in the size of the property and

recalled the lengthy grounds to the rear of the buildings.

"Do you live alone, Mrs Gray?"

"I do, yes," she replied, seeming a little confused at the question.

"Must be a lot to manage. Three B and Bs, plus some camping plots."

"It gets busy in the summer. We close the huts off for the colder months."

"I don't suppose there's much call for sleeping in a hut in the winter, is there?"

"You'd be surprised," she said. "But the guests tend to create mud down there. I got fed up with having to reseed every spring. Sorry, you mentioned Mr Wilson. Will this be a long discussion? I've got sheets to wash and I haven't even cleaned the Barn yet. I've got a handover at two o'clock."

"Yes," Freya said. "We're trying to track down Mr Wilson. He isn't at home."

"So how did you know he was here?"

"His credit card," Freya said, to which the woman seemed curious.

"So, he is in trouble then?"

"I'm sorry, but—"

"He checked out this morning," Miss

Gray said. "He only stays for one night at a time."

Freya digested the statement.

"You mean he stays here regularly, does he?" she said, to which the woman nodded as if it was common knowledge.

"Once a month."

"And was he on his own?"

"Who? Mr Wilson? No, he's never on his own. His wife was with him. This isn't some seedy house of disrepute, you know?"

"No, I wasn't suggesting that it was–"

"I make it quite clear to my guests that I shall tolerate nothing of the sort."

"His wife," Freya said. "Describe her to me, will you?"

She pondered the question for a moment, using the uniform pattern in the paving to clear her mind.

"About my height. A pretty redhead–"

"Red hair?" Freya said.

"Yes. Not unlike yours, if you don't mind me saying."

"And does his wife stay with him whenever he stays?"

"Always," she replied. "Why wouldn't she?"

"Oh, no reason," Freya said. "I'll let you get back to your cleaning." She turned back to her car and opened the door.

"Is that all?" Miss Gray called out, as Freya climbed into her car. She stared at the woman, seeing far more of herself in her than she cared for. Perhaps that was her calling. Perhaps that would be her retirement, offering a place for people to stay in the wild fenland. If she did, it would be a place like Wyatt's Farm. Clean and tidy.

She retrieved a contact card from the little pile in her centre console and handed it to the woman.

"If you do think of anything else," Freya told her, as the woman accepted the card.

"I just thought you'd have asked me about the other one," she said, and Freya's eyes narrowed. "The other person who stays with them."

CHAPTER TWENTY-ONE

"They let you through then?" Katy Southwell said. She was one of six technicians, each wearing identical PPE – a face mask, goggles, hood, and accompanying white coveralls. Even their hands were covered in matching blue, latex gloves. They were like a group of friends going to a fancy dress party as Oompa Loompas, Ben thought.

Ben glanced at each of them, finding all pairs of begoggled eyes staring at him. He ruled out two of them due to their smaller size and one of them due to his large frame. Another he ruled out due to the lack of hair beneath his hood, which left just two.

Then one of them raised a hand.

"Ah," he said. "There you are."

"All look alike, don't we?"

"It's what's beneath that counts, isn't it?" he said.

She sat up, removed her goggles and mask, and slid from the stool she had been using to examine something minute through some weird-looking piece of technology that, if truth be told, Ben thought might be a microscope but knew enough about the developments of forensic science to know not to make assumptions.

"Coffee?" she said, leading him from the lab.

She opened another door and held it, making it clear that in his state of undress, he wasn't really welcome anywhere else. She followed him through into a little kitchenette, where Ben leaned on the counter. Katy clicked the switch on the kettle and then pulled two mugs from a cupboard, both identical, and both bearing the University of Lincoln logo.

"I'm guessing you're here to give me the hurry up?" She turned to look over her shoulder at him. "Unless this a social call, that is."

He smiled sheepishly.

"The former, I'm afraid."

"Ah," she replied.

"And you're right. I've been tasked with giving you the hurry up."

"Ah again," she said, spooning some instant coffee into the mugs. "Sugar?"

"Not for me, thanks," he said. "I appreciate it's a bit of a minefield, what with all that mud and whatnot."

"Well, it certainly wasn't the easiest scene I've had to investigate," she said, pouring the water. She set the kettle back down and then bent to collect a small bottle of milk from a nearby fridge. "But we're happy we covered it all. Lucky we did, too. What with all this rain we're having, our window of opportunity was quite narrow."

"From what I've heard, the site is a complete washout. With us lot down there, then the search team. I'm afraid there'll be no revisits."

She slid one of the two mugs across to him with little ceremony, then clasping her own with both hands, she settled in to lean on the counter opposite him.

"Come on then," she said. "Let's hear it.

What part of our investigation are we pushed to complete?"

"I think it would probably be easier to know where you're at with each of them," he replied, to which she nodded, apparently impressed at his response.

She sipped at her coffee and her nose twitched slightly like a hamster's might, or a rabbit's.

"Groundworks," she said, by way of an introduction. "Boot prints have all been analysed against our database. There are more than two dozen manufacturers of Wellington boots that use that sole. As for size, I'm afraid there wasn't a single full print, which means we don't have a heel-to-toe from which to measure."

"Which means you can't tell me the size of the boot?" Ben said.

"We have the width to work with, which is something. Unfortunately, we can't narrow it down any further than a sized thirty-eight to forty-two, which I think I mentioned whilst we were on site."

"What's that in English?"

"From a size five to a size seven," she said.

"Okay, so small man or large woman."

"I'm a six," she said, then raised her eyebrows.

"Okay, so a small man or an average woman?" he replied. "Not that you're average, of course."

She grinned for a moment, clearly not as easy to upset as Freya.

"What is becoming a challenge is the lack of blood spatter," she continued. "I would have expected to find some traces of blood on the ground or the surrounding trees after a blow like the one the victim received. We found nothing. We ran a black light across the scene and the surrounding area but found nothing."

"Have you spoken to Pip?" he asked.

"Doctor Bell, you mean?" she said, taking another sip of her coffee. "Yes, she sent a package earlier by courier. It's in the queue."

"It's a soil sample," he said, then saw the look of surprise on her face. "Not that type of soil sample. It's an actual soil sample. That and some bark, I think."

"Oh, interesting."

"She seems to think there's a difference between the bark found on the head wound and the bark she found in the victim's clothing."

"All right," Katy said, slowly and thoughtfully.

"We're working with the idea that she was killed somewhere else," Ben explained. "I'm hoping that the sample from her clothing will give us an idea of where that location might be."

"Which would explain the lack of spatter or bodily fluids at the scene," she remarked. "Sorry, I was thinking aloud."

"That's it," he said. "That's all we have."

He took a sip of his coffee. Over the past year or so, Freya had turned him into a coffee snob to the point where he actually had a favourite bean – a fruity yet bitter bean from Ethiopia. But it was good to drink an instant again. It was like walking into a cocktail bar and asking for a pint of lager. Sometimes the fancy stuff was surplus to the occasion.

"Which leads me to the exhibits found by the search team," she said. "All of which are mundane items that I'd expect to find in any little forest which teenagers might use. Cigarette packets and papers. Plenty of evidence of somebody smoking cannabis, although much of it is far older than our crime scene. What we did find interesting were the wine bottles."

"Yes, we were hoping they might lead us somewhere."

"Well, they are interesting," she said. "But as for leading you somewhere, I'm afraid I'm going to have to dampen your excitement."

He stared at her, confused.

"Three bottles," she said. "All of which could have been bought from anywhere that sells alcohol. All of which are easily two years old. And all of which are empty."

"Probably the same kids smoking the weed," Ben said. "But it wasn't the origin of the bottle that interested us. It's the head wound. It was made with something hard and round, not unlike a bottle."

"I understand," she said. "Two of the bottles are covered in prints. However, the prints are as old as the bottles."

"You can tell that?"

"Of course," she said. "Dirt builds up over time. It stands to reason that the dirt on top of a print is newer than the dirt below it."

"I suppose it does," he replied. "And the third bottle?"

She shook her head.

"Wiped clean."

"Wiped clean? What do you mean? The neck, or..."

"All of it," she said. "No dirt, except the area that was sitting in the mud. The rest of it was completely clean."

"That doesn't make sense," Ben said. "Have you run it under a blacklight?"

"It's as clean as a whistle," she said. "Not a single droplet of blood, not a single fingerprint, and obviously no DNA of any kind."

He took another sip of his coffee and then set it down.

"Well, it's most likely the weapon then, isn't it?"

She shrugged.

"Unless some spotty teenager was worried their mother was going to fingerprint the bottle and find out her kid has been drinking," she said. "But that doesn't really add up, does it? I mean, how could the victim have been killed somewhere else when the weapon was found beside the body?"

"Unless the killer took it with him or her?" Ben said. "I mean, they wiped it clean.

Why risk a second hiding place for the bottle?"

He swallowed the rest of his coffee and then placed the mug in the sink.

"Oh, and for what it's worth, the fingernails are also clear. No DNA beneath any of them."

"And the wool? Did you get the strand of wool Pip sent?"

"We did," Katy replied, placing her mug beside Ben's. "It's wool."

"I know, but is there any way we can identify the wearer?"

"Well, I was hoping to save that little nugget for another time," she said. "Maybe lunch, or dinner, or something."

"Dinner?"

"Yeah, you know. New girl in town. Attractive man shows her the sights." He smiled weakly, not wanting to offend her. "You're not interested, are you? It's okay."

"No, listen–"

"No, it's okay. I just thought I'd ask. Don't tell me, you're married. I didn't see a ring, but I suppose that doesn't mean anything, does it?"

"And I'm guessing new girl in town hasn't

really got to know her colleagues too well?"

She peered through the door into the lab.

"New girl finds colleagues a little on the dry side," she replied. "Not very talkative. Especially Pat."

"Well, if new girl does manage to speak to her colleagues, she might learn that the attractive man you spoke of, for which I'm actually quite flattered by the way, isn't really looking for another relationship with a crime scene investigator."

She looked shocked.

"Doctor Fell? Michaela?"

He nodded.

"The woman I took over from? You're the one who–"

"Who what?"

She silenced, realising she had said too much.

"Nothing," she said eventually. "I just heard about how it ended, that's all."

"It wasn't pretty," he replied. "Thanks for the coffee, though."

He pulled on the door and she followed him out into the lab, where she directed him to the exit.

"Oh, seeing as you're not in the market

for an investigator," she said, as they parted. He stopped in the doorway, waiting for her to finish. "The wool. I'm quite certain that it's from a hat. The skin cells and hair. You wouldn't get that on a scarf or gloves, say. Not in that volume. Homemade, and worn by a woman with dyed brown hair and grey roots."

"The victim?" he said, and she nodded.

"Maybe she knitted while her husband... what was it?" she replied.

"Played with his choo-choo," Ben said with a little laugh.

"Right," she replied, then offered him a sympathetic smile. "It looks like we both hit a dead end."

CHAPTER TWENTY-TWO

Freya's career to date had given her the opportunity to work from five primary locations, those locations being police stations of varying shapes and sizes. Two had been built to spec, taking in the PCDG regulations for the custody suite and cells, allowing the free flow of foot traffic and segregation of prisoners. Others, especially those in central London, had to be adapted to meet the requirements, which was costly and mostly resulted in a higher budget to accommodate complex fit-outs and less budget to spend on the other, less regulated areas. Areas such as those places only staff and officers saw.

In short, older police stations generally

had awful facilities for staff. Stations such as the one she and Ben worked from were little more than a terrace of old houses that had been converted and extended, and then extended some more and converted some more until its original purpose was barely discernible yet somehow retained the vernacular.

Lincoln Police Station, however, was entirely different. Compared to Freya's station, it was space age. Captain Kirk might have walked through the doors with his friend, Spock doing that thing with his fingers and she wouldn't have batted an eyelid. The building itself was nothing special – a brick and glass structure that only drew the attention of passers-by because of the police cars and service vehicles parked inside the chain-link car park. But it was the size and range of services housed there that impressed Freya. Not only was it home to Lincoln's finest, but the fire and ambulance service also. It was as if some bright spark had dreamed up this utopia of services that, being housed in a single building, could improve the communication, reporting, and overall level of services.

And then the top brass had moved in, installed their policies, and wondered why response times hadn't improved and their officers received so much abuse from the frustrated public.

The good news was that the reception conformed to the standard set by every other police station across the UK, regardless of its base in a converted row of houses, a purpose-built brick and glass eyesore, or in a shipping container in the corner of a field somewhere. The plastic seating was blue and bolted to the ground, God forbid anybody should want to sit and enjoy some privacy. The drab posters on the wall told the same standard, moronic stories – don't drink and drive, stay away from drugs, and try not to burgle people's houses. But the chances were that if somebody was sitting in the police station and found the posters useful, then it was already too late.

And of course, a police station wouldn't be a police station without the soulless effigy of an officer who had been dumped behind the glass window, probably because their personality needed a little sharpening.

"Now then," he said, without looking up.

Freya approached the desk and withdrew her warrant card. Which he somehow managed to read, absorb, and then follow the little flowchart in his mind for the next step in that particular procedure.

"Who are you visiting, please?"

"The duty sergeant will be fine," she said. "I'm just passing through."

"Do you have a name?"

"Actually, no. I'm sorry. This isn't a scheduled stop. But I thought he might be able to help me with a particular investigation. It's the murder investigation in Boothby Graffoe."

Every ounce of the man's power lay in the ability to raise his arm, protrude his finger, and push the button beneath his desk that would release the electromagnetic lock and give her access to the familiar stark corridor that would lead down to the custody suite.

The corridor would be at least fifteen metres long to allow for the noisy, shouty, and often drunk guests, especially those who hadn't seen the moronic posters in time, to shout and hurl abuse without disturbing the yet-to-be-detained members of the public out front who might be developing a back problem from sitting in one of those terrible, blue, plastic chairs.

"I need a name, I'm afraid, ma'am," he replied.

"Oh dear, really?" she said, rummaging in her bag. "I'm sure I made a note of it."

"Barrow?" he said. "We've got a Sergeant Barrow on right now."

"Is he around six-foot-two? Reddish hair with glasses?"

The description perplexed the officer as intended.

"No, I'm afraid not," he said. "But we do have an officer that fits that description. Brown. Sergeant Brown. I believe he was leading the search team."

"Actually, I tell you what I'll do. I'll go out to my car to find the number he gave me and I'll call him to come down," she said. "I'm so sorry to have bothered you."

The decision seemed to please him. He collected up his pen, retracted that immensely powerful finger of his, and returned to whatever it was he was doing, which was probably filling in his timesheet.

"Just one more thing," she said. "In case I need it, may I take your name, please?"

"Me?" he said, a little wide-eyed at the question. "PC Venables." He turned his shoulder for her to read the number on his epaulette.

"Thank you so much," she said. "Enjoy the rest of your day."

She left the building and hurried to her car where she sat, made a note of the names and numbers, and then made a phone call. She waited for the ringing to stop and then spoke immediately, doing away with any frivolous greetings.

"It's me," she said. "I need you to listen to what I say. Don't speak, just listen."

CHAPTER TWENTY-THREE

The lane on which Ben and Freya had parked when they had attended the crime scene the previous day was a dead-end road named Far End. A handful of large houses were set back on either side, and it looked to Ben, who was the first male in his family for generations not to go into the family farming business, that many of the houses were originally part of a large farm or estate. Apart from one or two, they all shared a look. Barns and out-buildings had been converted into homes, and as Gillespie had alluded, many of the drives were long and the doorways concealed, meaning doorbell footage was of no use to them.

When he had been there the previous day, the narrow street had been closed and there had barely been a space to park due to all the service vehicles. But today, the circus had left town. He saw Gillespie's car and a single liveried police car parked in a little space outside of a spectacular-looking property that defied all rules of vernacular and tradition, with solar panels and huge sheets of glazing, a wild contrast to the old, stone homes it sat between. But somehow, it worked. Somehow the new and the old sat in harmony, each enjoying a wonderful view from the top of the Lincoln Edge.

He parked behind Gillespie and was thankful that he couldn't see the big Scotsman sitting in his car, whiling away the hours in the relative warmth.

In a few moments, he had donned his Wellington boots, pulled on his raincoat, and was making his way across the paddock down to the kissing gate that led out onto the footpath carrying a cardboard tray with two coffees on. The muddy path that thousands of boots had carved into the grass had been cordoned off with police tape, so he kept to one side, watching where he trod.

As he drew near to the little gate, a few bright yellow jackets caught his eye. The uniformed officers were moving slowly north, on either side of the footpath heading towards Coleby, three of them were side by side on their hands and knees, while two more followed on foot.

"Here he is," a voice said, rough and Glaswegian. Ben turned to find Gillespie to his left, standing near the entrance to the small copse of trees where the body had been discovered. "Is one of them for me?"

Ben took his own coffee and handed the other one to Gillespie, leaving him to deal with the cardboard tray.

"Thought you might like something to warm you up," Ben told him.

"Not quite what I had in mind," he replied, tapping one of the uniformed officers on the arm and handing him the tray. The officer took it before he knew what he was doing, but by the time he'd worked out that he'd been tricked, it was too late, and Gillespie and Ben were in front of the search, walking slowly.

"What did you have in mind?"

"Oh, you know. The arms of a good

woman," Gillespie replied. "Come to think of it, any woman would do. Did you make it to the lab?"

Ben, who walked on the left side of the path, scanned the ground to the left, leaving Gillespie to check the right. There was no harm in doing a preliminary search before the team followed up behind them.

"I did," Ben said. "Paid a visit to Pip, too."

"Oh, aye? How did it all go?"

"Plenty of information, mate. Sadly, nothing that moves us forward," he said. "It turns out that there's a good chance Linda Wilson was murdered somewhere else and then dumped back there in the trees."

"Somewhere else? Like where?"

"The lab technicians are looking into it," Ben said. "Pip found some debris in her clothing that was different to the debris found stuck to her head wound."

"In her clothing? You think somebody carried her out here?"

"She wasn't exactly heavy," Ben said. "And it's not far to the road. They could have carried her from Castle Lane to the south, or Far End from the east, where we're parked.

But it does mean that whoever did it knew about this spot."

"Aye, I mean, I've lived in this area for donkey's years and I've never been up here," Gillespie said. "Bloody stunning though, eh? It's the type of place I'd come if I had a dog. They say a nice view is good for the mind, don't they?"

"Do they?" Ben said. "Maybe I need to go and find myself a view then."

"Are you referring to the news you broke this morning?"

"I suppose," Ben said, pleased to have the grassy slope to his left to avert his eyes. "Listen, mate. I'm sorry. I feel really bad."

"What about?"

"About not telling you."

"Ah, for Christ's sake, Ben. Do you honestly think that none of us knew about it? You've been in each other's pockets for a year. Thick as thieves, you are. We're not bloody stupid."

"You knew?"

"Of course we knew," Gillespie said, releasing a roar of laughter. "Anna and I have a bet on which one of you will transfer when Granger finds out."

"Granger can't find out," Ben said. "Not that there's anything to find out about anymore. Not after last night, anyway."

"Ah, you'll get it together, Ben," Gillespie said. "You're all right together. You know that, eh?"

"Freya and me?"

"Aye, like a perfect match or something, if ever there was such a thing. I mean, she's like this well-to-do, domineering lass on the outside, but I'll bet she's as soft as the rest of us on the inside."

Ben thought about it.

"She is," he said. "Yeah, she is."

"Aye, and you're the rough and ready farmer's son, not exactly raised on a silver service, aye?"

"What are you trying to say?"

"I'm saying that you're opposites," Gillespie said. "Like polar opposites. Something works there."

"Do you think I should see if I can sort it out?"

"Sort it out? Ben, you had an argument, you daft, wee doughnut. You're soft in the head, you are. It's an argument. All couples have them from time to time."

Ben stopped, so that he could turn and look him in the eye.

"I never thought I'd be coming to you for relationship advice," he said.

"Me? Oh, I'm all right at giving the advice, Ben," Gillespie replied. "Taking it is my problem."

They were on a rise in the footpath, standing close to an electricity pylon, with its cables stretching east and west across the fields.

"You'll get there," Ben told him. "I was planning on being single for as long as I could. But you'll find someone, mate."

"Aye, maybe," he said. "Listen, I've been thinking."

"More advice?"

"Eh? No, that's me done for the day, Ben. I can't give away all my secrets in one hit," Gillespie said. "No, I've been thinking about what you said. About the murder taking place somewhere else."

"Wow, free relationship advice and an idea about the investigation. You're on a roll, Jim."

"You said that she had debris from some other place in her clothing, aye?"

"That's right."

"What if she was hit somewhere else and then legged it?"

"Ran, you mean?"

"Aye, chased. What if somebody clobbered her with the bottle, or whatever it was, and she ran? Christ, Ben, she could have run through here all the way from Coleby."

From where they were standing, the houses at the edge of Coleby were in view to the north, as were those of Boothby to the south. The well-trodden footpath was muddy and bore the prints of hundreds of boots.

"It's possible," Ben said. "And it would eliminate the need for somebody to have carried her."

"She would have been bleeding," Gillespie said. "Pretty heavily, too."

Ben eyed the path in both directions, contemplating calling Freya. But he thought better of it.

"Let's get CSI back," Ben said. "Have this entire footpath blacklighted. It's been raining all bloody day, but you never know. She might have grabbed onto something."

"What about the boss?"

"Leave her," Ben said. "Probably best if we keep this quiet until we know for sure."

"Aye," he agreed, nodding his head enthusiastically. "How about CSI? Do you want to call them?"

Ben gave it a thought, then smiled to himself.

"No, you do it. Ask for Katy Southwell," he said. "Tell her you've had an idea and need her with her blacklight."

"What are you smiling about? Is there something wrong with her?" He raised his index finger as a warning. "Is this some kind of stupid prank, Ben?"

"It's not a prank, Jim," Ben said and then slapped the big Scot on the shoulder. "But it might be worth mentioning how hungry you are. When you're done here, of course."

"What about you? Where are you going?"

"Well, she won't be here for a while," Ben said, starting along the footpath again. "There's a pub in Coleby. Fancy it?"

CHAPTER TWENTY-FOUR

On a sunny, summer's day, The Tempest Arms would have boasted one of the most glorious views in the area. The peaceful village of Coleby lay behind and to its side, while the Trent Valley sprawled westward, from the Lincoln Edge as far as the eye could see.

But the sky was not a pleasant blue. It was a mixture of dull shades of grey, darkening as it neared the horizon, where rain clouds brooded like an army regrouping in preparation for another wave of attacks.

The pub had been rendered smooth and then painted white, allowing its windows and roof to stand out in contrast. Outside, a little triangle of grass lay in the intersection of where the High Street came down from the north, then split to join Blind Lane, one arm heading east, the other heading west. Ben was standing on the grass with his phone to his ear in a spot from which he could see up the High Street and Blind Lane in both directions. The call went unanswered, and he was directed to voicemail, so he hit the red button and pocketed his phone.

"Had an epiphany?" Gillespie asked as he came to stand beside him.

"A what?"

"An epiphany," Gillespie said. "You know, like a revelation or something."

"Not really," Ben replied thoughtfully. He lingered on a memory for a while, then smiled it off. "I used to come here, that's all."

"To the pub? With a wee lass? Ah, come on, don't stop there. I want to hear the details."

"No, with my brothers," Ben said. "You should see the place in the summer. It's heaving. Good food, good beer, and bloody good view to enjoy meanwhile."

"I know what you mean," Gillespie said, and Ben turned to look at him. "Anna was right about me. I hate to admit it but she was. And if I'm honest, the days of looking for a decent pub with good food, good beer, and a nice view are over. Nowadays it's a bag of peanuts, a few pints, and a glimpse of the barmaid's backside. Sad, eh?"

"It's not sad, Jim. You're just at a stage in your life where everyone you know is either married with kids or moved away. You'll find someone."

"Aye, that's what scares me," he replied, and he turned away to look up the road to the west. "I'm not sure I even know how to do it anymore. You know, the whole dating thing. I mean, what do I have to offer? Really, Ben? What have I got that a woman is going to fall head over heels for? My car is falling to bits, the house is pretty much exactly as Anna described it, which I must say, I find a little bit odd, and I spend all my time in the boozer. I mean, if I met a girl who loved dry roasted peanuts, a decent pint, and watching football with the sound off, I'd be in. I'm sure of it."

"So, stop spending all your time in the pub. Maybe you should get a hobby?" Ben said. "You know, my brother's a bit like you."

"Which one?"

"Jeff," Ben told him. "He hasn't settled down. Likes to play the field, and I'm pretty sure that some of the cars I've seen parked outside his house belong to other men's wives. You know? Flash saloons and SUVs with kids' toys in the back and a Child on Board sticker."

"He could have been babysitting for them."

"Yeah, he could. But he wasn't. The thing is," Ben explained, "he told me once that if you go clubbing every week and meet a girl and fall in love, guess what she's going to want to do every week?"

"Go clubbing?"

"Exactly. He doesn't like clubbing. That's the problem. So, he has to make do with chatting up women he meets wherever he can. If they're married, which most of them are, then so be it. I'd still be single if it wasn't for Freya coming to Lincolnshire. I mean, if it wasn't for her, I'd finish work, go home, and happily stay there, and I doubt very much any woman is going to knock on my door."

"What are you saying, Ben? With all due

respect, mate, this feels a little like one of those lectures people's dads give them."

"I don't know what I'm saying, Jim," he said, then turned to meet his stare. "Don't look to me for advice. I mean, I'm in love with a psychopath, for crying out loud."

He slapped him on the shoulder again and started towards the pub.

"So, what are you saying? I need to get out more? Is that it?"

"It works for my brother," Ben called back over his shoulder.

"Clubbing? I haven't been to a nightclub for about fifteen bloody years."

Ben turned on the spot.

"All I'm saying is that it happened for me when I wasn't looking for it. And it doesn't happen for my brother when he does look for it," Ben said. "Make of that what you will, my friend."

"But you reckon this Katy lass is up for it, eh?"

"Up for what, Jim?"

"Well, I don't know. A night out, maybe?"

"And where would you take her? Your local? I'm not sure if she's a dry-roasted-peanuts and pint-of-bitter type of girl, and if she is, then I suggest you try not to sneak a peek at the barmaid's backside. They don't like that sort of thing, you know."

Ben pushed open the pub door and made a show of waiting for him.

"I don't know then," Gillespie said as he edged past Ben into the pub.

"Well, where do you normally take the women you meet?" He kept his voice low and discreet, not wanting the conversation to be overheard.

"Back to mine," Gillespie replied, with an expression that suggested that Ben was mad for asking.

"You don't take them out?"

"Aye well, sometimes. Normally, we have to go way out where they won't be recognised."

"Right," Ben said, nodding to be polite, but inside, he was questioning the man's lifestyle. He stepped up to the bar, where a young man was preparing slices of lime.

"Help you?" he said, without looking up.

"Just looking for the landlord," Ben replied, flashing his warrant card so that it could be seen in the mirror behind the bar.

The young man put the knife down, leaned to one side, and called through a door.

"Stevo? Somebody here for you."

He didn't wait for a response, nor did he turn to face Ben. He simply picked up his knife and continued to cut the limes, dropping each cut segment into a dish.

"Look," Ben said to Gillespie. "She's a nice girl. She's new in town, and she's looking for somebody to show her around. All you have to do is be yourself. Maybe get your hair cut and have a shave."

Gillespie felt the stubble on his chin thoughtfully.

"What do you think she likes?" he said. "There's a tapas bar in Woodall. I hear good things about that."

"I went there with Freya. The food is amazing. But I'd say that was more of a second-date place. It's quite intimate."

"Ah, you're right."

They heard the sound of approaching footsteps from inside, so Ben looked to finish his man-to-man chat with the big Scot.

"Look, if she's keen to be taken out," Ben said, "find somewhere nice. Somewhere that does good food, a nice glass of wine maybe, and you never know, maybe even a decent view."

"Now then," the man Ben presumed to be Stevo said. He was a small man with broad shoulders and a deep chest that seemed to have swallowed his neck. "Looking for me, were you?"

Ben smiled inwardly as the penny finally dropped for Gillespie, and he turned back to the landlord, presenting his warrant card again.

"Detective Inspector Savage. This is Sergeant Gillespie," Ben said, as he pocketed the wallet. "I wonder if we might have a little word."

CHAPTER TWENTY-FIVE

The man named Stevo turned out to be a Colin Cross. The reason for his nickname was one Ben planned on getting to later. To his credit, he hadn't played the hard game like many landlords might have. But then, with a pub like The Tempest, the man very likely had little to hide. It wasn't a rundown drinking hole on a backstreet in the wrong part of town. It was a stunning and re-spectable establishment in an affluent village that served good beers and wines to the drinkers, quality food to the foodies, and al-lowed pets and children, the latter of which was crucial for any Lincolnshire pub if the owner planned on operating for at least the next few months.

Cross had led them to a corner seat where he had taken the seat nearest the bar, from where he could keep an eye on the rest of the pub, while Ben and Gillespie sat opposite.

"Geoffrey Wilson, you say?" he said, with a hint of a north-west accent. Not Scouse, but somewhere close. "I see him from time to time. Why do you want to know about him? What's he done?"

"Nothing I can really go into now," Ben said, maintaining eye contact to drive the message home.

"You said you see him around," Gillespie added. "Come in here, does he?"

"From time to time. Sundays mostly. Says it saves him from washing up."

"That's not really a review I'd scream about."

"He comes back, doesn't he?" Cross said. "That's all the review I need, thanks." He turned his attention back to Ben.

"I'm guessing he didn't come for his dinner last Sunday," Ben said.

"Not that I recall," he replied thoughtfully. "No, I don't remember seeing him. But then they were in on the Saturday. And of course, there was the quiz night. He and his wife sometimes come in for that."

"What nights are they on?"

"Last Wednesdays of every month," he replied. "Good turnout, it is. Fancy your chances?"

"Were the Wilsons in for the quiz night then?" Ben asked, to which Stevo made a show of recalling the evening.

"You know what, I can't be sure. Gets busy in here, you know?"

"And the staff? Would they remember?"

"My son," he replied, flicking his head over to the bar. "I'll ask him, but like I said, I doubt he'll have been in."

"Your son calls you Stevo?" Gillespie said, to which the man laughed quietly, as if the joke was private and that they wouldn't get it.

"Everyone calls me Stevo."

"Your wife?"

"Even her," he replied, grinning to let them know that it was a secret he wasn't about to give up, not to two detectives anyway.

"This quiz night," Ben said, starting a new

angle. "You said that he comes with his wife. What, are they brainiacs or something?"

"What makes you say that?"

"I say that because having a team of two in a quiz night would be a severe disadvantage. People take this seriously, don't they?"

"They do," Cross said. "And no, they aren't brainiacs. They come in with friends. Kyle and Faye."

"Kyle and Faye?" Ben said, and he fetched his notepad from his pocket, clicked his pen, and after a sly glance at Gillespie, made a note of the names. "Last names?"

"Look, whatever this is—"

"I can assure you, it is all above board," Ben said. "We just need to find Geoffrey Wilson to ask him a few questions. He's not in any trouble. You telling us is not a betrayal, if that's what you're thinking."

Cross sat back, stretching his arms along the top of the back cushion. He was comfortable in his own place and it was probably the seat from where he did all his dealings with suppliers.

"Butters," he said. "Kyle and Faye Butters. They're down in Boothby. Kyle comes in most evenings on his dog walk. But he keeps himself to himself."

"Thanks," Ben said, again making a note.

"Is that it?" Stevo asked.

"I don't suppose you know where we might find him?"

"Geoff or Kyle?"

"Geoff," Ben told him, and again Stevo sat back in the seat stretching his arms out.

"A man who comes in here for his Sunday lunch when his wife is away and the occasional quiz night? No sorry. I just hand him the card machine and he pays. He asks how I am and I reciprocate. He eats, drinks, and then leaves. As far as I know, he doesn't really talk to anybody else in here."

"Only his wife, and..." he referred to his notes as part of his act. "Kyle and Faye Butters."

"That's it," Cross said.

"So, is it fair to say that nobody in here would have reason to hold a grudge against him or his wife?" Ben asked, to which Cross sat forward, a serious expression forming on his brow.

"Is this about the woman?" he said,

keeping his voice quiet. "Down in Boothby? The one they found on Sunday morning."

"I can't really–"

"It is, isn't it? It's her."

"Look, we just need to find him."

"You want my advice?" Cross said, and he looked between them, finally resting on Ben. "Talk to his neighbour," he said, then clicked his fingers as he recalled the name. "Kevin. Kevin Hart. Ask him about the Wilsons. I'm sure he'll have plenty to say."

CHAPTER TWENTY-SIX

It was early afternoon when Freya returned to the office. The car park was filled with the usual suspects minus two, which pleased her. An hour or so without disruption would be good for her soul. Perhaps she'd even calm down enough to make the afternoon's briefing a little more bearable than the morning's had been. Nobody on the team had said anything of course, but it was obvious that they were all thinking about it, and she'd be a fool to think they hadn't spoken about her demeanour when she had left to visit Wyatt Farm.

It was all par for the course, she told herself. Everybody has bad days, it's just that

when she has one, she still has a job to per-
form, whereas others might just go quiet or
into themselves for a while. She didn't have
that luxury.

The stairwell was empty, and her heels
licked on the concrete steps. She wondered if
they could hear her and if they'd stop the
chitter-chatter. But when she stepped onto
the first-floor corridor, the hum of voices
from inside the incident room told her that
was not the case. The hum wasn't loud. Not
like it would have been if Gillespie had been
there. It was just a bunch of women nattering. But what they were nattering about was
a question Freya wasn't really in the mood to
find out. The days of listening in as she and
Ben used to do, were well and truly over.

She pushed through into the room and
the hum fell quiet in an instant. They were
all seated, which was nice to see, as opposed
to the usual drama she walked into when
Gillespie was leading the affray.

"Now, now, girls," she said. "No need to
hush just because I'm back." She dropped her
bag onto her desk and sought a whiteboard
marker.

But still, the hum didn't return.

"I mean it," she said and then turned to face them all, perching on her desk as was her habit. "Look, I owe you all an apology. I wasn't very personable this morning, all right?" She held her hands up. "We all have bad days, don't we?"

There was a moment of silence, and then Nillson spoke.

"No worries, boss," she said.

Cruz raised his hand, looking a little confused.

"Cruz, what is it?"

"You said, girls, boss," he replied.

"That's right," she replied, and his head cocked to one side.

"But I'm—"

"You don't need to apologise to us," Gold said to Freya. "We get it."

"You get what?" Freya said, as nicely as she could.

Gold stammered a little and looked to Nillson for support. In the corner of her eye, Freya saw Cruz shake his head and return to whatever he was doing on his laptop.

"She just means that we understand, that's all," Nillson said. "You had a rough

Sunday call out. Gillespie was playing up. It's fine, boss. It's nothing."

"Hmm," Freya said. "Good, well, why don't we get some coffees in? Might as well enjoy the peace and quiet without Ben and Gillespie around." She dragged her bag towards her, pulled a twenty-pound note from inside, and then held it out in Cruz's direction. "Cruz?"

"Boss?" he said, looking up from his laptop.

She waved the twenty at him.

"Coffee?"

"No, thanks. I'm trying not to drink too many," he replied, and he tapped his stomach which was as flat as it most likely had been since he was a child. "I've put on a few pounds since Hermione left me."

A few of the others smiled at her while Cruz returned to his work, referring to something on his screen, and then making notes on his notepad.

"Nillson, I hope you don't mind me asking, but have you put on a few pounds recently?" She winked to convey that it wasn't as inappropriate a comment as it might have sounded.

"I have, boss," she said, immediately seeing the angle Freya was taking. "Now, I used to be a steady fifty-seven kilos. Now I'm a fifty-seven and half. It's getting out of control if I'm honest."

"Chapman?"

"Definitely," she replied. "But then I rarely leave the office, do I?"

"Anderson?"

"Rock solid at sixty kilos, boss," she replied. "I find it seems to hang on my bum."

"That's interesting," she said, and still Cruz continued to work. "I said, that's interesting, Cruz."

The mention of his name caught his attention. He dropped his pen flat on the desk and then inhaled with that lovely, dopey grin of his.

"What's that, boss?"

"What's funny?" she said. "Well, nothing really. I mean, I shouldn't really have asked, not according to the HR regs. But you know how it is. We're all friends. Sometimes you just have to know, don't you?"

"Know what, boss? Sorry, I wasn't listening. I was busy."

"Oh, only that Nillson, Chapman, Anderson, and I aren't watching how many coffees we drink, and yet we all feel like we could lose a few pounds."

"Me too," Gold said. "Well, I'm still carrying the extra weight I put on when I was pregnant with Charlie. I've got used to it now. My mum's the same. She said she used to be a size six before she had me."

"Thank you, Gold," Freya said, and then rested her eyes on Cruz to enjoy that innocent expression of his fade as the reality dawned on him.

"Oh, come on," he whined. She waved the twenty-pound note at him. "But I don't want one."

"You said you wanted to lose weight," Nillson said.

"Yeah, none of us are bothered about how much we weigh," Anderson added.

"Oh, for God's..." He didn't even finish his sentence. He knew when he had been beaten. He shoved his seat back, dragged his Parka from the back of his chair and slid it on in one movement, which to his credit was a pretty slick move. He strode over to Freya, clearly unhappy about the task at hand.

"Flat white," she said as he took the cash.

"Make that two," Nillson added.

"Latte, one sugar for me," Gold said, and they all looked to Chapman.

"Ooh, I think I'll have one of those nice teas they do," she said. "You know, the fruity ones."

"Flavour?" Cruz said, sounding bored already.

"You choose," she replied. "Surprise me."

He marched out of the doors without looking back and they waited to hear the sound of the fire escape doors slamming behind him. Then they enjoyed a good laugh. And it was a good laugh. It was needed and somehow brought a warmth to the room.

"I really am sorry about this morning," Freya said. "I know I don't need to say it, but I feel better for apologising. It had nothing to do with any of you in here, so don't worry on that front."

"Oh, it's okay," Gold said. "Ben told us all about it."

The room silenced. Even the faint but incessantly humming fluorescent light tube seemed to hold its breath.

"Oh?" Freya said. "What did he tell you?"

It was obvious from the look on Gold's face that she knew she had put her foot in it.

"Oh, only that you and he had an argument or something. He didn't go into detail."

"Right," Freya said slowly. "And is that all he said?"

Gold had returned to her work, but must have felt Freya's burning stare. She looked up again, and then to Nillson, who took a deep, reluctant breath.

"He told us about the pair of you," she said. "He was just being honest with us."

"He told you all about the pair of us?" Freya said, standing. "Us?"

"You and Ben," Nillson replied, eyeing Gold with contempt for leaving it to her friend to break the news. "We were arguing, that's all. When you left we were arguing about why you weren't yourself."

"That's a very diplomatic way of putting it–"

"It's true," Nillson said. "I think he'd just had enough of us having a go at each other. He just stood up and took the blame for all of it."

"Right, so now everybody knows about my personal life. Is that right?"

Another silence ensued before Nillson, clearly the only one with the courage enough to speak out, replied, "If I'm honest, boss, I already knew."

"You knew?"

"Yeah, me too," Anderson added.

"Gold?" Freya said, lowering her head to coax the gentle DC back into the conversation. "Did you know?"

"I had an idea," she replied. "I mean, you spend enough time together."

"So, you all knew, did you?" Freya said softly then turned to Chapman, eyes wide expectantly.

"We're not blind, ma'am," she said apologetically.

"What about Gillespie and Cruz?"

"I don't know if they guessed like we did," Nillson said. "But they were in the room when Ben told us, so they know now."

She thought for a moment and found herself twiddling the marker between her fingers.

"There's nothing to worry about, though," Gold said. "We were all rooting for the pair of you."

Freya looked up, a little taken back.

"She's right, boss," Nillson added. "Us four have wanted you two to get together for ages. We've even steered Ben in the right direction from time to time to speed things up. Well, Jackie needed a bit of convincing, but..."

Freya looked at Gold, still shocked by the revelation.

"She's right," Gold said. "I always thought Ben and I would end up together. But when I realised that was never going to happen. Well, the two of you look great together, don't you? And I don't want him to be alone. He's nice is Ben."

"But haven't you just started seeing somebody?"

"I have," she said. "But this was way back before I met him."

"So, how long have you lot been talking about this?"

"Oh, since last November," Nillson said. "About a week after you arrived."

"Over a year ago? And nobody said anything?"

"None of our business, is it?" Anderson

said, which made Freya smile at the irony of it all.

"You do realise what would happen if anybody found out, don't you?" she said, which made Nillson smile, enough for Freya to seek some kind of statement.

"I don't think you realise who you're talking to, boss," she said. "We're all behind you. Even Cruz and Gillespie. Nobody is going to say a word to anyone."

At that moment, they weren't her team members. They weren't her subordinates or direct reports. They were friends. It reminded her of when she had been married and she used to go to coffee mornings on a Sunday with the girls from their friend group.

"Thank you," she said. "I'm touched. Don't get me wrong, I'm appalled that my private life is so public but I think I can look past that."

"So?" Nillson said, just as one of her old friends might have.

"So what?"

"So, are you going to sort it out with him?"

Freya thought about it, and if she was

honest with herself, she hadn't a clue what she would do.

"I suppose you'll have to just carry on wondering, won't you?" she replied, and then winked at Gold. "Just like he probably will be right about now."

CHAPTER TWENTY-SEVEN

A 1973 VW campervan was parked in the corner of a driveway that could easily accommodate eight to ten vehicles. The two-tone blue and white paint was intact, the arches and sills showed no signs of rust, and the rubbers around the windows were in good nick. Unlike the many others dotted around the county, under tarps or standing forgotten in a field, this particular example looked like a runner.

Ben pushed the doorbell and then stepped back to find Gillespie hovering around the van, peering through a side window.

"Ah, now this is a bit of me, this is," Gillespie said, and Ben smiled to himself, imagining the great hulk of a man driving the old bus, his long hair flapping about in the open driver's window. "They don't make them like this anymore, do they?"

"Thankfully, no," Ben said.

"Ah, come on. This is an icon."

"I couldn't agree more," Ben said. "But they weren't exactly comfortable, were they? I mean, the heating was awful, as was the cooling, they were slow, the steering was nothing short of an upper body workout, and thieves could get into them with a lollipop stick. But other than that, Jim, yeah, they were great."

He looked back at the front door, which was still closed, and then rang the doorbell again, this time less hopeful that Kevin Hart would be in.

"No luck?" Gillespie said.

"I doubt that old thing is his daily drive," Ben said. He pulled one of his contact cards from his pocket, along with his pen, and, using the van as a solid base, he wrote a short message.

Please call me.

He slipped the card through the letter box and then backed away.

"Might as well check next door while we're here," he said and walked slowly enough for Gillespie to catch him up.

"Ben?"

He turned on his heels, to find Gillespie at Kevin Hart's front door. The door was ajar and a young boy peered up at them. He must have been no more than six or seven.

"Are you all right there, wee laddie?" Gillespie said. "Is your daddy home?"

The boy stared at Gillespie as if it was either the first time he'd heard a Scottish accent or the first time he'd seen a man so dishevelled that he could have come straight from one of his books. The Twits, maybe, or The Gruffalo. Ben remembered reading it once to Jackie's boy, Charlie, while his mum was getting ready for work. He recalled the vivid description of the beast, which wasn't a far cry from Gillespie.

"There's nothing to worry about," Ben said as he approached, softening his voice so as not to alarm the boy. "We just need to speak to your daddy. Is he home?"

He nodded and his lank hair flopped to and fro.

"Do you think you could get him for us, wee man?" Gillespie added, dropping to a crouch. The boy's eyes widened in fear and he stepped back, barefoot, onto the hallway carpet.

"Jake?" a voice said from inside. It was a man's but light, much like Cruz's voice. "What have I told you about opening the door—"

Kevin Hart came to the top of the stairs, a towel wrapped around his waist.

"Mr Hart," Ben said, flashing his warrant card. "I'm DI Savage and this is DS Gillespie. Sorry to bother you, but we wondered if we might have a word."

"Now?" he said, holding his towel with one hand as he descended the stairs. With his free hand, he coaxed Jake back from the doorway and then leaned forward to peer out of the door; presumably to see if any of the neighbours were watching.

"It'll just take a few minutes," Ben told him.

"What about?" he asked.

His chest was entirely free of hair and his skin was so white that Ben doubted it had ever been exposed to the sun. The man's upper arms were as thin as Ben's wrists, and he had so little body fat that his ribcage was visible through his skin. He nudged his boy back into the house.

"Go on. Go watch TV for a minute, mate." The boy eyed Gillespie with caution as he backed away, and then turned and fled through an unseen door. "Is this about that Boothby thing?"

"What Boothby thing?" Ben asked.

"Oh, come on," he replied. "Place like this. News travels fast. Old Man Mason found a body, didn't he? That's what I heard."

"Actually, we're investigating the disappearance of Mr and Mrs Wilson," Ben said, jabbing a thumb towards the house next door. "Your neighbours."

"Oh," he replied, and his expression sank a little before it seemed to scrunch into a confused look. "Hang on. Disappearance? What do you mean, disappearance? They haven't disappeared, have they?"

"Unless you can tell us otherwise," Ben said. "We need to talk to them, and we seem to be having some difficulty finding either of them."

"Hold up. You don't think that I had anything to do with it, do you?"

"Anything to do with what, Mr Hart?" Ben said. "We're merely making enquiries, that's all."

He looked between Ben and Gillespie, trying to read their stoic expressions.

"Have you tried the library?" he asked. "I know Geoff helps out down there sometimes."

"We have. No luck, I'm afraid. I don't suppose you've seen or spoken to them in the past few days, have you?"

"Not since Saturday," he said, doing a good job of maintaining eye contact. Ben raised an eyebrow, hoping to coax him into embellishing the statement. "They were at it again," he said, then checked to make sure Jake wasn't listening. "All bloody night, I might add."

"At what, Mr Hart?" Gillespie asked. "What was it they were at?"

"Arguing," he said, pulling a face as if there could be no other reason. "Bloody rowing all night. I tell you, that woman is a lunatic. Like a dog with a bone. And he isn't much better."

"You heard them arguing, did you?"

"Heard them? I should have thought the entire street heard them. Bleeding effing and blinding at that time of night. It's hard enough trying to stop my boy from seeing that type of behaviour on the telly. The last thing I need is for him to hear it all through his bedroom window."

"Sorry, Mr Hart, what time was this?"

"What time?" he said, clearly exasperated. "It wasn't a specific time. It was all evening and most of the night."

"They argued for that long?" Gillespie said.

"On and off," Hart admitted. "I mean, I'm used to them arguing, but this was something else. For a man who calls himself the village warden, he wasn't giving much thought to the rest of us. Did you know, when the Dillons moved in and installed security lights, he had the audacity to go over and have a word about how bright they were?" He gave a crazed expression and tapped his temple with a rather feminine index finger. "They're security lights. The brighter the better, surely?"

"Oh, I see," Gillespie said. "What you're trying to tell is that Mr Wilson doesn't play by his own rules. Is that it? Must be quite frustrating, Mr Hart."

He composed himself before replying. Bringing his rant to a check.

"I'm just saying that people in glass houses shouldn't throw stones," he replied. "If he's going to police the village, then there are standards he should live up to, that's all." He eyed them with a certain disdain, appraising Gillespie from his dirty shoes to his messy hair. "But then, I suppose the standards in policing have dropped somewhat, in recent years."

"Mr Hart," Ben said before the topic shifted away from the Wilsons, "if you heard them arguing all day and night, then perhaps you could tell us what they were arguing about."

Hart appraised Ben's appearance in much the same way he had done with Gillespie but seemed to be assured by the slightly cleaner shoes, and slightly tidier hair. He took a breath, and Ben felt that shift in the mood that suggested the conversation was nearing an end. It was a sensation that came with experience, and in this instance, it was welcome.

"Same as always," he replied casually, as if Ben should have already known. "Sticking his nose in where it isn't wanted." He shook his head sadly. "I suppose she'd just had enough of it. She's probably gone to her sisters. They've got a place over in Boston. As far as arguments go, it was a bad one. I kept hearing her saying how she's sick to the teeth of everybody treating her like the enemy. How she just wanted to make friends but couldn't when all he does is poke his nose into other people's business."

They'd been standing there for more than five minutes. Hart's pale skin was nearly dry and the cold air had begun to take effect. He shivered slightly then rubbed a hand across his arm for warmth.

"Last question, Mr Hart. I promise," Ben said. "What time did the arguing stop?"

"I don't think it did," he replied. "They were still at it when I went to bed at around nine-ish. I got up in the night to use the loo, but I didn't hear them. My guess is that they collapsed with fatigue mid-argument. Why don't you give them a knock? You'll probably find them asleep at the kitchen table."

"We'll take a look," Ben said, pointing to the contact card now on the carpet near the door. "Thank you for your time, Mr Hart. In case you remember anything else."

Hart bent and collected the card, studied it briefly, and then, with a final cautious look at them both, began to close the door.

"Well, that was unequivocal," Gillespie muttered under his breath when they were halfway up the drive.

"There is another possibility," Hart added, and both Gillespie and Ben turned to hear his final comment.

"What's that?" Ben asked, seeing a grave expression on the man's face.

"She could have finally done us all a favour," he said, and his eyes darted to the Wilson house next door. "And I wouldn't blame her if she has."

———

The driveways on both houses were fifteen to twenty metres long and each house on the street appeared to be unique, as if they had been built at different times, as and when plots of land were sold off. Kevin Hart's house was a large, sprawling bungalow, while the Wilson house was more aligned with the look of an eighties family home – brick-built, dormer windows, and with an annexe or an office over a large, detached, double garage. There was one car on the driveway, a little Toyota Aygo, perfect for nipping around town and short runs to nearby villages, or even to visit a sister in Boston. And then, of course, there was the stunning loveseat in the corner, from where somebody might sit and watch the village.

Ben rang the doorbell and again stepped back, while Gillespie had a look through the windows, exactly as Freya had done.

"Nice place," Gillespie mused. "Is that them with their son?"

"We think so," Ben replied.

"Doesn't look much like a criminal, does he?"

"Depends," Ben said. "What sort of criminal are you talking about?"

Gillespie looked away from the window at him for a moment.

"What did Chapman say? Tax evasion?"

"That and fraud," Ben said. "Although, given the look of him, I dare say he'll find it hard to make friends inside. Looks like a stiff breeze would knock him over."

"Aye, that was my thought, Ben," Gillespie said. "Fancy a wee look around?"

Ben thought about the idea for a moment and contemplated the potential consequences.

"Given that Wilson has been missing for more than a day," Ben said, "I think we're safe to have a little walk around. Why don't you take the left and I'll take the right?"

They split up and Ben slipped into the side alley, which was home to a line of wheelie bins – a black one for general waste, green for recyclables, brown for garden waste, and purple for cardboard. He lifted the lids as he passed each one but saw nothing out of the ordinary.

A hose reel was fixed to the wall at the far corner, alongside a bib tap, and on the boundary wall separating Kevin Hart's property from the Wilsons', a triple ladder hung. For the time of year, the ground was relatively clean. Barely a loose leaf was in sight, unlike Ben's rear garden, where mounds of the things had built up in the corners of his patio.

He stepped out onto the rear patio, which was a neat affair. The furniture had been covered for the autumn and winter, as had a decent-sized barbecue. The lawn had had its last cut of the year, and the beds had been mulched. All that remained was to prune the shrubs and the rambling roses, which was probably best done in the spring, so his dad said, anyway.

"Anything?" Gillespie said from somewhere over to his left.

"Pretty neat and tidy," he replied. Gillespie was peering through the French doors, and Ben came to stand beside him. "Signs of life?"

"Not a thing," Gillespie said. "There's more life between Gabby's ears than in here." He placed a hand on the door handle and gave Ben a questioning look. "What do you think?"

"At this point, I'm concerned for the man's safety," Ben said.

"That makes two of us."

He pulled down on the handle and found

it to be locked. Then, after trying the other handle, he moved across to the next set of doors that opened into a kitchen.

The door opened immediately, and for a moment, they both stared at Gillespie's hand.

"All right," Ben said. "This changes things."

"Want to call it in?"

"No," he said, almost immediately. "No, let's have a look around."

He fished a pair of latex gloves from his pocket and gestured for Gillespie to do the same.

"What are you thinking, Ben?" Gillespie asked, snapping a glove into place.

"I'm thinking that Geoffrey Wilson is missing, his wife has been found dead, and the back door to his home is unlocked. You think we might find him in here?"

"I'm keeping an open mind," Ben replied. "But at this point in the investigation, nothing would surprise me."

"Police. Anybody home?" Ben called out.

The kitchen was neat as a pin. There wasn't a single appliance, dish, bowl, knife, fork, or cup out on show. The sink had been wiped clean, and there was a distinct smell of disinfectant in the air.

Nobody answered.

"Reminds me of my place," Gillespie joked. "Remind me to ask him which brand of bleach he uses."

"Anybody home?" Ben called out again, watching as Gillespie poked his head into the dining room and then the living room, returning with a curt shake of his head.

He made his way through the hallway ahead of Ben.

"Is anybody here?" Ben called out, again. "It's the police. We're coming upstairs. Make your presence known."

They took a few moments to listen for a response, and then slowly they climbed. At the top, Gillespie signed that he would check the front two rooms, leaving Ben to check the three at the rear. But before he'd even nudged open the first door, something caught Ben's eye. A smear of crimson red on the doorframe, and then on the cream carpet beyond, a few more tiny, dark stains. He waited for Gillespie to emerge from the second room, again shaking his head to signify that they were empty.

Silently, Ben pointed to the stains, and Gillespie seemed to stiffen in preparation for what would happen next.

With the toe of his shoe, Ben tapped the bedroom door open. The wall opposite was a fully mirrored, built-in wardrobe revealing the room foot by foot as the door inched open. Until finally, the door hit the bedside table and came to a juddering stop.

A large double bed was against the wall behind the door, and in the bay window sat a neat dressing table with glassware on a silver tray and a mirror.

"There's nobody here," Ben whispered, more to himself than Gillespie. He stepped inside the room, spying another smear of blood on the carpet, and then another. He followed the trail of them. A few here, a few there, each patch marking the path of something quite sinister, until he came to the window where, on the net curtain, another faint patch of dark blood could be seen.

Using the end of his pen, Ben pulled back the curtain, much as somebody else had, to peer into the garden where, between what looked like a door to a workshop and a tall monkey puzzle tree, a piece of turned timber lay on the grass. Even from afar, Ben could see the dark stain on one end.

"What is it, mate?" Gillespie asked.

Ben couldn't quite respond with any certainty, except to ask, "Have you called Katy Southwell yet?"

"Aye, I have. She's on her way to the crime scene again," Gillespie replied. "You seen something?"

"Well, we need her here. You'd better get on the phone with her again." Ben stepped to one side to give him a view. "And I'd suggest you postpone your invitation to dinner."

CHAPTER TWENTY-EIGHT

It was a rare joy for Freya to sit at her desk while the team worked quietly and efficiently. Nillson and Anderson discussed their findings, Gold and Cruz exchanged a few words every now and then, and Chapman's fingers seemed to have more endurance than the Duracell rabbit, stopping only to turn a page in her notebook or to sip her tea. Perhaps the earlier interaction had weakened Freya's defences but she found herself savouring the moment. Nobody was arguing. There were no sly comments or digs that, while they might have lifted a few spirits, only served to create drag on the momentum she tried to maintain.

The hum of men's voices in the corridor outside dampened the joy Freya was experiencing and she held her breath until the inevitable happened. Ben and Gillespie entered the room.

"Enter legends," Gillespie said to nobody in particular, and he swung his bag onto his desk. "I am breaking my neck for a jimmy." He stopped mid-stride when he saw the empty coffee cup on Cruz's desk. "Thought you were watching your figure, Gabby?"

Cruz made a show of finishing what he was typing, two-fingered and with the tip of his tongue poking from between his lips.

"Eh?" he said, slightly irritated.

"The coffee cup," Gillespie said. "Thought you were on the wagon in the hope of finding love at your toy train convention."

"Oh," he said. "I was, but the boss bought us all a coffee. Couldn't help myself."

Gillespie checked each of their desks, finding half a dozen empty cups.

"You had coffee? Decent coffee?" he said. "While Ben and I were out in the bloody rain? Have you seen it out there? It's hammering down."

"I'm well aware of the weather, Sergeant

Gillespie," Freya said. "Sadly, it has no bearing on my desire to drink coffee, or my desire to catch whoever killed Linda Wilson. So, if you need to use the washroom, then I suggest you do so." She looked up at them all. "That goes for everyone. Briefing in five minutes."

It was normal for the volume to increase as chairs were shoved back as each of them dashed for the little kitchenette to grab a drink and visit the washroom. Nobody wanted to be the last one back. What was also normal was for Ben to remain seated, leaving him and Freya alone. The abnormality was in the mood, when the team rushed to make drinks, the two of them usually shared an insight or two. But Ben was clearly making a point of staying silent, busying himself with his laptop, which almost never worked, and his notepad.

She wanted to say something. She wanted to tell him that she was sorry for her behaviour.

But she didn't want to be the first to speak. That should be him. It should be him to make the first move.

She checked her phone, sighed audibly,

and began a little charade of demonstrating that her focus was on the investigation and not on him. She flipped through her paperwork, slapping each piece of A4 from the folder into different piles, and when that failed to rouse his interest, she made one large from the three separate stacks and then slapped that into the folder.

"Right," she said, hoping to sound like she was undergoing some kind of preparation.

"This is going to be a tough one," he said, to which she straightened and glanced his way as casually as she could.

"Sorry?"

"The briefing," he said. "It's going to be a tough one. Lots of moving parts."

"Yes," she replied, holding his stare for a moment. "Yes, it is."

"How was the Airbnb?"

"Sorry?" she said again, having heard him perfectly well.

"The Airbnb," he said. "Find much?"

"Oh," she turned back to her folder, grinning inwardly. "Let's wait for the others, shall we? I seem to be hoarding information like it's a Christmas dinner. One more mouthful and I'll go pop."

He smiled at the analogy but felt its sting. Not long ago she would have told him everything she knew. Now he was just part of the team, the connection had been broken. He opened his mouth to speak but was silenced by the rabble re-entering the room, with Nillson clearly doing her best to wind Gillespie up.

"Ah, I tell you what, that coffee we had earlier was good. I think they've changed the beans."

"I noticed that," Anderson said, as they filed into the room. "Honestly, I can't remember ever having such a nice coffee."

"Did you manage to stop for one, Jim?" Nillson asked.

"As it happens, yes, I had coffee," he replied, which raised Freya's eyebrows. "Somebody bought it for me. A mate, you know? Oh, sorry, I don't suppose you know what they are, being the vindictive cow you are."

Nillson laughed it off. To a stranger, the back and forth could have been construed as abuse or a lead-up to something larger. But if anyone was going to give Gillespie stick, Nillson was the one to handle it. Having three older brothers had hardened the woman and she could be quite intimidating at times.

A move that Freya had learned from an old superintendent years before was to remain absolutely still at the front of the room, except for her eyes which watched each of them in turn. One by one, they would notice that she was watching and listening to everything they said and did and that she was ready to begin. It had taken a little perfecting, but when done well, it was a brilliant technique with which to utilise another.

The quiet.

"Okay then," she said, so softly that each of them stilled in order to hear her. She checked her watch and then pulled her blouse sleeve down. "It's two p.m. Linda Wilson has been dead for thirty-two hours. Let's see what progress we've made, shall we?" They said nothing, waiting to be called to give their updates, and still, Freya kept her voice low. "First things first, we still haven't had a formal ID on the body, and for that, we need either the victim's husband, who we can't find, or her son, who is currently in prison for tax evasion. Chapman, have we had any luck with her family? Any brothers, sisters, or parents?"

"A sister, ma'am," Chapman said. "I'm struggling to track her down. Other than her, it looks like Geoffrey was the only family she had. Her parents died within a few years of each other more than a decade ago."

"Which puts the pressure on," Freya said, turning to the whiteboard and selecting a marker. She drew a line from Geoffrey Wilson's name into a corner, where she scrawled four words.

Wyatt's Farm. Mystery guest.

She added a question mark at the end.

"Sorry, boss," Gillespie said. "Who's the mystery guest?"

"I'm wondering the same," she replied. "According to the owner of the Airbnb, Geoffrey Wilson stays there with who she believes is his wife, but in fact matches the description of Faye Butters, whom we also haven't found."

"So, she's the mystery guest?" Gillespie said.

"No, Faye Butters played the role of Mrs

Wilson every month. But on Sunday night, yesterday, they had a guest. A male with short, dark hair. Other than that, we've got nothing apart from the fact that he drives a large dark car." They all stared at her, saying nothing, but processing the information in their own way. "He hasn't been seen since."

"There's no activity on any of his credit cards, either," Chapman said.

"Ditto on his phone records," Gold added. "Last known call was made this morning at ten-fifteen to his wife." Gold looked a little sheepish, and added, "She obviously didn't answer."

"Ten-fifteen. He would have just left the bed and breakfast," Freya said. "I wonder if he was feeling guilty and had to hear his wife's voice."

"He could have been covering his trail," Cruz said. "A call to her knowing full well she wouldn't pick up and knowing that we'd be checking his phone records."

"True," Freya said, impressed at this new Cruz who, without Gillespie hovering over him, appeared confident and, dare she say it, mature. "Anderson, Nillson. What did we learn?"

Being younger and lower in rank, Anderson looked to Nillson, who spread a few sheets of paper before her.

"We've been through every name on the list Gillespie provided," she began. "Two names with previous, neither of whom has a conviction. "Theft and public indecency," Nillson replied. "The thief is a housewife named Victoria Hawes, a certified kleptomaniac currently undergoing a program of rehabilitation."

"Jesus," Gillespie said. "So, we, the taxpayers, are paying for a woman who can't keep her hands to herself to receive treatment? No wonder the bloody NHS is backed up."

"Who made you minister of health?" Nillson said.

"Nobody, it just makes me sick, that's all," he said. "Especially when you can't get a bloody doctor's appointment."

"Okay, okay," Freya cut in, catching Nillson's attention. "And the flasher?"

"Joseph Herbert," Anderson replied. "Sixty-one years old. Lives on the edge of the village in an old farmhouse. Apparently, he exposed himself to several women, the last of which was an off-duty police officer out walking her dog."

"There it is," Cruz said. "Bloody dog walkers. If they aren't finding dead bodies or being murdered, they're being flashed at."

"Have you finished?" Freya said, after a pause.

"Sorry, boss," he replied, then shrank into his seat a little.

"Anderson, Nillson. Do some work on the pervert."

"Got it," Nillson said, sharing a smile with Anderson, which left Freya the chance to move on to the last two members of her team; the reports she'd been waiting for.

Freya wrote the new name on the board, circled it, and then added three question marks beside his name. The board displayed an odd array of information. The foursome, which was the Wilsons and the Butters, were all interlinked, with Thomas Wilson off to one side, and then there was Mr Mason and Joseph Herbert, both of whom had no known connection to the foursome at all. They seemed to just muddy the waters.

"Right then," she said. "What I really want, DI Savage and DS Gillespie, is for one of you two to tell me you've found Geoffrey Wilson in the arms of his lover, and they are both downstairs in custody ready to sign a confession."

"I'm afraid not," Ben replied, which came as no surprise. "But would it please you if I said that we'd found a potential weapon?"

Not wanting to appear too eager, Freya kept a straight face and simply adjusted her bottom on the desk.

"Maybe," she said.

"Well, you should be more than happy, then," he said, and his stare was unrelenting. "Because we've found two of them."

CHAPTER TWENTY-NINE

"Two murder weapons?" Freya said, adopting a disbelieving expression which amused Ben. She sighed, and then shoved off from the desk, preparing to write his news on the whiteboard.

"One of the wine bottles that Gillespie's search team found," Ben began. "CSI has analysed it, and..." He lingered, hoping to build the tension. "It's completely free of fingerprints, DNA, and dirt."

"And dirt?" Freya said.

"As in, it was recently wiped clean, thoroughly."

"That strikes me as odd," Freya said,

clearly not wanting to commit to that being the weapon. "And the other weapon?"

Ben closed his useless laptop and slid a single sheet of paper in front of him.

"Actually, do you mind if I go through all of our findings?" he said. "I've got a lot to get through and it only really makes sense in a particular order."

"As you wish," she said. "Do we need another break before you do this, or is it a five-minute affair?"

"Five minutes is fine," he said. "I just don't want to miss anything. I think we've started to unravel the sequence of events."

"Go on then," she said.

"First of all, I paid a visit to Pip," he said. "There's not really a great deal to report there, other than the fact that she found some debris in Linda Wilson's clothing which does not match the debris found on her wound."

"Debris is debris, surely?" Gold said. "It's just dirt, isn't it?"

"To you and me, maybe," he told her. "But you know what Pip is like. She's like a bloodhound, especially when it comes to all things bloody and grimy. Apparently, the debris in both instances is made up of dirt, tree bark, bits of leaves, and that sort of thing. She seemed to think the debris found in Linda Wilson's clothing is different to the stuff found in her head wound."

"Correction," Gillespie said, holding his phone up and giving it a little shake. "I've just had a message from the very lovely Katy Southwell, Lincolnshire's latest lead Crime Scene Investigator." He spoke to the team but stared directly at Ben. "That debris in her clothing. Pip was right. It was different."

"Go on," Freya said. "Don't leave us hanging."

"Araucaria araucana," he said, reading the message aloud, though his pronunciation was more than a little dubious. "Or more commonly known as–"

"A monkey puzzle tree," Ben finished for him.

"A what?" Cruz said. "Is that one of those big, weird trees? Looks like a strange sort of Christmas tree?"

"That's the one," Ben said.

"And what does that mean?" Freya said. "You're acting like you've just solved the investigation."

"I haven't solved anything," he replied. "But it does give us a fairly good narrative. Gillespie had an idea, and I think he's right."

"Oh God, does it involve drinking beer or eating takeaways?" Nillson asked.

"No, but I bet there's an affair," Anderson said. "I think we should get him a dog, so he can take it for a walk and make Cruz's wishes come true."

"All right, all right," Freya said, smiling at them, but with a clear undertone. "Ben, carry on."

"While we were at the crime scene, we took a walk along Viking Way up to Coleby, where we had a chat with the landlord of the pub."

"Oh, I see," Nillson said. "Another one of Gillespie's ideas, was it?"

"Actually, it was mine," Ben said with a laugh. "And before you ask, we didn't have a drink. According to the landlord though, Geoffrey Wilson was in the pub on Saturday with his wife and two friends."

"And they are?" Freya said as if she hadn't already worked it out.

"Mr and Mrs Butters," Ben replied.

"What?" Nillson said. "So, they go as a

foursome? Even though two of them are having an affair?"

"I'm just telling it as I heard it," Ben said, holding his hands up. "The landlord, Colin Cross, who also goes by the name of Stevo – don't ask me why – also told us about the Wilsons' neighbour, Kevin Hart. He said Mr Hart might be able to shed some light on the Wilsons. He was alluding to them having frequent arguments."

"And did he?" Freya asked. "Confirm the arguments, that is."

"He did," Ben replied. "We paid him a visit, and he told us that the Wilsons were arguing all evening, apparently over something the husband had done."

"According to Hart, our man Wilson is a bit of a busybody," Gillespie added. "Has a habit of poking his nose in where it's not wanted."

"Okay," Freya said, clearly following but wanting more from Ben.

"We did have a quick look around the Wilsons' property while we were there." He looked up at Freya. "I know we didn't have a warrant, but given the circumstances–"

"It's fine," she said, cutting him off before

he could explain. "This is a murder enquiry and I would have done the same. Did you get inside?"

"The back door was unlocked. Blood trail on the landing carpet leading into the master bedroom, and eventually to the window."

"And?" Freya said.

"Do you remember what Chapman said about Geoffrey Wilson's hobbies?"

She gave it some thought for a moment.

"The model railway magazine?"

"And the wood-turning publication," he said. "I found a piece of rolled maplewood. A real nice piece of turning. It looked like a chair leg or something." He pulled his phone from his pocket, found the photos he'd taken and handed it over for Nillson to pass around.

"Jesus," Anderson said. "It's covered in blood. It has to be what he hit his wife with."

Ben nodded his agreement.

"Yes and no," he said.

"Because she didn't die from her head wound," Freya said, falling in with where Ben was leading them.

"Correct," Ben replied. "And this is where Gillespie's theory comes in. Imagine this.

Geoffrey Wilson argues with his wife, which according to Colin Cross, Kevin Hart suggests is a regular occurrence. He hits her. She runs. He panics and leaves."

"What about the debris?" Cruz asked. "The monkey bush, or whatever it was."

"Well, that's where it gets interesting," Ben said. "The chair leg was on the ground in the garden."

"Don't tell me, near a monkey puzzle tree?" Freya said. "Or under it?"

"Under it," he said. "So, for whatever reason, Linda Wilson was on the ground somewhere near the tree, close enough to have picked up some debris from the ground. It looks like she was hit with the piece of turned wood that we found. From there, she ran, presumably getting away from her attacker. But instead of going to a neighbour's house, she ran along the footpath at the top of the cliff."

"Viking Way," Freya said. "Can we assume that her busybody husband has alienated them?"

"Right," Ben agreed. "Presumably the attacker went after her and caught her in the little copse of trees where they finished her off."

"And when you say the attacker, you're referring to her husband, Geoffrey Wilson?"

Ben shrugged.

"They argue a lot. He's missing. The weapon was found in his garden. The debris in her clothing was from the tree in his garden," he said. "I don't want to jump to conclusions, Freya, but we've got to bring him in."

She nodded slowly and thoughtfully then stared at the whiteboard.

"What about the bottle?"

"What about it?" he said. "It doesn't have any blood on it. The chair leg does."

"So why wipe the bottle clean?"

"Maybe it wasn't him?" Ben said. "Maybe the bottle was just out there like the others were. Maybe it had nothing to do with the murder."

"Immaculate?" she replied, shaking her head. Then she succumbed to his and Gillespie's theory. "So, you're saying that Geoffrey hit his wife with a chair leg, then she somehow escaped and ran along Viking Way?"

"She would have been terrified, Freya."

"Okay, I get it," Freya said. "He went after her, caught her in the trees and finished her off, then went home to get his car, then drove to meet Faye Butters at the Airbnb? The question is, why would he want to kill his wife? What's the angle here?"

"Freya," he said, and she looked back at him, "I know we don't have the answers. I know we haven't got a clear motive, but we've got to bring him in."

"I think he's right, boss," Nillson said. "There's too much evidence that points at him."

She inhaled long and deep, then licked her lips slowly in thought.

"If we do this," Freya replied, "then we'll have thirty-six hours to build a solid case. That means finding out why the bottle was wiped clean, finding out exactly what the sequence of events was, and who the third person was at the Airbnb. Any unanswered questions will give his defence grounds for reasonable doubt."

"Understood," Ben said, clearly enjoying interacting with her again. It felt normal, if not a little stilted. It almost felt like the old days, before they were an item. Before he'd ruined it. She'd have to remind him at some point that he was far from forgiven. "So, what's the plan then, boss?"

From the corner of her eye, she saw Chapman slowly raise a hand to get their attention.

"What is it, Chapman?" Freya asked, to which she shook her head, perhaps a little unsure of herself.

"Well, it struck me that Geoffrey Wilson hasn't been seen now for two days."

"One day," Freya said. "He left the Airbnb this morning."

"Right, but he hasn't been home and he hasn't been to work, and as you said, he's no longer at the Airbnb."

"Okay," Freya said. It was rare for Chapman to voice an opinion she didn't truly believe in. She was a risk-averse introvert with an eye for detail unlike any Freya had come across before.

"And the son, Thomas Wilson, is currently in prison," Chapman continued, then stopped allowing them to connect the dots.

"Which means his house is empty," Freya

mused aloud, then turned to stare at Ben. "You asked what the plan is."

"I did," he replied.

"There's your answer. Take Gillespie," she said. "Find Geoffrey Wilson and bring him in." He exchanged glances with Gillespie, who seemed happy at the prospect of getting back out of the office. "Oh, and one more thing," she added, stopping them both as they gathered their belongings. He stared at her longingly. "Don't come back until you have him."

——————
CHAPTER THIRTY
——————

"Right then," Freya said when the hustle and bustle had died down. She stared across at the remainder of her team, each one of them attentive, switched on. "While Ben and Gillespie find Geoffrey Wilson, we have some serious work to do. But first of all, let me ask you all something. The majority of murders are solved within twenty-four hours. Can anyone tell me why?"

A silence followed, cut short by Cruz, which came as a pleasant surprise. Had Gillespie still been present, perhaps Cruz would have thought twice about offering input.

"They're emotional, boss," he said.

"Can you expand on that?"

He shifted in his seat and leaned on his elbows, fiddling with a pen while he composed himself.

"They're not planned. They're reactive. The killer is reacting to something. Some kind of trigger."

"Give me an example," Freya said.

"Abuse," he replied, instantly. "A victim of abuse might bottle up his or her feelings for so long that they simply reach a breaking point. They lash out. We've seen it before."

"Good. Anybody else? Any other examples?" she asked the room.

"Desperation," Nillson said. "The victim might have seen or heard something the killer doesn't want known. The only way to silence them is to make sure they can't give them away."

"Premeditated?" Freya said.

"Not necessarily," Nillson replied. "Often the killer acts without thinking. Without thinking of the alternatives. They're desperate, and as a result, they're dangerous. For example, a man catches his wife having an affair. The man acts on impulse. It's a heat of the moment thing."

"Good," Freya replied. "So, what you're

not saying is that one of the reasons most killers are caught within twenty-four hours is that the murders are unplanned. They aren't thought out."

"That's right," Cruz said. "A professional hitman or an organised crime gang would take days or weeks to study the movements of their target, and they would ensure they left no evidence behind. Even the average person premeditating a murder would go to lengths to make sure that even if they were questioned, no evidence could be found to incriminate them. They'd wear gloves, hats, masks, they'd leave their phones somewhere else, drive a different car. A person acting on impulse has done none of those things."

"I think it's safe to say that we're not dealing with a professional hitman, but I take your point," Freya said, trying to keep the conversation light and flowing. "If our killer is Geoffrey Wilson, would he have planned the attack?"

Another silence followed while each of them gave it some thought.

"If he did plan it, then there's a strong chance it didn't go to plan," Anderson said, then caught Freya's expectant expression, and then continued. "Ben said the chair leg was left lying on the ground covered in blood for a start. If it was planned, then surely he would have given some thought to disposing of the weapon he intended to use."

"Good," Freya said, offering an encouraging smile.

"And I very much doubt if he intended for his wife to run away, or even have the ability to run away. I mean, how far is it from the Wilson house to the crime scene?" She turned in her seat to look at the map that Cruz had pinned to the wall. "What is that? A kilometre?"

"As near as damn it," Freya agreed.

"Surely that can't have been planned. Nobody in their right mind would plan to murder their wife in their back garden in a quiet, little village like Coleby, or on a public footpath."

"Ah, there we have it," Freya said. She clicked her fingers in the air and smiled. "Nobody in their right mind." She shoved herself off the desk on which she was perched and began to pace away from them. She took four steps, then turned on her heels. "If Geoffrey Wilson murdered his wife, then he was desperate. Desperate for what? What did she know, see, do, or threaten to do to make him act in such a way? We know the couple were arguing, from the neighbour's account, and we know they were arguing about Geoffrey poking his nose into somebody else's affairs. Whose affairs was it? What were they really arguing about?"

"I thought they were arguing about him and Faye Butters?" Cruz said.

"Is that a motive?" Freya asked. "Put yourself in Geoffrey's shoes. Your wife finds out you're having an affair with your friend. You argue. She threatens to leave?"

"I'd kick him out," Nillson said, earning herself a spread of agreeing looks from the team.

"Right," Freya agreed. "Easier said than done, but are we talking about Geoffrey Wilson being threatened with losing his house here? Is that the motive?"

"He's not short of a few quid, ma'am," Chapman said, seeming to read Freya's mind. "He wouldn't be sleeping rough, that's for sure."

"No, he wouldn't. So why kill his wife?

What would he gain? Or what would he lose that a divorce wouldn't provide?"

"He wouldn't have to sneak around behind her back," Gold suggested.

"He wouldn't have to sneak around behind her back if they were divorced either," Freya said. "It's not emotional enough. There isn't enough of an immediate consequence to her surviving for him to kill her."

"What are you saying, boss?" Nillson asked.

"I'm saying that I don't think the affair was the motive. I'm saying that Linda Wilson knew or saw something that he couldn't let go of. Whatever it was, her knowing it created too much risk."

"Like what?" Cruz asked.

"Well, that's my point," Freya said. "So far, all we really have to go on is the fact that he's missing and he's having an affair with a friend who is also missing. Sure, we have a chair leg that is likely to be the weapon used against her, but other than that. I can see no motive."

"You don't think it's him?" Nillson said.

"All I'm saying is that while Ben and Gillespie bring him in, we need to find some kind of motive. He had the means to kill his wife. He had the opportunity. But if we can't explain why he did it, then we've got nothing."

"What if he didn't kill her?" Gold asked. "I mean, he obviously loved her, or at some point had loved her enough to marry her and have a child, but what if it wasn't him who did it? What if we're looking at this wrong?"

"Go on," Freya said, and Gold nodded at the board. "Let's say Linda Wilson knew about the affair somehow. Who had the most to lose?"

"Geoffrey Wilson and Faye Butters," Cruz said.

"Right, and we've already established that Geoffrey Wilson couldn't really have gained anything from her death that he couldn't gain from a divorce. But what about Faye Butters? We know she was in the area, which gives us the opportunity. Ben said he walked around the side of the house to gain access through the back door. Maybe she did the same thing? Maybe she walked around the back, found something to whack Linda with, and it all started there. She's the one with the means, motive, and opportunity."

"She wouldn't even have needed to do that," Freya said, then turned to Chapman. "Find me Geoffrey Wilson's phone records," she said, then turned back to Gold, hoping to build on her idea. "Imagine this. Geoffrey Wilson and his wife argue all night long. But it's not about him sticking his nose in. The real crux of the argument is the affair. She threatens to tell Faye Butters' husband." She turned back to the board to remind herself of the name. "Kyle. Geoffrey tries to stop her from leaving. He hits her with the first thing he finds."

"A chair leg," Cruz said, following her trail of thoughts.

"But it doesn't kill her. She goes down, sure, and there's a struggle, but she doesn't die. She escapes. She runs along Viking Way not to get away from her husband, but to tell Kyle what has been going on." She stared at Cruz, enjoying the spark in his eyes, and then jabbed an index finger at him. "You're Geoffrey Wilson. You've been arguing all night. You've just told your wife about the affair and she's on her way to your lover's house to tell her husband. What do you do?"

"Go after her?" Cruz said.

"You can't. You're injured. She fought back and somehow you can't run. Humour me."

"I suppose I'd call my lover to warn her," he replied, and she clicked her finger in response.

"There," she said. "Chapman?"

All eyes fell on the petite researcher who found the piece of paper in her file and held it up for them to see.

"Eight minutes past six," she said. "Geoffrey Wilson called Faye Butters. The call duration was thirty-six seconds."

"Enough time to warn her that Linda was on her way and she had to be stopped," Anderson said, voicing her thoughts.

"But Faye Butters was walking her dog with her husband. She couldn't risk him hearing the news from Linda," Freya said.

"So, she told him about the affair," Cruz said, mimicking Anderson's thoughtful musings.

"No," Freya said. "No, if Faye had told Kyle about the affair, then there'd be no reason to murder Linda. She would have lost everything anyway. Telling him would eradicate any emotional consequence of murder."

"But she had to get rid of him," Nillson said. "She created an argument. In your report from Sunday, you said that Kyle left his wife halfway through the walk because they had a disagreement. She could have started a disagreement about anything and stormed off. Or he could have stormed off in a huff."

"Leaving her alone to intercept Linda Wilson," Freya said, then eyed the map on the wall. "Nillson, how long does it take you to run a kilometre?"

"Eh?"

"How long does it take?" Freya repeated, to which Nillson shook her head. "Come on, you're fit."

"I don't know. A few minutes. Four maybe."

"And like I said, you're fit," Freya said. "Linda was a woman in her late fifties, and I've seen her physique. I doubt very much she could manage it in anything under six or seven minutes. Ten, more likely."

"Which would have given Faye time to prepare," Cruz said. "Maybe she found the wine bottle and whacked Linda as she ran by? If I was her, I'd be considering the outcomes while I waited. I'd try to talk to her, you know? Try to stop Linda from destroying my marriage, but if she refused to listen, then maybe I'd have a plan B. I don't think it's reasonable for the average person to have planned an attack like this. But it's not unreasonable to think Faye could have tried to scare her. Maybe she held the bottle up to threaten her? Maybe Linda was adamant about speaking to Kyle?"

He stopped, and the team pictured the scene. It was plausible. It would be hard to prove without a confession, but Freya knew that quite often, just telling the tale as she saw it would incite the truth from a suspect.

"It takes a lot for a normal person to hit somebody with an object. There's something about the violence that deters the average person from that type of behaviour. Even if she held the bottle in the air to threaten her, actually going through with it is another thing entirely."

"So, she suffocated her instead?" Gold said, and there was a sadness to her tone. "She suffocated her and the sound Mr Mason heard wasn't an orgasm or relief. It was despair."

"It was fear," Freya told her. "It was the realisation of what she had just done."

"There's another call from Faye Butters to Geoffrey Wilson at six twenty-three?" Chapman said, phrasing it like a question.

"Faye Butters heard Mr Mason or his dog," Freya replied, staring at the board now, seeing the narrative come alive in those scrawled names. "She ran south, the only way to avoid being seen. She wiped the bottle clean and tossed it away, and then called her lover who picked her up on Castle Lane, which is why nobody saw anybody walking around the village, and from there, they went straight to the Airbnb."

"So, who was the third person?" Cruz said. "You said there was somebody else at the Airbnb. And also, you can't check in usually until two p.m. Sometimes not until four p.m. Hermione and I stayed at this place once..." He realised his anecdote would break the flow of information and then faltered. "Anyway, they went somewhere else."

"The son's house," Freya said. "The only safe place for them to go."

"So why have an Airbnb then?" Gold asked. "If they could hide in Thomas Wilson's house then why book an Airbnb every week?"

It was a good question and one that Freya thought she knew the answer to but didn't want to reveal her cards. Not yet anyway.

"If the third person knew about Thomas Wilson's house, then the house would no longer be a safe place, would it?" she said cryptically.

"I suppose," Gold replied thoughtfully, and Freya winked at her.

"Right then," she said, clapping her hands once. "Here's what we're going to do."

CHAPTER THIRTY-ONE

It was amazing what a single clap could do to an already energised team. Each of them was ready for a task, hungry to bring something to the table. Sure, Ben and Gillespie were out rounding Wilson and his lover up. But the hard work, the frustrating and often tedious work, was developing the case for the CPS. If there was a shred of doubt that Geoffrey Wilson and Faye Butters were the killers, then they would have to let them both go. If the defence lawyer had even the smallest thread to pull on, to plant doubt into the minds of the jury members, then the CPS would either reject the prosecution or suggest a different charge such as manslaughter.

But manslaughter just wouldn't cut it. Not when Geoffrey Wilson hadn't shown his face since his wife had been killed. When he hadn't even the courage or respect for the mother of his child to hand himself in and own up to his mistake. And definitely not when he was most likely lying in the arms of the woman who choked Linda Wilson's final breath from her.

"Ben suggested that CSI were attending the Wilson house," Freya began. "I need two volunteers to conduct a search of the property as soon as they're finished."

"We can do that," Nillson said.

"Or we can," Gold added, then shied. "That is if you had something else that you'd rather Anna and Jenny be doing."

Chapman was the only one not to volunteer but that was understandable. She rarely left the office, and if Freya was honest with herself, she was grateful for the young researcher's introverted nature. She far preferred her own company to that of the general public, and finding young officers who preferred paperwork to getting out on the street was a task in itself. Freya had struck it lucky with Chapman and she knew it.

"What I want is for the house to be turned upside down. Laptops, phones, and tablets confiscated. Photos, letters, bloody Christmas cards, anything. I want it all bagged and tagged and taken away. If I can get us a custody extension, we'll have thirty-six hours to go through it all to build our case, which means that this could be a late night."

"Fine by us," Nillson said, after exchanging nods with Anderson.

"Gold?" Freya said, knowing she was the only one with a child and external responsibilities.

"It should be fine," she replied. "I'll ask Darren if he can help me out. He'll understand."

"Who's Darren?" Cruz asked, with one side of his top lip rising into a sneer, not unlike a poor Elvis impersonation.

"It's her new boyfriend," Nillson said. "He's a paramedic."

"Oh yeah? Things are moving fast then, are they?" Anderson said, smiling, to which

Gold shied again and shrugged. "Like a man in uniform, do you?"

"He's a nice bloke," she replied. "If he can't help out, then I'm sure my mum won't mind having Charlie for a few hours."

"Good. Make the arrangements, please," Freya said. "I'm afraid I need your attention to detail on this."

"Will do, ma'am," she replied.

"I also want to search Faye Butters' house," Freya continued. "Same rules apply. Everything bagged, and I'm sorry to say, I want special attention paid to the bins of both properties."

"I can do that," Cruz said, which seemed to surprise everyone.

"That's very forthcoming of you, Cruz."

"Well, I might as well volunteer for it before it gets assigned to me," he replied.

"Should we request help from uniform?" Gold asked. "It's a big job, and what about the husband, Kyle? What if he tries to stop us?"

"Unless Faye Butters has turned up since we saw him last, which I very much doubt, Kyle Butters will be grateful for anything we can do."

"So, do we tell him she's a suspect in a murder investigation?"

"No, not yet. Let him work it out for himself," Freya said, after pausing for thought. "And as for bringing in uniformed officers to help, unless we really need to, I'd prefer to keep this in-house if we can."

"Surely a few extra pairs of hands would help us out, boss?" Anderson said. "I mean, you said it yourself, we're going to have thirty-six hours on this at best. Twenty-four if you can't get an extension."

"Whether or not a few extra hands would be useful or not all depends on whom the hands in question belong to," Freya replied cryptically, and she gave a Nillson a knowing look by way of an explanation.

"She's right," Nillson said. "We'll be fine. The last thing we need is to have half a dozen men getting in our way."

"But–" Anderson began.

"So, there we are," Freya said, raising her voice to regain their attention and bring the focus back to her. "This is the narrative we're going with. Geoffrey and Linda Wilson argued into the night, resulting in him striking her with a chair leg. I don't know how long she lay there, but when she finally came around, she made a run for it. Presumably, she was making an attempt to speak to either Faye Butters directly, or her husband, Kyle. When Geoffrey realised she had gone, he called Faye. We've got the record of the phone call and we know she was out walking her dog with Kyle. At that time. Faye Butters then created an argument with her husband, who left to go home, while she waited to intercept Linda Wilson as she made her way down Viking Way. What we can't be sure of is if Faye intended to murder Linda or if things got out of control. But either way, all the evidence points to her. She knows the area, so when she saw or heard Mr Mason, she left the crime scene using the path to the south and then called Geoffrey Wilson to come and get her. Neither she nor Mr Wilson have been seen since, but we do know they checked into the Airbnb sometime in the afternoon. Is that clear?"

"Yes, boss," Nillson said, while the others simply nodded.

"Good, let's get out there and prove that's what happened. Nillson and Anderson, load your car up. You're searching the Wilson house. Gold and Cruz, you've got the Butters' house. Chapman, go through the phone records. I want to know who both of them have spoken to in the last few days. Look for common numbers. The key to this is the third person in the Airbnb. If neither of them are willing to speak, then perhaps whoever that third person is will be."

"Yes, ma'am," she said, seeming slightly distracted. "One more thing."

"What is it?"

"I think I've got something here," Chapman said, her eyes never leaving her computer screen. Her index finger scrolled the mouse wheel to and fro, and her glasses magnified her large, brown eyes.

"Go on," Freya said, recognising the look on Chapman's face. It was the look she wore when she knew she had something, but often she would wait until she was certain. A real pro.

Chapman waited a few moments and then that look of certainty surfaced.

"Kevin Hart, ma'am. The neighbour that Ben and Gillespie spoke to." She scrolled once more with the mouse and then turned her screen for the others to see. "It looks like he and Geoffrey Wilson have been at logger-heads for some time. These are incident reports. Complaints filed by Kevin Hart against Geoffrey Wilson."

"What for?" Gold asked.

"Excessive noise, parking across his driveway, barking dog."

"Wow, serious stuff, then," Cruz said. "This Wilson chap is a dangerous man."

The comment earned Cruz a polite glare from Freya who put the behaviour down to spending too much time with Gillespie, who she was sure would have said something similar. As if to prove her point, Chapman then clicked another tab.

"These, however, are complaints made by Geoffrey Wilson against Kevin Hart," Chapman said. "There's one here claiming Hart was driving an untaxed car. And look here. Wilson called the police on Hart claiming that his wife hadn't been seen for weeks. This was last month."

"What was the outcome?" Freya asked, to which Chapman shook her head.

"NFA," she said. "No further action."

"So, are you saying that there was some kind of neighbourly dispute between them?"

"It looks like it, ma'am," Chapman replied.

"Do you want us to question him while we're at the Wilsons'?" Nillson asked. "It's only next door."

"No, leave him to me," Freya told her. "We've got our narrative. Let's see it through to the end. I'm sure whatever dispute there is between Kevin Hart and Geoffrey Wilson is just that. A dispute."

CHAPTER THIRTY-TWO

The sky was darkening by the time Ben and Gillespie turned into the little street in Timberland. It was a twenty-minute drive from the parents' house in Coleby, fifteen if the weather permitted. The roads east from the Lincoln Edge were often swathed in fog in the colder months, and despite them being near arrow straight, the rises and falls in the topography and the numerous potholes were enough to keep any driver alert. But the evening was clear – cold, but clear. Huge puddles lay in wait at the edges of the road, some of which concealed the notorious potholes, some of which stretched across one of the two lanes, forcing the driver into the on-coming lane periodically. But besides the perils of the roads, Ben's window wipers weren't doing much in the way of wiping his windows, making the whole journey far more anxiety-inducing than normal.

"Well, you're definitely in her bad books, my friend," Gillespie said, adjusting the passenger seat in Ben's car so he could stretch his legs out and lean back a little. "Yep, mark my words, Benjamin Savage. You are well and truly on your way down the ladder."

"What are you going on about?" Ben said.

"The boss. Your missus."

"She's not my missus," Ben told him. "Not any more at least."

"Aye, she's still your missus, Ben," Gillespie said. "If the pair of you were over, then you wouldn't have been brooding since we left the station, would you? You'd have spent the past half hour insulting her. Then you'd probably break into some kind of denial, maybe telling me how she was wrong, and how could she even think ill of you. Then you'd probably start spewing all kinds of rubbish about how you're going to get out there and back in the game."

"Is that what you'd do, is it?"

"Aye, it is," Gillespie said. "It's the break-up cycle. We all do it, you know?"

"Well, we're not all like you, Jim. Some of us handle things differently, and as for getting back out there in the game–"

"You're not getting back out there, are you?"

"Well, no–"

"Because deep down, you don't believe it's over."

"What?"

"You don't think it's over, Ben. You're still clinging on," he said. "And if you don't mind me saying–"

"How can I possibly stop you?"

"So does she."

"Sorry?"

"So does she," Gillespie said. "She still wants you. I watched the pair of you during that briefing. You're not over. You never were." He sat up a little now that he had Ben's attention, and he spoke with an authority, undeserved or not. "You're like dogs."

"We're like what?" Ben said, half of him finding the comment amusing, the other half finding it insulting. "Dogs?"

"Aye, dogs. Look, when you put a bunch

of dogs together, they'll have a wee sniff here and there, work out who's who, and then one of them will kick off. He, or she, is the boss. That's what they do, and that, my friend, is what your missus is doing. She's letting you know who the boss is." He took a deep breath, clearly pleased with his analysis of the situation, and then pointed to a house on the right. "It's that one there, by the looks of things. Car out front, too. What does Wilson drive?"

"A Kia, I think," Ben said, still reeling from Gillespie's dog analogy. "And for what it's worth, mate, she does not wear the trousers."

"No?"

"No. We're equals."

"That's a Kia," Gillespie said. "Looks like he's home."

Ben pulled the car up beside the curb a few doors down from Thomas Wilson's house.

"The question is, is he alone?" Ben asked.

"Equals, yeah?"

"Yes, Jim. We're equals," Ben said, snapping off his seatbelt. "Look, it's over, mate. She made it pretty clear."

"We'll see," came the reply. They both closed their doors and walked side by side towards the house. The horizon was a pastel orange while the sky above them was heavy with clouds. A ground floor light was on inside but the curtains had been drawn.

"What do you mean we'll see?" Ben hissed, keeping the noise to a minimum. "Look, she asked me to do something I wasn't prepared to do. As far as she's concerned, it's a betrayal. It's nothing more than a demonstration of me not supporting her needs."

"Something you weren't prepared to do?" Gillespie said, and he dropped a hand to his backside. "You don't mean–"

"What? No. What's the matter with you?"

"Well, I just thought–"

"It's not..." Ben began, but began to grow exasperated. "Look, I can't say what it is. But trust me, it's nothing sexual. She needed me to do something, to risk everything." He shook his head sadly. "I just can't do that, not for her, not for anybody. I just can't."

They turned into the driveway and appraised the house and its exits. The house was semi-detached, offering just one gateway to the right-hand side in case either Wilson or Butters made a run for it.

"Well, if you ask me, mate, as far as she's concerned, you're still an item."

"Oh, really? Considering I had to give you relationship advice earlier, why on earth would I listen to you?"

Gillespie reached up for the doorbell and gave it a push.

"First of all, if it was over, she would have made arrangements to collect her things from your house. Has she?"

"Well, no, not yet–"

"And secondly," Gillespie said, as he bent down to peer through the letterbox. "You're with me."

"What?"

"You're working with me."

"What are you saying, that working with you is a punishment? That somehow by working with you my prospects have shifted? I'm now the lowest of the low, am I?"

Gillespie stared at him, a bemused expression forming on his face.

"No, Ben," he said. "It just means that you can't access the rest of the team. My guess is that she's having a word with the girls. You know? Getting their opinion. You know how girls talk, mate. You'll be all right. You'll see."

Ben opened his mouth to speak but found himself speechless. Instead, he reached past Gillespie and slammed his hand on the door three times.

"Geoffrey Wilson, we know you're in there," he called out. "It's the police. We just want a word with you."

He bent over to peer through the letterbox, just as Gillespie had done, but saw nothing except for light spilling from the living room into the hallway.

"Open the door, Mr Wilson," Gillespie called through the letterbox. "We need to speak to you about your wife."

The two men stood side by side while Ben contemplated their next move. Without uniformed assistance, breaking the door in would be a challenge. He opened his mouth to whisper an idea to Gillespie but was silenced by his raised hand as he tuned into something he'd heard. And then Ben heard it. The gentle sound of feet on concrete. Almost imperceptible noises of minuscule stones grinding beneath soft-soled shoes. They craned their heads away from the door, both staring at the passageway to the side of the house just as two figures emerged slowly, using the shadows to conceal themselves. They stopped when they realised they'd been seen.

"Ah, Mr Wilson," Gillespie said, loud and brash as he often was. "And is that your wee friend there? Faye Butters?"

"How did you find us?" Wilson replied, holding the woman by the arm. "We don't want any trouble."

Ben let his warrant card flop open and then stepped closer to allow them to read it.

"DI Savage," he said. "This is DS Gillespie. We've been looking for you two."

"Police?" Wilson said, almost breathless with anticipation. "You're the police? Oh, thank God." He dropped to his knees, at Ben's feet, letting go of his bewildered lover's hand, breathing hard. "Oh, thank God for that."

Ben glanced back at Gillespie and gave him the nod to step forward.

"Geoffrey Wilson and Faye Butters," Gillespie began. "You're both under arrest on suspicion of murder. You do not have to say anything. But it may harm your defence if you do not mention when questioned something which you later rely on in court. Anything you do say may be given in evidence."

"Arrested?" Faye Butters said, her contorted expression almost grotesque in the dim light. "We're being arrested for murder? Who the bloody hell are we supposed to have murdered?"

It was a sight to behold, thought Ben. The man who had led her out under the guise of protection was close to tears on the ground while she demonstrated no emotion but anger and outrage. Wilson looked up at Ben as if he was waiting for him to say the name.

"Linda Wilson," Ben said calmly, and the man on his knees closed his eyes and nodded slowly. "It's your wife, Mr Wilson."

CHAPTER THIRTY-THREE

"The chair leg was found over there beneath the tree. We'll be going over the area in a while," Katy Southwell told Nillson.

It was the first stop on their guided tour of the property, which was more to prevent any obstructions to the work and any contamination of evidence. The garden was a good length and just as broad. Nillson gauged it to be at forty metres by forty metres, give or take. A few floodlights on tripods had been installed to light the scene, giving the space the feel of a stage play.

A workshop-type building was at the end of the garden, its door was open and the lights were on, and from where she and Anderson were standing, they could see a wood rack on the far wall.

Southwell followed her gaze. "It looks like he was a keen woodturner," she said. "We've been over the inside. Nothing out of the ordinary, I'm afraid. Just a few old lathes, a stack of wood, and various carpentry tools. Not to mention Yorkshire."

"Sorry?" Anderson replied.

"Yorkshire," Southwell said. "At least it looks like Yorkshire to me."

"I think our esteemed colleague is suggesting there's a model railway inside," Nillson said, pleased to see that the new CSI lead at least had a sense of humour.

"You know what boys and their toys are like," Southwell added.

"Well, that's something we can look at later. Ben mentioned blood upstairs?" Nillson said. "Can we see it?"

"Yes, of course. We're just finishing up there."

She led them into the house, and thankfully, they were not asked to don the cumbersome shoe covers they usually had to wear. With the CSI team having nearly finished their work, all they had to do was be mindful of the little flagged areas – handprints on doorframes, droplets of blood on the carpet. A few flags had been deposited on the stairs, and each of them was cautious to step over them, then ease past a man in a white suit and mask taking photographs. It was the usual scene. The photographers employed by CSI were often qualified in their field. The cameras were of the highest grade, full-frame Canons which, when combined with a variety of top-quality Canon lenses and ring flashes, probably added up to somewhere close to Nillson's annual salary. The subjects were the only downside to the role. They weren't shooting weddings or portraits, or even architecture. They were most often photographing the finest droplets of blood on a carpet or a weapon in situ. Fifty or more shots sometimes of the most mundane objects and finds, all of which they would have to trawl through later to find the images most worthy of adding to the case file. They photographed the bodies, of course, but they were few and far between. More often than not the focus was on those dull little flags and the evidence they marked.

"This is it," Southwell said, stepping to

one side to allow them into the master bedroom, which in this instance was to the back of the house.

A few more little flags marked the deposits of blood on the carpet and the doorframe.

"Not much to go on," Nillson remarked. "Is this the only room in question?"

"The bathroom," Southwell said. "Do you want my theory?"

Both Anderson and Nillson stared at her. "Why not?"

Southwell stepped into the room, edging past Nillson politely.

"The attack happened in the garden. Linda Wilson was knocked to the ground, where she was left while Geoffrey Wilson cleaned up. Judging by the blood on the curtains, he came in here, peered out of the window to make sure she was still down and then washed his hands. He might have changed his clothes, but if he did, then he took them with him. I think he returned to the window after washing his hands and found her gone. There are some watermarks on the net curtain, giving us a before and after of the clean-up."

"Sounds plausible," Nillson agreed and noted the neatly made bed. "He didn't sleep."

"No. No, none of the beds have been slept in."

"According to the neighbour, they were arguing all night. Plenty of crying and shouting."

"Well, it looks like it all came to a head down there."

"But you said the workshop was clean?" Nillson said, peering out of the window. "Why on earth were they down there?"

She looked at Anderson for some sort of clue but found only a perplexed expression. It was Southwell who wore the knowing smile. It wasn't a smile of happiness. Instead, it was a polite way of letting them know that the worst was yet to come.

"I think you should follow me," she said, aiming her way towards the stairs. "I've saved the worst bit for last. I hope you don't mind." She edged past the photographer again and then peered up at them. "I wanted you to see this beforehand. It was the only way to make my theory make sense."

"Fine by me," Nillson replied. "If it makes

our lives easier, then I'm all for it. I wonder if you're any good at writing up reports?"

"I am, as it happens. Sadly, they're the boring type. Filled with technical jargon, you know? We're usually pushed to deliver as much information as we possibly can, only to have them skimmed over in the courtroom. It's a bit like writing a novel without the support of a publishing team to get it in front of readers."

"Well, I have an idea when this particular investigation goes to CPS, we'll be needing all the help we can get," Anderson said, as they made their way out into the garden and onto the lawn where two more white-suited investigators were snapping the locks closed on several large Peli cases.

The borders were neat and consisted mostly of shrubs which were easy to maintain, and which probably enjoyed the shade that the huge monkey puzzle tree cast over the bottom half of the garden.

A safe trail had been formed of stainless steel steps to preserve the evidence in the lawn, which Southwell bypassed as she led them down to a little space behind a small yew to one side of the workshop. A mound of earth sat to one side, and when Nillson peered into the hole, she saw nothing.

"Was he digging a pond?" she asked to which Southwell responded with a curt nod of her head towards the foot of the yew, where a hessian sack had been placed in an open plastic box. "What's that?"

"Not what, who?" Southwell replied. She took a few steps over to it, and crouched, opening the bag enough for them to see inside.

"Ah, for God's sake," Anderson said, the sight catching her off guard enough to let her professionalism slip.

"A dog?"

"The family dog," Southwell said for clarity. "She's in a few photos in the house, too."

"How long?"

"Has she been dead?" Southwell finished for her. "My guess is that she died at the weekend."

"I know you're not a veterinary pathologist, Katy, but I don't suppose–"

"Head wound," she replied, again cutting Nillson short. "Several blows with something hard and heavy."

"The chair leg," Anderson suggested.

"It's likely. We'll be analysing the blood deposits on that, of course," Southwell said. "And before you ask, we'll also be fast-tracking the results. You'll have them tomorrow."

"Why on earth would somebody do that to a dog?"

"I don't know why anybody would do that, but it explains what the Wilsons were doing at the bottom of the garden when it all kicked off. They were burying her."

She could feel Anderson's stare boring into her but took a moment to compose herself, to get her head around what Southwell was showing them before turning to her colleague. The look was knowing. It was one of those expressions Nillson had come to know over the past nine months or so since Anderson had transferred from the Met.

"If he can do this to a dog and then attempt to kill his wife," Anderson began, but she left the second half of the sentence for Nillson to complete.

"Then he's unhinged," Nillson said, sure it wasn't exactly how Anderson had intended the statement to end. "You better tell the boss, and while you're at it, get Ben on the phone. He needs to know who he's dealing with here."

"Geoffrey Wilson?" Southwell asked, clearly pressing to be part of the conversation. Nillson nodded.

"Beating your wife is one thing," she said. "But doing this to your pet dog? The man needs locking up."

"Animal lover, are you?"

"They're kinder than humans," Nillson said, finding herself staring at the sack on the ground. She tore her gaze from the sack and dabbed at a rogue tear that threatened to reveal the heart she fought to conceal. "At least, they're kinder than most of the humans we get to meet in this job."

CHAPTER THIRTY-FOUR

"Thanks for letting me know, Nillson," Freya said, and she ended the brief call, before appraising the property.

An old VW bus sat on the driveway, reminding Freya of a time long ago when a similar model had trundled along her father's driveway and a spotty, long-haired youth in a denim jacket had climbed out. Her father had, of course, been well-mannered enough not to intervene when it turned out that the individual in question had not been there to give the place the once over in order to perhaps return at a later date to rob it but rather to escort Freya to dinner. Although the dinner hadn't exactly been a dinner by her father's definition – a Wimpy burger with a strawberry milkshake could hardly be called a dinner – that didn't matter. It was the look her father gave her as he whispered something into her suitor's ear, while she climbed into the passenger seat.

Her father had not been a fighting man in the slightest. But there was something in his eye that day, at that moment – something wild and alpha.

They had driven away in silence. To this day, she had no idea of what her father had said to the boy whose name she couldn't remember. But it was severe enough that none of that young lad's fingers had eased their way through her hair or under her blouse, which, on reflection, was a pity.

"Now then," a voice said from behind her, and she turned on her heels to find a slight man wearing a polo shirt buttoned to the neck, a look Freya despised and found so unnecessary.

'Top buttons are fastened in the presence of a tie,' her father would have said.

"You must be Kevin Hart," she said, composing herself and adjusting her posture. It was like being sucked from the past into the present in the space of a heartbeat.

"S'right," he replied, as she fished her warrant card from her pocket.

"DCI Bloom. I wondered if might have a word."

"I had a word yesterday. Two of your lot came."

"That's right," she said. "My colleagues summarised your account. However, since then my researcher has discovered a series of complaints made by Mr Wilson against you."

"And I'm the only one am I?" He laughed. "I'm surprised he didn't have a hotline to the local nick."

"You're the only one who made a series of complaints in return," Freya told him, and she stepped closer to him giving her time to read his eyes in detail. "Shall we go inside, Mr Hart? I'm not a fan of standing in the dark. You never know who's lurking in the shadows, do you?"

"Do I have a choice?"

"Of course," she said, as pleasantly as she could. "I mean, you could always come to the station and tell me how the Wilsons' dog died."

"You what? Mindy's dead?"

"If Mindy is the dog that you raised several complaints about Mr Hart, then yes."

———

"If you don't mind me saying, Geoffrey, considering the gravity of the situation, having a legal representative present would be most advisable. We're happy to wait."

Ben gave the advice freely for two reasons. The first reason being that he would have a solicitor of sorts in his phone contacts and wouldn't require legal aid. During investigations as serious as this, the presence of an experienced lawyer added certain credibility to the processes, ensuring there could be no claims of misconduct at a later stage in the prosecution. The second reason was far simpler. The man was broken. His eyes were distant suns in the infinite space, their lids were drooping, and it seemed that every muscle in his face had succumbed to gravity, hanging lifelessly.

Despite being a man who had apparently been playing away, he was, in Ben's opinion at least, not exactly a shining example of masculinity. Flakes of skin on his forehead were mid-peel and his hands appeared to have been dunked in acid or hot oil up to his rolled-up shirt cuffs, with angry, red skin and swollen joints. He saw Ben staring at his sores and folded his arms, doing his best to conceal them.

"I'm happy to proceed. He can catch up when he gets here," Wilson said. "There's not much to say anyway."

"And you understand why you've been placed under arrest, do you?"

"I killed my wife," he replied, matter of factly. "It's not complex." It took a brave man to openly admit that he'd committed such a crime – brave or desperate. Ben was beginning to believe it was more of the latter than the former. "I'm just glad it's all over."

Even Gillespie, who sat beside Ben managing the recording and taking notes, appeared slightly perplexed at the ease at which the confession had come. His eyes widened momentarily and he sighed heavily, puffing out his cheeks. In short, he was as unsure of the man as Ben was.

"Perhaps you can tell us what happened?"

Ben said, keen to get the confession down on recording before he changed his mind.

"What does it matter what happened? I did it," Wilson replied. He spoke as Ben imagined a parent might speak to a child – with compassion. Making a case of spilt paint on an oak floor seem as if it was nothing to worry about. "It's over now. It's all over."

"If I'm honest, Mr Wilson, nothing is over," Ben told him. "In fact, I'm afraid it's only just beginning. Do you want to know what's ahead of you once we've finished here?"

Wilson stared up at him from across the table, eyes fixed, but there was nobody home. His mind was elsewhere. It was like explaining something to Freya while she waited for her turn to speak. A polite gaze.

"You'll be formally charged," Ben explained. "You'll be held in a cell until we can secure a place on remand. You'll be up in front of the judge to hear your plea, and a date for your hearing will be announced. Now, that could be days, weeks, or months away. If you can tell us exactly what happened, then that process could be significantly shortened. If you maintain a guilty stance, you wouldn't need to go through the ordeals of a trial. But unless your account closes off our enquiries in full, then don't expect to start hanging up family photos on the wall of your prison cell in the not-too-distant future, because believe me, Mr Wilson, your feet won't touch the ground. But then, I suppose you know all about the judicial process, don't you? Especially after watching your own son endure them."

It wasn't a harsh comment, Ben thought. Not below the belt, at least. Maybe a shot to the midriff, painful enough to deliver the message that they knew all about him and his family so there was little point in telling lies.

Wilson blinked his initial response and a single tear broke free and carved a track across his unshaven cheek.

His mouth opened. Just a crack. Enough for Ben to catch a glimpse of his front teeth which were yellow with age rather than ill-health. He ran a hand across the top of his head, which did little for his appearance. If anything, it just dislodged a few flecks of skin and made the few hairs he did have stand up and then lean in various directions, giving him the look of a mad scientist. He was not an attractive man, which may be in his favour when the cell door would finally slam and his future cellmate introduced himself.

"What happened, Geoff?" Ben said softly. "Can I call you Geoff?"

He nodded in a way that suggested it didn't matter and then blinked away the few tears that had followed the pioneer.

"I didn't mean for any of this to happen," he said, his voice carried by the croak of a lifelong smoker. "Nobody was meant to be hurt. Nobody was meant to die. I was just..."

He stopped, and for a moment Ben thought he might have to call the on-duty medic. Wilson appeared to be struggling for breath. His fingers splayed on the table and his red eyes widened.

"You okay there, Mr Wilson?" Gillespie asked, his eyes dancing from Wilson to Ben and then back. "Can I get you something? Water maybe?"

"I'm fine," he said finally, balling his fists and regaining composure. "I'm fine. Let's just..." He motioned with his hands in a circular fashion. "Let's just get on with it, shall we?"

"We can take a break if you need to," Ben added.

But he was cut short with a curt response, "No, I have to do this. I have to face it."

"You do," Ben said after a moment of reflection. "You do, and if it helps at all, most people feel better when they get it off their chest."

"Is that supposed to help?" Wilson replied.

"Whether it helps or not, it's true. Ask any therapist."

"I wouldn't know. I've never seen one."

"Well, the prison service offers counselling, so you'll have plenty of opportunity to start. Although, that might not be for some time if we keep going at this rate."

"I hit her," he said, then threw his hands up. It was as if the sudden outburst and movement were meant to shut Ben up. "I hit her. She kept going on and on. Bloody hours, it was. On and on. The same old story." He leaned forward, placing his elbows on the table, and pointed a finger at Ben. "Now, I'm a reasonable man. Ask anyone–"

"We have," Ben said.

"So, you'll know then. I'm the bloody village warden for crying out loud. People look up to me. They come to me with all sorts of..." He paused, as if refraining from swearing, then settled with, "Crap. And I listen. I listen because I care. I can empathise."

"What sorts of problems are we talking about?"

"Oh, anything. Village stuff mainly. The stuff people moan about but are too bloody lazy to do something about. But that's not the point. The point is that I'm a pillar of the community. If it weren't for me, we'd probably have bloody street lights in the village and one of them mobile phone mast things. We'd probably even have an army of them bloody boat people camped on the green, too. I fight for us. I'm a good man." He stopped to regain his breath and to lick his lips and then delivered what he must have deemed to be his punch line, shaking his head as he did. "But there's only so much a man can take. Especially from his own wife."

"What was the argument about?" Ben asked, to which he shook his head again and then tossed his hands up. It was the third time he'd done the same thing, and Ben figured on seeing the habit a few more times before the interview was over.

"Does it matter?" he said. "It's husband and wife stuff. Private stuff. All that matters is that she was going on and on and I snapped."

"And where was this? Where did this happen?"

"At home, of course. Where do you think it happened?"

"Specifically, Mr Wilson. Where in your home did this take place?"

The anger was paused and his voice rose in pitch as the memories flooded back.

"I was in the garden. My workshop. It's where I always go when..." He paused again and closed his eyes to whatever horror he was reliving.

"When you argue?" Ben suggested. "Is that what you're trying to say?"

He nodded and his nostrils flared with a long exhale.

"It's my escape," he said finally. "I make furniture, see? Chairs and whatnot."

"We found the chair leg, Geoff," Ben added, hoping to ease the man past the hardest junction of his confession. "It's being analysed by our investigators as we speak."

"Well, there you have it," Wilson replied. "There it is."

It was so far from the detail that Ben needed that it almost seemed inconceivable that Wilson should believe the interview was even close to ending. But it was enough for the time being. Enough at least for Ben to open another door.

"Geoff, we've searched your home."

He let the news permeate, watching as Wilson's face ran through a series of emotions. There was an anger there that he did well to keep hold of. A tightening of his lips and a glare in his eyes that softened after a second or two into pure helplessness.

"When I'd done it," he began. "When I'd, you know..." He gestured again, hoping that Ben would fill in the details.

"After you'd struck your wife?"

He nodded again, closing his eyes as the harsh reality was verbalised.

"I went inside. I couldn't think straight. She was just lying there on the lawn. She wasn't moving. There was blood, so much blood. I just thought to myself, I have to wash my hands, I have to change my clothes. I ran upstairs and checked her from the window. The bedroom is in the back, see? She hadn't moved. The security light was on. It turns on if there's movement outside, and I saw her lying there."

"What time was this?" Ben asked, to which he shook his head.

"Early. It was dark still, I know that much. But I couldn't tell you an exact time."

"And after that?" Ben said. "After you checked on her?"

"I told you. I washed my hands. I went back to our bedroom to get changed. I remember thinking about what to do. I knew I should have called you lot. I knew it. But there was something inside me. I don't know what it was. A fight or flight thing, I suppose." He was breathless from his account but was mid-flow, so Ben simply gestured his understanding, not wanting to break his stream of thought. "I checked again. Out the window, I mean. Only this time, the light was off. It's on a timer, see? I wanted to get changed. I wanted to burn my clothes but all I could think about was her lying out there in the cold." He tossed his hands up again, but the effort was weak. "So, I went back down. There's a switch by the back door in the kitchen. I remember reaching up to turn it on and stopping. It was like if I don't turn the light on then she won't be there. Then all of this would have been a bad dream or something."

"But?" Gillespie said before Ben had a chance.

"But I did," he replied. "I turned it on."

CHAPTER THIRTY-FIVE

"Do you know who Geoffrey Wilson is?" he asked.

The kitchen was modern, and the lights from beneath the cupboards were just enough, not too bright like the overhead lights would have been, but not too dim. It was the perfect lighting for a couple to share a glass of wine, perhaps with some soft background music. But Kevin Hart was not about to pop the cork on a nice Chianti. He flicked the kettle on and, as many people Freya spoke to did, he kept his distance, leaned on something solid, which in this case was the large American-style refrigerator, and then folded his arms, a defensive posture despite the effort to appear nonchalant.

"I feel I'm getting to know him better as each day passes," Freya replied. "Perhaps you could help me cut a few corners in that regard?"

"Have you spoken to anybody else?" he said. "In the village, I mean. Have you asked around?"

"My colleagues paid a visit to the landlord of The Tempest. I believe it was he who directed us to you."

"Stevo?" he said with a laugh. "I imagine he did. Not a lot goes on in the village without him knowing about it."

"Busybody, is he?"

"Stevo?" he said with a laugh. "No, salt of the earth is our Stevo. As good as they get. People talk to him, and believe me, in a place like this, somebody always has something to say." He sucked in a deep breath. "No, him next door is the busybody. Walks around here like the bloody Gestapo, he does. I tell you, if he sees anything out of place, he's on to you. It's all right for him, he's retired. He's got the time to do the little jobs. But us working folk–"

"I thought he worked at the library."

"Oh, aye, he does. Only part-time, mind. Though, God knows why. It's not like he's short of a few quid. Him and the other one. The pair of them are right old menaces."

"The other one?"

"Aye, the other one. Kyle Butters' wife. Faye. She works there, too. The pair of them are always scheming."

"I feel like we're getting off-topic," Freya said, hoping to take back control of the conversation, which Hart obviously recognised. He reached up to a cupboard, withdrew two cups and a teapot, and then set them down, using the move to turn his back on Freya. "We noticed a few complaints between yourself and Geoffrey Wilson."

"Aye," he replied curtly.

"Noise complaints–"

"Aye."

"Barking dog."

"Aye."

"Missing wife." Even with her limited view of his face, Freya could see the comment had raised a grin. "Care to tell me about that?"

"Aye," he said, although this time with the

weight of regret in his tone. He turned and carefully placed the teapot onto the kitchen island, and then added the cups, saucers, a sugar bowl, and a small milk jug. It was nice to see things being done properly.

"Not much to say," he replied.

"Well, as I understand it, somebody from Lincoln Police attended–"

"And I told him exactly what I'll tell you," Hart replied. He finished pouring the tea, then set the pot down before leaning on the island opposite Freya. "It's none of your business." He slid one of the cups, complete with saucer, across to Freya. "I don't know how you like it, so help yourself."

Freya added a tiny dash of milk, then stirred, setting the teaspoon down on the empty plate.

"Sadly, I think it is my business," she said. "You see, the Wilsons' dog has been killed."

"You said. Tragic," he replied, his tone a contradiction to his choice of words.

"And his wife was found dead on Sunday morning."

The comment garnered a brief pause for digestion and reflection, followed by a hard swallow.

"Now that is a tragedy," Hart replied, with a little more enthusiasm in his voice. "She was all right, she was." He turned to look at the Wilson house through the kitchen's side window. "What she saw in him, I can't tell you. Takes all sorts, I suppose."

"So, you can see why your wife's whereabouts is, in this instance, Mr Hart, pertinent to say the very least," Freya said.

"Pertinent?"

"Despite what the TV might lead you to believe, suspicious deaths are few and far between. Rarely is coincidence a suitable explanation for such matters." She sipped at her tea and was polite enough to offer him a grateful nod. It was a good brew. "Of course, as yet, we haven't really had cause to look into your background. You're not a suspect," she said, with a polite chortle, then allowed her expression to settle into something far more serious. "At least that is, not yet."

"What do you mean, she wasn't there?" Ben asked.

"She was gone," Wilson replied. He ran a

hand across his forehead and Ben was slightly sickened at the dry skin that fell to the table. Wilson was either used to it or hadn't noticed, as he carried on regardless. "I couldn't believe it. I even fetched my glasses to check I hadn't missed her. But she was gone. I mean, I saw where she'd been lying. The grass was all flattened. But she wasn't there."

"And what did you do at that point, Geoff? What was your thought process here?"

"I..." he began, then hesitated. "There's no way she could have survived. There was no way at all. Her head. It was..." He brought his hands to his head and then demonstrated what Ben could imagine were supposed to be horrific wounds. But he gave up trying to convey the injuries and let his hands fall to the table. "There was just no way."

"Did you go after her?"

"Go after her?" he said, almost letting an incredulous laugh escape. "And do what?"

"So, what did you do?"

"I panicked. What would you have done?"

"Gone after her," Ben suggested, to which Wilson simply dismissed with a shake of his head.

"I called a friend," he replied. "Someone I trust. Someone who knows me, who knows her. Knows what she's like."

"Does this friend have a name?" Ben asked, to which Wilson turned his head to look at the door. "Faye Butters? Is that who you called?"

Wilson nodded once more then leaned back in his chair, covering his face with both hands.

"For the recording, please," Ben said.

"Yes," he said, although his hands muffled his voice until he let them drop to his lap. "She was out with Kyle and the dog, but she said she could get away. I picked her up in Boothby. I just needed someone to talk to, that's all. Someone who would understand what she's like."

It was often best to let the story come naturally. The hardest part was over. What remained were the parts that filled the blanks in the narrative they had developed. The theory. More often than not, it was these times that Ben enjoyed the most. Especially when he shared them with Freya, who, on many an occasion, offered an alternative theory. They are about to learn which of them had been right.

"We went to Thomas's house. The sun was coming up. She said that I should get somewhere, somewhere safe. So, we went there," he continued, retelling the tale as if it had indeed been a nightmare that made no sense in the waking world. He laid his hands flat and thought for a moment, before looking up at Ben, pleading with his eyes. "Can I see her?"

"Your wife?"

"Yes. You know? Before you take me away," he said. "I just want to see her one more time."

It was as if he thought Ben owed the man a favour for his confession. That somehow by freely giving the information up, he had earned some kind of respect.

But there was still the matter of identifying the body. There was absolutely no question that Linda Wilson was lying in one of Pip's drawers right now. But legal processes had been designed to eradicate mistakes, and any flaws in the prosecution would give the defence lawyer an unnecessary advantage. Besides, Freya would hit the roof if they missed an opportunity to tick that particular box. By rights, they shouldn't even be investigating until they had a confirmed ID, but given the husband's initial disappearance, and subsequent confession, they would have enough to satiate any twitching eyes belonging to clipboard-wielding nerds hell-bent on making the process of upholding the law even more difficult.

"Why don't we talk about that when we're finished here," Ben said, as diplomatically as he could. "I'd really like to understand your relationship with Faye Butters. Could you describe it?"

"My what? My relationship with Faye?" He looked slightly perturbed, confused even by the question. "We're friends."

"Good friends?" Ben said, pushing for more.

"Well, yes. Of course."

"And there's nothing more than that between you?"

"What? No." Wilson scrunched his nose in disgust. "What on earth?"

"There's no need to take offence, Geoff," Ben added. "But from our perspective, we have a man who, by his own admission, has delivered a potentially fatal blow to his wife. He didn't look for her when her body disappeared and instead called a female friend, who he then spent the next two days with, hiding out in his son's house."

"I told you," Wilson cried out. "I panicked."

"And Faye? Did she panic too?" Wilson took a moment to think about it. He swallowed hard and licked his lips. "She was gone for two days, too," Ben added. "In fact, on Sunday, just before the coroner removed your wife's body, Kyle Butters came to us. His wife hadn't come home, and he'd seen the various vehicles and activity on the road. He was quite obviously worried, Geoff. Can you blame him? I mean, Did Faye even call him?"

"I don't know," he said. Another shake of his head. "Not that I know of."

"Why do you think that is?" Ben asked. "Why would a woman not contact her husband in two whole days? Can you see now why I asked if there was something more between you and Faye? Can you see how this looks, Geoff?"

"I don't see what Faye has to do with any of this. She was being a friend. She wanted to call Kyle, but I begged her not to. I begged her. Don't you get it? She's a friend, that's all."

"You can't see?" Ben said. "You can't see how that looks?"

"No. No, honestly, I can't. And even if there was something between us, which there isn't, what does this have to with what I did to my wife?"

In his peripheral, Ben saw Gillespie turn his head in Ben's direction. But he didn't meet his old friend's stare. He didn't want to break away from Wilson's defiant glare.

"Geoff, there's something you need to know," Ben said, and he slid a sheet of paper from his folder that Chapman had prepared. "These are your phone records. It supports what you said about calling Faye." Using the end of his pen, Ben tapped on a single line on the phone records. "What about this one?" he said. "It looks like Faye Butters called you at six forty-eight. Why?"

"To pick her up," he replied. "She didn't want Kyle to see her, so she cut through to Castle Lane."

"Geoff, what was she wearing?"

"Who, Linda? I don't know. Um, jeans, I think. A sweater? I can't remember–"

"Faye," Ben said. "What was Faye wearing?"

"Faye? I don't know. She was out walking her dog when I called her. A raincoat, I think."

"If she hasn't been home since Sunday morning, does that mean that she's wearing the same clothes now?"

"No. No, she changed into some things that belonged to Thomas's ex."

"So, her dirty clothes are still in Thomas's house?" Ben asked, to which Wilson shrugged.

"I suppose, so. Why?" Then his expression altered entirely. "Oh no. No, you don't think..."

"You called Faye to tell her what you'd done, Geoff. Faye then created an argument with Kyle, knowing full well that he'd storm off, leaving her to wait for Linda."

"Oh, come off it. Faye wouldn't do that. She hasn't got it in her." Ben linked his fingers and waited for the reality of what he'd said to sink in. It took a few moments, which was fair considering the stress the man was under. "Hang on. Hang on, are you saying—"

"Your wife didn't die from the injuries you gave her, Geoff," Ben said quietly. "She was suffocated."

"She was what?" he said, his bloodshot eyes widening to the point of becoming grotesque. "But that means—"

"That you were not directly responsible for your wife's death, Geoff," Ben added. "And it also means that I might be able to arrange for you to see her." He leaned forward on the table, resting his chin on his knuckles. "Unless, of course, you know of any good reason why we shouldn't charge Faye Butters for murder?"

A few long seconds passed. The air was still and the slamming of a door, far away, was the only distraction.

"Mr Wilson?" Ben said, then nodded to Gillespie, when Wilson failed to drag himself from his thoughts. "In that case, you should know that we'll be charging Faye Butters immediately." He collected his files and slid them back into his folder. "I will of course arrange for you to see your wife." Ben stood, sliding his chair back across the painted concrete floor. "Interview terminated at—"

"Wait," Wilson said.

Ben paused and looked down at Wilson holding his head in his hands.

"There's nothing between us," he said. "Between Faye and me, I mean. There's nothing there. We're friends, that's all."

"I'd like to think that none of my friends would murder my wife, Geoff," Ben said.

"She didn't," he replied. "She couldn't have." He sucked in a deep breath and rubbed at his eyes before staring at Ben like a man who had put his fortune on red, only for the ball to land on black. "There's something you should know."

CHAPTER THIRTY-SIX

A plaque on the wall informed Freya that Lincoln Central Library was erected in 1913. It was a marvellous building. The type that modern construction firms simply couldn't build today with its cornices and dome. It wasn't so old that thousands had to be spent each year to maintain it, unlike the Cathedral, which was worth every penny in Freya's opinion. And it wasn't so new that its designers had placed large panes of glass where ornate features and cornices might have lived, in search of simple beauty. The former would have been a sight to behold yet cold, and the latter rarely worked in Freya's opinion. She appraised the building from the far side of the road deeming it somewhere be-tween the two. The shadowy niches in the walls were out of reach of the streetlights, adding drama to the design, a beauty that no pane of glass could ever achieve.

They hadn't had the time to stop and ad-mire the building when she had visited with Ben, and if she was honest with herself, there hadn't been much time to stop and admire many of the buildings in Lincoln and she'd been living in the county for a year.

"It's Bloom, isn't it?" a voice said from be-hind her. She turned to find a familiar, squat lady with short, grey hair in an unfortunate side parting. She wore large glasses with no makeup or jewellery and beneath her eighties herringbone jacket, the collars of a man's white dress shirt protruded.

"Shelley James," Freya said. "And yes, it's Detective Chief Inspector Bloom. You have a good memory."

The woman smiled, which she hadn't done the first time they had met.

"My mother was a Bloom," she replied. "Maiden name. In some ways, I wished she had kept it. It's a lovely name."

"Well, thank you," Freya said. "I don't

often meet other Blooms. Anyway, I'm glad I bumped into you. I wondered if either Geoffrey Wilson or Faye Butters had been in touch at all?"

She laughed and shook her head sadly.

"No, and I doubt they will. It wouldn't be the first time I've had employees walk out and not come back, but it's the first time I've had two go together."

"Why do you think that is?"

"Well, I know the money isn't great, but they took the job, didn't they? If the remuneration was a problem then why take the job in the first place?"

"Here's the thing about people," Freya told her. "People work for people, not for money."

"What are you saying?"

"I'm saying that if somebody leaves stating the money is bad, then that's just an excuse. It means they haven't the heart or the courage to tell the truth. And seeing as you're the boss, I'd say it's more of the former than the latter." She watched as Shelley deciphered the compliment, but couldn't be sure of her conclusion. "It means you're a nice person, Shelley." She finished with a smile that seemed to hit the spot.

"I'm so sorry," Shelley said. "Here's me going on about myself. Did you need to speak to me?"

"I did actually, yes."

"Well, I'm just heading home," Shelley replied, then gestured at the dark sky above. "Gets dark earlier every day, doesn't it?"

"Until they don't." Freya watched her. She was a nervous-looking woman, unable to hold eye contact for too long, and when she did, it was clearly an effort to do so. "Do you have a family, Shelley?"

The question was a curveball that anyone with a reasonable IQ could have seen through. Freya wondered if Shelley was one of them.

Shelley glanced back at the library and then at Freya.

"How long do you need?"

"Five minutes," Freya replied. "I suppose the cleaners are doing their thing, are they?"

Another curve ball.

"It's not locked yet if that's what you're asking. Still open for an hour or so. What is it you need to know?"

With her hands plunged into her coat pockets, Freya pulled her jacket around her and took two steps towards the roadside.

"When I was here before, you told me that Geoffrey and Faye were close. You suggested they were having an affair."

"That's right. I mean, I don't know for sure, but–"

"Geoffrey Wilson is retired, officially anyway," Freya began. "Whatever he did beforehand, he did it well." Shelley gave her a quizzical look, and Freya made a show of leaning closer to whisper. "He's loaded," she hissed playfully, and Shelley's quizzical expression took on one of intrigue. People were like that. They enjoyed being part of a secret, a rumour, or as Freya had learned a long time ago, an investigation. It was exciting. It made them feel important.

"So why would he work at the library?"

"Not for the money," Freya said. "If there's one thing he isn't short of, it's money. The question is, what is he short of?" Shelley gazed across the footpath at her, biting down on her lower lip in thought. "What does a library have more of than anywhere else?"

"Books?" she said, and Freya's opinion of her plummeted.

"Information," she replied, and she stared at the old building in wonder. "The question is, what information was he after?"

———

It was six p.m. when the well-spoken lady on the other end of the phone announced to Ben that the person he was calling was unavailable. He wondered if Freya should perhaps record a new message. Something along the lines of, 'The person you are calling is able to take your call but would prefer to leave you hanging at this moment. Please leave a message after the tone.' Freya was never without her phone. He had a good mind to go upstairs to use Chapman's phone. Freya would recognise the number and probably answer. But that would give her ammunition to deliver a mouthful of abuse, no doubt spouting how devious and deceitful he is.

"Freya, it's me," he said after the tone. "I've got some news. Give me a call, will you?"

He ended the call in time to see Gillespie poke his head out of interview room two. He saw the phone in Ben's hand and looked awkwardly at him, clearly realising he had been trying to contact Freya.

"We're ready," he said and gave him a nod as if to say, 'in your own time', before ducking back inside, leaving Ben to pocket his phone and wonder where the hell the interview would lead them, and what the hell Freya was doing.

He caught himself groaning then checked to make sure nobody had heard before he made his way down to the interview room. He was just about to enter when the door to the front desk clicked open with an angry, warning buzz.

"Inspector Savage?" a voice said, and he turned to find Sergeant Hawkins leaning into the corridor.

"Kev," he replied. "Sorry, mate, I'm just about to go into an interview. Can it wait?"

"Not really, mate. I've got an irate customer. Says he needs to speak to someone in charge of the Boothby murder. I can't seem to get hold of Chief Inspector Bloom."

Referring to a visitor as a customer was a

bit of an in-house joke. It was a way of describing somebody as politely as possible, whilst conveying the old sentiment that the customer was always right, which in Ben's experience of police matters, they most certainly were not.

"A witness?"

"No mate. Some bloke named Kyle Butters. Ring any bells? He says you've got his wife or something. He's ready to make a complaint."

"Oh joy," Ben said, then he peered into interview room one where he had recently finished interviewing Geoffrey Wilson. "Send him through, mate. This one's empty."

"Cheers, Ben," Kevin replied, and Ben took a slow walk over to the seat he had not long ago vacated. A few moments later, he heard the door to the reception buzz open and the rumble of voices from outside. Then Kyle Butters emerged followed by Sergeant Hawkins.

"I'll take it from here. Jim's next door. Can you let him know where I am? I'll just be a minute," Ben said, not bothering to stand. He was sprawled on the chair, his legs outstretched before him. "Take a seat, Mr Butters."

Kevin had the good grace to close the door, and Ben watched as the retired gentleman slowly and cautiously took the seat opposite.

"She called me," he said. His tone was bitter as if his temper was frayed, but he was holding onto his manners. "She said you've arrested her."

"That's right, Mr Butters," Ben said, casually, to which the older man simply shook his head in disbelief. "She's in the room next door waiting to be interviewed."

He stared at the wall as if he might have developed some kind of superpower enabling him to see her.

"What for? She said you arrested her for murder. Is there something wrong with your head?"

"Well, we're all on the spectrum, Mr Butters, aren't we?"

"Murder? My wife? She wouldn't hurt a fly. You've got it all wrong."

"What can you tell me about her relationship with Geoffrey Wilson, Kyle?" Ben said, still with his legs outstretched like he was chatting with Gillespie in the incident room. He waited with his eyebrows raised, making it clear that he would continue the line of questioning regardless of Butters' evident fury.

"What's that supposed to mean?"

"Do you want me to rephrase the question?"

Butters took a moment, then sank back in his chair, deflated or exasperated. Either was preferable to the tense, old man with the artery popping from his temple.

"They're friends," he replied, to which Ben nodded.

"Good friends?"

"I suppose," he said. "As good as any we have."

"Good friends, as in you attend the quiz night in The Tempest on the last night of every month, or good friends as in lovers?"

"What? No. Geoff and Faye? Are you having me on?"

"Just answer the question, Kyle, please," Ben said and checked his watch. "It's seven o'clock. The sooner you tell me what's going on between your wife and Geoff Wilson, the sooner I can let her go. But I have to warn you. It's been a long day, and it just might have to wait until the morning." Butters sneered at him in disgust, then sighed. "Paperwork takes a long time, as you can imagine."

"Alright," he said. "What is it you want to know?"

Ben pulled his legs in, then turned in his seat so he faced Butters.

"Does your wife own a woolly hat or scarf?"

"What?" he said, then saw that Ben was serious. "Yes. Yes, she has. What on earth–"

"What colour are they?"

"I don't believe this," Butters said, then made a show of thinking about it. "Red. They're red."

"Right," Ben said, and he slowly pulled his notepad from his pocket and made a note of the response.

"Do you remember when we spoke on Sunday morning?" Ben asked. "You walked down to my car on Boothby."

"Yes. Yes, I remember, why?"

"You said something about an argument with your wife. What was it about?"

Butters said nothing.

"The clock is ticking, Kyle—"

"All right, all right," he snapped. "I'll tell you. Just give me a minute, will you?" He brought his hands up to his face and squeezed his eyes closed.

"You look tired, Kyle."

"I haven't slept," he replied. "Not since Sunday." He dropped his hands to his lap and exhaled heavily. "I was worried about them."

"Them?"

"Her and Geoff," he said. "Who else?"

"But if you said that there's nothing between them and that she wouldn't hurt a fly, then why worry?"

"Because she didn't come home," he said. "Because she wasn't answering her phone. Nor was he." He stared at Ben. "And because of what happened to Linda."

"I think you need to start talking, Kyle."

Butters said nothing at first. Ben had seen it before. The narrative was coming. It was just being put into an order that suited Butters.

"My wife," he began, then gave a little laugh. "My wife, she's what you might call a busybody." Ben sat back in his chair, stretched out his legs again, this time to one side of Butters, and gave an expression of utter boredom and disbelief. "It doesn't normally hurt anybody. Just upsets them, if you know what I mean. Causes unnecessary tension."

"I get it," he said.

"She's the village warden in Boothby. Geoff is the warden for Coleby. But the two of them, they're like the bloody fun police. I don't know why she does it. She never used to be like it. She used to be normal. But she and Geoff, when they're together, it's like they look for things to moan about. I mean, there's enough going on in the world to moan about without going looking for it, isn't there? But no. They write notices for people who park a little bit out of alignment or have their music loud during a barbecue. Do you know what I mean? Petty stuff."

"I think I know what you mean, yeah," Ben replied, leaving it open for Butters to continue.

"I suppose you've looked into Geoff, have you? I suppose you know about his boy?"

"Thomas? Yes, we know all about him. Naughty boy."

"Well, he's just as bad," Butters said.

"When we were out walking that morning, Faye stopped and told me she had something to say. Something I wouldn't like."

"Hang on one moment," Ben said, and he stood. "I'm just getting a colleague."

Kyle Butters gave a look of utter contempt but said nothing as Ben slipped from the room and opened the door to interview room two.

"Sorry about this," Ben said, holding the door open. The duty solicitor sat opposite Gillespie, who sat quietly watching Faye Butters. "Jim, a minute, mate."

"Will this take much longer?" Faye asked. "I'd like to see my husband."

Ben didn't reply. He held the door open for Gillespie and led him into the next room, where Kyle Butters looked up from his seat.

"You know Kyle Butters, I presume," Ben said.

"Aye, Ben, I do," Gillespie said. "How's it going, Mr Butters?"

"My wife has been missing since Sunday and I've just learned that you have her here. How do you think it's going?"

"Ah, well, when you put it like that."

"Mr Butters was just telling me about the

argument with his wife last Sunday, Jim," Ben said, retaking his seat. He waited for Gillespie to sit, and then gestured that they were waiting for Kyle to continue.

"As I was saying," Butters said, "we were out walking. It must have been six-thirty or thereabouts. Light enough for a dog walk but dark enough to watch where you trod, if you get my meaning."

"Aye, I know what you mean," Gillespie replied, always far more verbal than Ben.

"She had a phone call or a text or something. I mean, I didn't even hear it ring, and she didn't say anything. But I saw the phone in her hand and she stopped me. We were on Viking Way up near the pylons," he said. "Anyway, she told me about something that Thomas had mentioned during Geoff's last visit."

"Thomas Wilson," Ben said, for Gillespie's benefit. "Apparently, Geoffrey Wilson and Faye Butters collectively police the villages and the son seems to have inherited the long nose."

"Aye, right. Busybodies, you mean?"

"Right," Kyle said, clearly not warming towards Gillespie. "Apparently, Thomas told them about somebody who had just been released. A murderer."

"A murderer?" Gillespie said. "And they released him?"

"Well, manslaughter. But it's all the same, isn't it?"

"Well, not really, no. But go on," Gillespie said.

"Apparently this bloke and his mate were caught on camera moments before an attack took place. The victim later died. But because it happened off-camera, the jury couldn't be sure which of them actually delivered the fatal blow. All they could ascertain was that both of them were there. That's a murderer in my book."

"What's his name?" Ben asked.

"John Briggs. He's from somewhere out Newark way, somewhere in Nottinghamshire, anyway. Well, when he was sent away, his parents had to move house. Couldn't stand the grief the locals were giving them for what he'd done. They didn't want a murderer as a next-door neighbour. And bloody right, too."

"Well, manslaughter isn't exactly murder," Gillespie said. "Technically speaking."

"They moved to Boothby," Kyle said, ignoring Gillespie's comment.

"Ah," Gillespie replied. "And that's what Thomas told Geoff, is it?"

Kyle shuffled in his seat a little, looking embarrassed on his wife's behalf.

"They've been trying to find a way to get them out of the village," he said. "That's what they do. They push people out. They get the neighbours on their side, the ones that matter anyway, and they isolate the wrongdoers until they can bear it no longer."

"And how long has this been going on for?" Ben asked.

"John Briggs was released three months ago," Kyle said. "They've never done anything this serious before. I thought that they'd have the sense to leave someone like that well alone."

"But?"

Kyle sighed again and buried his face in his hands.

"We all went for lunch at The Tempest last Saturday," he replied. "Faye and I were going to walk home along Viking Way but Geoff and Linda said we should go for drinks afterwards at their place. It's nothing out of the ordinary. We do it often."

"But?" Ben said again.

"But this time, when we got back to their house, the back door was open," he replied, and his eyes watered in the short hesitation that followed. "The dog was lying on the kitchen floor. Oh God, you should have seen the poor thing."

Ben cast a confused look at Gillespie, who looked equally as surprised.

"Are you saying that Geoffrey Wilson didn't kill the dog, Kyle?"

He peered over his hands with eyes as wide as saucers.

"He couldn't have. He was with us at the pub. Somebody had beaten her to death," he replied, shaking his head. "Geoff said it must have been a burglar. Somebody must have broken in and disturbed her. I helped him bury her. I dug the bloody hole in the garden and we all stood around and said a few words, you know? Poor Linda was distraught. She loved that dog. But we had no idea then, did we, Linda and I? We didn't know about John Briggs. We didn't know what Geoff and Faye were up to."

"Did anybody call the police, Kyle?" Ben asked, feeling a vibration in his pocket. He gestured for Kyle to continue while he pulled it from his pocket, and saw Freya's name on the screen.

"Sorry, is this not interesting enough?" Kyle said.

"No, of course," Ben said. "Sorry, I'm just expecting a call, that's all." Kyle stared at the ringing phone until Ben hit the red button to decline the call. "Go on," he said. "It's nothing important."

"Geoff said he would do it."

"There's no record of a complaint," Ben replied to which Kyle simply shrugged.

"We left them to it. Linda was upset. She was shouting at Geoff. He was shouting back," he said. "So, we took our leave. We went home. I mean, nobody wants to be in the way of an argument, do they?"

"And you believe this John Briggs had something to do with this, do you? You think that because they were trying to get him and his parents out of the village that he killed their dog, like some kind of warning? Is that right?"

He placed his hands on the table, nervously picking at a piece of hard skin, then looked between Ben and Gillespie.

"When Faye stopped me on the walk, she said they found something that would get rid of Briggs," he said quietly as if someone was listening in. "She said they had irrefutable proof. I told her to stop playing Sherlock Holmes, and she told me they'd got some private investigator in and that they were going to meet him. Some chap named Sloane, or something."

"Proof?" Ben said.

"That's what she said," Kyle blurted out. "Look, I've told you everything. Can't you just let her go?"

Ben glanced at Gillespie, looking for some kind of support, but only received a casual shrug and a soft shake of his head.

Ben considered it. He thought about Freya's reaction to letting Faye Butters walk. He thought about the endless misery Freya could put him through, just when he had an inclination that she was coming around.

"Your wife is a suspect in a murder enquiry, Mr Butters," he said, as he shoved the chair back, stood, and caught Gillespie's attention. "Take her back to her cell Jim, will you?"

"What?" Kyle said. "You can't do this. You bloody well know it wasn't her. I've told you all about John Briggs."

"I can and I am. I suggest you go home," Ben told him, as he pulled the door open and waved to get the attention of a uniformed officer to escort Kyle back to reception. "And if you're that worried, Kyle," Ben said, then waited for him to lift his head and stare at him, "I'd lock your doors tonight."

CHAPTER THIRTY-SEVEN

Ben drew the car up outside his home and sat there for a while with the engine running. The house was one of three laid out in a horseshoe shape. Aside from the row of labourers' cottages further along the lane, one of which Freya used to rent, they were lonely, old buildings. The central and original house of the three belonged to his father, and his father before him, and before him men of the Savage family for generations. On either side of the original building was Ben's house and the house his two brothers occupied, both of whom still worked for their father, and would no doubt inherit everything when the time came. But that suited Ben. As long as he got to keep his house, he didn't mind. They deserved it.

The light was on in his father's kitchen, and although the curtains were drawn he was sure of the scene inside. It was eight p.m., which meant that his father would be sitting at the kitchen table with the wireless on. Talk radio, of course, specifically BBC Radio Four. The stations that played modern music would be an insult to his senses, and the others were just boring drivel. He would have the crossword in front of him from Sunday's paper, and maybe some cheese and crackers. Ben often envied his dad's simple life. The way he held onto those traditions and practices, not through an utter disdain for the future, and not through stubbornness, but because those things that he did, he'd been doing since he was a child. So, why change for the sake of change?

He had an office as large as the kitchen. It was neat and organised, and the chair was comfortable. He had what he called the parlour, a living room with a comfortable, three-piece suite, a turntable complete with a handful of old records that belonged to Ben's mother, and a little drinks cabinet. Now he thought about it, Ben couldn't remember the last time that particular door had been opened, certainly not during one of his visits anyway. But despite the comfort and conveniences the old man had at hand, he chose to spend his evenings sitting on an old, wooden chair in his draughty kitchen, because that's what he knew. One day, Ben would look at that old house and remember him. He'd remember his funny ways with the sadness that only the bereaved feel. As cantankerous as the old sod could be, Ben would miss him when the day finally came.

He switched off the engine and climbed out of the car, dragging his laptop bag with him. Rarely did he lock the car door when it was outside his house, but he preferred not to tempt fate by leaving his bag inside.

The front door swung open and banged against the wall behind, and he was greeted by the cold embrace of the dark and lifeless house. In the living room, he kicked off his shoes and dropped his bag onto the little dining table, and he walked to the kitchen pulling off his tie, which he tossed onto the banister as he passed it. But before he reached the kitchen, he stopped, sniffing at the air. The house was slightly dusty but clean in the way that unused houses often were. It wasn't sullied by dirty footprints, dishes, and food stains, but it was tainted with dust on those surfaces he rarely used, which meant that when the aroma of wildflowers hung in the air, it was as remarkable and distinguishable as neon light, and yet somehow it was familiar. He switched on the kitchen light, finding the space empty, so he made his way back to the living room, where the scent seemed yet to penetrate. It was prominent in the hallway, though. And on the stairs, it was even stronger.

He hadn't seen another car outside, but then he had been preoccupied with his father's house. He was tempted to open the front door and look, but he was on the stairs now, climbing one by one sniffing the air like a bloodhound, unsure if it was hope or dread that he felt when he imagined Freya waiting for him in his bedroom. The light was off, but he knew her well enough to know that lying in the darkness ready to surprise him somehow was not beyond her imagination. She could be very creative in the bedroom when she put her mind to it. Or rather, when her imagination wasn't clouded by an investigation.

At the top of the stairs, he stood in front of his bedroom. If she was going to tease him then he would play her at the same game. He stood there in silence, staring into the darkness, allowing his eyes to adjust to the darkness. He thought he could make out her form on the bed. A gentle shape, evident only by the gradient of shadows on the sheets.

The question was, would she be dressed, and if so, in what exactly?

If he knew her as he thought he did, then she would have opened a bottle of red wine. Something expensive, as was her taste, and it would be sitting with two glasses on her side of the bed.

He unbuttoned his shirt, then tugged the tails free of his trousers. That was enough. He didn't want to leave her completely redundant. He could smell her and even remembered the little Parisian shop where she had bought the perfume. The aroma was strong now, stronger than it had been downstairs. In fact, it was so strong that he was sure he could follow the scent to its source. To that little spot on her neck where she dabbed sparingly each morning.

He stepped inside the room, listening hard for her breathing. He could almost picture her smiling at him. Or perhaps there was no smile, and all this was simply her way of apologising for her behaviour. She would, of course, never formally verbalise such an admission of being wrong, such was the narcissist inside of her. But an act such as this? Yes, that was Freya to a tee.

He took another step, almost certain he could make her out, lying on her side, resting her head on one arm. The other was draped across the bed, ready for his touch. Ready to grab him, perhaps? He sniffed the air, loud enough for her to hear. Loud enough that she would realise he was tracking her and he imagined that knowing grin of hers. With one knee on the bed, he lowered himself gently, reaching forward as he let the soft mattress take his body weight, inching his face closer to her, fighting the urge to speak, until his lips were just inches from that dark mass before him, only darker than its surroundings by just a few degrees of shade.

And then he reached forward, closing the gap with his moist lips poised for a kiss.

———

Freya's lips met the hard, cold touch of the wine glass. She sipped once, savoured the aroma, and then took a large mouthful of the Chianti, before setting the glass down on the bedside table beside the bottle. She snatched another of the tissues from the box, wiped her eye carefully, and then tossed it onto the floor with the others before shoving herself off the bed and walking over to the window. The moon was low and to the west. The bench on the green was empty, and the shadow across the grass was long. The wind was up and it was trying to rain again. No doubt the clouds would creep back across the sky sooner or later.

She stepped back to the bed, whipped up the documents she had asked Shelley to print, and then made her third attempt to read them before tossing them to one side, deeming the wine far more appealing. She sat back and eyed her phone on the bed, and instead of placing the glass back on her bedside table, she held it to her bosom. There had been no more missed calls since he had tried to get in touch earlier on, the call that she had almost answered. It would have been nice to hear his voice.

But not now.

Refusing to help her had been one thing. It was a betrayal of sorts. But his excuse had been feeble. The chances of him losing his job over making some enquiries on her behalf were slim to none.

But now she knew why.

She shoved herself off the bed and, taking her wine glass with her, made her way into her dressing room. The three names on the piece of A3 she was using had meant so little. And even when she added Ben's name into the mix, along with the name she had learned at Lincoln, they still meant almost nothing.

- PCSO Harris – RTA
- Sergeant Sanderson – Complaint
- Sergeant Godfrey – Press leak
- Sergeant Brown – Search team
- DI Ben Savage

The road traffic accident had been the first time Freya had an inclination that something was awry. She had been greeted on her doorstep one morning by two uniformed officers from Lincoln Police Station, claiming that her car had been involved in a hit-and-run. It had taken them longer to return her car than it had for her to prove her innocence. But still, the mistake should never have happened. There were hundreds of black Range Rovers on Lincoln's roads, so why had hers been the one they had targeted?

The complaint, at first, had felt like she was back in the Met. It was a spiteful, back-stabbing move that could have been avoided with a frank conversation. An apology even. A seasoned officer with the rank of sergeant should have enough backbone to take criticism on the chin, learn from a mistake, and then move on. They shouldn't – in fact, no – a sergeant would never feel compelled to go above Freya's head and make a formal complaint. After all, she had only commented on the man's experience and maybe given her opinion on his competence. And sure, all that had been in front of a junior officer, but even then there were far more professional ways to deal with an unofficial grilling than to throw them under a bus.

And then there was the press leak. The most recent of the apparent faux pas designed to put Freya under Granger's spotlight. Thankfully, Gillespie had been idle in his car. God knows what garbage the local rag would have printed, no doubt showing a photo of Freya in the most unflattering of candid shots they could get their hands on.

Brown had been added purely on a whim. Her reasons were so farfetched that somehow they made sense – to her, at least. Only time would tell if her gut feeling was correct.

And then there was Ben. She had left a space between the names of the Lincoln officers and Ben's and she was close to drawing a line to connect them. But nothing did.

Nothing connected Ben to the incidents, except for one name. A name that Nillson had sent her. She hadn't baulked at the risk. She was a true friend.

Freya downed the rest of her wine, her mind stepping up into a higher gear as all kinds of ideas and memories came to her fervent mind.

And then she wrote it.

And the whole jigsaw began to make sense.

CHAPTER THIRTY-EIGHT

"What the bloody hell..." Ben said, reaching for the bedside lamp.

He switched it on, knocking over a framed photo of his mum and dad back in the days when they were young and free. He stared down at the bed beneath him, finding not Freya, but a pile of her clothes, some clean, some used. The source of the scent was the blouse she had worn on the Friday night when she had stayed at his house.

But the clean clothes had been a mystery. As far as he remembered, she kept them in the side of the wardrobe he didn't use. But now the light was on, he could see the door was open and the weekend bag she used when she came to stay was left on the chair in the corner, pulled open as if it was ready to be filled.

He fell onto his back, feeling as stupid as they come, and to his surprise, he even found himself wiping a tear from his eye and issuing a single stab of laughter.

But he could still smell her. The blouse was beside his head and he pulled it closer, holding it to his nose and inhaling long and hard.

It had all been a pipe dream. She wasn't waiting to surprise him on his bed, of course she wasn't. She would never apologise even if it was with actions rather than words. She wouldn't prepare a bottle of wine, or dress up for him.

She wasn't even speaking to him. She wasn't even responding to his calls.

"What an idiot," he said aloud to only himself. "What an absolute idiot I am." He slammed his hands onto the mattress, which did little but rock one of the piles of clothes he had thought was Freya so that it spilt onto the bed, and then slowly to the floor.

He shoved himself off the bed, yanked open the wardrobe door, and saw a large, empty space. It was everything. Everything she had kept at his house, the comfy track-suit bottoms, the t-shirts, the dressing gown, and even the underwear. It was all on the bed and now the floor, too. He stepped over to the chair, finding it empty save for her wash bag, in which she kept a toothbrush and a few other bits and pieces, including the special toothpaste she insisted on using. She had said once that selecting a toothpaste based on its flavour or price was tantamount to inviting tooth decay or gum disease. He'd never really thought about the toothpaste he used. He liked the flavour and the price wasn't astronomical. But he'd never considered that it was inferior in any way shape or form. It was toothpaste. There were far more important things to think about.

He tossed the bag to the floor and leaned against the wardrobe, just long enough for him to consider his phone. She hadn't answered his call, which was nothing unusual when she had a bee in her bonnet, but for him not to answer her caused a swarm of the bloody things. She must be seething. He must have totally underestimated how much she believed in the whole out-to-get-her thing.

He snatched up his phone, found her number in his recent call history, and then hit dial. With his phone to his ear, he began to pace the room. The dial tone began as he bent to pick up the clothes he had knocked over, and he was on the second ring when he dropped them onto the bed. It was on the third ring when he straightened the photo of his parents, and the fourth when began to give up hope.

He stepped from the room onto the landing, still catching the remnants of her scent, which he inhaled longingly. He paced, as he often did, stepping into the spare room, and he stood before the corkboard.

The sixth ring was ending when he felt the draught on his bare feet and that irritating woman began her speech, informing him that the person he was trying to call was not available. That's when something clicked, and he studied the open door, and the pit of his stomach lurched as if it had just fallen to the floor, taking every hope of saving their relationship with it.

CHAPTER THIRTY-NINE

The rain fell in sheets. The windscreen wipers on Ben's old Ford Focus were working overtime. Changing the blades had been one of those jobs he had meant to do during the summer. It had been long enough, that's for sure. There was no excuse. He found himself blinking repeatedly, trying to find a clear space between the swishing wipers and the thrumming raindrops. The rear lights of the car in front were his only real clue as to the road ahead. If the driver of the car decided to turn off before Ben, he'd be in a little bit of trouble.

But as it turned out, the car in front was Gillespie's, who, after a tumultuous journey, pulled into the station car park, enabling Ben to follow. He parked in the first space he saw, as opposed to his usual spot, and prayed silently that the rain would ease before he had to drive again.

The anxiety of driving quickly faded and was replaced by another cause for concern. Freya's car wasn't there. In one way, he was pleased. She would no doubt make an interaction of any sort difficult given what she must have surmised from her discovery.

Gillespie was at the door to the custody suite, holding it open for Ben while he ran across the car park.

"Bloody hell," he called out, shaking his mop of hair like a dog under a hosepipe. "I haven't seen it this bad for years. I swear, if we stay out there long enough, we'll see Noah floating past."

"No doubt he'll be speeding," Sergeant Priest said from behind the desk.

He was a stocky Yorkshireman approaching retirement, with rosy, red cheeks and bright eyes. Ben couldn't remember how many times he had mentioned that he was the longest-serving officer in the station. There had been times, over the years, when various senior officers had tried to entice him into a higher rank, but Priest enjoyed what he did, and had dug his heels in. It was an admirable move, Ben thought, and one which had earned him much respect from nearly every officer in the station. Perhaps it was the collective admiration he enjoyed that allowed him to be so jovial. Nothing was ever too much trouble, and even the suspects that were dragged before him were treated with more respect than they deserved.

"Either that or his passengers will prove to be an unstable load."

"You want to nick Noah for an insecure load?" Gillespie said.

"I didn't say I want to nick him," Priest replied. "There are times when I believe that the exacting standards of the law aren't always appropriate for the situation."

"Such as acts of God, or acts on behalf of God?"

"Aye," he replied. "Aye, that's it." He put his head down and continued to fill in some form or other. "The paperwork on that one would be a challenge, that's for sure."

The comment raised a chuckle, and he

reached below the desk for a folder in which to slot the form.

"How are our guests?" Ben asked. "A good night, was it?"

"By all accounts," he replied. "I've only been on for an hour, but they've enjoyed the delights of a bacon butty and a lukewarm tea with no complaints. That's always a good sign. Will you be charging them today, Ben?"

"I don't know yet," he replied. "We still have a few unanswered questions that CPS will want answers for."

"Well, be sure to let me know. I've got transport coming later. If they're to be re-manded then I'd like to make sure there's space."

"Are you looking to free up your cells, sarge?" Gillespie asked. "Expecting an influx of prisoners, are you?"

Priest eyed him, clearly amused.

"Aye, as it happens," he replied. "Two sheep, two cows, two rabbits, and two deer, and I'll be calling on you to help clear the mess up when they've gone."

Ben laughed aloud and nodded a farewell to the jolly man behind the desk and then he and Gillespie pushed through into the corridor.

"So, we're not charging them, then?" Gillespie asked as they entered the fire escape stairwell and began the climb to the first floor. "After all that."

"You heard what Wilson said yesterday, Jim. He might have hit her but he didn't kill her. I'm sure there are grounds for GBH or something, but that's not going to help us. We need the individual who held Linda Wilson to the ground and suffocated her."

"And that isn't Faye?"

"I'm not ruling her out, but my gut says there's more to this," Ben said, stopping at the top of the stairs. "I want to look into this John Briggs bloke, and I want to speak to the PI they hired."

"And what about the boss? What do you think she'll have us do today?"

"God knows," Ben replied. "But given the weather, I imagine it'll be outside, uncomfortable, and insignificant."

"Just a normal day for me, then," Gillespie said.

They pushed through into the incident room, and a conflicting wave of relief washed over Ben. Everyone was there, save for Freya. He stared at her empty desk where she should have been perched. And at the whiteboard that she would normally have fixated on. And at the team, to whom she would normally have set tasks. But instead, there was a hum of chitter chatter, the positive type. It was the reassuring hum of a team that was hard at work, exchanging opinions, information, and, since Ben had stepped inside, concerned glances.

"Ben?" Gold said. Her voice registered in some far-flung corner of his mind but failed to rattle enough of his conscience to break his train of thought. "Ben? Are you all right?"

He looked up at her, finding himself blinking away a teary veil.

"Sorry?"

"I asked if you're all right," she said. "You look like you've seen a ghost."

He gave a laugh, and even he knew how weak it sounded. "I'm soaked through," he replied, then glanced around the room at the faces he knew and loved. "No sign of Freya, then?"

"Not yet," Nillson said.

"She left me a message," Chapman cut in.

"She's taking the morning off to run a few errands."

All eyes returned to Ben, and Gold raised her eyebrows expectantly.

"Right then," he said, clearing his throat while formulating a plan. He made his way to the desk that Freya usually sat on, but chose to remain standing. "Looks like it's down to me, then."

"Aye, just like the old days, eh?" Gillespie said.

"Something like that," Ben replied, then took a breath to find some semblance of a structure to the briefing. "So, as you should all know, Jim and I were told to bring in Geoffrey Wilson and Faye Butters. Meanwhile, I believe you were all tasked with developing a case for the CPS. Where are we with that?"

"Pretty much the same place we were yesterday," Nillson said, assuming the role of spokesperson for the team. "We have had a few updates. CSI can now prove that Geoffrey Wilson struck his wife with the chair leg, or whatever it was. It's her blood on the wood, and his prints, so that's an avenue for us."

"GBH at best," Ben said. "Apart from

giving us a beginning to the whole sordid affair."

"What about the dog?" Nillson said. "He bloody well killed the dog, didn't he? Surely if he killed the dog in the same way, there's cause for attempted murder?"

"I wouldn't put any money on that, Anna," he said. "Have we finished searching the houses?"

"Yes, we found a dead dog with the same injuries as Linda Wilson," Nillson replied.

"Just trust me, will you?" Ben said, grinning at her tenacity.

"The Butters' house is clean, too," Cruz added. "Jackie and I tore the place apart, pretty much. And that doorbell camera came in handy, too. It clearly shows the couple leaving with their dog around six a.m., and only he came back. The next time it was triggered was when he came running down the road to tell us his wife was missing."

"Did you check the bins?"

"I did," he said, wide-eyed. "All I can say is that they eat a lot of vegetables and that they should really consider composting. It was basically decomposing slime in one bin and the TV-bloody-Times in the recycling."

"So, we're sure she didn't return home, which gives Kyle Butters' statement some credibility. We can at least be certain that he left his wife and took the dog with him, and that she met with Geoffrey Wilson directly from the dog walk."

"Oh, here we go," Cruz said. "So, we're sure they were having an affair, are we?"

"Actually, no," Ben replied. "In fact, I'm certain that they are not having an affair."

"You what?"

Ben smiled at the young DC and it felt good.

"Last night, when all of you had gone home, Jim and I interviewed Geoffrey Wilson and Kyle Butters."

"Kyle Butters?" Jackie said. "I thought you were supposed to arrest Faye Butters?"

"Oh, we were, and we did. She's downstairs," Ben said, checking his watch. "And we've got her for another eighteen hours or so before we have to make a decision."

"I'll make a decision," Nillson said. "She did it."

"It's not as simple as that."

"Oh really? You spoke to Geoffrey Wilson, you said."

"That's right."

"And what did he say, Ben? Did he admit to hitting her?"

"He did, as it happens."

"Right, so we've got him killing his dog, and then attacking his wife in exactly the same way, probably with the same weapon, or something similar. We've even got the phone calls between him and Faye. What did he have to say about that?"

"He said that he called Faye when he realised his wife had gone," Ben said. "He left her in the garden thinking she was dead."

"So, he tried to kill his wife, and then not only left her in the garden, but he called his lover?"

"Something doesn't add up," Ben said. "It's not black and white. You heard what Freya said. We need answers to everything. We need black and white, and this..." He faltered, struggling to find the words. "This isn't. It just isn't."

"You really don't think she did it, do you?" Nillson said, her head cocked as if she was trying to peer into his mind. "This isn't about insufficient evidence. This is you not believing that she did it."

He stared at Nillson, one of the few people he trusted. Which, in theory, should earn her the right to be told the truth.

"What else do we have?" he asked. "Aside from the blood in the house, and the dog, what else do we have?"

"Nothing," she said eventually. "Apart from a few anomalies with Wilson's credit card, that is."

"Oh?" Instead of replying, Nillson eyed Chapman, signalling that she should state her findings. "Denise?"

The quiet, young researcher was as reliable as a golden retriever, though somehow comparing her to one felt like an insult rather than the compliment it was meant to be, so he kept it to himself. She wore a floral blouse beneath what appeared to be a hand-knitted cardigan. Her watch was plain, and Ben couldn't remember ever seeing her wearing jewellery such as rings or bracelets.

"It's a card from another bank, Ben," she said, flatly and by way of an explanation. "That's why I didn't pick it up the first time around. As far as I can tell there's only one card associated with the account, so any transaction had to have been made by Geoffrey Wilson."

"What did you find, Chapman?" Ben pushed.

"There are a few transactions that caught my eye," she began. "Six hundred pounds each. All to the same account, and all two weeks apart."

"I'm guessing it's not a subscription to Woodturners Weekly?"

"It's a private investigator," she said. "I contacted the bank last night. They responded this morning. It's a man named Scott Sloane."

"Sloane?" Gillespie said and eyed Ben with far less of a poker face than Ben would have hoped for. It was enough for Nillson to pick up on.

"What?" she said. "What is it? Why is that name familiar?"

"Only that Kyle Butters mentioned him last night. I was hoping we could check him out today. In fact, I was hoping that you would, Anna. Find out some more about him. Chapman, maybe you could do some digging? Is he local? Where does he live? Is he married?"

"Why the interest in him?" Gold asked. "I mean, aside from the money."

"Because it turns out that Geoffrey Wilson and Faye Butters are what you might call busybodies," Ben began.

"Hence the complaints to the police," Chapman added, and Ben nodded.

"They take it upon themselves to keep their villages in order. Butters in Boothby and Wilson in Coleby."

"And they team up when the going gets tough," Nillson said, a statement rather than a question.

"When Kyle and Faye were out walking their dog, Faye received a call from Geoffrey. Until now, we thought the two were having an affair, but I don't think they were. I genuinely believe they were just friends with a common interest."

"Policing their villages?" Cruz said.

"Right," Ben replied. "Only this time it seems they have picked on the wrong target. You all remember that Wilson's son is in prison?"

"But that was tax fraud," Chapman said, clearly not following yet.

"It was. But, when Geoffrey paid him a

visit in HMP Lincoln, Thomas Wilson gave him some news, which he then passed on to Faye Butters. Chapman, look up a man named John Briggs. He's originally from Newark somewhere."

Chapman set to work. It would take her moments if she was already logged into the database and Ben studied the rest of the faces in the room while he waited. Cruz waited calmly, alert and attentive. Gold's eyes seemed to bore into him, not with regards to the investigation, but rather his mental health. Anderson busied herself with her laptop, and Nillson watched his every move disapprovingly.

"Balderton?" Chapman said. "I've got a John Frederick Briggs from Balderton. Sentenced to twelve years for manslaughter at HMP Lincoln. Paroled after eight years. He was released a few months ago."

"That's him," Ben said, then prepared to deliver the punchline. "When he was convicted, his parents found living in the area somewhat awkward. The neighbours disapproved if you know what I mean?"

"So, they relocated to Boothby?" Nillson

said, following on exactly as Ben hoped she would.

"And when Geoffrey Wilson visited Thomas Wilson and asked him about any news, Thomas told him about John Briggs living with his parents in Boothby."

"And Faye obviously wanted him out."

"Hence the private investigator," Ben said. "At least, I think that's how he's connected. According to Kyle Butters, Sloane found irrefutable evidence relating to the original case. He's still on parole so if the authorities, A.K.A us, get wind of it, then he'd be back inside before you could say good behaviour."

"But why did he only get manslaughter?" Cruz asked.

"Apparently, he was caught on camera with another man moments before the attack."

"But the murder took place off camera?" Nillson said, and Ben nodded. "So, they know he was involved, but couldn't prove which of them actually did the murder so they both got manslaughter."

Ben nodded. It was a problem they had faced before and one that a tiny hole in an investigation could produce if the defence was any good at any rate.

"The problem is that if Kyle is right, and it was Briggs who killed the Wilsons' dog, and then Linda, then we have a murderer on the loose who is looking to keep his past a secret, and to top it off, he's prepared to do almost anything to achieve his goal."

"But how come there wasn't a Briggs on the list Gillespie gave us?" Cruz said, his face crumpling like a teenager facing an algebra problem. "Jackie and I went through every name in the village from when Jim had been knocking. There wasn't a John Briggs, I'm sure of it."

"Maybe they were one of the ones that didn't answer the door?" Gillespie said.

"Double check the electoral register," Ben said, finding Nillson looking as perplexed as he felt. "In fact, no. Jim, find me the names of everyone who was at the crime scene on Sunday."

"Sunday?"

"Yes, you know, when the whole village descended on us. You took their names, right? Freya asked you to."

"Aye, I did."

"Crosscheck the names on your list with Cruz's list of the houses you knocked at and the electoral register. If I'm right, then there'll be a name that doesn't match, and that's our man."

"You think the killer was there on Sunday, standing beside half of Lincolnshire's police force?"

"Where would you be if you'd just killed someone?" Ben asked, smiling as it began to come together. "You wouldn't be at home waiting for a long-haired, Glaswegian detective to come knocking on your door, would you? No, you'd be hiding in plain sight, masquerading as a concerned villager so you can see exactly what's going on and perhaps send us in the wrong direction."

"I don't get it," Cruz said, never one to shy away from revealing his innermost thoughts, despite the backlash it often provoked.

"You don't get what?"

"This John Briggs bloke. So, we're saying that he killed the dog to warn Faye and Geoffrey off?"

"That's right."

He hesitated, and his eyes flicked towards

Gillespie, clearly expecting some kind of childish rhetoric to follow his next statement.

"So why did he kill Linda Wilson?" he said. "If Faye and Geoffrey were the ones who were trying to get him out of the village, then why kill Linda? She didn't even know about their investigation. And why not kill the Butters' dog, too?"

It was one of those times when Ben wanted to go over and shake the young constable's hand. Nobody else had raised the question. None of them. Yet they were all keen to go out and bring Briggs in.

"Well, as far as warnings go," Ben said, "killing a dog is about as clear and direct as they come. As for Linda, I have a feeling she was in the wrong place at the wrong time."

"That's a pretty big mistake to make," Gillespie said. "For someone on parole, I mean."

"It is a big mistake," Ben agreed. "But not as big as ours will be if we don't find a way to prove it and bring him in."

CHAPTER FORTY

"So, what's the plan, then?" Nillson asked. "Do we go after this John Briggs character? Anderson and I can be at his house in under half an hour."

"No," Ben said, hearing the urgency in his tone and adjusting it accordingly. "No, he's already been convicted of manslaughter, so we can assume he's not afraid of going above and beyond. If we hit him, then I want uniformed officers there."

"So, let's do it," Nillson said. "Let's get things moving."

"Let's just wait a while. I don't want a ticking clock adding even more pressure. When we bring him in, I want an infallible case to submit to the CPS. No unanswered questions." Ben paced away from them, playing it over in his mind. It was all there. All roads led to John Briggs. But once more, there were far too many ifs and buts to build a solid case. "How long have we got left on Faye Butters' custody?"

"A little under eighteen hours," Gillespie said. "Same goes for Geoffrey Wilson."

"Good, at least they'll be safe here until then. In the meantime, let's see what this Scott Sloane has to say. Chapman, get me his address, will you?"

"Already done," she replied. "It's in your emails along with details of his car."

"Excellent, thanks."

"So, we're just going to let this Briggs bloke run amok while we build a case? What if he does a runner, or goes after someone else?"

"He won't run," Ben said. "He can't. He's got nowhere to go. He has no money. He's living with his parents, and he's on parole, which is a good point. Can somebody get in touch with his parole officer? Ask to be kept abreast of any communications, or failure to report in."

"If he's on parole, then he'll be on a tag?" Anderson said. "Most likely a curfew tag." She waited a moment for the others to catch up with her idea. "They have GPS," she added.

"Which means the monitoring team will be able to tell us where he was," Ben replied. "Get onto it."

"That's all well and good, Ben," Nillson said. "But Briggs will still be running free while we do all this."

"I'm not bringing him in with nothing to go on, Anna," he said. "We've got one shot at this, and while those two are downstairs, we know he can't get to them. I tell you what, Cruz, Gold, when you've got that rogue name, I want to look into it. Pay whoever it is a visit."

"Eh?" Cruz said, his face a picture of perplexity. He snatched up the papers in front of him and held them up. "I've got a name that doesn't match. But I don't see how that helps us."

"What's the rogue name?"

"Steven Yates."

"Right," Ben said. "So, if John Briggs was at the crime scene last Sunday, and he told

Gillespie his name was Steven Yates, which let's face it, if he's on parole he most likely would have given a false name, then his parents won't be expecting a knock on the door from two police officers asking for Steven Yates, will he?"

"Well, what do we say to them? What if he answers the door and says he is Steven Yates?"

"Then we'll know he hasn't done a runner," Ben replied. "You can ask him to clarify his whereabouts."

Ben added the name to the board, just as Freya would have done, and then circled it, stabbing a full stop to finish.

"But what if he denies all knowledge of knowing who Steven Yates is?" Cruz asked, and Ben closed his eyes while his disappointment dissipated.

"Then you take his details for your report," Ben replied, pulling his coat from the chair. "And he'll know we're on the right path. Either way, we'll put the frighteners on him." He pulled on his still-wet coat and checked the weather through the window. The rain had eased a little but not entirely, and there was every chance of another deluge. Gillespie followed suit and, still seated, slid his arms into his coat which hung on the back of his chair, and then shrugged it onto his shoulders. Ben held up a hand to signal he should stay put for a moment and then tapped Nillson on the shoulder. "A word, Anna."

"But what if he gave Gillespie a false address?" Cruz argued. It was a shame. The young constable had proved himself a competent officer but lacked the confidence to answer the questions himself.

"What address did he give?" Ben asked.

"Um, it's a house on Main Street."

"And according to the electoral register, who lives at that address?"

Cruz flicked through some papers on his desk until he found what he was looking for, then took a moment to find the address.

"A Mr and Mrs Briggs," he replied, closing his eyes at his own stupidity. "John Briggs' parents."

Ben smiled at him and finally, Cruz's anxiety was satiated.

"We got there in the end, didn't we?" he said. "When you're ready, Anna," He stopped at the door and looked back at them all, feeling that surge of adrenaline pump through his chest. It was the mark of progress. "Gillespie, change of plan."

"Aye?" the big Scotsman replied.

"Call down to Sergeant Priest, will you? Ask him to get Faye Butters in an interview room. Call the duty solicitor in, too."

"Your wish is my command," he replied, shrugging off his coat and letting it fall onto his chair behind him.

Ben left the room and waited. As soon as Nillson stepped outside the incident room, he caught hold of her wrist and dragged her as politely as he could further along the corridor towards the restrooms where nobody could overhear them.

"Ben?" she said, snatching her arm back. "What the bloody hell–"

"She knows," he hissed.

"What?"

"Freya," he said. "She bloody knows."

"So, you drag me up the corridor? Let me tell you something, Ben. If you ever grab hold of me like that again, I'll break your arm."

She was serious. Her eyes and tone left little room for misinterpretation.

"Sorry," he replied. "Sorry, I just had to tell someone, and–"

"I'm the only one who knows?" Nillson said, and her anger finally abated. "How did she find out?" She studied his face, and it was all he could do to focus on a dirty handprint on the wall that had been there for as long as Ben could remember. "You don't think that I told her?"

"No, no, of course not," he said. "It's my fault. I ignored her calls yesterday. I wanted to make some progress to show her that..." He stopped and sighed.

"To show her what?"

He smiled and even he knew it was a boyish smile of immaturity.

"To impress her," he replied. "I wanted her to know that I'm still me. That I'm still a good detective and that I'm on her side, regardless of what she thinks."

"So, you did that by ignoring her calls?"

"I was in an interview with Kyle Butters. I couldn't exactly step outside and have a personal chat with my boss about our relationship," he said. "Anyway, when I got home, I found the door unlocked."

"The front door?"

"No. The bedroom door. My spare bedroom."

Nillson's eyes widened and her mouth fell open until she bit down her lower lip and grimaced.

"And you didn't get rid of it all like I told you to? Why not, Ben?"

"No, I didn't," he said. "And because I'm stupid. I'm a stupid, stupid man, and now she probably thinks I'm investigating her for murder. Has she called you? Has she said anything?"

Nillson looked sheepish, but it didn't last. She was far too brazen and confident in her own actions to reveal anything but a fleeting weakness.

"She called me a couple of days ago," she admitted. "She asked me to look into a few names."

"Oh, for God's sake. Not this again."

"She thinks she's the target of some internal attack," Nillson explained. "She thinks that somebody is manipulating officers in Lincoln, in order to get her sacked or humiliated, or something."

"And did you do it?" Ben asked, and again Nillson looked away. "Anna, did you do it?"

"What did you expect me to do? The woman was in bits the other day about you two. She wouldn't show it, of course, but we all knew. We could all see it."

"What do you mean, you all?"

"Us," she said. "The girls. Me, Jenny, Jackie, Denise, and Cruz." Ben gave her a quizzical look at the last name and then saw the thin slice of humour in it. "She was asking for advice. Not directly, but it was obvious."

"What kind of advice?"

"Whether or not she should fix whatever happened between you two. She said you let her down. That you were unsupportive or something. She didn't go into detail. But the point is that we convinced her, or at least I think we did, to let it go. We told her that we all knew about the two of you and that your attempts at hiding it were pathetic." The comment raised Ben's eyebrows and he smiled at the thought of it. "Well, not quite on those words," Nillson continued, softening. "There's still a chance, Ben. Don't you see?"

"Not anymore," he replied sadly. "Me

being unsupportive and letting her down. She asked me to look into the names."

"And you said no?"

He nodded. "The thing is, it's too risky. If the IOPC got wind of it–"

"The IOPC? It hardly warrants an internal inquiry, Ben."

"Right," he said. "But if my computer account was flagged for looking into police officers that she later goes after–"

"Then the IOPC could potentially see who else you've been investigating. They'd know you were looking into Freya."

He nodded.

"And they'd see what I found." Nillson stared at him, too polite and professional to push for any more information. But he said nothing. "So, what did you find, anyway? Is there any truth in these names?"

Nillson nodded. But this time she didn't turn her head. She just stared at him with dread and regret in her eyes.

"What is it?" Ben said.

"There was a name," she replied, checking over her shoulder to make sure they weren't being overheard. "I messaged her last night. One name that linked every officer on the list. They all reported into him at some stage in their career and they've all run background searches on the boss."

"So, she was right?"

He kicked at the wall and slammed his hands against the plaster, realising at that exact moment how the original handprint had come to be there. He turned to face her, unapologetic for his outburst, to which she closed her eyes and turned away, perhaps from shame, or maybe even regret, forcing him to duck to intercept her gaze, and then draw her attention back to him.

"Who was it, Anna?" he said, his voice monotone and unwavering.

She sighed and her nostrils flared. She was a pretty, young woman. Masculine, but pretty. She took care of herself and everyone on the team knew of her penchant for a good chase and a rugby tackle to bring a suspect down. It was something to do with having multiple older brothers.

"Steve Standing," she said quickly and quietly as if she was ripping the plaster off a fresh wound.

"Steve Standing?" he repeated. "As in, Steve Standing the ex-detective-chief-inspector that she locked up for murder? As in, the bloke that made our lives hell when he was here?"

"There's more," she said, stopping him from entering into a rant, and he sensed something awry. "There's one more person who also reported into him and whose name was flagged on the system for running background checks on her."

He crumpled against the wall he'd just given a hard time and let his head fall back. He wanted to smash it backwards several times to knock some sense into himself, but he knew it would be fruitless and only risk somebody from the incident room taking an interest in their conversation.

"Did you tell her that last bit?" he asked dryly.

"I'm sorry," she replied. "But she would have worked it out eventually. She's not stupid, Ben."

"No, she's not," he replied, taking a heavy breath. "No, that she certainly is not."

CHAPTER FORTY-ONE

The sticky, blue mattress, bacon butty, and lukewarm tea that Priest had provided had clearly been less than adequate for Faye Butters. Her red hair was pulled back into a ponytail and the makeup she had been wearing the previous day was now smudged and cracked, making her the Hollywood depiction of a lady of the night, especially with the long overcoat she had wrapped herself in. She had a stare that could have cut glass, a bitterness that was rooted deep inside, and if anything, the sour expression only added to the unfortunate image.

Sitting beside her, the duty solicitor

looked up briefly, then returned her attention to the file the team had provided. It was due process to submit relevant evidence against a suspect to the legal representative. But in this case, the evidence only served to support her innocence.

Gillespie took his seat and prepared the recording, leaving Ben to take the seat opposite Faye. He said nothing, choosing instead to prepare his files until the time was right. A long, hideous buzz announced the commencement of the recording, and even then Ben waited a few seconds to begin, starting first by introducing himself and Gillespie to the recording. The duty solicitor then introduced herself as Mary Haggerty, and all eyes fell on Faye, whose voice cracked when she said her name, a sign of fatigue brought on by the emotions, the fear, and most likely, the uncomfortable night.

"Mrs Butters, I'm obliged to remind you why you're here. You have been arrested on suspicion of the murder of Linda Wilson. You do not have to say anything. But it may harm your defence if you do not mention when questioned something which you later rely on in court. Anything you do say may be given in evidence. Do you understand the charges against you?"

"I do," she said softly. "Would it make a difference if I told you that I'm innocent?"

"Yes, as a matter of fact," Ben replied. "But what I'd like to do before we get there is to hear your version of events. I've provided your legal aid with the evidence against you. Have you had a chance to discuss the points?"

"We have," Haggerty said. "And I'd like to raise several points."

"All in good time," Ben replied before they both ventured down the path of innocence. "As I said, I'd really like to hear your account. When we're done, you'll be given the opportunity to raise any questions. Does that sound fair?"

Faye nodded slowly, her lips parted revealing a glimpse of healthy teeth.

"So, let's start with Saturday evening, shall we?" Ben said, glancing across at Gillespie to make sure he was ready to take notes.

"Saturday?"

"Yes, how did you spend your Saturday evening?"

"I was home. I was with Kyle."

"All night?" Ben said, leading her in the direction of dinner with the Wilsons, without actually pointing the way.

"Well, no. We spent the afternoon with Geoff and Linda," she replied. "We had dinner in The Tempest. It's the local pub in Coleby."

"Good food?" Gillespie asked, and the question seemed to rattle her.

"Of course. It's why we go there. Well, that and the views, that is."

"And a good time was had by all, was it?" Ben asked.

"Whatever do you mean?"

"Well, I was just wondering if there were any little tiffs or ill-feeling of any sort, between Linda and any of you."

"No, of course not," she replied, appearing horrified. "We're friends." Ben raised his eyebrows at the present tense. "We're friends," she said softly. "We're good friends."

"Would you say that your friendship, in particular, was stronger with Linda or her husband, Mrs Butters?"

"Sorry?"

"Should I rephrase the question?"

"No. No, there's no need. But you're

wrong. We were all friends. The four of us," she said, slipping into past tense. "It's true that Geoff and I are close, but no closer than Linda was with Kyle."

"But you and Geoff work together at the library," Ben said, and she saw the angle Ben was coming from.

"Yes, we did. We both share a common love of literature."

"Literature?" Gillespie said, almost scoffing.

"Books," she said with more than a hint of malice in her tone. "Reading. You should try it sometime."

"Ah, I get enough to read, I can assure you," he said. "The last thing I want to do is read a fictional whodunnit when I spend my days sitting here doing this."

It was a decent comeback but one which did little to progress the interview, and even less to get Faye Butters on side.

"What time did you leave The Tempest?" Ben said, to which Faye spent a moment or two thinking.

"Sometime between five and six," she replied. "It was dark but not fully."

"And did you go straight home?"

Faye sighed and wiped her eye with the back of her hand, giving Ben an excuse to pass her a tissue.

"Okay this is the hard part," she said, leaning forward and clearing her throat. "Linda invited us back for drinks. It's something we did often. Boothby doesn't have a pub, so we invariably end up at their house after The Tempest." She paused for a moment and fiddled with her fingers. "Only this time, when we got back, we found something. We went around the back. Theirs is one of those houses where the front door is seldom used. In fact, I don't recall ever using their front door. Not in recent years anyway." She cocked her head to one side thoughtfully and wet her lips with a flick of her tongue. "Geoff went to unlock the door, but it was already unlocked, which was odd. One minute we were laughing and joking, and the next minute the mood had changed." She clicked her fingers. "It was just like that. We all sensed something was wrong. And it was."

"What did you find?" Ben asked, feigning ignorance.

"Mindy, their labrador," she explained.

"She was lying on the kitchen floor. She'd been..." She shook her head and put her hand to her mouth.

"She'd been killed?" Ben suggested, and Faye nodded and then gave a loud groan of despair.

"It was a little chaotic after that. Linda was distraught. Geoff was angry. They started arguing. Blaming each other, and I suggested that Kyle and I leave them to it. But Kyle was keen to stay. He said he'd help Geoff bury her. God knows it's hard enough to bury your pet, but to dig the hole too? So, Kyle dug the hole for them. When we were done, they were still at each other's throats. So, Kyle and I found an old blanket and a sack in Geoff's workshop, and we laid Mindy on it so they could say their last words to her in their own time. We left shortly after. We didn't say goodbye. It didn't feel right, somehow."

"And then you and Kyle walked home?"

"That's right. We walked along Viking Way as we always do."

Not a single word of the account was news to Ben. If anything, it confirmed his thoughts and corroborated what he'd heard from her husband. But the account of the next day was where the difficulties would come, and difficulties usually provided one of two things: lies or confessions.

"And did you speak to either Linda or Geoffrey later that evening?"

"No. We wondered if we should call them, but we daren't. Not the way they were going at each other."

"So, you just went to bed, did you?" Ben asked. "Your best friend's dog has just been bludgeoned to death, and you simply went to bed?"

"What were we supposed to have done?"

"Call the police?"

"Geoff said he'd do that."

"Well, clearly he didn't," Ben said, doing his best to hide his joy at her taking the bait. "Why didn't he call the police, do you think?" She stumbled on the question, delaying her response by taking a quiet word with Haggerty. "Perhaps he forgot?" Ben suggested, looking at Gillespie for some support.

"Aye," he replied. "Maybe they just went to bed, too."

"No," she said. "No, they were upset."

"So why wouldn't he call the police? Somebody had broken into his house and murdered his dog, Faye. You understand why I find that a little perplexing, don't you?"

"I do," she said, balling her fists, clearly fighting with some internal dilemma. "It's just..." A breath fell from her lips as if she no longer had control over her body.

"Mrs Butters, are you okay?" Ben asked. "We can take a break if you want."

"No," she said, her throat so tight that the word sounded childlike, high and from the back of her throat. "No, just give me a minute, will you?" She closed her eyes and entered into some kind of breathing routine to control her nerves. The wait was easy. Ben already had the answers. He knew what she should say. The guilt and complexities would only arise should she decide to keep something back or lie. "You obviously know about Linda's boy, Thomas?"

"We do," Ben said. "Dreadful business, tax. But nothing is more certain than death and taxes. That's what they say, isn't it?"

She dismissed the comment with a shake of her head as if it had muddled her mind.

"Geoff went to see him. He gets those VOs, or whatever they're called–"

"Visiting orders?" Gillespie said.

"Yes. Linda can't bear to go," she said, then realised her mistake of using the present tense, but didn't correct herself. "Apparently, Thomas had been speaking to some other prisoners in there. He does quite well, apparently. We all thought the sentence would destroy him, but he's no threat to anyone else and he knows the financial systems like the back of his hand. So, it seems he's won himself some exclusivity."

"Small wins, Mrs Butters," Gillespie said. "Small wins."

"We have to hold onto what we can," she replied. "Anyway, it turns out that one of the men he spoke to was moving to Boothby when he got out. His parents moved there when he was put away. Thomas told Geoffrey and Geoffrey told me."

"Did it concern you?" Ben asked innocently. "What does it matter if a man who had served his time, paid his penance, and was looking for a new start was to move into Boothby?"

"It matters a great deal, Inspector," she replied haughtily.

"Oh?"

"We have to maintain the standards our villagers are accustomed to. Don't you see?"

"Standards?"

Having to explain herself was clearly making her cross. She was fighting the urge to snap at him.

"If we let a man like him in, then who knows who'll be next? Before you know it, we'll have God-knows-who living next door and our house prices will hit the floor." She stabbed her index finger onto the table. "We're proud of our village," she said. "And you might not mind living next door to a murderer, but I certainly do."

"I think you'll find it was manslaughter," Ben said.

"Whatever," she replied, and he waited for her to catch up, which she did eventually. "What did you say?"

He grinned at her.

"I think you'll find John Briggs was convicted of manslaughter."

"You knew?"

"Of course," he replied. "Your husband told us."

"My husband? You've spoken to Kyle?"

"This is a murder enquiry, Faye," Ben said. "We don't just sit around hoping that murderers will come to us and confess."

"What else did he say?"

"It's not what he said that bothers me if I'm honest," Ben said. "I mean, he did his best. But I suppose when you were out walking your dog on Sunday morning, you didn't have much time to tell him the full story, did you?"

"I'm not following."

"And if I'm being honest," Haggerty said, her voice shrill and headmistress-like, "I'm wondering why the evidence you've submitted has no mention of this."

"Because it's not evidence," Ben replied. "It's information. It'll become evidence when we can use it to prove your client's guilt or her innocence, and when we do that, we'll submit it." He turned back to Faye while the solicitor licked her wounds. "Geoffrey called you while you were out walking. What did he tell you, Faye?"

Ben was pleased with how the interview was going. He'd given enough for Faye to know that he was aware of most of the facts, but she had no idea of the extent of his knowledge, which made lying and hiding details more difficult.

"He just..." she began. "He said that he'd done something terrible. He said that he'd hit her. That he thought he'd killed her. But that she'd somehow woken up, or come around or something."

"And?" Ben pressed, and she inhaled long and hard.

"And that she was very likely on her way to my house to tell Kyle."

"I see," Ben said. "Tell him what exactly?"

"About John Briggs. About what I'd done."

"About how you and Geoffrey had tried to force John Briggs and his family from the village? About how you'd overstepped the mark on this occasion? Or picked on the wrong person?"

"Kyle hated what I did. He said it made the neighbours hate us."

"And so, you kept it from him. And now

Linda was on her way to tell him. So, you told Kyle before she could. Is that right?" Faye nodded and swallowed hard enough for her guilt to rise and fall. "And you knew he'd be angry. Angry enough that he'd leave you out there on your own."

"If she had got to him before me, I wouldn't need a defence lawyer. I'd need a divorce lawyer."

"Which must seem like a far more preferable option right now," Ben added. "So, you waited for Linda. You intercepted her. Tell me about that, Faye. Tell me what happened next."

She fumbled with her fingers again, picking at her nail varnish with her thumb. Then she wiped the flakes of paint onto the floor and linked her fingers, releasing a deep breath.

"Faye?" Ben urged. "This is where you tell us what you said to Linda."

"I didn't speak to her," she said. "I saw her. She was staggering along Viking Way. It wasn't quite light, but it had to be her. I was down on the lower path at the bottom of the edge and she was up the top. I could see her against the sky."

"Did you call out?"

"No. No, I saw her approaching Kyle. They were a few hundred metres away, so there was no chance of intercepting her."

"So, she spoke to Kyle?" Ben said, and Gillespie did little to conceal his confusion. "You're sure about that? You said it was dark and you were a few hundred metres away. Are you sure it was Kyle?"

She said nothing. Instead, she frowned as she relived the memory.

"Faye, this is important. Are you sure it was Kyle that you saw?"

Again, she seemed hesitant to speak. A worried look washed over her face.

And then she shook her head.

"No," she said. "No, I can't be sure. I didn't stop to see."

"So, what did you do? Where did you go?"

"I made my way down to Castle Lane, then gave Geoff a call. He was in right old state."

"Seems like a strange decision to make, Faye, given the circumstances."

"Not really," she replied. "You see, John Briggs isn't the first person I've upset by keeping our village up to scratch."

"Oh?"

"I don't why, but Kyle says I'm interfering," she replied, and the muscles in her face softened. "The last time this happened, he said he'd leave me unless it stopped."

"Ah," Ben said. "Hence why you and Geoff both kept it quiet."

She nodded and dabbed at her eye with the tissue.

"The last words he said to me," she said. "He told me that I shouldn't bother going home. He said he'd pack my bags and call me when they're ready to be picked up."

"So, you saw Linda making her way along Viking Way. You saw a man waiting for her, whom you thought was your husband, and then you got into Geoffrey Wilson's car, and..." Ben said, holding his hands up, hoping that she would finish the sentence for him. "Where did you go?"

Haggerty leaned across to speak quietly into her ear and Faye nodded, offering her a grateful but weak smile.

"You know where we went," she said. "It's in the evidence you submitted."

Haggerty seemed pleased with herself, having stalled the progress Ben was making.

It was a common tactic for defending solicitors to do what they could to interrupt a line of questioning, casting doubt over either the questioning officer's competence or the credibility of their evidence.

"Well, here's the thing, Faye. We know you went to the Airbnb in Ashby de la Launde with Geoffrey Wilson. We're also aware that Geoffrey hired a private investigator named Scott Sloane." He looked across at Haggerty. "Before you ask, you won't find that in the submission. Not until it's confirmed as evidence." He looked back at Faye. "What I'd like to know is why you met with Scott Sloane, and what was said. I can only presume you went there to discuss the investigation against John Briggs. But most of all, I'd like to know why on earth, after what he did to the dog, you wanted to carry on?"

"It's not like that," she snapped, then took a moment to compose herself. "We'd been working with Scott for a couple of months. He came highly recommended, he was discreet, but most of all he was aware of the John Briggs case."

"The manslaughter charge?"

"That's right," she said. "We wanted him

to reexamine the evidence. We couldn't get him out of the village unless we could prove without certainty that he was actually guilty. Then we could have pushed for a retrial. He could have served the rest of his time, as he should have done in the first place."

"Assuming he is guilty," Ben added.

"Right," she replied. "We used the Airbnb every couple of weeks. It was a safe place we could meet and go over what we'd all found. We were supposed to go on the Saturday night. Geoff and I usually went when Kyle and Linda had gone to bed, but what with the dog and that. So, when he picked me up, we went there. It was already booked. Scott was already there and he wasn't too happy with us, but when we explained what had happened, he understood. He said he was onto something but needed another day or so."

"And was that the last time you saw Scott Sloane?" Ben asked, to which she nodded.

"We're supposed to meet him today. That's if I'm released. Will I be?" she asked. "I've told you everything. Will I be released?"

She stared at Ben in earnest, and he checked his watch. Her custody clock would time out that evening, and after all she, her husband, and Geoffrey Wilson had said, there was a slim chance that she was responsible for Linda Wilson's death.

"No," he said. "No, I'm afraid you'll be here a while longer."

"My client has given you all the information you need to drop the charges, Inspector," Haggerty said. "Or at least release her on bail."

"Has she?" he replied, collating his files, and giving Gillespie the nod to prepare to end the recording. "Because from where I sit, nothing has been proven. And until I can demonstrate that your client is innocent, then she'll remain in custody." He turned to look at the defeated Faye Butters, whose shoulders sagged at the idea of another twelve or more hours in the cell. "Where I can keep an eye on her." Haggerty looked displeased but said nothing. "And her partner in crime," Ben added.

The lull in debate was decidedly cold, and Ben took pleasure in the fact that Haggerty seemed not to have a suitable response. He glanced across at Gillespie, then checked his watch.

"Interview ended at ten forty-five," Ben said, then turned to the woman before him. "I suggest you take the time to think long and hard about the consequences of your actions, Mrs Butters. Long and hard."

CHAPTER FORTY-TWO

It was as if the weather Gods had been watching Ben, toying with him in his already frustrated state, in the same way that his father's sheep used to recognise when he was having an off day and decide that that would be the day to break a fence and escape into a field of crops or avoid the pens he was driving them into, making the job take twice as long as it should have. He stood at the door to the custody suite, overlooking the car park, where the puddles were slowly deepening and spreading, inching themselves closer to each other to form a single large puddle. The rain had eased whilst they had been in the station, but now that he was ready to leave, the clouds appeared to be re-forming to join forces above him.

"Bugger this," Gillespie said from behind him. "I tell you, Ben, if ever I want to kill somebody, Cruz, most likely, remind me to wait until the summer."

The comment had caught Priest's ear and Ben grinned as, over Gillespie's shoulder, he saw the old Yorkshireman shake his head in disbelief, and then return to his work at the custody desk.

"Probably best to do it in the rain," Ben told him. "The chances of getting me to stand out in the rain looking for evidence are much slimmer."

"True," Gillespie said, gesturing at the car park with a nod of his head. "Shall we?"

"You can drive."

"Eh?"

"My wipers need changing," Ben told him. "The last thing I need is a pull from our friends in white hats and a ticket for driving without due care and attention."

"I erm..." Gillespie started, seeming to search for an excuse.

"What is it?"

"Well, it's just that...my car, I haven't got

around to cleaning it."

"I'm sure a bit of a messy car is better than having to call a tow truck to drag it out of a dyke, Jim."

"Aye," Gillespie said, sucking in a deep breath. "Right then."

He edged past Ben, and they ran through the rain to his old estate, where he fumbled with the lock on the driver's door, jiggled a few times, and then slipped inside. The car rocked to one side as it took Gillespie's weight, so Ben tried his door handle, very aware that in under thirty seconds, he had become soaked through. A big hand reached across and tugged on the door handle from inside, and his door opened. Ben climbed in, slammed the door closed, and then set about unfastening his coat and pulling on his seat belt.

"Hasn't this got central locking?"

"Well, it used to have it. I just haven't got around to getting it fixed."

It was only when his seat belt was clipped in that Ben noticed the smell. It was like Jim had collected socks from the homeless and stored them all in his car somewhere.

"What the hell is that smell?"

"Bad, isn't it?" Gillespie said, peering into the back. "Not sure what it is, if I'm honest. I had a wee look, but couldn't really see what it is."

"The McDonald's wrappers?" Ben asked, pulling a few brown bags from the footwell and dumping them into the back, where he was even more surprised to find old shirts and jumpers on the back seat, and another footwell filled so high with discarded wrappers, drinks cans, and God knows what that the carpet wasn't even visible. "Jim, this is a state. In fact, it's more than a state. When you said you hadn't got around to cleaning it, did you mean ever?"

"I've a busy life, Ben. We don't all live a cosy, little life on Daddy's farm, you know?"

Ben was aghast and completely lost for words.

"I feel like I need a bath."

"Oh, come on. It's just a few old wrappers and that."

"Are you still planning on taking Katy Southwell out?"

"Eh? Oh, aye. I spoke to her down at the crime scene. She seemed keen," Gillespie said. "I owe you a thanks, mate."

"Where are you taking her?"

"I was thinking about The Tempest in Coleby. Seemed like a nice place. No chance of bumping into an ex-girlfriend down there, either."

"You're not taking her in this, are you?"

"Eh?"

"Jim, you can't. Get a taxi or something. You can't let her see this. She'll run a mile, mate."

"Ah, Ben. You know your trouble, mate? You're too soft." He shoved the car into drive and it lurched forward out of the parking spot. The only things that seemed to be functioning well were the window wipers, so Ben supposed it was a marked improvement on his old Ford. "Where are we going anyway?"

Ben fished a slightly damp piece of paper from his pocket, bearing Chapman's neat handwriting which had been slightly blotted.

"Ashby de la Launde," he said, as Gillespie pulled out of the car park and the suspension gave an unhealthy series of clunks. "That's if we actually get there. God forbid that this thing breaks down. We'll have the choice of standing in the rain or sitting in this dump and risking the prospect of contracting some sort of nineteenth-century lung disease."

———

The main road through Ashby de la Launde was a single, winding country lane, wide enough for two cars to pass, but narrow enough that should a driver find themselves stuck behind one of the many tractors in the area, they would be in for a lengthy wait. Ashby, much like Boothby Graffoe and Coleby, were very much unchanged since Ben had been a teenager blasting around on his old motorbike.

The property was on the right, just outside of the village, and almost missing the turning, Gillespie broke hard. At least he stamped hard on the brakes, producing a terrifying grinding sound and the car slowed marginally faster than it had done when Gillespie had braked with moderation.

"For God's sake, Jim. This is a bloody deathtrap."

"Can you see out of the windscreen, Ben?" he replied, fighting with the steering wheel to make the turn.

"Yeah, it's about the only thing that is working."

"Well, then it's better than your car, isn't it?" He straightened the car onto the long drive, and while Ben held the bitter retort on his tongue, he was quite taken and distracted by the landscaping.

Even in the rain, the property was simply stunning. The driveway was lined on either side with small trees that in the late summer, Ben guessed would be filled with blossom. When they reached the end of the drive, they were greeted with the sight of a large house, reminiscent of an old Roman villa, or the Sphinx, with two bold arms protruding from each side to form a central courtyard which appeared to be where the owner preferred the cars to be parked. Little signs marked the designated parking for each of the Airbnbs and those that were reserved for the owners.

A Volkswagen SUV was parked in one of the spots closest to the house, connected to an EV charger by a thick, black cable. In one of the other spots was a dark blue Volvo estate, newer than Gillespie's old Volvo and one that Ben surmised did not smell like a marathon runner's underpants.

"Aye up, duck," a voice said, as he climbed from Gillespie's cesspit, and he turned to find an attractive, middle-aged woman standing in the doorway to the main house. She was holding a caddy filled with all kinds of cleaning equipment. "Won't be a minute. I'll just put these away and I'll show you in. The door is open if you want to get out of the rain."

"We're not here to stay," Ben called out over the thrum of rain on the car's body-work. "We're looking for Harriet Gray."

"That's me," she said and then set the caddy down inside the front door. She tugged her light waterproof coat closed and ran the zip up. "And you are?"

Ben let his warrant card fall open and he held it up long enough for her to see.

"Detective Inspector Savage," he said, then pointed at Gillespie who was still in the car struggling to get his wet coat on. "That's Sergeant Gillespie. I wondered if we might have a word with one of your guests."

"Oh, not you lot again," she replied. "Is this about Geoffrey Wilson?"

"It is," he replied, his intrigue stirring, which he made obvious enough for her to continue.

"I had one of you lot here earlier."

"Sorry?" Ben said.

"She left about an hour ago," she replied. "It was that posh woman with the big car."

"Detective Chief Inspector Bloom? Reddish hair?"

"Aye, that's her. She was here a few days back and I saw her again this morning."

"You spoke to her today?"

"No, I saw her. She was coming out of the stables," Harriet replied and then nodded at the arm of the building on the far side of the courtyard, where a wooden sign had been neatly painted with the words, The Stables. "There's a fella in there. Not sure of his name, but he normally comes to see Geoffrey Wilson when he stays."

"Mr Sloane?" Ben suggested.

"Like I said, I don't know his name. Mr Wilson booked the room but he hasn't turned up. Nor has his wife, come to think of it. But seeing as he usually accompanies them, I didn't say anything. Why would I?" She gave the pair of them a quizzical look.

"Here, they're not up to no good, are they? I don't want any funny business going on. I've got a business to run. The last thing I need is bloody police cars and whatnot coming in and out. You know what neighbours are like. I'll be in tomorrow's bloody local rag if they get wind of anything."

"Oh, God no," Ben said. "But would you mind if we had a quick word with your guest? We're not here to cause trouble. We just have a few questions for him."

"Be my guest," she said. "As long as he doesn't leave a bad review."

Ben smiled appreciatively at her.

"If the interiors are as nice as the exterior, Harriet, I'm sure he'll be leaving a glowing five-star review."

"All right," she replied, backing away and holding the lapels of her raincoat together. "But don't cause him to be late checking out. I'll be in there at two o'clock to get it ready for tonight's guests."

"Trust me," Ben said. "I'll make sure he's checked out by two, and I can assure you, when we're done, we'll leave your guest in peace and your neighbours won't even know we've been."

CHAPTER FORTY-THREE

"This is nice, isn't it?" Cruz said as Jackie pulled up outside the given address. She appraised him and couldn't help but smile to herself. He sat as her grandmother used to, with his hands folded on his lap, peering out of the window, watching as the world went by.

"What is?" she asked.

"This? Us. You know, getting out and about. Unshackled from the office, and all that."

"We're investigating a murder, Gabby," she said. "And if Ben's right, then the suspect could be behind that front door."

"I know, but still," he said, then laughed.

"I suppose it's just nice to have completed a journey without being insulted, put down, or abused in some way."

"Is Gillespie that bad?"

"He's a git," Cruz said flatly.

"He is a git," Jackie agreed. "But he has your back. You know that, don't you? He might be hard on you, but that's just his way. But when push comes to shove, he has your back."

"I know. And it makes it all the harder to despise him."

"Oh, come on, he's not that bad."

"You don't know what he's like when it's just us. I don't know how he does it, but whatever happens, I always either seem to get it in the neck or somehow end up worse off. He does it all the time, to the point where I go home and daydream about him getting his comeuppance somehow. But then he does something like lend me a few quid at the end of the month, or help me decorate my house–"

"And you find yourself with conflicting feelings?" Jackie asked, and Cruz turned to look out of the window again.

"All I'm saying is that it's nice to be

treated kindly for once. I don't dislike him, he's a good bloke, and all that. But working separately from him has been…" He paused to think of the right word. "Enlightening. I think I might ask the boss if this could be a more permanent thing."

"But what will Gillespie do? He can't work on his own."

"I don't know. Maybe he'll be assigned one of you?"

"What?"

"It makes sense," he continued, seemingly oblivious to Jackie's reaction. "I mean, Ben and the boss aren't working together right now. Maybe it's time to have a shift around?"

"What about Anna and Jenny? They're good together."

"I know, but surely we'd all get along better if we had the opportunity to work with others. I mean, the boss could work with Nillson, Ben with Anderson or me."

"And Gillespie?"

"With you, I suppose."

"What?"

"Think about it. It makes sense, doesn't it?"

"No!"

"Chapman doesn't need to work with anybody. But I'd be happy to work with someone else–"

"Gabby, think about this for a moment," she said. "Just think about what you're saying. If you go to the boss and ask to be moved away from Gillespie, what will she think of him?"

"Eh?"

"He'll get into trouble. You don't want that, do you?"

"Well, no–"

"You said he was often nice to you. You said you were conflicted, right?"

"I suppose–"

"Do you really want to land him in a load of trouble?"

"Well, no, I suppose not–"

"So perhaps it's best not to meddle, Gabby." She gave him the look her own mother often gave her to add weight to a piece of advice. "Come on. Let's get this done." She gave his leg a playful slap, shoved the car door open, and climbed out, meeting Cruz on the pavement outside the house on Main Street. "What did you say the name was?"

"Steven Yates," he said, staring up at the

old cottage, his nose wrinkling with the effort. "If I'm honest, I'd prefer it if we had a bit of backup. What if he goes for us?"

She studied him a moment, wondering if one day, when they were both approaching retirement, they might meet and if he'd have matured into a man.

"Then I'll expect you to protect me," she told him, leaving him standing there with his imagination. He ran up the few steps to catch her up as she rang the doorbell.

The cottage was pretty with a neat garden. The beds were mostly herbs — rosemary, thyme, sage, and a few pots of mint set to one side. The grass was cut short and the edges trimmed. The shrubs to the front of the property were kept well. It was almost as if Jackie's mother had done the gardening. Maybe it was a generational thing, she thought, and then briefly let her mind wander to the future when there would be no front gardens, each of them being turned into low-maintenance driveways.

The lock on the inside of the door turned and they saw a hand through the frosted glass, but it wasn't the lithe hand of a thirty-something-year-old man.

The door reached the extremities of the security chain and the face of an elderly woman appeared in the crack, sizing them up with a scrutinising glare.

"Yes?" she said, her voice younger than her years.

Jackie raised her warrant card and let it fall open, and Cruz followed suit.

"Hello. I'm DC Jackie Gold from Lincolnshire Police. This is my colleague, DC Cruz. We're looking for a..." she began, then made a show of retrieving her notepad from her pocket and checking a blank page. "Steven Yates. Is he in?"

"Who?"

"Steven Yates, ma'am," she said. "We're investigating a crime that took place last weekend, just down the road there. Mr Yates told one of our colleagues that he lived here."

"There's no Steven Yates here, love," the woman replied.

"Oh," Jackie said. "Well, may I take your name, please? There must have been some kind of mistake."

"My name?"

"Yes, it's just for our records, ma'am. It's

okay, we won't be contacting you for anything."

"Oh well, I see. It's Dorothy Briggs," she said, then pointed a finger at Jackie's notebook as she wrote the name. "That's two Gs."

"Thank you, Dorothy. May I ask if anybody else lives at the property? A husband maybe?"

"Of course," she said. "His name is Michael. He's down at the allotment at the moment, but he shouldn't be too long."

"And he's a Briggs too, is he?" she said, making a note of the husband's name for show.

"That's right. Michael Briggs."

"That's great," Jackie said, stabbing a full stop after the name. "Is it just the pair of you that live here?"

"It is, yes," she replied, and her expression stiffened. "Although I should mention that our son is staying here."

"Your son?"

"Yes, John. He's..." she began, then faltered, as if deliberating on the correct choice of words. "He's between jobs right now, so he's just staying here until he's back on his feet."

"Ah, it must be nice to have him at home so you can spoil him," Jackie said, doing her best to sound as friendly as she could.

"Yes," the lady replied. "Yes, it is." Her voice trailed off as if she had stopped herself from saying too much.

"I wonder if you could help me," Jackie said. "You see, we're trying to determine the whereabouts of the local residents last Sunday morning. One of our colleagues has already been through the village, but there were a few addresses that failed to respond. Yours is one of them."

"Right?" she said, with more than a hint of caution in her tone.

"I wonder if you could tell us where your husband and your son were on Sunday morning?"

"On Sunday?"

"That's right," Jackie said. "It's just for our records, that's all."

"Well, they were here, I suppose. No reason for them to be anywhere else."

"Your husband and your son?" Jackie said.

"They were both here, were they? They didn't go out to walk the dog, or—"

"We haven't got a dog. I'm allergic."

"What about your son? I mean, I have a nine-year-old, and it's hard enough to keep track of him. I couldn't imagine keeping my eye on a grown man. He was in, was he? He didn't stop out for the night?"

"No," she said. "No, he couldn't have."

"And you're sure, are you?"

"Well, I'm as sure as I can be."

"You don't sound certain, ma'am," Cruz added, speaking up for the first time. It was all part of an act, and Jackie thought he had fallen in quite well. He turned to Jackie. "I wonder if it's best if we speak to them directly."

"Yes, it might be for the best," Jackie said and then addressed Dorothy Briggs. "You see, if we go back to our boss without answers, she'll hit the roof. I don't suppose you could tell us where the allotments are, could you? We'll pop down there now just to check them off our list."

"They were home. I'm sure—"

"I think we should let them speak for themselves," Jackie said. "You can never be too careful with these things. Besides, they might have seen or heard something that would help our enquiries."

She looked uneasily between them, clutching the front door with a gnarled hand.

"Mrs Briggs. Is everything okay?"

"Yes," she said defensively. "Yes, they're in the field. It's just behind the house on Castle Lane. You can't miss it."

"A field? Not an allotment."

"Well, it is a field. Only small, mind. It came with the house, you see. I said we should sell it, but Michael wanted to keep it. Said the old barn would come in handy for storage."

"And he's there now, is he? With your son?"

"We turned one of the corners into an allotment," she told them, her voice sad as if she was somehow betraying them. "But you'll find them there or thereabouts. They can't have gone too far. It's nearly two o'clock."

"Have you given them a curfew?" Cruz joked, and the muscles in Dorothy's face tensed.

"Lunch," she said haughtily. "I expect

they'll be wanting lunch after all that digging."

"I expect they will," Jackie said. But there was something in Dorothy's stare that suggested sadness. Perhaps it was the way her grip on the door loosened. Or maybe it was the almost imperceptible quiver of her lower lip. "Thanks for your time, Mrs Briggs," she said and then lingered for a moment. "Go on. Get yourself back in the warm. I'm sure they'll be back soon."

CHAPTER FORTY-FOUR

"Oh Christ," Gillespie muttered. The door to what was signed as The Stables had opened at Ben's knock, and following a cautious look from Gillespie, he had stepped inside only to be greeted by the sight of a middle-aged man sprawled across the little two-seater sofa with his shirt unbuttoned. But it wasn't the state of the man's undress that had shocked them. It was the man's tongue that hung limply from his lips, tinged with blue, and red eyes that seemed to stare into the distance.

"Call it in," Ben said, as he stepped cautiously to the man's side to check his pulse.

He snapped on the latex gloves he kept in

his jacket pocket and crouched down. It seemed rather ridiculous, but searching for a sign of life was part of the process that had been drilled into every officer in the country. He found no pulse, despite trying various parts of the man's wrist and neck, so he laid his head to one side close to the man's mouth, to listen for even the faintest sound of breathing. But there was none.

"And Jim—"

"Aye?"

"When you speak to Chapman, ask her to be discreet, will you?" Gillespie pulled a confused expression. "Just trust me will you? I don't want anybody else knowing about this. Not yet."

Gillespie stepped back inside a few moments later, pocketing his phone. He said nothing, leaving the obvious question to the doubtful look on his face, and Ben shook his head.

"ID?" Gillespie asked, and Ben gestured at the jacket that was laid over the back of the chair in the corner of the room. While he looked for the ID, Ben checked the body for a cause of death, which was a challenge to do without disturbing the scene. There were no marks or bruising on the neck, and as far as he could tell no puncture wounds. The whites of the man's eyes were red, and there were traces of blood in his nostrils.

"That can't be right," Gillespie said, then tossed Ben the man's wallet for him to see. "That can't be him."

Ben studied the name on the driving licence.

"Scott Sloane?" he said. "Brilliant." He tossed the wallet back to Gillespie, who caught it, then took a moment to stare at the photograph in disbelief. "What is it, Jim?"

"This can't be Scott Sloane."

"Why not?"

"This is the bloody reporter."

"The what?"

"The reporter," he replied, gesturing wildly at the corpse. "He's the bloke who got through the barrier at the crime scene."

"You're sure?"

"Aye, I'm sure," Gillespie said. "I'm bloody positive. I remember his eyebrows. They're like a caterpillar."

"Well, perhaps next time a reporter gets through, you should check their credentials a little more closely."

"Aye, well," Gillespie replied, then moved the topic away from his mistake. "There's no sign of a struggle. Any ideas how it happened?"

"Well, I'm not Pippa Bell–"

"Thank God."

"But he seems to have similar signs to Linda Wilson."

"You mean he's lying down and not moving?" Gillespie said. "You're in the wrong game, Ben."

"Slight bleeding from his nose, discoloured lips, and do you see all those blood vessels in his eyes?"

"Aye, looks like he had a better night than I did."

Ben ignored the rhetoric and pushed himself up away from the corpse.

"How long?" he asked.

"Uniforms are on their way, as is the ambulance, and Chapman is calling Doctor Saint."

"And CSI?"

"I thought I'd give Kate a call."

"Kate?"

"Aye, Kate. The lass I'm taking out."

"You mean Katy Southwell? Doctor

Southwell?"

"Aye, her."

"Right. So?" Ben said.

"So what?"

"So why don't you call her? Or better still, why don't we go through the right channels and maintain a paper trail? Chapman will need to issue a crime number. We can't submit a request for CSI with a note from some desperate detective who wants to take the investigator out."

"Eh?"

"Call Chapman back. Ask her to make the arrangements, Jim. We're playing by the rules, remember. If a defence lawyer finds us cutting corners, they'll pull us apart in court."

"It's just a phone call, Ben."

"Right, it's just a phone call, Jim. Just a phone call."

"What's got into you?" Gillespie asked, and Ben sighed. "You're a bit tense."

Ben presented the dead body with a sweep of his arm.

"Scott Sloane is dead, mate."

"Right, so?"

"And Freya was here."

"The boss was here? Why?"

Ben shook his head and stepped over to the window. The view of the courtyard was slightly obstructed by a few, tall potted plants, but not enough to obscure the Volvo estate.

"Ben?" Gillespie said, coming to stand beside him. "You all right, fella?"

"Yeah, sorry mate."

There was no real need to apologise to his old friend. As well as a mop of thick hair, and a six-foot-something frame, the Scotsman enjoyed the benefits of a thick skin, which he made use of at least several times per day.

"Why do you suppose the boss was here?"

"See that car?" Ben asked, and Gillespie followed his eye line to the estate in the spot allocated to The Stables.

"Aye. Mine used to look like that."

"Do you know that Freya was followed to work the other day?"

"Eh? Who by?"

"I don't know. It was the morning after we'd had the row. I was driving down the lane towards the station, and I found her standing on the S-bend. Her car was parked a hundred feet further along."

"What was she doing?"

"I don't know. She said somebody was following her. She kept asking me if I'd seen a dark blue estate car go the other way."

"And did you?"

"I was concentrating on the road. I didn't see much."

"Wipers?"

He nodded but veered into another train of thought.

"It just seems odd to me that a dark blue Volvo estate should follow her, and then we find out she's been here." He turned to study the room. Gillespie was right. There was no obvious sign of a struggle. He strode over to a leather satchel, finding the two brass buckles unfastened. Inside was a mobile phone, which was turned off, a pen case, and a notepad. "Faye Butters said they came here to go through the investigation," Ben said.

"Aye, it's their safe place."

"So where are the investigation notes?" He flicked through the notepad, finding nothing but the type of scrawls somebody makes when they're on the phone, or to remind themselves to do something. "The way she was talking, Sloane had found something big. There should be notes or files or photos or something. There's nothing here."

"Maybe it's in that notepad?"

"No, that's not evidence. It's more like his to-do list," Ben told him, and then they looked back out of the window. "Car keys?"

After a quick rummage through the jacket pockets, Gillespie produced a set of keys, one of which was a Volvo key.

They left the room and ran over to the car, this time almost indifferent to the rain. Gillespie pushed the button on the fob, and Ben, who was still wearing his gloves, yanked the door open. He opened every door, checked the glove box, and then finally the boot.

"Nothing," he said, spying an inquisitive-looking Harriet Gray at the front door of the house. "Harriet?" he called, and she stepped out of the house, pulling on her waterproof jacket as she walked. "You said our colleague was here earlier."

"That's right," she replied. "She left about an hour ago."

"Was she carrying anything?" Ben asked.

"I didn't see," she replied. "I passed her on the driveway when I was coming back."

"Coming back from where?"

"Oh, I just had to pop down to Metheringham to get some bleach," she replied. "Why? Is everything okay?"

Gillespie gave him a look as if to say, 'You're the boss. It's your call', and Ben winced at what he had to say.

"What's happened?" she said. "You're scaring me."

"I'm sorry, Harriet," he began. "But the chances are that your neighbours will know we're here. In fact, I'm quite certain they will."

CHAPTER FORTY-FIVE

In an ideal world, Ben would have loved to have restricted the number of vehicles to a maximum of two or three. But a murder was a murder, and the owner of the property's desire to avoid bad publicity was nearly always trumped by police procedure. It wasn't quite a convoy, as many of the vehicles arrived at different times. But even so, an hour had passed since they had discovered the body of Scott Sloane and the courtyard was rammed. There was Gillespie's car and of course Harriet Gray's. Then there was Scott Sloane's car, which Ben had asked a young PC to tape off to prevent disturbing any evidence. Next was Doctor Saint's car, a rather nice Mercedes, which in Ben's view was a touch boring but it likely drove well and offered a suitable level of luxury for a man who could be called from one side of the county to the other in a heartbeat − or in this instance, a lack of one. The three bays allocated to The Toolshed and The Barn were occupied with three little, white vans belonging to the Crime Scene Investigators − one for the photographer, one for Katy Southwell and her many boxes of equipment, and the other filled with empty boxes that might soon contain evidence. Not that there was much evidence to take away. Four police cars lined the driveway, parked beside those wonderful, little blossom trees, and finally, parked at the centre of the melee, was an ambulance, a fixture that reminded them of why they were there. It was often the case that the ambulance was the centre of attention and a scene of urgency. But the rear doors were closed and the two paramedics were waiting beside an empty gurney for the all-clear so they could remove the body from the scene.

"Here," a voice said, one that Ben was beginning to learn and recognise. Harriet Gray stepped between him and Gillespie with a tray containing two mugs of tea. "Thought you could do with these. At least the weather's holding for a while."

"That's very kind of you," Ben told her.

"Ooh, look at that. Now that's a proper cup of tea. We'll have to leave a review," Gillespie joked. "The accommodation was a bit cold and stiff, but the tea was good."

Had the comment been voiced in front of the team in the incident room then there was every chance it might have raised a smile or two. But in front of Harriet Gray, it was nothing short of bad taste, and her discouraging glare confirmed her agreement.

"It's his way of dealing with the sight," Ben said, which seemed to go some way towards appeasing her. "Something to do with having a traumatic childhood. He uses humour to mask his true emotions."

"I see," she replied, as Ben took their teas, handing one to a red-faced Gillespie. "Just leave them on the step when you're done."

She dropped the empty tray to her side, glanced at all the vehicles, and then, wearing a brave face, she made her way back into the house.

"Actually, now that you're here," he said. "I wonder if I might have a word."

"I've told you everything I know," she said, stopping her retreat, but making no attempt to return to his side.

"It's about our colleague. DCI Bloom. You said that she visited earlier."

"That's right. I was out when she left though. As I said, I passed her on the driveway."

"But you were here when she arrived?" Ben said. "Otherwise, you would have stopped and spoken to her."

"What makes you so sure?"

"Because you recognised her," Ben told her. "And if the police were driving down my driveway, I'd want to know why."

Her expression altered. There was little to gain from lying, and she was smart enough to recognise that.

"Shall we talk inside?" she asked, and Ben nodded for Gillespie to follow. "I'm afraid you'll have to excuse the mess," she said, holding the front door for them.

She closed it when they had passed through, and then led them through to a large sitting room. The floor was solid teak and well-polished. The furniture was an expensive collection of leather sofas and solid, wooden cabinets, and the drapes wouldn't have looked out of place in the home of the local gentry. As far as mess was concerned, Ben couldn't find a thing out of place, and should he have run his finger along a surface, he doubted that he'd find a single fleck of dust.

"It's a beautiful home," he said.

"Thank you," she replied. "It was a dream of my late husband's. It's his design, most of it is his handiwork, and Ashby is where he grew up. He used to tell me how he used to cut through this farm to get to the fields when he was a boy. I'm just living his legacy, I suppose. The barn, stables, and toolshed were all run down when we bought it. But he had a vision, and he had the capital." She stared at him sadly. "And he was dying. So, what was I supposed to do, deny him his life's dream?"

"I suppose not," Ben replied.

"But you didn't want to speak to me about the house, did you?" Her eyebrows flicked up and down knowingly, and she waited, hand on a round but firm hip.

"My colleague," Ben said.

"The posh woman? She arrived an hour or so before you, just as I was leaving. She told me that Mr Sloane was expecting her, so I left them to it."

"Bit risky, wasn't it?" Ben said. "For a woman so keen to maintain standards, I mean."

"Believe me. Geoffrey Wilson and his wife have rented The Stables enough times for me to know that nothing untoward takes place during their visits. I had no reason to think that it should be any different this time, especially given she's a police officer. Although come to think of it, there's enough in the news about you lot that perhaps I would have been better off asking a few more questions."

"We're not all bad, Harriet," Ben told her.

He strode over to the front window, from where he could overlook the activity outside. Katy Southwell emerged from The Stables, yanked off her hood and freed her hair from her ponytail, giving it a good shake. She was pretty and had Ben met her now, without having met Michaela or Freya, he might have taken her up on her offer. "Was she alone when she arrived?"

"She was, yes. She was alone both times, but listen. I was just heading out when she arrived."

He pictured the courtyard free of the service vehicles, with only Harriet's, Sloane's, and Freya's cars. He imagined her climbing from her car, addressing Harriet, and then sauntering off to the Airbnb.

"What was she carrying?" Ben asked.

"Sorry?"

He turned to look at her.

"Was she carrying anything? A handbag or…"

"I don't recall," Harriett replied.

"Think," he said. "She never reverses into a spot. She should have parked beside the Volvo. Is that right?"

"It is," Harriet replied, eyeing him with what looked like suspicion.

"She nearly always checks her phone before getting out of the car. She likes to make people wait for her."

"She did just that," Harriet replied, slightly startled at the insight.

From beside the window, Ben stared hard at her.

"So now you can see her in your mind's eye, perhaps you can remember if she was carrying something?"

Harriet gave a little laugh, almost incredulous.

"She had a bag," she said. "Not a handbag though. It was a tote. She had it on her–"

"Left shoulder," Ben finished for her. "And you're sure nobody else paid Mr Sloane a visit today?" She appeared to still be a little taken aback by the way Ben had awoken her memory, and how well he knew the woman. "You said you were only going for ten minutes. Could somebody else have stopped by in that time?"

"I doubt it," she replied. "But now that I think of it, there was somebody else here. I remember now."

"When?" Ben said. "When was this?"

"Early," she replied. "I was feeding the chickens out the back. I heard the tyres on the gravel, but I suppose I thought it was Geoffrey and his wife."

"You didn't see them?"

"I was out the back," she replied, her

tone hinting at indignation. "It was more than likely them though, wasn't it?"

He felt Gillespie's awkward glance and briefly matched it.

"Probably," he replied. "I'm sure everything is above board."

"Inspector Savage, is there something you're not telling me? How exactly did he die?"

"That's what the post mortem is for," he replied. "It'll be a few hours before we know for sure."

"But it wasn't natural causes. Otherwise, you wouldn't have half the police force here," she said, not letting her eyes waver from Ben for a second. "I have a right to know, don't I?"

"As soon as we know for sure, we'll let you know," Ben told her. He walked over to her and handed her his empty mug, gesturing to Gillespie that they were leaving. "And I'll see what I can do about getting the place cleaned up for you when we're done."

"Is that supposed to appease me?" she said.

"Thanks again for the tea, Harriet," Ben said quietly, as he made his way to the front door. "Oh, and if you get a call from the press..." Her eyes widened and she looked horrified at the prospect of her property being in the press. "It might be for the best if you thought about what to say."

"I won't tell them anything," she said.

"On your head be it," he replied. "I should be telling you not to say anything, but in my experience..." He opened the front door and let Gillespie out into the light drizzle. "If you give them nothing, they'll print anything. Maybe give them something to chew on. No names, no mention of the police. Maybe something to say how much of a nice person the victim was."

"I'll bear that in mind," she replied, unconvinced that it was the best idea.

He smiled briefly, then stepped out into the rain.

"Suspect?" Gillespie asked quietly as he shoved his hands into his pockets.

"No," Ben replied, as he started towards Doctor Saint, who had just emerged from the stables. He called back over his shoulder, "Not yet at any rate. Don't you think we have enough suspects to work with?"

"Hold on a wee moment," Gillespie called

out, and Ben turned to find him standing in the same spot, his hands firmly in his pockets. He raised his eyebrows in question, waiting for the big Scotsman to say what was on his mind. "What was she doing here?"

Ben glanced at The Stables and the spot in which she had parked. Not for any good reason, but in the hope that a revelation might come to him.

"Her job, I imagine," he replied, although with far less conviction than he was aiming for. "At least, that's what I keep telling myself."

CHAPTER FORTY-SIX

Doctor Saint was one of life's big men. Standing a couple of inches taller than Ben, who was usually the tallest in whatever room he was in, Saint's features were also seemingly unstoppable. His ears, nose, hands, fingers, and God knows what else, were all oversized.

But by God was he friendly. He was probably one of the friendliest people Ben had ever met, and when he extended one of those giant hands, and beamed down at him, genuinely pleased to see him, Ben couldn't help but warm to the man.

"Busy week," Saint opened with, still clutching Ben's hand. "Chief Inspector

Bloom isn't looking too good." He nodded over to the cars, where Gillespie was standing with a few unformed officers giving instructions to cordon off the entrance in case the press got wind of the incident, one hand pointing down the driveway, the other scratching his backside. "Has she done something with her hair?"

Ben gave as much of a laugh as he could muster.

"She's working on a lead," he said, lying through his teeth, but without the first clue as to what to say.

"Right," Saint replied, and then finally let go of his hand. "Well, you'll be glad to know I've taken a look and made some notes. I'll be sending my report through to Pip later on."

"Asphyxiation?" Ben said, and Saint made no show of hiding his pleasure.

"Very good."

"In an ideal world, I wouldn't have been able to guess. But at this rate, I'll have my doctorate in a few months."

"Sad times, Ben," he said. "How's my old friend Granger doing?"

"He's still the boss. He was made Detective Super a few months back when Arthur..." He stopped mid-sentence. "Well, you know how it is."

"The old make way for the young," Saint replied. "Freya made DCI, and you're a DI now. About time, too, if I might say."

"Well, we'll see about that," Ben said, keen to move the topic away from Freya. Yet Saint seemed content on remaining there. "Anything else I should know about?"

"How long has it been since we spoke, Ben?" he said. The comment knocked Ben off guard, and he stepped back, just enough to give him room for a distraction, which came in the form of Katy Southwell through the stable window. Saint followed his line of sight and smiled broadly. "Perhaps we can go inside?"

There was very little difference in the mood inside where Scott Sloane was still sprawled across the sofa having his last photos taken, compared to outside where the rain seemed not to be falling from the sky, as it had been, but instead rode the very air, saturating everything in sight.

"It's a sorry sight," Ben said. "The owner

isn't too happy about having us lot here. It's not going to do much for her business."

Saint lowered himself onto one knee, rather awkwardly due to both his size and his age. But from where he had positioned himself, he could lean across the corpse with ease, using the back of the sofa for support.

Then, quite oddly, he beckoned Ben to join him on the floor.

"Come," he said, and Ben dropped to one knee beside him. "You see, after I'd taken the vitals–"

"The vitals? I thought that's what a doctor does."

"I am a doctor," he replied. "Granted, my patients don't often have a pulse, and their blood pressure is usually pretty low, but I still take a few readings – temperature for example, which helps us determine an approximate time of death, plus a few more I won't bore you with. And when I'm done doing that, I like to have a look around to see if there are any physical signs to support my analysis."

"Hence why you look like you're about to propose?"

"Hence why I'm on my knees," Saint said.

"Your initial observations were good. The tinged lips, the bloodshot eyes, and the lack of a physical wound all suggest asphyxiation, among other things, but asphyxiation could mean strangulation, suffocation–"

"I get it," Ben said, and Saint seemed disappointed to be cut off. His expression saddened a little. "Sorry, I'm just having an off day."

Saint smiled warmly.

"That's all right," he said, then sucked in a breath, a precursor to him continuing. "So, I peered down his shirt." Ben felt his head cock to one side. "I don't think he'll mind, do you?"

There was something in the gentle giant's tone and mannerisms that was somehow far more palatable than Gillespie's crude rhetoric.

"I don't suppose he will."

As if to confirm, Saint leaned forward and peered into the man's shirt collar again.

"Want to take a look?" he said, and Ben saw Katy Southwell's head turn and behind her goggles, her eyes revealing her mild amusement.

"Why not?" Ben sighed. "My day couldn't

get much worse. What's a little bit of indecency going to do to it?"

He joined Saint up close to Scott Sloane's pale face and peered into the shirt, but saw nothing. Just the chest of a slightly overweight man, past his best years, and with a few suspect moles that he needn't worry about any longer.

"What am I looking at?" Ben asked, and Saint smiled.

"Look closer," he said, and Ben took another look, this time leaving room to study Saint's face as he did. The old man saw the change and inhaled as if he were smelling the sweet aroma of a country garden in summertime.

And then Ben followed suit, recognising the smell immediately.

He sat back, cleared his throat, and then climbed to his feet.

"I'll have to include it in my report–"

"Of course," Ben said. "You do what you need to do, Peter." He turned to leave, then stopped at the door, hoping his final comment might let them part on good terms. "You ought to advertise that nose of yours.

I've seen trained spaniels who wouldn't have picked that up."

Saint was on his feet now and straightening his jacket which had ridden halfway up his back.

"I'll just finish up here," he said and offered one of those thoughtful but beaming smiles. "You take care, Ben. You've come a long way. You've done well, and I dare say nobody begrudges you your success. Can I offer you some advice?"

"You can," Ben replied, though he was sure to convey his cautiousness.

"Just make sure you have your priorities in order. Do what's right, Ben."

"The trouble is that isn't always a straightforward option, is it?" he replied, and Saint stared at him, his expression one of understanding.

"Let your mind be your rudder," he said. "And let your heart be the wind that blows you off course. My dad told me that."

"Your dad must have been a wise man."

Saint smiled appreciatively.

"Like I said, take care of yourself, Ben."

"You too," he replied and then left before he said something he might later regret.

He stepped out, grateful for the refreshing droplets of rain on his face, then let his head fall back to savour the invigorating fine mist.

"That was tense," a female said from behind him, and Katy took her place beside him. Her tone was akin to Freya's when she was fishing for information, with a slight rise in pitch nearing the end of the sentence. "It's not getting personal, is it?"

"Oh, I don't think so," he lied. "He's a good man, that's all. He's just looking out for me." He turned to face her. "Much as he will for you when you get to know him."

"Speaking of good men," she replied, and his eyes darted across the courtyard to where Gillespie was standing. "It's funny because, after your visit to the lab the other day, Jim Gillespie called me."

"Oh?" Ben said, feigning surprise.

"He said that he tried to talk to me at the crime scene in Boothby, but couldn't find the right moment."

"I dare say that it's difficult to make small talk whilst standing over a dead body."

"I dare say it is," she concurred. "He also mentioned that I'm new to these parts and that he wondered if he might show me around."

"Gillespie isn't really known for being an introvert."

"No, I'd agree with that. It's just that I don't remember telling him that I was new around here. It's odd that he should ask the exact same question I asked you."

"It is," Ben said, realising that he'd been found out, but still wanting to play the game. "Did you agree?"

"Should I?" she said. "What's he like?"

The distraction was exactly what Ben needed. He stared across at Gillespie who was in the process of handing a note to a young PCSO, presumably to go and find coffee.

"Jim is one of the kindest people you'll ever meet," Ben began. "He's not had it easy, and I'm not sure if you've noticed but he's not from around here, either."

"I did notice," she replied with a smile. She was pretty with good teeth and eyes that belied the serious nature of her profession. They were playful, bright, and dare he say it, lovely. "So, should I?"

"Should you let yourself be guided by Jim?

I think so. Just..." He stopped, unsure if he should say the words.

"Just what?"

"Just look after him," Ben said, as he prepared to go and join the big, daft Scotsman. "He's a gentle soul. He needs somebody to look after him." Ben turned back to her, and she cocked her head, inviting him to elaborate. "If you don't think you care for him, then maybe you should turn him down."

"And if I thought I could?"

"Then jump in with both feet," Ben replied, as Gillespie called out to the young PCSO not to forget the sugar, followed by a playful threat to send him back to the shop on a police space hopper if he forgot. "Do us all a favour, and give him somebody he can channel all that unspent affection into."

CHAPTER FORTY-SEVEN

"Any news from Freya?" Ben asked nobody in particular, as he and Gillespie entered the incident room. He slung his bag down and draped his jacket over the back of his seat.

"Not yet, Ben," Chapman said, her voice tinged with sorrow. "Should I call her?"

"No," he replied, then heard just how childish he sounded. "No, let her be. We've got plenty to be getting on with. Let's have a catch-up in ten minutes. I just need to see Granger."

He shoved his way through the double doors before anybody could say anything to distract him, and then taking a few steps to the right, he rapped twice on Detective Superintendent Granger's door before entering.

"Ah, Ben, how are things moving?" Granger said, habitually closing the file he was reading, and then politely sliding it to one side – a sign that Ben had his full attention. "I understand from the team that Geoffrey Wilson and Faye Butters are yet to be charged. Does this mean you have somebody else in mind?"

"I do, guv," Ben replied, then took the seat that Granger proffered with an outstretched hand. "It turns out that the pair we have downstairs are a meddlesome duo. They have the outward appearance of respectable retirees, but they are hell-bent on upholding the standards of their respective villages, those being Boothby Graffoe and Coleby. Sadly, on this occasion, their efforts have rather sullied the reputations of the villages."

"Oh, that sounds interesting," Granger replied. "Far more appealing than the grubby, ne'er-do-wells we usually deal with."

Ben smiled politely.

"There may be some grubby ne'er-do-wells just yet," he said. "You see, the Wilsons have a son. Thomas. He's currently serving time for tax evasion."

"Oh dear–"

"He's in Lincoln nick, guv. Apparently, he got wind of another prisoner staying at his parents' new house when he was released. A man called John Briggs."

Ben watched Granger's face for any sign of recognition, but he remained impassive.

"What did he do?"

"Manslaughter. It turns out though that he would have got murder if the CCTV that caught him and his friend had been positioned a few inches to the right."

Granger nodded thoughtfully, interlocking his fingers briefly before laying his hands flat on the desk.

"And this house was in one of the two villages, was it?"

"Boothby, guv," he replied. "Faye Butters is the village warden. From what I gather, she and Geoffrey Wilson have been conducting their own investigation into the individual. It looks like they reached the limits of their resources and so hired a private investigator. A man named Scott Sloane."

"Oh Christ, I can't stand PIs. As if the

job isn't hard enough. The last thing we need is to add a local wannabe Sherlock Holmes into the mix," Granger said.

"He's dead, guv," Ben told him and then watched Granger's expression soften into something more akin to shame. "We found him earlier today."

Granger nodded his regret but was man enough to stare Ben in the eye.

"Am I to presume he didn't die of natural causes?"

"Similar MO to Linda Wilson."

Granger swivelled his seat to stretch his legs out to one side, allowing him to face the door. He linked his fingers on his lap again and then licked his teeth, which ended in a loud pucking sound.

"So let me see if I've got this right," he said quietly. "This Linda Wilson was murdered by John Briggs, was she? So you're beginning to believe, anyway."

"That's right, guv."

"Asphyxiation?"

Ben gave a curt nod.

"All because her husband and Faye Butters were building a case to get John Briggs sent back to prison."

"It was six a.m., guv. Dark enough for him to mistake Faye and Linda quite easily."

"But light enough to see her coming," Granger mused. "But he somehow learned that they had hired Scott Sloane to help them, and you think this John Briggs murdered him in a similar fashion?"

"That's right, guv. We still need to prove it. I've got the team working on it now."

"I doubt he'll be keen to go back inside, Ben."

"Well, luckily for us, he's on a curfew tag. If he left the village then we'll know."

"And his parole officer?"

"Chapman's on it."

"What about now? Have we got eyes on him?"

"He can't leave the country, guv. He'll be stopped at any border he tries to get through. But I don't think it'll come to that. I don't think he'll try to run."

"Why's that?"

"Well, if he feels so strongly about not being sent back to prison, then he'd just go, wouldn't he? He wouldn't stick around to murder two more people beforehand. He wouldn't risk adding two more life sentences to his charge sheet."

"So, you'll be releasing the meddlesome duo, will you?"

"Not for the time being, guv. I want to get something on Briggs first."

"Two bodies not enough for you, Ben?"

"Wilson can stay on a GBH charge at the very least. Attempted murder, ideally. He confessed to striking his wife with a chair leg. Faye Butters could be released, but I'm inclined to keep her in for a bit."

"On what basis?" Granger said. There was a hint of doubt in his voice. "If we've nothing on her, and we're looking at another possible primary suspect, then she needs to go."

"I just want to keep her a while longer, guv," Ben told him. "Just until we've wrapped this up."

Granger was unmoving. Perhaps he still looked at Ben as the young DC he once was. Perhaps he still felt a need to protect or mentor him. But eventually, he acceded.

"Very good," he said, then inhaled long and hard. "Well, it looks like you're on top of all this."

"Well, we don't have much to go on, but we're piecing it together."

Granger listened, blinked a confirmation, then bit down on his lip.

"And what about the elephant in the room?"

"Guv?"

"DCI Bloom, Ben. Don't be coy. I might be sitting in an office now, but I worked the streets the same as you. I can spot a mistruth when I see one."

He straightened in his seat, slid the file back in front of him, and laid his hands on it, a sign the conversation was nearly over, but not quite.

"She called in. She needs a day for something personal," Ben said, reciting Chapman's explanation. But Granger was far from convinced. Not a muscle in his face moved. The weight of his stare bore down on Ben, and a lesser man might have caved. But Ben held his nerve, returning the stare with innocence. "Guv?"

"Be careful, Ben," Granger replied, collecting his pen from the little pot on his desk, which was the invitation for Ben to leave. But accepting the invitation would be an admission of guilt. What was required in that instance was to stay and question the statement, albeit a risky move.

"Guv?" he said, which Granger seemed to be expecting.

"You do know that not everybody in the force is as supportive as your team, don't you?"

"Sorry, I'm not following."

"Don't play games with me, Ben. Have you any idea how embarrassing it was to be told by the deputy chief constable during the monthly meeting that he chairs that two of his senior officers are in a relationship?"

"I see," Ben said quietly.

"Not only are the two individuals in a relationship, but they have even spent weekends away together. Under my nose, Ben."

"Weekends away, guv?"

"Paris, Ben. You travelled by Eurostar. First class, I might add. Do you need me to state the name of the hotel you stayed in?"

"No, not really, guv."

"Listen, Ben," Granger said, his tone softening to something far more reasonable. "DCI Bloom is an attractive woman, and she's a bloody good detective. But I can't help feeling that she's not the right road for you."

"Guv, I–" Ben began, but Granger held up one of his hands to silence him.

"You're well-liked, Ben. In fact, I'm not sure I've heard anybody speak ill of you," Granger said. "Until now, anyway."

"Sorry?"

"You may be liked, Ben. But Freya Bloom is not. I don't know if it's because she's not from around here or if it's because of her confidence. But she rubs people up the wrong way. She's made enemies in the short space of time she's been here. Powerful enemies, too, some of them are, anyway. Don't get mixed up in it, Ben. You're better than that. You've come this far. I can still remember when you moved across from uniform, believe it or not. You were exactly what the team needed. A fresh mind, keen and hungry. You know, David Foster and I used to bet on which of the team you would end up with. Only a pound, nothing serious. But deep down, we knew that when the day came, it would put an end to that hunger of yours."

"Who did you bet on?"

"Me?" Granger said letting a chortle escape. "I had my money on young Jackie Gold. She's always had a soft spot for you."

"And DI Foster? Who did he have his money on? Nillson?"

"God no," Granger said. "I thought you weren't really her type, anyway."

"We all thought that," Ben replied. "But it seems she now has a man. A white cap from Nottingham."

"Traffic police? Well, that does surprise me. No, David hedged his bets on one of the younger officers in uniform. I can't remember her name now. But the point is that we knew that if you got together with somebody from this station, it would be the end of your career."

"I don't intend on letting anything end my career, guv."

"Well, I'm glad to hear it," Granger said. "And one day I hope you'll be sitting in this chair at this desk."

"I sense a but coming, guv," he said.

"But if you carry on with her, then those chances become slim. If she goes down, she'll take you with her."

"She's not like that," Ben told him.

"It wouldn't be her decision," Granger retorted. "She has eyes on her from above. Eyes that even Freya cannot shield you from whilst you're standing beside her." He flipped open the file but held Ben's stare. "Now then. I hope you make the right decision, Ben." He nodded at the door. "Dismissed."

Ben turned and opened the door but was reluctant to end without saying all he had to say.

"You should be pleased to know that..." he started, then found a weak smile more suitable to finish the sentence than a poor selection of emotionally cracked words. "Well, there's no risk of the DCC pulling you to one side for any more chats."

"Oh?"

"We've decided to call it a day, guv," Ben said. "It was all too much, what with risking top brass finding out."

"Are you sure about that?" Granger said.

"Am I sure about what?"

"Are you sure the pair of you have seen sense?"

"Quite sure, guv," Ben said. "Freya isn't one to mince her words. The last thing anybody could accuse her of is beating around the bush."

"Well, that is a surprise," Granger said. "Because I had a call from the superintendent at Lincoln. It turns out that he had an email from Freya last night," Granger said. "She was asking for details of the teams there. It seems DCI Bloom is looking for a transfer, Ben."

Granger stared hard, just as one day, a long time ago, he might have stared down a suspect on the far side of an interview room table, and much like the suspects he had interviewed, Ben dizzied a little, and he sought to conceal his emotions.

"She's a DCI now, guv. For her to move any further up the ladder here, she'd need you to step down. In the city, however, she could make that move within a few years, providing the opposition has been dealt with."

"I daresay DCI Bloom can deal with her opposition, Ben. I can't help but feel a little used."

"And if she transferred?" Ben said. "Would I enjoy your confidence as I used to? Or would Lincoln be too close?"

"My concerns regarding your relationship with DCI Bloom were not based on breaking the rules, Ben. We're a small, rural station and you're a red-blooded man. Even I know when to turn a blind eye," Granger said. "No, my concerns were with your choice of partner." He glanced at the closed door briefly then back at Ben. "If you're going to break the rules, Ben, then for God's sake do it with somebody who won't drag you down when she falls."

CHAPTER FORTY-EIGHT

"Right then," Ben said, and he re-entered the room. He clapped his hands once, just as Freya often did. But the action was subconscious, and he saw the recognition in their faces. "If anybody needs a drink or a pee, go now." To Ben's surprise, nobody moved. They all stared at him, eyes open, and pens in hand. "Good. Jackie, let's start with you and Cruz. Tell me about your visit to John Briggs. Or was it Steven Yates?"

"It was John Briggs, Ben," she said. "And you were right about the rogue name on Gillespie's list. But he denies all knowledge of being at the crime scene."

"Does he have an alibi?"

"He does. His dad. We knocked on the house first of all. His mum said they were in the field behind their house. It's like a small piece of land with an orchard and a barn that came with the house. They use it to grow their vegetables. According to the dad, Michael Briggs, they rent the rest of it out to a local family who graze their horse there from time to time."

"A small field with a barn and an orchard? Not the field off Castle Lane?"

"That's it."

"The one that whoever murdered Linda Wilson would have had to cut through to escape the crime scene? For God's sake."

"That's the one," Gold said, and Ben took a few steps toward the end of the room and then turned.

"The crime scene had three possible exits. North to Coleby, east into Boothby through the paddock, or south through the field and onto Castle Lane. No wonder none of the locals saw anybody." He returned to the desk where Freya often perched and thrust his hands into his trouser pockets.

"And when Linda Wilson was murdered? Where was John Briggs?"

"At home," she said. "Both the mother and the father confirmed this separately."

"What about his curfew tag, Chapman? Did you get hold of the parole officer?"

"The data from the curfew tag will be of little use to us," Chapman said. "But we do have a reason to bring him in."

"Oh?"

"The conditions of bail stipulate that an individual on parole with a curfew tag must allocate two hours per day to charge the tag," she said, and Ben felt the muscles in his face slacken.

"And he didn't?"

"The parole officer, a Susan Bennett, was processing Briggs' rearrest when I called," Chapman told him. "But I've managed to convince her to hold off for the time being."

"Good work, Denise," Ben said.

"We'll have to move fast, though. She took some convincing, and I'm afraid she has protocols to follow just as we do. If we haven't picked Briggs up by the end of today, she'll be sending somebody to collect him tomorrow morning, and then we'll be doing our questioning in the prison."

"I'm certain we'll get to him before then," Ben said. "Anything else?"

"Actually, yes," Nillson said. "Jenny and I looked into the murder investigation that John Briggs was previously sent away for."

"Okay," Ben said, intrigued, and although he was doing his best not to mimic Freya, he sat back on the desk and folded his arms.

"The victim was a man named Lee Frost. A decade ago, he was beaten to death in a dead-end alleyway of Monks Road in Lincoln. A nearby CCTV camera caught John Briggs and his accomplice, Darren Hunter, entering the alleyway shortly after Lee Frost. They walked out of shot and then the camera shows them leaving a few minutes later."

"Calmly?" Gillespie asked.

"They were running," Nillson replied. "Frost, however, did not leave. He was found dead the next day by a local shopkeeper emptying the bins. Nobody else entered the alleyway in that time."

"So, the investigating officer could confirm that either Briggs and Hunter killed Frost, but as it was out of the camera shot, they couldn't prove which of them actually did it."

"Hence the manslaughter," Ben said. "So, who are these individuals, Frost and Hunter?"

"Well, Frost worked for Michael Briggs. He had a small construction firm. His son and Darren Hunter also worked for him. According to the file, the SIO deduced that Frost had been passing on information of Briggs' developments. What properties he was going for, where he was getting his materials, how much he was paying. The firm was losing money hand over fist. Another developer was snapping up the properties and even using the same suppliers and local tradesmen. So even if Briggs managed to secure a development, he couldn't get the people or materials he needed to complete on time."

"So, they killed him?" Ben said. "Not much of a motive. Did they link Frost to this other developer?"

"They did," Nillson said. "And the loss to Briggs' business was seven figures."

"A million quid?"

"Several million," Nillson said. "The firm

folded a few months after John was sent away."

"So, you've just recited what the previous SIO found," Ben said. "What do you have to add to that?"

Nillson smiled and slid a piece of paper to the edge of her desk. Ben stood and walked across the room, feeling the eyes of the team follow him.

"What's this?" he said, then read the document. "It's a statement of accounts for Briggs Homes Limited." He shrugged and stared down at Nillson. "What am I looking at?"

"Read it," she said, and Ben scanned the printed names down one side of the sheet. Then he saw it. A single name that might as well have been printed in bold and italic font. "Scott Sloane?"

The smile Nillson bore grew in strength and she sat back in her seat twirling her pen in her hands.

"Scott Sloane used to work behind the scenes. He'd find suitable properties or greenfield pieces of land, and then he'd build a case to develop them. John and Darren would pressure the owners to sell and then

Michael would move in. What Frost was doing was passing Sloane's hard work onto another developer. Once the owner had agreed to sell, they would go in with a better offer."

"Hold on," Ben said, and he turned to Gillespie. "Faye Butters said that Sloane was familiar with Briggs, didn't she? That was why they selected him."

"Aye, I think you're right," Gillespie replied. "Want me to check the recording?"

"Hold that thought, Jim," Ben told him, then addressed the room. "So, Geoffrey Wilson hits his wife and she goes down hard enough for him to think he's killed her. However, by the time he's cleaned himself up, she's gone. She makes her way along Viking Way en route to the Butters' house. Geoffrey calls Faye, and Faye instigates an argument with her husband, knowing full well that he'd walk off in a huff, leaving Faye to intercept Linda. Faye saw Linda–"

"Wasn't it dark?" Nillson asked, and she flicked through her notes. "It was early, wasn't it?"

"It was six-thirty. The sky would have been getting lighter. Faye was at the bottom of the Lincoln Edge. She saw Linda against the skyline. She also saw a man nearby and presumed it was Kyle. But it wasn't Kyle. It was John Briggs."

"Brilliant," Cruz said. "Now all we need to do is prove it and close off the loose ends, such as the wine bottle, Scott Sloane, and of course the sound of death that Mr Mason heard." He made a show of checking his watch. "We should be done by dinnertime."

"There is something else," Ben added, and the hum of laughter died like the door had been closed. "Scott Sloane is dead."

"Eh?" Cruz said.

"Gillespie and I found him at the Airbnb earlier today. CSI is finishing off, but from what we can tell, the MO is the same."

"Bloody hell."

"Should I contact DCI Bloom, Ben?" Chapman asked.

"No," he said. "No, if she's taking a personal day, then let her do what she needs to do. In the meantime, let's have some theories."

A few of the team looked around the room for somebody to start, and as usual, it was Gillespie who opened his mouth first.

"How about this?" he began. "Scott Sloane discovered something that proved John Briggs was guilty. We know that Scott had found something new. That's why the Airbnb was booked."

"So, he killed Linda Wilson?" Nillson said. "Doesn't make sense."

"Not unless he thought she was Faye Butters," Ben added. "It was dark enough to make that mistake, and if he'd been watching Faye's movements, then he would have known she liked to walk the dog out there."

"He's ticking them off," Gillespie said. "He's bloody ticking them off. He hasn't charged his curfew tag so nobody could prove where he was."

"Or where he wasn't," Ben said. "He's risking a sentence for breaching his parole terms, but it would be far less than that he'd get if proof of the murder was discovered."

"I don't understand. How would Briggs have known about the Airbnb?" Cruz said. "The whole idea of them booking the room was to go through their investigation somewhere secret. Somewhere that Linda or Kyle wouldn't even know about. So how did John Briggs know about it?"

"When Linda Wilson's body was found, did she have a phone with her?" Gold asked.

"No, she didn't have anything with her. It took us long enough to find out who she was if you remember."

"So maybe Briggs took it? All he would have had to do would be to search the messages."

"You're getting mixed up," Ben told her. "Linda wouldn't have known about the Airbnb. Only Faye and Geoff would have known. Briggs wouldn't have even known about Scott Sloane."

"So, somebody told him," Nillson added. "Somebody who knew about the investigation, knew about John Briggs, and knew about the Airbnb."

"Darren Hunter," Chapman said, as she finished typing something with a flourish and then sat back. The team all turned to face the quiet, fresh-faced woman. "He was released a week before John Briggs. It stands to reason that if Sloane was investigating the original murder of Lee Frost, then it also stands to reason that he approached Hunter. If Hunter tipped off Briggs about Scott

Sloane, then all Briggs would have had to do was follow him."

"Ben, did Sloane have any files with him when you found him?" Nillson asked. "If he was there to go through his findings with Faye and Geoffrey, then surely he would have had some kind of paperwork."

"Not a scrap," Gillespie said.

"Do you have an address for Darren Hunter?" Ben asked, snatching his coat from the back of his chair and giving Gillespie a brief nod.

"On its way to your inbox," Chapman replied, and just as Ben made towards the door, she added something that made the hairs on the back of his neck stand on end. "There's something else. I've been looking through Sloane's bank records. There are payments here from Lincoln Police. Somebody on the force was paying him for something."

A myriad of possibilities crossed Ben's mind, one of which was far more prominent than the rest.

"It's not uncommon for the force to use PIs for surveillance. A station the size of Lincoln would do it all the time. Especially when resources are tight," he said. "Let's focus on the theory. If we bring Briggs in, then we'll need evidence." He opened one of the double doors and held it there. "And I don't think I need to remind you that so far, we have no evidence at all. Not a bloody shred."

CHAPTER FORTY-NINE

"So?" Gillespie said, somehow managing to convey a whole number of difficult questions into that single-syllable word.

"So what?" Ben replied. They were on the new bypass road that encircled most of the city. Ben distracted himself by tossing the rubbish in the passenger footwell into the rear. He cracked the window a little to allow some fresh air inside, but not enough that the pouring rain would soak his jacket.

"You know," Gillespie said knowingly. He had a relaxed driving posture with the seat reclined beyond what Ben would find comfortable, but which afforded him easy access to the cup holder in the centre console.

"Sloane is dead. The investigation files are missing. He took payments from somebody in the force. And yet, the team investigating the man's murder aren't even aware that she was there."

"You're reading too much into the whole payment thing," Ben muttered. "I imagine every PI in Lincolnshire has done a job or two for the force at some point. It's their bread and butter. Why do you think we don't sit outside suspects' houses watching them? Because it's a waste of police resources, Jim, that's why."

"Aye, you're probably right," Gillespie said, in a tone that somehow made Ben doubt his sincerity. "I mean, we shouldn't even mention it again, right? And as for the boss being at the Airbnb, she was probably just making a booking or something, right? She probably just spotted Sloane and thought she'd have a wee word–"

"There's something you need to know," Ben said, cutting him off before the whole sarcastic account ventured beyond the bearable.

Gillespie silenced. Despite his free-flowing whims, he understood more than anybody when a line had been drawn. "Go on," he said.

"It's about Freya."

"Mm-hmm. I guessed that much," Gillespie replied.

"You see, I told you about our argument."

"Aye."

"And I told you about what she said afterwards. About me not supporting her–"

"Aye," Gillespie said.

"Can I just tell my story without you butting in with your 'ayes' and 'mm-hmms?'" Ben said. "Please?"

Gillespie focused on the road ahead, cleared his throat and then muttered quietly.

"Aye, sorry."

Ben gave a heavy sigh. He could have just stopped there. He wanted to. But he'd started now, and if he didn't finish, then Gillespie's wild imagination might fill in some blanks, and God only knows what that might look like.

"Freya thought she was being attacked."

"Eh? Attacked?" Gillespie said, then held up a hand. "Sorry, sorry."

"Not physically. Do you remember somebody made a complaint about her during the old lady investigation? You know, the one in Navenby?”

“Oh, aye. Said she belittled him in front of his officers or something.”

“That’s right. Then there was the RTA. Somebody linked her car to a crime, despite it being blatantly obvious that it couldn’t have been her.”

“Ah, it was enough for her to be carted off to Lincoln Nick though, eh?”

“And then there was the press who turned up last Sunday. The guy you stopped from entering the crime scene.”

“Oh him, aye.”

“And there’s more. They are the only ones she can put a name to but there are more. She’s got it into her head that somebody is trying to make her lose her job or worse.”

“And those names?” Gillespie said. “She wanted you to look into them?”

“She did, yes.”

“And you said no?”

“Of course I said no. If anything happened to one of them and they found out that I’d been looking into them–”

“Hence why she’s given you the cold shoulder. I see. Well, Benny boy, you certainly know how to dig yourself a hole, don't you?"

"There's more," Ben said.

"For Christ's sake. What is this, an episode of The Bill?"

"I think I've really messed things up," Ben said, and the void that followed beckoned him to continue. But when push came to shove, he simply couldn't betray her. Not even to Gillespie. "It doesn't matter?"

"Ben?"

"Look, just forget I said anything, all right?"

"Ah, I see." He sucked in a deep and concerned breath. "Well, I can't help you out of the hole unless you give me a spade?"

"Did you get that from a fortune cookie?" Ben asked, guiding him onto a side road, where they were immediately greeted with the sight of two liveried police cars blocking the road with their blue lights flashing. A familiar white tent had been erected at the front door of one of the properties, and a uniformed officer stepped over to the car.

"No, I just made it up," Gillespie replied. "I think it was quite good, actually." He lowered his window and peered up at the man.

"What's happening here?" he asked and flashed his warrant card, which seemed to ease the officer as he leaned on the car door, and bent to see inside the car. Ben held his warrant card up from the passenger seat.

"We're looking for a Darren Hunter," he said, then checked the address on his phone. "He lives at number seven."

The officer glanced at the commotion in the street behind him.

"Well, you found him," he said. "But I doubt very much he'll be able to answer any of your questions." The officer straightened and then peered up at the sky with a look of dismay on his face. "Want me to get the gaffer?"

"No," Ben said, not wanting to get too involved.

"Hold on. Here he is now," the officer said and then waved at a man in a suit that looked far more expensive than police officers usually wear. "Guv? Got a sec?"

He held a plastic file over his head and was making his way to a fairly new Mercedes when he looked over, and then, obviously irritated by the diversion, made his way over to Gillespie's car.

Even the moisture-filled air and car fumes did little to mask the man's musky aftershave. He had a face that looked as if it had been carved from granite, hair so slick that Ben could have cooked his sausages in it, and fingernails so polished and neat they could have rivalled Freya's after one of her nights in that she liked to call me time.

"I've got two officers from North Kesteven, guv," the uniformed officer said. "Said they were looking for the victim."

"I hope you weren't hoping for a statement?" the older detective said, bending down to peer into the car with obvious disdain that seemed to grow in weight as he took in the state of Gillespie's car.

"Mr Hunter is a witness in an investigation we're working on," Ben said, again letting his warrant card fall open. The officer studied his ID, and almost immediately his tone altered.

"DI Savage?" he said, then introduced himself. "DI Rawling. Sorry, mate, you're out of luck. Mr Hunter was found dead earlier today. A neighbour put some mail through his door. Found it unlocked and then smelled him."

"Sorry, did you say smelled him?"

"He's been there a day or two. FME seems to think he was murdered sometime last weekend."

"Don't tell me, he was suffocated," Ben said, and Rawling was suddenly interested in what he had to say. "We've got two more. Same MO. I believe they're linked to a historical crime."

"Right, that explains it," Rawlings said.

"Explains what?"

Rawlings thought for a moment, staring back at the crime scene and the melee of uniforms going about their duties.

"Listen, if you think you're taking over—"

"I'm not taking over anything," Ben told him. "Trust me, we have enough on our plate. But we will need to collaborate. You give me what you've got and I'll do the same."

"All right," he replied. "What's this historical crime you think he was mixed up in?"

"He served eight years for manslaughter. He was released a few months ago."

"And?"

"There's a chance that Hunter and his accomplice are guilty of murder and that somebody had proof."

"And they're cleaning up, are they?"

"That's our theory," Ben told him, then waited for the man to reciprocate.

"All right," he said. "Give me your details and I'll send you what we find."

Ben fished one of his cards from his inside pocket and held it out, then retracted it when Rawlings reached over.

"You must have something," Ben said. "CSI is here, the FME has been and gone, and you've got more uniforms on the scene than we have in our entire station. They locked stares for a second until Rawlings eventually let out a long and tired breath.

"All right," he replied. "Someone was seen leaving the house this morning. We're not sure if it's linked yet."

"Someone?" Ben said, still holding the card hostage.

"The neighbour spoke to her," Rawlings said. "Some posh tart in a black Range Rover."

CHAPTER FIFTY

"We're bringing John Briggs in," Ben said. He held his phone up on loudspeaker for Gillespie to hear the call as he drove. "Darren Hunter is dead. Lincoln Police are all over the scene."

"What?" A light, male voice erupted on the other end of the call and Ben realised the call was on loudspeaker. "He's bloody picking them off," Cruz finished.

"That's exactly what he's doing," Ben replied. "Chapman, stay in the office and co-ordinate. We need uniformed support, we need transport, and given the state of the bloody NHS, you might as well get an ambulance on standby. The rest of you, get yourselves to Boothby but be discreet. Park up and wait for everyone to arrive. No heroes, okay? Nillson, take the reins until I get there."

"Got it," Nillson said, and Ben pictured the feisty sergeant rubbing her hands together at the prospect of some action.

"He's not at home," Cruz called out before the call ended. "He's at the field I told you about. I think they'll be there all day."

"What makes you say that?" Ben asked.

"Well, they were burning stuff. They had a fire going in one of those metal dustbins. You know, the type with holes in."

"An incinerator?" Ben said. "What were they burning?"

"I don't know," Cruz replied. "I didn't think to ask if I'm honest. I thought they were going to go for us."

"Right, Chapman, I want CSI on the scene. I want to know what they've burned before any evidence is gone forever. We're coming in from Cherry Willingham," Ben said, and he glanced over at the speedometer, noting the focused expression on Gillespie's face. "We'll be there very soon."

He ended the call and then lowered the window a little.

"Speaking of burning," he said. "Maybe you can make use of the fire and set light to this thing. I can barely breathe in here." He turned in his seat and leaned into the back. "Is there a local map under all this crap?"

"Oy," Gillespie replied, and he tapped the dashboard affectionately. "She does have feelings, you know? And yes, there is one in the back somewhere. Have a look behind me."

"It's a car, Jim. It doesn't have feelings. It's an inanimate object. It doesn't see, hear, smell, or feel." He bit the bullet and plunged his hand into the mess, trying hard not to think about what was in there as he groped for the OS map.

"Aye, right. Like a certain DCI we both know?"

"Sorry?" Ben said, finding what he was looking for and retracting his hand from the filth.

"The boss, Ben," he said.

"What about her?"

Gillespie rolled his eyes, pulling off the new bypass road, and onto the Sleaford

Road, from where it was a clear run down to Boothby Graffoe.

"Don't you think the team might have benefitted from knowing that she was there?"

"We don't know that she was," Ben replied.

"Oh, come off it. Posh tart in a Range Rover? At the scene of a murder? Where, need I remind you, she was at around the same time that Sloane was killed."

"We don't know it was her, Jim," he said. "How many women drive Range Rovers around here? Dozens, if not hundreds."

"I hope for your sake that you never have to sit opposite me in an interview room, Ben."

"And why's that?"

"Because you're a lousy liar, that's why. We both know it was her. Now either you tell me what you're up to or I ask Anna."

"Anna? What makes you think she knows anything?"

"Because the pair of you have been thick as thieves, Ben," Gillespie said, and then his demeanour shifted. "And you trust her. You just put her in charge, didn't you?"

"Until I get there, yes. She's a sergeant. What should I have done, asked Cruz to step up?"

"A sergeant. As am I."

"But you're with me, Jim. What is this? Are you suggesting that I favour Nillson over you?"

"I don't see her knocking on doors, mate," Gillespie replied. "And if I weren't a detective, then I might not have noticed how she always seems to get the preferable leads, whilst me and Shank's pony get to go waking up the neighbours."

"You need to have this conversation with Freya."

"I thought I was," he replied. "Or, as close as I can get to her, at least."

"Jim, look–"

"I'm just asking you to be frank with us, that's all. With me. I'm your bloody pal, aren't I?"

"Of course–"

"Well, stop treating me like the enemy then. Talk to me. Tell me what's going on. Tell me why Freya was at the Airbnb and why she went after Darren Hunter. I can help you, Ben. I might not be Anna-bloody-Nill-son, but I can help you."

"Can you?" Ben said, and he stared through the passenger window.

"Aye, I can. Do you think she's involved in something? Is that what all this is about?"

"Not really, but–"

"Then what's with all this tension? What's going on?"

Ben considered what to say. He clearly wasn't going to get away with saying nothing.

"She thinks somebody's out to get her," he said finally.

"Aye, you told me. And you know what? It's mental, Ben. It's so bloody farfetched–"

"That it could almost be true?" Ben said, finishing the statement for him. "The thing is. What I didn't tell you, was all of the officers she thinks are involved all link to one name. All of them, at some point in their careers, reported into one man."

"Who?" Gillespie said. "Someone from Lincoln?"

"Standing," Ben told him.

"Steven Standing? As in ex-DCI Steven Standing, currently serving a life sentence for rape and murder? Ben, this is nuts, mate. You even sound like you believe her," Gillespie said and took his eyes off the road long enough to look Ben's way. "You bloody do, don't you? You believe her."

"There is another name that crops up," Ben told him. "Do you remember Chapman revealing that Sloane had received a payment from Lincoln Police?"

"Aye, but like you said. That could have been anyone. I mean, how many officers across Lincolnshire could authorise a PI to cover the grunt work of an investigation? Anyone from a DI up. I mean, even you could, couldn't you?"

"I could," Ben agreed. "And you're right, it could have been any one of a hundred officers. Including me."

"Right, so..." Gillespie said, clearly unsure of where Ben was leading him. "Was it you? I mean, you were pals with Steve Standing at one point, weren't you?"

"I was. Years ago, before Freya arrived. But I wasn't exactly on his side, was I? I helped to bring him down for God's sake."

"So, what are you saying, that he has some kind of die hard fan group out to exact revenge?"

"It doesn't matter what I think. It matters what Freya thinks," Ben said, and took a deep breath. "And she thinks that I'm part of it."

"Eh?" Gillespie said. "Why the bloody hell would she think that? Just because you wouldn't help her?"

"Because she thinks that I was investigating her."

"What?"

"Can you just keep your responses calm and keep to using full sentences, Jim? It's like explaining something to a teenager."

"Aye, right," Gillespie said, calming himself as he turned the old car into Boothby Graffoe. "It sounds to me like she's lost the plot, Ben. Why the bloody hell would she think that you're investigating her?"

They drove past Far End, the dead-end lane they had closed off when Linda Wilson had been found, and then turned into Castle Lane where several liveried police cars were waiting, along with Nillson's hatchback.

The road followed the descent of the Lincoln Edge, a shallow hill compared to the Wolds or the Peaks, but in the context of the surrounding Fens, it was a noticeable decline.

At the foot of the hill, some three hundred yards away, and close to the gate to Briggs' field, a black Range Rover had been parked on the verge. They both saw it and Gillespie drew the car up behind Nillson's. He killed the engine and waited as if he knew what Ben was going to say.

"Because I *was* investigating her," Ben said, quietly, and before any of the others joined them. "I was investigating her for her uncle's murder."

Gillespie opened his mouth to convey his surprise but thought better of it, and took a breath to digest what Ben had told him.

"You were investigating her for murder?" he said.

"It's a long story," Ben told him. "And I'll tell you one day. But suffice to say that she found my investigation notes and then put two and two together."

"And made five?" Gillespie said to which Ben nodded. "So now she thinks that you're part of this whole Standing thing? Which is why she hasn't been into work and why you've been playing secret squirrel. Now I get it." He rested his hands on the steering wheel, and then his forehead on his hands.

"So many questions," he said. "I don't know where to start, Ben."

"Well, why don't we start with John Briggs?" Ben suggested. He shoved the car door open, and then leaned back inside, hopefully for the last time. "Then perhaps she'll tell us exactly what she's been doing."

CHAPTER FIFTY-ONE

The map was shameful, even Gillespie had to admit it. He had folded it to show Dunston, Nocton, and Wasps's Nest during a previous investigation and hadn't touched it since. It had just been sitting there in the footwell behind the driver's seat, slowly buried by coffee cups, takeaway wrappers, and God knows what else.

Ben managed to unfold it without conveying his disgust at the stains across Dunston, and he laid it across the bonnet, then stabbed an index finger at the top of Castle Lane.

"Right, so we're here," he began, then checked to make sure the wider team were involved, including the uniformed officers. "In the corner of this field, behind this property, there is an old barn. That's what we're hitting. Our target is a man named John Briggs. He's currently on parole after serving eight years for manslaughter. We believe he's dangerous, so pair up." He grouped the six unformed officers into three pairs and gestured for them to lean into where he was pointing on the map. "I want one pair here, up on Far End. Another pair here at the top of Main Street, and one pair here further down Castle Lane. That will lock the village down. Nobody gets through unless they've got a blue light flashing, understand?"

"Got it," one of them said, while the rest of them nodded their confirmations. "Good. Gold and Cruz, I want you out on Viking Way in case he does a runner. Nillson and Anderson, you'll be up at the house in case he gets out that way. Keep off the radios unless either of you see him running or you hear one of us."

"What about you two?" Nillson asked, clearly disappointed at the somewhat sedate assignment.

"We'll be going in alone."

"Just the two of you?" she said and eyed him as if he had lost the plot.

"Just stay where I've asked you to. You can be there in under a minute if we need help," he said, "as can Gold and Cruz, and the pair on Castle Lane."

"You said yourself, Ben. He's dangerous—"

"There's ten of us, Sergeant Nillson," he told her. "I'm not going in heavy-handed unless I need to. Just trust me, will you?"

She was either placated or she was professional enough not to press it in front of the others, and she nodded once, which to those who didn't know her might have seemed like a submission. But those who did know her knew that she wouldn't let him forget it. Gillespie knew all too well what Anna Nillson was capable of. She didn't so much hold a grudge as wrestle the bloody thing into submission like a python.

"Right," Ben said, balling the map and stuffing it against Gillespie's chest. "In your positions. Two minutes until we move in. Remember, the best-case scenario is that Gillespie and I walk him out of the field quietly. Worst case, well, just be ready to run. I have a feeling this one doesn't want to get caught."

The uniformed officers moved off in pairs, as did Gold and Cruz. Gillespie fought with the map, trying to make sense of the fold lines.

"I'll meet you up there," Nillson told Anderson and then loitered while Ben prepared himself. "Do you want to talk about the elephant in the room?"

"What elephant is that, Anna?" Ben replied, retying his bootlaces to make sure they were tight.

"The black Range Rover parked at the bottom of the hill," she said. "I know you've seen it."

"It's just a car," he said. "That's all."

"It's the boss's car, Ben."

"Have you checked the number plates?"

"I have," she said. "It's hers."

"Well, seeing as she isn't on duty, I don't see what that has to do with this investigation, do you?"

"Ben, come on. This is Freya. If she's here somewhere, then why don't we get her involved?"

"No, Anna," he said. "My focus is on John Briggs. If she wants to go rogue, then that's her business."

"She hasn't gone rogue, Ben."

"My main concern is removing a killer from the streets," he said, cutting her off. "What's yours?"

Gillespie tossed the map into the mess onto the back seat of his car and closed the door.

"She's right, Ben."

"Oh, not you as well–"

"Yes, me as well," he said. "We're talking about the boss here. She might be in trouble, mate."

"She's not going to go after John Briggs on her own. She's not that stupid."

"She went after Sloane," he said, which came as a surprise to Nillson.

"She did what?"

"Aye. The lass that runs the place saw her literally hours before we found him. Dead, I might add."

"Well, we know why–" Ben started.

"And Hunter?" Gillespie said, speaking directly to Nillson now. "Found dead this morning. And guess who was seen leaving his place?"

"No," Nillson said in disbelief. "Surely not."

"Some posh tart in a Range Rover were the officer's exact words."

"Ben, why didn't you say?" Nillson asked her expression more one of hurt than inquisitive.

"I don't see the relevance," he replied, then checked to make sure they weren't being overheard, lowering his voice. "So what? She was there. She didn't do anything, did she? And to quote you, Jim, this is Freya we're talking about."

"Ben, she could be in that bloody barn. For all we know, they could be bloody burying her. Or worse, she could be bloody well burying him."

"I know," he said, far louder than before, and he stared at them both. "I know, all right. I just didn't want you both to think..."

He paused as if the words were somehow out of reach, or too out there to believe.

"You didn't want us to think she was involved?" Nillson said, and he nodded slowly.

"You both know far more than anybody else," he said, holding his hands up and turning to Gillespie. "The murder I told you about. It happened years ago. When she was a teenager."

"Ben—"

"Look, I know what it looks like—"

"We've got eyewitnesses placing her at two bloody murder scenes."

"I didn't want this to be about her," Ben said. "It's not about her. It's about John Briggs. If I'd made a song and dance about her, then everyone would have to know. I can't have that, Anna. Jim, you understand, right? She's not a bloody killer. She's going through a hard time, and as much as I want to help her, I can't get close." He stopped to take a breath. "She's not a killer. She's Freya, right?"

"Aye," Gillespie replied, giving himself a moment to control himself, and his thoughts. "Aye, I know that mate. I know that you know that, and Anna knows it. But the fact of the matter is that we've been here ten minutes now, and I don't know about either of you two, but I haven't seen her walk out of that wee barn over there."

Ben turned and leaned on the bonnet. He closed his eyes and let his head hang between his shoulders.

"All right. As far as everyone else is concerned, this is about John Briggs."

"Aye," Gillespie said. "And if it becomes more than that? If Freya is somehow involved?"

"Then we'll deal with that if and when it happens," Ben told him, shoving himself upright and zipping his jacket closed. "I can't think about that right now. Right now, I want to get in there, I want John Briggs in custody, and I want Freya safe. Whatever happens after that is out of my control."

CHAPTER FIFTY-TWO

The small field was more of a grassy paddock, around an acre in size and surrounded on all sides by mature trees – sycamores, limes, and even an ash or two. The faint trail followed the path of least resistance, then forked to create three broad green patches. The first fork led further up the hill, working its way towards the distant rooftops that peeked over the trees, and presumably to the Briggs' rear gate. The second fork took a wide detour, following the contour of the land to the far corner of the field, where an old barn or shed stood, but only barely. The structure reminded Ben of the original wooden barn on his father's farm, which had long been super-seded by newer buildings of steel and concrete.

From behind the barn, thick, silver smoke rose into the air like the shadow of some great bird taking flight, its form broken only by the occasional gust from the west, after which a new form took its place.

They stopped outside the barn doors and listened. Men's voices grumbled softly and the fire crackled angrily. He half expected to hear Freya's velvety, alto voice, creamy and smooth against those men's rough tones.

A few hundred metres away, way down the lane, the first pair of uniformed officers waited, watching for a signal.

"Ready?" Ben asked, and Gillespie nodded. "I'll go through, you go around."

The barn door was open just a few inches and it creaked at Ben's touch. At the corner of the old building, the noise stopped Gillespie in his tracks, and he glanced back at Ben, who gestured for him to go on. Just as Ben had thought there might be, there was another pair of doors at the back of the barn. One of them was ajar, leaving a small gap through which thick smoke poured, collecting in the ancient eaves like a storm cloud, rolling and seeking a way up and out.

The space was mostly empty. A few old benches lined one wall, adorned with bags of compost, potting materials, and a few basic gardening tools. Another wall housed larger tools such as spades, shovels, forks, and some machinery, including an old two-stroke rota-vator, a scarifier, and even an old generator. There was very little on the shelves that Ben hadn't expected to see in such a place – fuel cans, weed spray, and rolls of netting.

Quietly, he made his way to the rear of the barn and stood with his back to the doors, where he took a few deep breaths. Through an old, dusty window in the side wall, he saw Gillespie ease past, making his way through the overgrown vegetation as quietly as he could. Ben waited, gauging when his old friend would be ready to round the corner into view.

And then, with a final deep breath, he kicked the door wide open.

"Lincolnshire Police," he called loud enough for Gillespie to know it had begun. He held his warrant card up before him. "Stay where you are."

Two men and one woman were sitting in old, teak chairs with a matching table before them. They held steaming, plastic mugs, and on the table was a tartan flask.

None of them moved a muscle.

Gillespie came to stand at Ben's side, searching around them for signs of anybody else.

"John Briggs?" Ben said to the youngest of the men, and he nodded. "I'm arresting you on suspicion of the murders of Linda Wilson, Scott Sloane, and Darren Hunter–"

"You're making a mistake," the older man said, unperturbed. But Ben continued regardless.

"You do not have to say anything. But it may harm your defence if you do not mention when questioned something which you later rely on in court. Anything you do say may be given in evidence. Do you understand?"

"I do," Briggs replied, loud and clear.

"On your knees, please. Hands behind your back."

The young man set his tea down on the table, staring arrogantly at Ben. He eased himself from the chair and then dropped to his knees, placing his hands, as requested, behind his back. Gillespie moved in to secure his wrists with zip ties and then hauled the man to his feet.

"Anything to say?" Ben asked.

"No comment," he replied.

"I said you're making a mistake," the man who Ben surmised to be the father said.

"Well, if I am, then I'm sure that will all be made clear at the station," Ben told him.

"He's no murderer, you know?"

"Even if you're right, Mr Briggs, he's still breached the conditions of his parole. I'm sure his parole officer will want to have a few words with him."

"Oh, I already have," the woman said, and she too set her drink down on the table to fish her identification from her pocket, which she duly held up for Ben to see.

"Susan Bennett," she said. "I've just been talking to your suspect here about a harassment claim."

"A harassment claim?"

"As far as I can tell, since his release, Mr Briggs has suffered undue harassment not only from certain members of the local community but now, in light of a recent incident, from the Lincolnshire Police Force."

"It sounds like you've picked your side, Miss Bennett."

"It's Mrs Bennett, and I have not picked sides, but I do believe in the system."

"I was told he'd breached his parole conditions," Ben said. "Or doesn't that count in your definition of the system?"

"Which is the purpose of my visit," she said. "There was a fault with the GPS transmitter. It logged his whereabouts but failed to send the data to our monitoring team. I can assure you, it's all been rectified now."

"So, you can tell me where he was on Sunday morning, then."

"Oh, I can do more than that. I can verify that he hasn't been more than two hundred metres from his house for the past two weeks. And it's hardly a wonder, is it? Considering he gets accused of some new crime every time he steps foot off of the property."

"So you won't be charging him, then?"

"I won't be charging him, no," she replied. "And unless you want a full-scale enquiry, I suggest you retract your statement and let

John Briggs go, and before you ask, I am happy to testify to what I've just said."

"We have evidence," Ben said.

"I doubt it," she replied and reached into her bag, from which she withdrew a tablet. She clicked a few buttons and then handed it to Ben. The device showed a heat map depicting Briggs' movements over the past two weeks. There were two areas of bright orange. The first was the house, at the other end of the field, and the second was the barn where they were standing, with weaker oranges across the field.

There was a small yellow trail on the screen that led from the Briggs' front door to Far End and back again.

He handed the tablet back to Bennett and appraised John Briggs and his father.

"So why did you give a false name on Sunday?" Ben asked, and the man shrugged.

"Wouldn't you? I'm trying to start afresh," he replied. "I don't want people to be afraid of me. I just want to blend in."

Ben nodded and turned to the fire.

"What are you burning?" he asked.

"Just some debris from the storm," he replied. "Isn't that right, Dad?"

The older man nodded.

"Sticks and whatnot," he said. "That's all. Bloody everywhere, it was."

"And if I was to extinguish the fire to have a look?"

"Then I would see no option but to pursue the harassment claim, Inspector," Bennett told him in no uncertain terms.

"Against me?"

"Against your entire team," she said. "Starting with your boss."

"My boss?"

"I prefer to deal with the organ grinder where possible," she said. "It's a DCI Bloom, isn't it?"

She stared him down, studying his eyes for some hidden truth. But it wasn't the first time he had encountered allegiance with the downtrodden within the force and its wider factions.

"John Briggs served eight years for manslaughter following the death of Lee Frost," Ben said as if Briggs wasn't even there. "As did Darren Hunter."

"I'm well aware of the circumstances, Inspector."

"Darren Hunter was found dead this

morning," he told her. "As was Scott Sloane. Recognise that name from your file?"

She shook her head but said nothing, and it was the old man who spoke up.

"Scott is dead?" he said, incredulous.

"He died this morning, sir," Ben replied.

"He worked for me did Scott. Good bloke, too. Bloody smart man."

"And what was it he did for you, Mr Briggs?" Gillespie asked, to which the old man inhaled long and hard.

"I was a developer," he began. "I bought old buildings from desperate owners, turned them round, and then flogged them. The idea was for John here to take over from me." He looked across at his boy with pride. "There wasn't a homeowner in the county he couldn't talk around when he put his mind to it."

"They don't sound very desperate to me," Ben said.

"They were," he replied. "And if they weren't, then they were by the time he'd been round there and pointed out the damp, the rotten roof, and the cost of building materials. It was legit, you know? We didn't prey on anybody."

"You just helped them see sense?" Ben suggested.

"Aye, we did. That is until we started losing properties."

"Go on," Ben said, intrigued.

"Well, Scott used to find the properties. He would go through the surveys, the land registry, and whatnot. He'd find potential properties and we'd assess them. If we thought that we could restore the building, and turn a small profit, then John and Darren would go in. But there came a time, see, that they'd go to talk to the owner, and find out that another developer had already been to see them. It was a few at first. Inconveniences. But then it was more and more. We started losing money."

"And it turned out that Lee Frost was leaking information to this other supplier?" Ben asked, to which the man nodded.

"If it's true about them both," he started, "then it's a shame. It's a bloody dreadful shame. They were good men, both of them. And I'll tell you exactly what I told that other one when all this nonsense started up again. My boy had nowt to do with what happened to Frost, and if you want to push the matter, then you'd better be prepared for a war. Because I've just about had enough of it."

"I see," Ben replied, and he looked to Gillespie for some kind of support but received only a helpless shrug. "Well, I think it's best if we go away and have a rethink. If we need a statement to help our enquiries, I hope that wouldn't be asking too much, would it?"

"I'm happy to make a statement," John Briggs said, his expression as sincere as any Ben had seen. "I just want my name cleared, that's all."

"Well, we'll leave it there then, shall we?" Ben said, and he started back through the barn door, where he stopped and turned. "Just one more thing. When you said, that other one, you were referring to Geoffrey Wilson, I presume?"

The old man laughed aloud.

"Geoffrey Wilson? No, I wouldn't give him the time of day," he replied. "Him or his poor, dead wife."

His tone shifted. His eyes told a far different story than before.

"So, who did you speak to?" Ben asked.

"Who did you tell, Mr Briggs? Who did you warn?"

"It's funny, isn't it?" the man said, and he stepped up to Ben, as bold as brass. "How life has a way of going round and round. It catches up with us in the end, doesn't it? Karma, I think they call it, don't they?"

"What do you mean?"

He looked to his boy and the parole officer, and then back at Ben, and for a moment, he could have been a young man, a fit man, with his life's work on the brink of success.

"Just over eight years ago, I lost everything. I lost my business, my livelihood, my house, and I lost my boy, and all because I was too scared to stand up for the truth." He shook his head. "I swore I would never give in again, and I swore, the day my boy was sent down, that I would be back." He grinned. "And that I'd make this right, Inspector, and by God I have."

CHAPTER FIFTY-THREE

She trod the Viking Way with care. The path was muddy and slippery, perhaps more so due to the dozens of officers that had been through there on their hands and knees.

But it was silent, and she needed the silence to compose her thoughts. She needed the silence to be sure she was alone out there, as she pulled the wire fence down, and stepped over it.

There was no turning back now. She had crossed the line.

The rear garden was long and narrow, and she imagined the views must have been spectacular in the summertime, although the winter winds would wind their way along the

Edge, ready to tear across the open Fens beyond Boothby and out across the distant Wolds.

She shouldn't have been alone. Not by rights. By rights, she should have had a whole team behind her. But things didn't always work out. People weren't always predictable.

Sometimes you have to go it alone. Sometimes the rewards outweigh the consequences.

Sometimes you win, even if the odds are stacked against you.

"All units, return to the cars," a voice said on the radio. Ben's voice. She pictured his disappointment, how he beat himself up over the smallest mistake, so much so that he often failed to see what was staring him in the face. "We're calling it off. Nillson, get hold of Chapman, will you? I want to know who owned the business that Lee Frost was supposed to have been leaking information to."

A crackle of confirmations and questions came back, but she had heard all she needed to hear and pocketed the radio.

Along one side of the long garden, fruit trees, bare in their winter form, created a veil of branches and gnarled trunks, through which she could pick her way almost to the house. She crossed the open ground with care and peered through the rear window into an open kitchen diner, with views through to the driveway, where a car was parked, its boot lid open.

The back door was unlocked and nothing moved when she entered, save for the dog, a labrador, which raised its head from slumber at the sound of the closing door, and who was far more interested in the box of dog biscuits that she scattered across the floor before giving it a gentle pat on the back. The house was a bungalow and clearly very little expense had been spared in its interior design. The wallpaper was Philip Jeffries, or a close copy at least. The furniture wasn't too dissimilar to that which Freya had selected for her own little house, although this particular house demanded far more pieces than her little cottage. Even the floors were luxurious, and she felt the warmth from the underfloor heating rising up from beneath the vinyl tiles. It was no wonder the dog was content to sprawl across the kitchen.

A loud zip came from the front end of

the house, long and hurried, followed by opening drawers and cupboards, and heavy footsteps. She crept towards the noise, along a wide hallway with walls adorned with family photos. Times. Memories. She wondered how many of them were lies.

And there before her was what she had expected to find. A bathroom and a bedroom, and a door open just far enough for Freya to spy a pair of matching suitcases on a floral bedspread. It didn't matter how well the house was finished or how expensive the brands were, the layout dragged them all down with its lack of ambition and imagination. It was a large, two-bedroom bungalow dressed up in designer furnishings.

The contents of the cases had been hurriedly packed, with grey trousers spilling over the edge, along with white, button-down shirts. She stopped at the doorway and listened, trying to place him inside the room. To gauge his movements, and the moment she should burst in.

But the silence was broken by a soft crackle from inside her pocket, and Nillson's voice, scratchy and tinny came across the radio.

"Ben, come back," she said, as a gentle breath washed over Freya's nape. "Chapman has just come back to me about the owner of the company. It was–"

Freya turned the dial and the radio clicked off. She cleared her throat.

"I hope you weren't planning on going somewhere," she said and then turned to face him. He was the same man she had spoken to before, but that naivety was gone and in its place was urgency, irritation, and anger. The clincher, if indeed there was any doubt in her mind, was the blue, woolly hat that he wore.

"I could say the same to you," he said with a smile, and then his hands grabbed her throat.

CHAPTER FIFTY-FOUR

Freya's boot heels dragged across the hallway carpet as she scrambled for purchase and she kicked one of them off, leaving it lying in the hallway. His grip on her throat was tight, too tight for her to pull apart, so she reached out for the kitchen door frame, forcing him to let go of her throat and grab her hands. He pried her fingers free, and before she could stagger to her feet, the back of his hand connected with her face, sending her sprawling onto the kitchen floor, where the dog was still collecting the treats she had scattered. She began to push herself up but his hands grabbed onto her ankles and tugged her backwards, further into the house. She kicked and writhed, connecting a few times, but not hard enough to stop him in his tracks.

It was only when he pulled her onto her back and knelt on her shoulders that she finally acceded to his greater strength. Breathless, he held onto her wrists, pinning her down with his face just inches from hers.

"They're coming for you," she told him. "There are police covering every road in and out of Boothby."

"I don't believe you," he replied, his breathing relaxing.

"Why don't you go and have a look?"

"Yeah, right."

"It's over," she said. "The longer you stay here with me, the harder it will be to get away."

"Shut up," he hissed, and he glanced towards the front of the house, then back at her.

She smiled at him and then licked the blood from her lip.

"Did you mean to kill her?" she asked. "Did you really mean to kill Linda?"

"I said shut up," he told her.

"What about Scott Sloane and Darren Hunter?"

"I'm trying to think," he said, and there was a weakness to his voice. A doubt.

"Do you know what I think?"

"I don't care what you think."

"I think you made a mistake. I think you didn't mean to kill her. I think it was a mistake."

"Yeah?" he said. "Well, you think wrong then, don't you?"

"I think things just got out of hand. They spiralled. The deeper you went, the harder it was to contain."

His lips drew back, and for a moment, she thought he might slap her again, or worse. He drew his hand back, and just as he was about to strike, the doorbell rang.

"I'm guessing that isn't the Avon lady," Freya said, which amused her briefly but only served to anger him.

With one hand on her wrists, he used the other to whip his belt from his trousers then dragged her across the room by her hair to a radiator. In a few short moments, she was tied down, and he glared at her.

"If you scream, I'll kill you. Keep quiet," he said, "and you just might survive."

"You won't get out of here," she told him, as the doorbell rang for the second time. "They'll have the place surrounded by now. You took too long. You'll probably die in prison. Did you ever consider that?"

He ripped the hat from his head, crouched down beside her, and stuffed it into her mouth, forcing Freya to breathe through her nose.

"That's where you're wrong," he said, and he strode over to the large range, where he began turning all the dials, releasing gas into the air. He stared back at her, his eyes wide with fear. "I have absolutely no intention of going to prison."

———

The heel of Ben's boot connected with the front door just beneath the lock. But it held fast.

"Round the back," he yelled to Nillson and Anderson. "Find a way in." He pointed to two of the uniformed officers. "You two, go with them. I want two more of you at one end of the street and two more at the other. Nobody gets in or out."

Then he turned and lunged at the door. The door still held, but this time, the solid thump he had heard on the first kick was accompanied by a loud crack. It was giving way. He crouched and peered through the letterbox.

And then he saw it.

Her boot, lying on the carpet near the kitchen door.

"Freya," he called out. "Freya, are you in there?"

"Want me to have a go?" Gillespie asked, gearing up for a turn at the door. But Ben held him back.

"No, I've got this, mate," he said, then met his stare. "She's inside."

"The boss?" he said, then pulled his radio from his pocket. "All units. Suspect is inside the house. Police officer inside, possibly captive, possibly injured." He stopped for a moment, then added drably. "Situation unknown." He let the radio hang by his side, and then as Ben prepared for another kick, he spoke into it once more. "Gold, we're going to need that ambulance."

"Copy," the response came almost instantly, and Ben pocketed the radio, leaving him to focus on the job at hand.

The final kick connected well. It was a combination of timing, weight, and force. To surge forward gathering momentum, to plant the boot in the exact spot at the exact moment that bodyweight and the extension of the leg were at their optimum, to create the maximum velocity.

That velocity transferred to the door. The latch gave under the sudden stress and the door slammed back into the wall, juddering to a stop as Ben stepped inside. The door to a bedroom on his left was ajar and suitcases were open on the bed, half-filled with clothes and shoes.

He gave the door a nudge to check the rest of the room but found it empty. Gillespie moved past him, ducking into the next bedroom and the bathroom, then returned with a shake of his head.

"Police," Ben called out. "My name is Detective Inspector Ben Savage. If you're home, then make your presence known."

Nobody replied and they both glanced at the kitchen door. Ben moved forward cautiously, sensing Gillespie behind him. He kicked at Freya's boot to ensure that Gillespie had seen it. At the threshold of the kitchen, Ben stopped, took a breath to prepare himself, and then sniffed again, recognising the smell immediately.

"Out," he said, shoving Gillespie back towards the door. "Out now."

The big Scotsman caught a whiff of the gas and dragged Ben with him. They tumbled through the front door.

"Radio," Ben said. "Fire brigade. And we need more uniforms. I want the bloody village closed off and I want the neighbours evacuated."

"Right," Gillespie replied.

"And get Faye Butters here. Get Sergeant Priest to send her here. I don't care how, just get her here. Think you can do that?"

"Aye," he replied. "But what are you going to do? You aren't going back in there, Ben. I can't let you do that." He reached up and grabbed hold of Ben's shoulder. "Sorry, Ben, but I can't."

"I don't have a choice," Ben replied, then tore his shoulder free of his grip. "Just do as I ask, will you?"

"Ben–"

"That's an order, Jim. Get everyone back here to help you," Ben said, and the look on Gillespie's face told him that he understood the reasons why but wholeheartedly disagreed. "You take control for me, big fella."

CHAPTER FIFTY-FIVE

The sight of his six-foot-something frame stepping into the kitchen could have been joyous had it not been for the stench of gas that filled the room. She was drunk on fumes or the lack of oxygen. It was hard to tell which. She raised a hand to stop him. To wave at him to leave. But her arm hung uselessly at her side as if it belonged to somebody else.

He stood there, appraising the situation, and it was all she could to blink at him – a sign that she was awake, yet not fully compos mentis.

"You don't have to do this, Kyle," Ben said, his words sounding distant, as if it was all a terrible dream, or as if they were underwater.

Kyle Butters leaned with his back to the range, his finger poised on the ignition button, and Ben's eyes hung there for a moment, before staring at the man.

"I'm just going to open the door," Ben said to which Butters flinched.

"Stay where you are," he said. "One push. That's all it'll take."

"But what will it prove?" Ben asked. "What will you gain?"

"I've nothing left to gain," Butters replied. "I've nothing left to live for."

"What? You're talking rubbish, Kyle," Ben said, holding his sleeve to his face to filter the air. "What about your wife?"

Butters gave a little laugh.

"You think she'll want me now? You think she'll want me when she learns about all of this? When she learns about how I paid for all of this? How my business did so well? Do you think she'll even look me in the eye?"

"She loves you, Kyle. She's on her way here now. She loves you, mate. She won't care about what you've done."

"No?"

"No," he said. "That's the thing about love. True love. It's unconditional. Those things don't matter. The past doesn't matter. What matters is honesty."

Butters seemed to process the information and just might have been on the cusp of being convinced when the reality of it all returned.

"And what is she supposed to do, love me while I'm locked up in a prison cell?" he said, then nodded at Freya. "She said it the way it is. I'll die inside. I won't see daylight again." He shook his head. "No, it's better this way. This way she can move on. Her and Geoffrey–"

"There's nothing between them," Ben said.

"No, there's not. But they'll have each other, won't they?" He stiffened and his hand tensed.

"Think of the lives you'll ruin," Ben said, searching for a different angle, his eyes flicking down to the ignition button. "Think of the devastation. Don't you think you've caused enough heartache?" Ben stood, ready to jump into action, leaving Freya to slowly work the belt behind her back. The thick leather cut into her wrists and the buckle was just out of reach of her probing finger.

"I know what happened, Kyle," Ben said. "I know what happened to Lee Frost. I know it was you who killed him." He took the opportunity to move closer, staring into the garden beyond. Butters let his head fall back as if he sought to inhale the toxic air, and his shallow breaths rasped. "And I know you framed John Briggs and Darren Hunter."

"It wasn't meant to happen like that," Butters said. "He wasn't supposed to die. I didn't mean to frame them. There was just no way out. He wasn't supposed to die."

"Just like Linda wasn't supposed to die?"

"She was going to ruin it all," Butters yelled. "She was going to go to the police."

"And you couldn't let her go?" Ben asked. "What were you afraid of, Kyle? Why couldn't you let Linda go to the police?"

"She didn't know. Nobody knew. Nobody had to know. They wouldn't have known, either, if Faye hadn't—"

"Hadn't what? Poked her nose in?" Ben said. "Yes, I imagine that was the straw that broke the camel's back, wasn't it? You'd got away with it for eight years, hadn't you? You thought it was all over."

"It was over. It should have been. Do you know how many sleepless nights I had? Do you know how long it took me to come to terms with what I had done?"

"When did it start, Kyle?" Ben said. "Was it when Faye reached out to the only half-decent PI in the area? Is that it? Imagine if you were Scott Sloane. You'd witnessed a murder and you'd been paid well for your silence. Then, out of the blue, eight years later, Faye comes along and wants to give him more money to prove John Briggs is guilty, when you know damn well he's not. What was he supposed to do? On one hand, he could have been honest and shopped you in. On the other hand, he could have just gone along with it, taken the money, and led them down a very long and winding garden path."

"I should have known never to trust him," Butters said.

"Ah, yes. Is that because it wasn't Lee Frost who was passing information from Michael Briggs' firm to you, was it? It was Scott Sloane. You already had a working relationship. Briggs paid him to find potential properties and then he sold the information to you. But when it got out of control, when firms began to go under, someone had to take the fall for it. And that person was Lee Frost, wasn't it?"

"He didn't have to die," Kyle said. "How many more times?"

"So now you're a murderer and the only person who knows is Scott Sloane. What do you do? You pay him and you pay him well. Perhaps at around the same time that you folded your business and retired. It was all going so well, wasn't it, Kyle? Everything was going as planned. The only thing you hadn't planned was Michael Briggs. You thought he'd just go away and leave you to it, didn't you? You framed his son, Kyle. You framed John Briggs and Darren Hunter. What did you think, that he was just going to roll over and let you get away with it?"

"Well, I didn't expect him to move to our bloody village, did I?"

"You also didn't count on him being smarter than you," Ben told him. "Much, much smarter. You see, by the time your wife first contacted Scott Sloane, the Briggs were living in Boothby. A dozen doors away, Kyle.

Not far. So now let's think about Scott Sloane again. Let's think about what he would do when Faye gets in touch and explains about this John Briggs bloke who's moved into the village, and about how he was convicted for manslaughter. Imagine Sloane's ears pricking up. I can see the dollar signs rolling in his eyes, Kyle, like a fruit machine." Ben took a few steps, more to test the water with Butters than to help him think. "Now here comes Faye Butters, willing to pay him handsomely to prove that John Briggs is guilty of murder, not manslaughter. But Sloane knew he was innocent. So, he took the money from your wife and Geoffrey Wilson. He played the game. You know, if I was Scott Sloane, I would have come to you, Kyle. I would have come to you and said that my silence demanded more money."

"He did," Butters said. "And I told him where he could go."

"You should have paid him."

"If I had paid him any more, what was to stop him coming back and asking for more? Where does it end? No, the way to deal with people like Scott Sloane is to let them know who's boss."

"Oh right. And how did that work out for you?"

Butters shifted on his feet.

"I see," Ben said. "So, Sloane gave you a month or two to come to a decision. He was in no rush, was he? After all, Faye and Geoffrey were already paying him, and paying him well I might add. But when you refused to pay for his silence any more, his allegiance shifted. Now, who do you think would pay handsomely for that type of information? Who would be willing to learn the name of the person who was responsible for his son going to prison?"

"He didn't have to do that," Butters said. "That was a low blow."

"Maybe," Ben said. "But then, we've already concluded that Sloane wasn't to be trusted, haven't we?" He took a few more steps, glancing out into the garden briefly. "So, what does Michael Briggs do? Let's put ourselves in his shoes for a moment. On one hand, our son is out of prison, and we just want to get on with our lives. Start afresh, if you like. On the other hand, we have an opportunity to exact revenge on the man who ruined their lives. What did he do, Kyle?

What did he say? Was it money that he wanted? What was it?"

Butters closed his eyes to Ben's words and Freya's finger slipped into the belt buckle, tugging it free from the little, leather loop.

"He wanted Faye to stop," he said quietly.

"Sorry?"

"I said, he wanted Faye and Geoff to stop. He said that if they didn't stop their investigation, then he'd make me suffer."

"Is that all?"

"Isn't that enough?"

"For some. But not for someone like Michael Briggs," Ben said, and Butters sighed.

"He wanted money."

"And you paid him?"

"Of course not. I didn't pay Scott and I didn't pay Michael Briggs."

"And that's where it all went wrong, isn't it? Ben said. "That's why he killed the Wilsons' dog. It was a warning."

"He couldn't come to our house, could he?"

"No, you've got a camera and the Wilsons haven't," Ben said. "So, you get back to the house after the pub and you find the dog. You feel guilty and help bury the dog–"

"It wasn't like that–"

"And then you leave them to it. Geoffrey and Linda talk. They grieve their dog. He comes clean about the investigation and they argue all night."

"I don't know about that–"

"They did. We have witness statements from their neighbours," Ben told him. "And somewhere in amongst all of that, Geoffrey flips. He lashes out. So hard that he thinks he's killed her. And this is where things become a little hazy. You see, if I was Linda, and my husband had just tried to kill me, would I go to the police about the investigation or the fact that my husband has just tried to kill me?"

Butters stared at him but said nothing.

"Or would I go to my lover?" Ben said, and Butters' tense shoulders sagged under the weight of the truth. "I would go to my lover and ask him to take me to the police. But you – my lover – would know that if the police were called then the dog would have to be explained, and that would lead back to Michael Briggs, and then Lee Frost. Essentially, a can of worms would have been opened. And then to take it back a few steps, that's why Geoffrey lashed out, isn't it? Because she told him about the pair of you. It's all beginning to make sense, Kyle. On one hand, you have Scott Sloane and Michael Briggs threatening to ruin you, and on the other hand, you have Faye and Geoff doing everything they can to expose you. So, when Linda, the last person you can rely on, comes along and wants to go to the police..." He stopped, and Freya organised the narrative in her mind. He had done well, far better than she had. "You lost it. You saw no way out."

"I didn't mean to," Butters said.

"You killed her," Ben said. "You put your hands around her neck and you killed her because you were scared of the truth coming out. How did it feel, Kyle?"

"Stop it."

"What was it like to feel her life ebbing away beneath your fingertips?"

"Stop!"

"Did it remind you of Lee Frost? Is that it? Is that why you cried out?"

"It hurt," he screamed. "If you must know, it hurt to do it. But I didn't have a choice, did I? I'd be sent away. I loved the woman. Of course I did. What did Faye think would happen when she and Geoff spent all their free time at the bloody library? Who did she think Linda would turn to?"

Ben leaned against the wall beside the back door and Kyle eyed him cautiously, his finger still hovering over the ignition button.

"So, what do you do?" Ben asked. "See, this is what we do. Part of our job is to look at evidence and find a motive. But that isn't always possible. Not without becoming the victims or the suspects. We have to em-pathise. I have to mentally put myself in your shoes, Kyle. Here I am, with my secret about to be exposed. My life is about to be ruined. Everything I have worked for is about to be lost. And just when I thought that was bad enough, I murder my lover. The last person who truly cares for me," Ben said. "But there is a way out of all of this. There is a way out of the mess and to bury the truth forever. Blame John Briggs. That's easy enough. He was convicted of manslaughter, so how hard would it be to position him as the murderer? All you had to do was come down to the sta-tion and tell us about the investigation your wife and Geoffrey were working on. And we walked right into it, didn't we? We fell for it. But you had to get rid of Sloane. Sloane was the only one who knew the truth. But why stop there? From Scott Sloane, you went to Darren Hunter, leaving a trail of destruction in your wake. A trail that could only lead to one person. One convicted man who linked all of them. John Briggs."

A single tear fell from Kyle Butters' eyes and rolled down his cheek.

"It's over, Kyle," Ben said, and he stepped forward, only for Butters to stiffen at his approach.

"No closer," he said. "I'll push it. We'll all go up."

"No," Ben said. "No, you won't push it."

He moved forward again.

"I will," Butters said, "I'll bloody do it. It's over for me now."

"The way I see it, you have two options," Ben told him. "You can come with me and face the music like a man. You can show people that you really are a man. That all you wanted was to provide for your family."

"Or?" Butters said, and Ben inhaled long and hard.

"Or you can push that button," he replied. "And the world will know that Kyle Butters was a coward who not only cheated on his wife but let an innocent man lose eight years of his life in prison, and killed three people to cover the truth and to save himself, not to mention killing two police officers in the process."

Freya stretched her legs before her, watching Butters' finger trace the outline of the button. He stared down at her as if somehow she held the answers.

"What's it going to be, Kyle?" Ben said.

"Get out," he replied. "Just go, will you? And take her with you."

"We're not going anywhere," Ben told him. "Do you really want to do this? Do you really want the world to know you were a coward?"

"I don't care about the world," he said. "I made a mistake, that's all. Lee Frost was a mistake and I've had to live with it all these years." He sniffed and wiped the tears from his eyes with the back of his free hand. "It's never going away, is it?"

"You need to make peace with the world," Ben said. "With yourself. The only way you can do that is to face your punishment, Kyle."

"No," he said, shaking his head. "I can't. I can't. I won't survive. Look at me. I'm an old man. I'll die inside."

"A least you'll die at peace," Ben said, and when he glanced at Freya, she saw a confidence in his eyes. "Step away from the oven, Kyle. Step away and make this right."

Butters stared at the floor, his eyes vague and lost in the mess he had created, the mess his life had become.

Then he looked up at Ben and slowly shook his head.

"I'm sorry," he whispered, then sniffed to clear his nose. He took a few deep breaths and then looked Ben in the eye. "I'm sorry, but I can't. I just can't do that."

And then he pushed the button.

CHAPTER FIFTY-SIX

His finger pushed down on the button and three little clicks accompanied three tiny sparks at each hob.

But nothing ignited.

He pushed again and a confused expression began to form on his face. And again, three little clicks accompanied three tiny sparks.

"What the...?" He turned to face the oven, turning the dials to maximum, and then retried the ignition button. And then he saw something through the window and his body, which until now had been rigid with tension, seemed to fold on itself. He slumped over the oven. "You tricked me."

Ben gave a wave through the window and beckoned somebody in.

"They disconnected the gas ten minutes ago, Kyle," Ben said.

Nillson entered through the back door with two uniformed officers and a very excited Labrador.

"You let me say all that. You let me tell you everything."

"I needed time to let the gas dissipate," Ben explained.

"I would have, you know? I would have done it."

I know. At least this way you get to make peace with yourself. It's for the best, Kyle."

He turned and stared at them all, a broken man, and then slowly, he nodded.

"Faye can't know," he said suddenly. "She can't find out about Linda and me—"

But Ben winced slightly, and before he could answer, a voice came from the hallway.

"I already know," it said, and Faye Butters stepped into view behind Ben. "I heard it all, Kyle. I heard every word."

"No," he said. "No Faye, I can explain."

"It's too late, Kyle," she told him. "I think I understand everything now."

He took a step forward and reached for her, but Ben held him back with a hand on his chest.

"Kyle Butters," he began. "You are under arrest on suspicion of murder. You do not have to say anything. But it may harm your defence if you do not mention when questioned something which you later rely on in court. Anything you do say may be given in evidence."

He nodded for Gillespie, who had led Faye in through the front door, to lead him away, and the big Scotsman stepped up to Butters, pulling his arms behind his back.

"Come on then, Mr Butters," Gillespie said. "Let's go and see if we can't find a nice wee room to sit down in, shall we? Then you can tell us all about it in your own words."

But Butters fought back at the door. He turned to his wife.

"Faye. Wait for me, darling, will you?" he said. "Promise me you'll wait for me. It's the only thing that will keep me going."

She stared at him at first then slowly she made her way across the room to him, and Ben nodded at Gillespie to give them a moment.

"In light of everything I've just heard? I'm sorry, Kyle, but I just don't think I can," she said, and she shook her head. "No more lies."

"I can do that," he begged. "From now on. I'll tell you everything. I can't do this without you, Faye."

"Well, you'll have to. Because even if you do live to be released, I won't be here, Kyle. I can't be. You understand that, don't you?" she said, and she stared him in the eye. "I think this is where we go our separate ways."

She smiled sadly then turned and walked away into the back garden, escorted by the uniformed officers and Nillson.

"Faye, come on," Butters shouted. "Come on, this is us. I did it all for you."

"Take him away," Ben said to Gillespie and then looked at Freya on the floor beside the radiator. "And give us five minutes alone, will you?"

He watched Gillespie leave with Butters and then took a few steps over to where Freya stared up at him. The first thing he did was pull the hat from her mouth, which he took the time to bag and then set down on the kitchen work surface.

"You got there in the end," she said,

licking her lips. "I wondered how far behind me you would be." But Ben said nothing. He pulled a glass from a cupboard, filled it from the tap, and then held it to her mouth, and she drank, letting it spill down her coat. "Thank you," she said and then gestured at her restraints. "A little help?"

"In a minute," he said and then dropped to the floor, where he sat beside her against the radiator.

"In a minute?"

"There are a few things I want to say first," he said and then eyed the belt that bound her hands. "It's not often I get your undivided attention."

"Ben, this is absurd."

"I know you found your way into my spare bedroom," he said, staring at the wall opposite, where photos of Kyle and Faye Butters had been neatly placed. "And I suppose, by way of an explanation, I should treat you in much the same way as I treated Kyle Butters."

"You didn't tie him up," Freya said.

"No, he wasn't going anywhere. Anyone could see that."

"And if Nillson hadn't disconnected the gas supply?"

"Then this might have ended very differently," he replied. "But I feel like the only way to explain myself, and what I did, is to put myself in your shoes."

"You're empathising?" she said. "With me?"

"You have a feeling that you're being pushed out," he said. "The RTA, the complaints, the reporter, which by the way was Sloane—"

"I know—"

"And I didn't help you. I said that I couldn't help."

"I know that too," she replied.

"And when you walked into my spare bedroom, you saw why I couldn't help."

She felt her body stiffen and then sighed.

"Yes, Ben. I did."

"But not because of the reasons that you're thinking," he told her. "You see, I know that Anna helped you. I know what she found."

Freya opened her mouth to speak but he held his hand up.

"Don't make me use the woolly hat," he said with a grin.

"You wouldn't."

"I would if it meant I could talk to you for five minutes without being interrupted," he said, and she let him go on. "You see, if somebody who knew how to analyse saw who had looked DCI Freya Bloom up on the police database, on the central records, and any other piece of software we have at our disposal, they would find one name. Mine. Ben Savage."

"I know that as well. Tell me, Ben, are you going to tell me everything I already know? Or is there some new piece of information coming that you're hoping will sway me into submission?"

"There's no new information," he said, with a shrug. "Just a new perspective. My perspective."

"Oh right," she said. "So, this is all about you, is it? Is this your defence, because I'm telling you now that you would certainly not be allowed to do this in court."

"Just shut up for a moment, will you?" he snapped, and there he was, in full strength. She quietened and grinned at how easy it was to stir a reaction from him. "The officers you're looking into all work from Lincoln. They all, at some point in their careers, worked under Steve Standing."

"As did you," she said, and he widened his eyes as a warning. "Sorry, go on."

"But if you think that I'm part of some wider plot to bring your career to an end, Freya, you are gravely mistaken. Those other officers were, and still are, loyal to Standing. But I most certainly am not."

"No? You're just investigating my uncle's murder for the fun of it, are you?"

"And if you think that was fun, then you're wrong again," he said. "Can't you see? I wasn't trying to prove you were guilty of that murder. In fact, I know that you were not guilty of that murder."

"Oh?"

"It's true," he said. "It's true and I can prove it."

"How?" she asked, and then saw deceit in his eyes, like a vivid reflection. "Sloane?"

He said nothing but gave a slight nod.

"It was you who paid Scott Sloane to investigate me," she said. "How can you tell me that you weren't trying to pin my uncle's murder on me?"

"Because I wasn't," he said. "I was trying to prove your innocence, Freya, for God's sake. And it wasn't about whether or not you did it, it was about whether or not you were able to be truthful with me. Murder is a big thing to hide. At least it is where I'm from. All I wanted to know is if you had anything to tell me that you hadn't."

"And?"

"And you haven't," Ben said, and then looked away at those pictures on the wall again. Pictures of an old man and his wife, enjoying their autumn years. "He found it. He found the truth."

"Who, Sloane?" she said. "The only half-decent PI in the area? Your words, not mine."

"How do you think I know he's the only half-decent PI around here?"

"So, what did he find?" she asked. "Or shouldn't I ask?"

He took a moment to gather his thoughts and to construct a sentence worthy of the charge.

"It was your dad, wasn't it?" he said eventually. "Your dad caught your uncle and he hit him. Then he made it look like a robbery."

"You'll understand if I adopt a no-comment response, won't you?" she said.

"The important thing is that I know that you had nothing to hide."

"The important thing is that you didn't trust me," she replied. "After all we've been through—"

"Oh, come on, Freya. You're like a closed book. Every time I ask you about your past, you clam up. I was just making sure that the person I want to be with was being honest with me."

"You should have just asked."

"Maybe I should have. But I'd always be wondering, wouldn't I? That's why I do what I do. Because I want to know. I want to be sure."

"And are you?" she said. "Are you sure?"

"I've never been surer, Freya. And do you know what? All those officers from Lincoln, the ones who are trying to get you kicked out, or force you into early retirement? Let's go after them. You and me. We can tackle it together."

"Oh, so you believe me now, do you? Now

that Sloane has found out what I could have told you. Now that you've been through an entire investigation into my past. What's changed? Why do you suddenly want to help me?"

"Because not only do I know that it wasn't you who killed your abusive uncle, Freya, but I'm also quite certain that you were right about how loyal some of the Lincoln officers are to Steve Standing. He might have been a loose cannon, and he might have done those awful things for which he's serving time, but he did have personality. He made Chief Inspector and collected quite a few fans along the way. There are plenty of people in Lincoln who took a disliking to you when you locked him up, and I don't think they're done with you. If you're going to face them, then you need someone by your side. You need a team by your side."

"So, what clinched it?" she asked after a few moments to digest his words and to gauge his sincerity. "What made you change your mind?"

He grinned at her.

"What is the only outstanding piece of evidence in the Kyle Butters investigation?"

She shook her head and then thought for a moment.

"The wine bottle," she said, to which he nodded.

"Wiped clean by one of Standing's loyal fans. It had to be. It doesn't fit anywhere else. One of the search team from Lincoln found it and wiped it clean, knowing it would create a diversion or a distraction, and would stop you from getting a conviction. It would mess your investigation up, Freya, at a time when, let's face it, your popularity isn't exactly soaring."

"And you're going to help me, are you?" she said. "Why should I believe you? This could all be part of it. You could be covering your tracks. You haven't even untied me, Ben. If you think that you're somehow winning my trust by leaving me like this so you can rant at me, then—"

"I want to help you, Freya," he said, and she silenced. He moved closer so that their faces were just inches apart.

"Really?"

"I do," he said.

"Why?" she asked. "After all of this, after everything we've been through, why should I believe that you won't just get fed up with the drama and walk away?"

"Because I want to be with you," he said. "I want you to trust me."

"How can I ever trust you again, Ben?" she said. "How can you possibly prove that anything you just said is true?"

"Quite simply," he said, and he shifted onto one knee before her, and looked deep into her eyes. She wanted to say something. She wanted to stop him before he said too much, but either her words or her heart failed her, and she just sat with her mouth wide open. "Marry me, Freya. Marry me, and we'll deal with this together. We'll deal with everything together."

The End.

Click here to download No More Blood.

NO MORE BLOOD - PROLOGUE

For Debbie Jarvis, life was one big game. Kevin knew it, her parents knew it, and she knew it. Everyone knew that if there was a win to be had, then Debbie was onto it. Her edge, she had called it once when they had sat chatting at the waterside. But Kevin knew it only as her narcissistic tendency. It was the one thing about her he simply couldn't bring himself to like.

A fire burned further into the field. There was always a fire at this time of year, despite the dozens of posters on the school walls, and even a local fire officer giving a talk on the danger of summertime fires, they still had them.

They were cautious enough, and it wasn't as if they had nothing to lose. If the trees surrounding the fields went up, then at least two of their houses would go up with them, and the blaze would probably take their parents, too.

"Shall we join them?" he said to her, but she shook her head. They were sitting at the edge of the field, closest to the little path that led back to his house.

"I'm going to stay here for a while," she replied. "I'm not sure if I can handle Ross right now."

"Don't worry about him," he said. "Come on."

"No, you go."

He climbed to his feet, and stared down at her, giving her once last chance to join him.

"I told you, I'm staying," she said.

"Debs, nobody cares what you did with him-."

"I told you not to mention that-."

"I know, but come on. If we don't go over there they'll only come over here."

"No, Seb won't leave the fire," she said.

"And Anna won't leave the wine. She'll be worried about somebody nicking it."

A scream rang out in the field, contained by the trees at every edge. Laughter followed, and he felt Debs scorn rather saw it in her eyes.

"She's a slut," she said, referring to the only other female in their group. "Every one of them lads has felt her up at some point."

"I haven't," he said, quite proud of being the odd one out.

"No," she said, with a laugh. "But you would if you had the chance, wouldn't you?" she grinned up at him, then took a swig from her wine bottle. "I've seen you looking."

"Look, are you coming or not?" he said, trying to change the topic.

"Only when you admit that you fancy her."

"I *don't* fancy her."

"So, I'll stay," she said, taking another swig of wine and resting back onto an elbow. "It's fine by me."

The sky was pitch dark, dothed with bright stars, and her skin appeared grey against the grass.

"Come on," he said. "This is ridiculous."

"Go," she told him. "You asked me to come tonight, and you said he wouldn't be here."

"Well, I didn't know he would be, did I?" he said. "For God's sake, Debs. What can I say to make you come with me?"

She rolled onto her back and stared up at the sky.

"You can tell him to go home."

"Oh, behave. I'm not going to do that."

"So, I'll stay," she said, and then her expression altered. She was onto one of her wins. "Okay, how about this for an alternative." She sat up, folded her legs, and beckoned for him to sit opposite her. So he dropped into a crouch, took a drink from her bottle, then handed it back.

"Go on," he said, and her smile reached from ear to ear.

"Tell me a secret."

"What?"

"Tell me a secret," she said. "Something that nobody else knows."

"I don't have a secret."

"Yes, you do."

"What?"

"Tell me."

He thought for a moment, but couldn't think of a single thing that he knew that nobody else did.

"I don't have a secret. I tell Seb everything, and if I don't tell him, I tell you."

"There must be something," she replied. "Something personal."

"What?"

"Something personal. What do you think about when you...you know?"

"What's wrong with you?" he said, and she laughed loud. "I don't do that."

"Oh really?"

"Really."

She gave another laugh, dismissing his weak denial.

"You're on your own then," she said. "I do it all the time."

The confession could have floored him, and he closed his eyes to clear the image from his mind.

"Are you picturing it?"

"Debs, come on," he said.

"Do you think about me?"

"What? No! Of course I don't-."

"I bet you do," she said, and then cackled when, even in the dim light, she could see his blushes. She sighed, as if relenting, and then rolled onto an elbow again. "Okay then. Last chance. If you really want me to come with you, then tell me about the box under your bed."

The last few syllables came at him like individual slaps to his face. He hesitated, realising that he should have at least made a noise to hide his guilt, instead of simply staring at her with his mouth hanging open.

"See?" she said. "You do have a secret."

"You're mental," he said, clambering to his feet.

"And you're sick," she replied. "But I'm not complaining."

He stormed off towards the fire, not looking back.

"Tell me about the box, Kev," she called out, in that tormenting sing song tone she was so good at. She cackled again, and it danced around the trees. "I know your dirty secret. I know your dirty-."

She stopped her tormenting, and he looked back into the darkness to where she was sitting. He was somewhere between her and the others; not just physically, but metaphorically. Seb laughed at something.

He was always laughing. He was always so carefree. One of them was playing music on their phone, but none of them were dancing. He could make Ross out, sitting on the far side of the fire, while the others were back in the shadows somewhere, away from the blazing heat of the fire.

They weren't missing him one bit.

He turned on his heels, and began marching back towards her, seething more and more with every step he took.

"Debs?" he said, trying to eliminate all traces of his usual friendly tone. "You about? Come on, don't play games."

But she didn't reply, she didn't step from the shadows, and her cackle didn't dance around the trees. Then he saw it. It was unmistakeable. A Vans shoe, her trademark footwear. He bent to pick it up. It was still warm from her body heat.

"Debs?" he said quietly, and for the last time.

And then he ran.

ALSO BY JACK CARTWRIGHT

The DCI Cook Murder Mysteries

A Winter of Blood

A Secret to Die For

The Wild Fens Murder Mysteries

Secrets In Blood

One For Sorrow

In Cold Blood

Suffer In Silence

Dying To Tell

Never To Return

Lie Beside Me

Dance With Death

In Dead Water

One Deadly Night

Her Dying Mind

Into Death's Arms

No More Blood

Join my VIP reader group to be among the first to

hear about new release dates, discounts, and get a free Wild Fens novella.

Visit www.jackcartwrightbooks.com for details.

Locations are as important to the story as the characters are; sometimes even more so. It's for this reason that I visit the settings and places used within my stories to see with open eyes, breathe in the air, and to listen to the sounds.

I have heard it said that each page should feature at least one sensory description, which in the age of the internet anybody can glean from somebody else's photos, maps, or even blog posts.

But, I disagree.

I believe that by visiting locations in person, a writer can experience a true sense of place which should then colour the language used in the story in a far more natural manner than by simply providing a banal description which can often stall the pace of the story.

However, there are times when I am compelled to create a fictional place within a real environment. For example, in the story you have just read, the fields, Viking Way, and the Lincoln Edge are all real places, whereas the houses that are described are not. The Tempest in Coleby is a real pub, and I wholeheartedly recommend a visit. It is, in my opinion, one of the best places in the area to enjoy a drink, a meal, and a spectacular view.

The reason I create fictional places is so that I can be sure not to cast any real location, setting, business, street, or feature in a negative light; nobody wants to see their beloved home town described as a scene for a murder, or any business portrayed as anything but excellent.

If any names of bonafide locations appear in my books, I ensure they bask in a positive light because I truly believe that Lincolnshire has so much to offer and that these locations should be celebrated with vehemence.

I hope you agree.

Jack Cartwright.

AFTERWORD

Because reviews are critical to an author's career, if you have enjoyed this novel, you could do me a huge favour by leaving a review on Amazon.

Reviews allow other readers to find my books. Your help in leaving one would make a big difference to this author.

Thank you for taking the time to read *Into Death's Arms*.

Best wishes,
Jack Cartwright.

COPYRIGHT